ECSTASY

# ECSTASY

# GWYNNE FORSTER

**HARLEQUIN**® KIMANI ARABESQUE®

Recycling programs
for this product may
not exist in your area.

ECSTASY

ISBN-13: 978-0-373-09128-7

First published by BET Publications, LLC in 1997

Copyright © 1997 by Gwendolyn Johnson-Acsadi

**⊖ HARLEQUIN®**

™ www.Harlequin.com

**Printed in U.S.A.**

## Acknowledgments

To my husband, whose love and never-failing support sustain me; Jeanetta Harria, who has shown me in hundreds of ways what it is to be a true friend; in memory of my mother, who gave me a love of books and an appreciation of the beauty and power of the English language; and in memory of my father, who instilled in me a sense of duty and responsibility and whose greatest joy was in seeing his children laugh.

My special thanks to librarians at the New York Academy of Medicine Library for assistance with medical issues raised in this story.

Thanks,

Gwynne

# Prologue

Mason Fenwick paced the length of his brother, Steve's, living room, turned and retraced his steps.

"I know you feel I've let you down, Steve, but that's the way it is. I'm quitting." He didn't have to glance at his older brother and surrogate parent to know that the beloved face held a mixture of sadness and incredulity.

"For good? You mean you're leaving medicine for good?"

"For good."

"Did you lose your nerve? If so, I can understand your doing this. The type of surgery you perform requires nerves of steel."

"No. I didn't, I've got the gall to do anything I ever did." He paused and walked once more toward the other end of the room. "What I lost, you might say, is myself. When I think of the chances I've taken with people's lives and gotten away with it, I get cold chills. I've healed a lot of people, but I could have killed every one of them." He stopped within inches of Steve and drew a deep breath.

"I relished the challenge that the disease's complications presented to me, as though it didn't affect a human being. As though the possibility of failure were implausible. I took the Hippocratic oath, and I've done my best to honor it but, for the last couple of years, I've only been serving myself. Risking human life for my own glory. Filling my calendar with names of rich, famous people who get a headache then schedule a five-hundred-dollar appointment with me. Living it up with people, who wouldn't know me from Adam if they saw me in jeans, a sweatshirt and a baseball cap. Choosing my dates from the socialites who call and beg me to take them to Mrs. X's party. Women who'll do anything to be seen with me. I've backed myself into a corner, Steve. When I had this horrible accident, some papers made a big deal of it, but not one of those people who swore I was indispensable to them called me. I sweated out three lonely and anxious weeks beside Bianca Norris's bed, doing what I could to get her out of the coma. And that wasn't much. I promised God that if she regained consciousness and survived, I'd quit pretending to be Him. I've got to straighten out my life."

"And you have to leave your practice in order to do it?"

"The kind of change I need to make has to be done decisively and completely, if I'm going to respect myself. I can serve mankind in some other capacity."

# Chapter 1

Alone in her little white-frame house, located in a picturesque valley in Pilgrim, New York, Jeannetta Rollins sat at her desk holding the telephone. With her lips agape and her eyes rounded with disbelief, she stared at the grains of sand that filtered slowly downward through her late father's hourglass, signaling the passage of time. It couldn't be. The great oak that she loved to watch from her window, no matter the season, the snow-covered garden and the brilliant blue sky blurred into nothing as she savored the incredible words. Her tests revealed the need for delicate brain surgery that most neurosurgeons hesitated to undertake. Without it, the prognosis for her sight was poor, and the longer she waited for treatment, the slimmer the likelihood that she'd be as good as new.

"I've checked with the surgeons to whom I normally refer patients, and none of them wants this job," Dr. Farmer said. "A Dr. Fenwick has had spectacular results with the surgery you need but, for personal reasons, he's terminated his practice and operates a travel business."

She hung up and looked around; within ten minutes, the world had become a different place. But she wouldn't give up. Surely that doctor would take her case if he knew about her. How could he not help her? She called her doctor back.

"Dr. Farmer, couldn't you talk with this Dr. Fenwick and ask him to take my case? Maybe if he knows that I'm young, that I'm a writer and that my livelihood depends on my eyes, he'll relent and perform the operation."

"Alright, Jeannetta, I'll try my best, but it's been a couple of years since he operated, and I'm sure a lot of people have wanted him to treat them. So don't hold out too much hope." Within the hour, she answered her doctor's call.

"I'm sorry to disappoint you, my dear, but he flatly refused, saying that he's no longer a doctor. I begged him, but to no avail. I'm sorry, indeed."

Jeannetta looked at the pages of her novel and thought of the deadline for its submission five months hence. She'd have to slave over it night and day to complete it on time. She'd have to… She sent the hourglass crashing against the door. She'd done nothing to deserve what she knew awaited her. But she was more subdued after reflecting on the uselessness of anger and vowed to find that doctor and convince him to help her. Calmer now, she got up and went to the kitchen for a glass of cranberry juice and sipped a little. Maybe the radiologist had read the test improperly. She ought to get another specialist.

She went out in the back garden and gazed at the snow-covered mountains rising in the distance and the maze of green pines that stood in proud contrast to the glistening white snow, a scene of which she never tired. She put food in the birdhouses, talked to the blue jay that ate from her hand, threw peanuts to the lone squirrel who came to greet her and breathed deeply of the crisp, late-winter air. Smoke curled high several blocks down the street, and she knew that Laura prepared to roast a turkey or a fresh ham on the outdoor rotisserie for her dinner guest. She'd have to tell Laura.

Her sister operated Rollins Hideaway, a ski lodge that had twelve guest rooms and two apartments and which they had inherited from their deceased parents. Jessie and Matthew Rollins had left the South shortly after their marriage, unwilling to raise a family in a climate of segregation, and had invested their savings in the ski lodge. The profitable venture had enabled them to raise their children comfortably and to send Jeannetta to college. Laura hadn't wanted to study beyond high school, so they had given her three-quarters interest in the lodge.

The odor of roasting pork perfumed the air as Jeannetta neared the lodge. She loved the smell of food cooking on a chilly day; it was as though you'd been invited to feel at home. She walked around the back, where her older sister poked at the hot coals.

"I hadn't expected you so early," Laura told her, reaching up to dust a kiss on Jeannetta's cheek. At thirty-five, Laura was older than Jeannetta by six years, a difference that had cast her in a protective relationship with her younger sister. "Come on inside. I saved you some apple cobbler."

Jeannetta had to force a smile; if she didn't show enthusiasm for apple cobbler, Laura would immediately become suspicious. She sat in her usual place at the kitchen table and picked at the cobbler.

"What's the matter?" Laura asked her. There was no use trying to postpone the inevitable, so she summarized the doctor's report. Laura groped for the back of a chair, nearly falling to the floor as she did so. She sat down, stared blankly, as would a catatonic and began to shake her head in mute denial. Jeannetta rounded the table and knelt to comfort her sister. She knew that, although their relationship had at times been troubled, they loved each other and could depend upon each other no matter what happened.

"What will you do?" Laura asked when she was able to control her near-hysteria.

"I'm going to find that doctor, get on my knees if necessary and convince him to help me. Dr. Farmer wouldn't tell me where he is, because he doesn't want my hopes raised. He considers Fenwick's 'no' as final, but I don't."

"Suppose he won't help you?"

Jeannetta whirled around, unwilling to entertain that possibility.

"He will. I won't take no for an answer. I'll remind him that he took that Hippocratic oath and that he'll have to answer to God if he has the skill to cure me and refuses to do it. He'll do it, or I'll be on his conscience for the rest of his life. I'll make certain that he doesn't forget me." She rose and had to grope for a chair, exhausted. "If he won't help me, I won't stop living—I'll learn how to live without that surgery. I won't be anybody's or anything's victim."

Laura looked at her as though seeing her for the first time. "I always thought you were fragile, but you aren't, are you?"

"No, I'm not, but you wanted to take care of me, so I let you."

"You'll find him. Something tells me that nothing will stop you. How are you going to convince him?"

"I don't know, but I will. Could you give me a pen and some paper?" She ignored Laura's obvious confusion—opening first one drawer and then another, as if she were lost in her own kitchen.

"You're going to write him?" Laura asked, a look of incredulity masking her face.

"I don't know where he is, but I know what he's supposed to be doing. I just hope he isn't headed for skid row and that his hands are steady." The apple cobbler suddenly had appeal, and she bit into a forkful of it, savored the cinnamon-flavored tart and ate some more. "I'm going down to New York City tomorrow," she went on, dismissing her sister's expression of amazement, "and while I'm there I'm going to the Metropolitan Museum of Art. I'm writing down a list of the paintings I want to see."

"Jeanny, for the Lord's sake, don't be morbid."

Jeannetta shrugged her left shoulder. "Morbid? Don't be dramatic, Laura, life's full of battles. You change what you can. The rest, you learn to live with. And I'm going to teach myself to come to terms with this, with or without Fenwick."

"I felt better when you swore you'd get him to help you. Now, you're..."

Jeannetta interrupted to put Laura's mind at ease. "Don't worry. I'll find him."

She promised herself that she wouldn't be disappointed if the first clues led nowhere. From the hospital at which he'd practiced, she learned that he'd given a post-office box as his forwarding address. After several days, she located a Fenwick Travel Agency in New York City and wrote for brochures.

"What are you planning to do with those?" Laura, a skeptic, queried.

"Learn all I can about him."

"Are you sure it's him?"

Jeannetta had had years in which to accustom herself to her sister's tendency to mistrust everything and everybody. "That's what I'm trying to find out." A smile moved over her smooth, ebony skin. The man guided a special round-the-world tour, a two-month venture with twenty personally selected individuals.

"You can't do that," Laura objected, when Jeannetta mentioned it. "That must cost a fortune."

Jeannetta pooh-poohed Laura's concern. "If I succeed, it will be more than worth the cost." She telephoned the agency.

"Is this the *Mason* Fenwick personally guided tour?"

"It is, indeed," a friendly voice replied. "Would you like to speak with Mr. Fenwick?" *Mr.* Fenwick, indeed!

"Yes, please," she replied, quickly remembering her goal.

"Mason Fenwick speaking. How may I help you?" She'd made contact. She knew where he was. But her elation was temporary; tiny hot pinions fluttered through her, crowding her throat, churning in her belly. His low, dusty and mellifluous voice disarmed her, robbed her of the aplomb so natural to her and left her speechless. "Fenwick speaking," he repeated patiently. Thinking fast, nervous and bewildered by her reaction to him, she asked for more details about the African portion of his tour.

"Any special reason why you're interested in that part of the tour?"

Though annoyed with herself, she couldn't still the dancing organ in her chest, nor the trembling of her fingers.

"I've never been there," she managed in a small girl's voice.

"Then you'll enjoy the countries we visit," he assured her and added, "I usually have a fascinating group, too. Most parts of the country, and different races and religions, are represented." His chuckle surprised her. "On every tour, at least one couple meets and later gets married." She tried without success to resist his seductive voice, and found herself imagining what he looked like.

"I hope you aren't too far from New York," she heard him say. "I insist on interviewing all prospective tour members in person. Two months is a long time to spend with nineteen incompatible people. Let my secretary know whether you're interested." He told her goodbye, and she heard the secretary's cheerful voice again. They agreed upon a date and time for the interview, and Jeannetta hung up, finally able to release a long sigh.

"How do you know you're doing the right thing?" Laura

wanted to know. "That man could be a charlatan and, from the looks of you when you were talking to him, he probably is. Anybody would've thought that was the first man you ever said a word to." She sat down, reached over and patted her sister's hand. "I'm not as smart as you, but I always had mother's wit. It doesn't make sense to take your savings and go chasing around the world with a bunch of strangers when you may need every penny."

"I know you love me, Laura, but I have to do this. I'll take every precaution I can, but I'm going to do it." Laura had never been easily placated when she set her mind on something, so Jeannetta let her have her say. Then she told her, "I'll hire a private investigator for a report on him. If it's negative, I'll ditch the idea. Okay?" Laura nodded.

Jeannetta contacted one the next morning and couldn't shake the feeling of guilt when the investigator assured her that he'd "get everything on him down to how many teeth he's had pulled."

Mason Fenwick dropped the receiver into its cradle, leaned back in his chair and closed his eyes. He sensed something strange about that telephone call. The woman had barely said a word and the few she'd uttered had been with what appeared to be an infantile, almost frightened voice. After musing over it for a few minutes, he dismissed his concern; as usual, he'd decide after the interview. The ringing phone annoyed him; he needed to get some work done.

"Miss Goins on three."

He wished Betty Goins wouldn't interrupt him during office hours. "Hello, Betty. I'm sorry. I meant it when I said we couldn't continue this…this farce. How can you be satisfied with this…vacuous relationship? I deserve better, and so do you, and I want to be free to look for what I need and to go after it when I find it. No, I won't change my mind. I can't.

In spite of the intimacy, we've never been more than friends;
let's remain friends. I won't call you again. Goodbye."

Thank God she'd had too much pride to plead. He wanted
more for his life than he could ever have with her. His fingers
brushed the keys that lived in his right pants pocket, the keys
to his late-father's house. The keys to the only place that had
ever been home. When he put medicine behind him, Betty
had lost interest in a future with him, told him that she wanted
a professional man. Travel agents—black or white—were a
dime a dozen, she had said. At the outset, she'd sworn what
they had was enough, that she would teach him to care for
her. But in his mind, she couldn't do that because she hadn't
loved him, hadn't cared, and he had suffered for the lack of
it. She had wanted a doctor, a man who'd give her the social
status she craved. But he needed a woman's love, a family of
his own and a door in which to put a lock that would yield to
the key in his pocket. He signed three letters, took them to
his secretary, walked back into his office and closed the door.
Freedom: how good it felt! He couldn't help jumping high,
clicking his feet together in the manner of a dancer and smiling broadly before sitting down to work.

A light snow blanketed the streets of New York the morning of Jeannetta's interview with Mason. She'd spent the previous night in the city to avoid being stranded in Pilgrim by
the late-March storm. She combed her thick, curly black hair
with unsteady fingers. Then she donned a fashionable rust-
colored woolen jacket and a matching knee-length skirt, pulled
on a pair of brown leather boots, slipped her arms into a beige
camel-hair coat, reached for a pair of brown leather gloves and
her brown Coach hobo bag and struck out for Mason's office.
She couldn't suppress the sensation that she journeyed toward
her destiny. Walking west on Fiftieth Street, she reached St.
Patrick's Cathedral and, as she had done many times, she

entered the Fiftieth Street door, paused for a minute to say a silent prayer, left by the front door and continued down Fifth Avenue to East Forty-sixth Street. Her steps slowed—but her heartbeat accelerated—when she reached the building. She should have consulted another specialist, she told herself. It didn't make sense to go to such lengths because of one man's word, but Dr. Farmer had consulted several specialists about her case, and each had referred him to Fenwick. She glanced up at the imposing structure, took a deep breath and opened the door. She looked neither left nor right, but counted the floors as the elevator sped to number twenty-six. Lead feet took her to suite twenty-six hundred. She reached out to ring the bell and withdrew her hand. A long masculine arm reached across her shoulder, rang the bell and pushed open the door.

"Who did you want to see?" That voice. A faint odor of sandalwood cologne reached her nostrils, but she knew at once that he wasn't wearing it. *I've got to handle this like a pro,* she told herself.

"I want to see Mr. Mason Fenwick," she answered, and made herself turn around and look at him. Her left hand flew to her chest as he stood smiling down at her. She couldn't shift her gaze from the blackish-green eyes that held her captive, entrapped. His smile evaporated and the deep, sensuous voice became crisp and businesslike.

"I'm Fenwick."

She had to be certain. "*Mason* Fenwick?"

His eyebrows arched sharply in a look of surprise. "Yes. I'm Mason Fenwick. And you are?"

"I thought I heard your voice," a woman who must have been his secretary said as she stepped into the little hallway. "Your coffee's ready." He told her he'd take it into his office, then gestured toward Jeannetta.

"She's here to see me. Get her a cup, would you?"

Jeannetta stepped into Mason's office, her poise intact. She

removed the sunglasses she'd worn to deflect the glare from
the snow and took the chair that he offered her. It wasn't his
physical appearance that unsettled her. He stood before her,
tall—around six feet, four inches, she surmised—very dark,
and, by any measure, handsome. No, it wasn't that. He had
an aura, a mystique, an appeal that sucked her in as though
he were quicksand. She got hold of herself.

"I'm Jeannetta Rollins."

He extended his hand, a bit reluctantly, she thought, though
the possibility perplexed her. Why wouldn't he want to shake
her hand? Without her sunglasses, his strange eyes had an
even more compelling effect, reaching inside of her, warming her, soothing her. She couldn't tear her gaze from them.

The buzzer on his desk went unanswered.

"Telephone, Mr. Fenwick."

If he heard, he gave no indication. Jeannetta watched, mesmerized, as his eyes darkened, losing their blackish cast, and
seemed to radiate warmth in a change so drastic and so sudden
that she hadn't time to hide her reaction. She gasped aloud,
drawing him out of his trance.

"Who are you?"

In control once more, she repeated her name. He waved
the words aside with a quick movement of his hand. "I mean,
*who are you?*"

"A prospective tourist," she told him, though she cringed
inwardly at the deceptive white lie. He picked up the black
folder on his desk, read her name and opened it.

"You haven't filled in this form."

Noticing that it included, among other questions, two on
the condition of her health, she told him she'd mail it.

"Better make it snappy. I have only four places left and
fourteen applicants."

Unwilling to risk missing the tour, she took the form and
completed it.

"You write sketches for stand-up comedians?" His voice held a note of awe.

"Among other things, yes. It's amazing what people will find comical."

He stared at her and shook his head as though disbelieving his ears. "Care to offer a sample?"

He didn't smile, so she couldn't know whether the request was a part of the interview or fodder for his curiosity. Well, she'd play it by ear.

"My samples are expensive," she told him, deciding that she wouldn't smile either.

"I'll settle for one of your cheaper ones." Not an expression on his face. Was he playing with her? She wondered what her demeanor conveyed to him when his peculiarly magnetic eyes became brownish and he leaned forward in an air of expectancy.

"Okay, here goes. Esther Ruth Hankin's good-for-nothing husband hadn't worked a full day in the twelve years since she'd married him, but Esther Ruth thought he was wonderful. Her hardworking, redneck father disagreed and threatened to stop supporting them. 'It's time you left that bum,' he told her. 'The man's an absolute failure.' 'He ain't a failure, daddy,' she pleaded. 'He just started at the bottom and got comfortable down there.' The old man then turned to his other daughter, who crocheted happily nearby, and complained that her husband was too stupid to keep a job and that he was also going to stop taking care of them. Janie Dixon looked her father in the eye and asked him, 'Who's smarter, the man who can own a Cadillac without ever doing a lick of work, or the man who works his tail off to give it to him?'"

Mason Fenwick continued to stare at Jeannetta until she wanted the floor to open up and swallow her. Then his wonderful eyes gleamed with mirth; laughter rumbled in his chest and spilled out of him. He leaned back in his chair and gave his amusement full rein. Astonished at the change in him, intuition told her that this man could only be reached at a primal level with gut-rending overtures, that he could intellectualize as irrelevant any other kind of approach.

"That's pretty good." He scanned the form, his face again solemn and unreadable.

"It had to be better than pretty good," she told him, not bothering to hide her annoyance, "otherwise you wouldn't have laughed your head off." His long brown fingers strummed his desk, and he leaned back and watched her intently, like a cat eyeing a mouse.

"You're right," he said, after seeming to weigh the effect of yielding to her. He scanned the form that she'd completed. "This looks okay, but I'll have to check your references. You should hear from us within a week."

They both stood. He walked around the desk and extended his hand and she felt her face throb with the rush of warm blood when she touched it. Did he grasp it longer than necessary? She didn't know, so caught up was she in his gaze, his whole aura. She never knew how she got out of his office.

He didn't move until the door closed behind her. He walked over to the window overlooking Forty-sixth Street and braced himself with both hands resting on the windowsill. What had happened in there? The churning in him couldn't have been more violent nor more enervating if he had just encountered a Martian. He couldn't help smiling inwardly; maybe he had. But he was master of his fate and he'd proved it. Starting over at age thirty-four in what, for him, had been uncharted waters, hadn't been without pitfalls, but he'd done it and it had given him a sense of accomplishment and a measure of inner peace. Now, this stranger had bolted into his life and nailed him with a wallop such as he hadn't known he could experience. She'd looked up at him, her eyes sparkling with some kind of gut-scaring, almost sad appeal, and he'd had a time steadying himself. If she had set out deliberately to pulverize his resistance to her, she had succeeded admirably.

"Well, what do you think, Mr. Mason?" He whirled around, strode quickly to his desk and punched the intercom.

"I haven't decided, Viv. What was your assessment?"

"I didn't see much of her, but I think she probably isn't demanding and won't be a troublemaker, since she didn't ask me a lot of questions about the other tourists, sleeping accommodations, that sort of thing—and nothing at all about you. Most single women under forty-five ask if you're married. She'll be okay."

"Hmm. Maybe." He hung up. Anybody as intelligent as that woman obviously was definitely should have asked some questions. He'd have to think about it. The buzzer rang again.

"She must be interesting, too, Mr. Mason. She's a writer, and she's got three books published. On top of that, she teaches writing at SUNY. Maybe she'll put the tour in one of her books, and you'll be famous again." He opened Jeannetta's file. Any writer had a perfect reason for taking a world tour, but she had stated "personal" in answer to the question. He recalled that he'd sensed an aura of mystery around her when they'd talked on the phone earlier; now he was sure of it. Well, he didn't have to take her. He had a peculiar feeling about her. Yet, she met his written criteria, and he prided himself in being fair. He'd sleep on it.

After that evening, Jeannetta sat on a hassock in Laura's tiny, cluttered office while her sister planned menus for the next week.

"Well, how'd it go with Fenwick?"

"You sure you want to know? That man's a keg of powder."

"Oh, Lord, don't tell me. I thought you were ready to move

in with him just from talking with him on the phone. What happened?"

"What happened was I looked at him and felt as if he'd slugged me with a sledgehammer. Laura, I've never been a pushover for any man, but *that man!* Honey, he was all around me, everywhere. I could feel him before he touched my hand. Just talking about him makes me want to… Gosh, I shouldn't be speaking to you like this."

"Shoot, honey," Laura said with her usual diffidence about such things, "at least let me live vicariously."

"He's a fantastic specimen, but it's more…I…I was practically traumatized, and he hadn't done anything but ask my name…and gaze at me. His eyes change from a blackish-green to brown when he smiles, and he… Laura, what if he's blunted my brain to the point where I can't persuade him to do what I want? Five minutes with him and I was a bowl of mush."

"I don't believe that."

"Well, maybe I've overstated it a bit, but not by much. Trust me."

"What was his reaction?"

Jeannetta hadn't thought much about that but, upon recollection, decided that he'd at least noticed her. She described their encounter.

"Sounds to me like he wasn't exactly immune to you," Laura said. "You watch it."

"Don't worry. This has to be business. If sex gets into it, I'll lose everything."

"I'd like to have that problem with him," Laura said dryly. "You always did have what it takes with men, and you never used it. I'm thirty-five years old and still waiting for the first man to tell me he admires something about me other than my business smarts and my cherry pies. I'd give anything to be tall and slim with your long legs and hourglass figure. I'd even exchange my straight hair for your wooly stuff. A lot of men look right past short, plump women."

"You don't want to exchange places with me, Laura. Maybe this is fate's way of evening things out. I look like Dad and you look like Mother. When I was little, you got the roles in school plays, because you're fair. Nobody up here ever heard of a black fairy queen."

"And I never saw a fat drum majorette. You were the toast of the Pilgrim football team." She turned off the computer and rested her chin on the heel of her right hand. "Sex or not, what choice do you have? You need him, and if you two fall for each other, you'll just have to deal with that. Just you make sure he doesn't turn out to be another Jethro. That man chased you right to the day he married Alma."

"I know," Jeannetta replied, shaking her head in wonder, "and he's still at it. He must be a masochist. I detest him, and I let him know it. How could he possibly think I'd give him a second look after he slept with my best friend, when he was engaged to me? They both got what they deserve—she tricked him into marrying her, and he's still trailing after me."

Laura waved her hand in a gesture of dismissal. "Alma never was your friend. Biggest actress ever to walk these streets. Forget about them, and be sure that, if you fall for Mason Fenwick, he feels the same way about you."

Mason telephoned his older brother, Steve, the person who had been his spiritual, psychological and economic anchor since they'd been orphaned at the ages of seven and twelve.

"I'll bring over some Chinese food and we can have supper together, if you're not busy."

"I'm free this evening," Steve assured him. "Why don't I make a salad and chill a couple of beers?"

Mason arrived at his brother's co-op apartment at about seven-thirty. The refined old building was situated on the

south side of the dividing line between Harlem and the rest
of mankind, as Steve liked to say, and was the only substantial gift he'd been willing to accept from his younger brother.
Steve put the food in the microwave oven to be warmed later,
divided a bottle of Heineken between two glasses and took
them into his living room.

"What's on your mind, Mason?"

He told his brother of his encounter with Jeannetta, by
phone and in person. "I never felt so unsettled, as if I were
in total disarray, unravelled, as I did when she left my office.
I have a premonition that nothing good will come of it if I
admit her to that tour."

Steve set his glass on the leather coaster and looked at
Mason. "If she meets your criteria, and you said she does,
you have no legal right or moral basis by which to exclude
her. And since when did you base your actions on hunches
and premonitions? It wasn't a premonition that led you to quit
medicine, was it?"

Mason expelled a long, labored breath. He'd hoped that his
leaving medicine wouldn't arise, but it nearly always crept
into their conservations.

"Steve, I know you're disappointed in me, and that you'll
probably always be, but I can't go back into that operating
room. It warped me as a human being."

"You mean you let it warp you."

"Whatever. You worked most of your life to send me to
school because I wanted to be a doctor, and you dedicated
yourself to helping me realize my dream. I think of it all the
time. You're forty-two, and you don't have a family, but you
would have had if you hadn't cared so much for me." He covered Steve's hand with his own, in an attempt to convey the
depth of his feelings.

"You weren't there, Steve. Everyone in that operating room
saw it. For some reason, call it Divine Providence if you want

to, I wasn't holding that scalpel right. If I had been, and my finger hadn't been as close as it was to the tip of that blade, Bianca Norris would be dead. She's in perfect health, and I don't plan to tempt fate ever again. I know it hurts you, and I lose more sleep over it than you can imagine, but that's the way it is."

"You'll go back. You'll have to. People need you. But you didn't come here to talk about that. You're here because of that woman."

Mason got up and walked the length of the long living room, stopped at a Shaker-style rocker and propped his right foot on its bottom rung, rocking it.

"I don't want to take her along."

"Why? Seems to me you'd be glad to have someone your age on that two-month-long tour. When were you ever scared of a woman?"

"I'm not afraid of her, for Pete's sake." *How would you feel about a strange woman strolling into your life and dulling your senses without uttering a word?* he wanted to ask.

"Then take her." His wicked laugh seemed to carry immense satisfaction, Mason decided.

"Get down on your knees, brother," Steve continued jovially, "and see what it's like. We've all been there." Sobering, he asked, "What are you planning to do about Betty?"

Mason shrugged elaborately and ran his long fingers over his hair. "That's history."

"I'm glad to hear it," Steve said. "And at the risk of pontificating, I have to tell you it never should have started. She wasn't for you, but I suspect you know that. Any doctor taller than she is would have sufficed. When are you leaving?"

"May twenty-second. I have to ask you to go with Skip to his school program June first. He graduates from elementary school, and I can't leave him stranded. He needs support."

"Tell him to call me." He paused as though reluctant to

raise an issue. "Mason, that boy's become so attached to you that, if you wanted to cut him loose, you couldn't."

Mason kicked at the carpet, as he frequently did when aggravated. "I have no idea why Skip began to tag along behind me. When my office was a couple of blocks from the Upper East Side branch library, Skip used to sit on the steps and, when I passed there every afternoon, he'd speak. I'd give him a thumbs-up sign and walk on. Seems he studied there to avoid the boys who were his neighbors in the projects. After a while he began waving at me when he spoke and I couldn't help noticing him. Neat. Always alone and with an armful of books. Then, he began to walk along with me without saying anything, unless I asked him a question. One day, he rushed to greet me as though I were an old friend, even used my first name. I talked with him that day and, from then on, he waited for me. I didn't think to tell him I was moving my office down to East Forty-six Street but, after a couple of weeks, he found me and actually gave me a tongue lashing for not having told him I intended to move. I'd missed him, too, and told him so. He got to know my coming and going better than I did. He trailed along with me for months before he got around to asking me if we could be brothers, since his only family was a sick aunt who'd raised him almost from birth.

"He asked me to come to his school one night to root for his debating team. I went. As team captain, he introduced each team member and, to my astonishment, introduced me as his best friend. That gesture was out of place, and he knew it, but I never saw such a proud kid. By now, he means as much to me as I do to him, so don't think I'm going to want to cut him loose."

"What if you want to get married and your intended doesn't like Skip?"

"I won't want to marry a woman who doesn't like Skip." He ignored Steve's gestures of disbelief. "I'll tell him to call you."

They warmed the dinner and sat down to eat. Steve always honored their late father's custom of grace before meals, but Mason admitted that he rarely thought of it. They discussed the relative merits of General Colin Powell and Brigadier General Benjamin O. Davis, Jr., each conceding that Davis might have been great had he operated in a racially less-difficult, less-troubled era, and that Powell had made a more phenomenal imprint on the history of his time.

"You could have done the same in the field of medicine," Steve griped. "You developed a method of operating successfully where most doctors would rather not venture."

It always came back to that. Mason put the remainder of the food in the refrigerator, rinsed the dishes and placed them in the dishwasher and prepared to leave.

"Is that the reason why you won't go into business with me? As partners, we could take turns touring, and one of us would always be in the office." When Steve failed to answer, Mason added, "I need you. If I ask often enough and long enough, maybe you'll give in." They embraced each other, as was their custom, and Mason left, knowing that Steve watched him from the doorway, as he had since their long-ago youth.

Mason took a taxi to the Amsterdam Houses on West Sixty-fifth Street, to the grim little apartment where Mabel Shaw lived with her nephew, Benjamin "Skip" Shaw. He surveyed the tidy but modest accommodation, wondering how Skip managed to study with the television, his aunt's only diversion from illness, blaring loudly, noise from outside and from surrounding apartments intruding and the smell of decaying refuse drifting through the window with the dank air. At times, he was tempted to take the boy home with him, but Mabel was confined to the house, and she needed her nephew. He gave her some bills and inquired of Skip's whereabouts.

"Thank you, Mr. Fenwick. We couldn't live on what I get

from the city, not even in this old dump. God bless you." Her weak hand dropped helplessly to her lap, and he knew a twinge of guilt. She needed better medical care and, under other circumstances, he could have gotten it for her.

"Where's Skip?" he asked again, and learned that the boy had gone to choral rehearsal. He told her he'd call Skip, and left. Two hours later, he walked into his apartment building to find the boy standing in the lobby wearing a hopeful look on his face. Although he'd eaten earlier with Steve, he sent out for pizza and nibbled some, while Skip devoured most of it.

"You don't need me to help you with your homework," Mason told the boy.

"Man, I have to know it's right. I have to stay at the head of my class.

Mason put the palm-sized calculator aside and looked Skip in the eye. "I do not like your calling me 'man'. How would you like me to call you 'boy'? I have a name, so use it."

"Yeah, but…"

"I don't care for that expression either, and I've told you so. The word is *yes*. Where's your math workbook?" Mason knew that what Skip wanted from him was attention. Though in junior high school, the boy's knowledge of math was nearly equal to that of a high school senior.

Skip confirmed that, when he said, "Man, I'm way ahead of my class in math."

"Then we'll work on your English. You're not ahead of anybody on that. I want you to drop that street language."

The boy's eyes rounded and increased in size. "You want me to talk like you? I can't do that, man. The guys'll gang up on me if I start acting smart-assed."

"And clean up your mouth. You are not going to be like them, and you're not going to talk the way they do. You hear me?"

"Okay. Okay. I'm gonna be just like you. Right? I'm gonna get an education and learn everything. Me and my aunt are

gonna move out of the projects soon as I get my first pay-
check."

Mason resisted an urge to pat Skip's shoulder, to relieve
him of his immense psychological burden. "My aunt and I.
Read this page aloud." He listened, enraptured, as the boy read
a long passage from Richard Wright's *Native Son,* interpreting
it, giving life to the writer's words. Chills streaked through
him as Bigger's furor, fears and then his dreams flowed from
Skip's mouth. How could a twelve-year-old express another
person's horror so eloquently? The boy had crossed Central
Park and walked another twenty blocks to get to Mason's
apartment near Eighty-seventh and Madison.

After Skip left, Mason sat alone, looking at the wood-
panelled walls of his study, glancing occasionally at the expensive Tabriz Persian carpet beneath his feet. Without his
brother's sacrifice, he'd have been like Skip—a good little
ship with no rudder—or worse. Quitting medicine had been a
tough decision, but living with it had been hell. He had gained
a measure of peace, had learned to be comfortable and relaxed
with himself and with others since changing his profession.
He got up and paced the floor, ill at ease now, stressed as he
hadn't been since he'd pulled off those surgical greens for the
last time, and he traced his discontent to Jeannetta Rollins. He
didn't understand his reluctance where she was concerned,
but he had to do what was right.

Mason didn't fool himself; his fitful sleep was due to his
unsettled feelings about the woman who, in the space of seconds, had jarred him out of his sense of contentment, his hard-
won equilibrium. He didn't doubt what would happen if he
spent two months in her company. Hell: two days. At first light
of morning, he called it a night, a sleepless one, dressed and
walked over to Central Park. He had searched for an apartment on the East River so he could see the sunrise from a balcony or a window. But people who had the kind of place that

he wanted could afford seldom vacated. He leaned against a huge oak at the park's edge and enjoyed the chirping birds that darted freely about as though claiming nature's beauty and bounty for themselves before humans laid waste to them. He crossed Fifth Avenue on the way back home and greeted the newspaper lady who worked the corner of Madison and Eighty-seventh, collecting papers that she sold for recycling. She stored them in her shopping cart, and he saved his copies of *The New York Times* and *The Wall Street Journal* for her. She was a businessperson, he remembered her having told him, and she didn't want handouts. At eight o'clock he telephoned Jeannetta.

"Hallo."

"Sorry to awaken you, but I thought writers started work early."

"They do if they get a good night's sleep. Who is…? *Mason?*"

"Right." So she recognized his voice and thought of him by his first name! He blew all the air out of his lungs. Maybe he ought to let nature take its course and stop worrying about what could happen. And he would, too, if he didn't have this strangely uneasy feeling about her.

"Do you still want to take the tour?"

"Yes. Does this call mean you're accepting me?"

"We fly out of Kennedy on the twenty-second of May. My secretary will send you a list of the countries for which you'll need visas and information about the required shots. If you don't have a health card, your doctor will give you one. Any problems, call me. I know you're interested in Africa so, before you give me your word, I want you to understand that we'll be going to Northern and Western Africa, but not to any countries in the southern and eastern regions. That suit you?"

"Fine. I can go to East Africa some other…"

"Some other time?" He wondered why she hadn't finished

the thought, and when she replied, "Well, maybe," he became curious.

"I know this trip is expensive. Most people who take it have saved for a lifetime."

"It damages your savings, alright."

He recognized evasiveness when he heard it and decided not to push her. "Next time you're down here in the city, stop by the office and pick up your carry-on bag."

"I have to be there Tuesday morning. Is that too early?"

Excitement coursed through him and he tried to suppress it. He wanted to see her. As soon as he'd heard her voice, his sexual energy had kicked into high gear and he'd felt the heat swirling in his belly. As though unaffected, he replied in a dispassionate voice, "That'll be fine. If you're free, say around one, we could have lunch, and I can outline our route for you."

"I… Thank you. I…I'd love that. See you around one on Tuesday."

He hung up, but didn't shift his gaze from the telephone. So she, too, was skeptical about a relationship between them. He fingered the keys in his pocket and told himself to stop thinking about Jeannetta Rollins. Not much chance of that…

Four days later, Jeannetta walked into Mason's suite of offices to find him standing by his secretary's desk with his right hand braced on his hip, examining his wristwatch. She'd tried to get there on time, she really had, but she hadn't been able to resist watching the harlequin-like couple in Grand Central Station who danced for their livelihood to the tune of Louis Armstrong's old recording of *Let's Do It*. The crowd had loved them, had showered them with money and they had shown their appreciation with dazzling bluegrass clogging.

"Sorry I'm late."

"Something tells me you say that often." The thrill of his deep, comforting voice washed away her cares. She didn't care if he showed displeasure, as long as he kept their date.

White shirt, red-and-navy-striped tie and dark gray suit. Did he dress that way every day? When she'd met him, he had looked good, Lord knows, but not that sharp. The thought that he might have dressed well for their luncheon sent her heart into a gallop.

"I can't resist enjoying things that are pleasing to look at," she said. "I hope you'll forgive me."

He asked if she liked Italian food and smiled his pleasure when her reply indicated they had that much in common. He took them to a restaurant on Sixth Avenue, not far from his office.

"Your usual, Mr. Mason?" the tiny dark-haired woman asked him. He nodded, and the woman led them to a small back room that had four well-separated and well-appointed tables. White linen cloths, vases of yellow, pink and white snapdragons, long-stemmed crystal glasses and porcelain dinnerware. Any ideas she had of insisting that they go Dutch went out the window.

"Do you eat here often?"

Amusement reflected itself in the gleam of his eyes, dazzling her. He held her chair, seated himself and leaned toward her.

"When I can find the time. Yes. Now, let's get something straight before we proceed. *If you're not at the boarding gate for flight SK620 on May twenty-second when the flight is called, I'll let the plane leave without you and I will not reimburse you. Got that?*" He didn't smile, wink, or do anything to soften the harshness of his remark. She avoided looking in his eyes and let her gaze find a spot over his shoulder, mulling over her reply before deciding to bait him.

"I won't be the first woman you left behind, but you'll be able to say you know at least one female who didn't chase after you."

"I'm serious, Jeannetta."

"Me, too, Mason." His handsome long brown fingers strummed the table lightly while his gaze fastened on her. "You aren't known for patience, are you?" she ventured.

"With people who don't deliberately provoke me into losing it, I've got plenty. Take you, for instance. You've got a built-in patience buster that stays on automatic pilot."

"How do you know all that?" she bristled. "We're strangers." She wished he wouldn't look at her so intently. Right then, his eyes changed color, jacking up her body's temperature and jellying her bones.

"Oh, I don't imagine that you do it deliberately. My guess is that you merely float around in your own world, laid-back, unperturbed, wrecking other people's equilibrium without meaning to." She shifted in her chair. Laura must have accused her of something similar dozens of times over the years. Without thinking, she asked him, "Are you a psychiatrist?" She watched the light in his eyes dim and a defensive shield steal over his face.

"Anyone who cares about people can learn to interpret human behavior—one needn't be a psychiatrist."

She told herself that she'd gotten too close there, that she had better be more careful. In his mesmerizing features, she had glimpsed pain; just for a second, it had been there. Unmistakable. Perhaps he regretted leaving medicine. Or maybe someone for whom he had cared had betrayed him. This man carried scars, and trust probably didn't come easily with him. It wouldn't do for him to know too soon why she had chosen his tour. The waiter took their orders. Shrimp scampi with rice and a salad for him; spaghetti with pesto sauce and a salad for her.

He folded his arms, grasping his biceps and leaned back in his chair. "Jeannetta, we might as well stop fencing with each other. It doesn't make sense and, besides, it's useless."

Tiny pricks of warm sensation shot through her and anticipation simmered in her breast.

"I don't know what you mean." She hadn't been able to steady her voice, and his expression said that he knew it.

"Alright. Stick your head in the sand, if you think you'll be more comfortable that way." Before she could speak, he added. "And if you like mind-blowing surprises."

"I'm taking this tour because I want to see the world." Realizing that her voice had sounded plaintive, she smiled to soften the effect and, to her amazement, Mason abruptly leaned forward, his eyes simmering pools of brown heat.

"I'll show you the world." Tingling excitement shot down her spine at the sound of his passion-filled lover's voice. "The world through my eyes is a wondrous place, Jeannetta. Sunrises that explode from a kaleidoscope of colors, great trees with leaves that dance in a wind you can almost see, foamy ocean caps, long stretches of virgin sandy beaches and moons that nourish your soul. I'll show you stars in your favorite colors, mountains topped with evergreen trees and pristine snow, green valleys with millions of wildflowers. If you travel with me, Jeannetta, you'll live in a new and different world. You'll bask in the realm of the ethereal."

She hid her trembling hands beneath the tablecloth, pressed her arms to her side and crossed her ankles. He wasn't speaking of the Fenwick Travel Agency tour, but of what she'd find in an intimate relationship with him. Strange that the picture he painted symbolized what she'd lose if he didn't help her. Somewhere from the archives of her mind came a reminder that if she fell for him all might be lost, and an admonishment that she ought to get away from him while she could. She knew she'd better get them back on an impersonal basis. But she sat there, imprisoned by his hypnotic stare, and said nothing.

"Well, what do you say?"

She called on her aplomb and managed to return his gaze. Sucking in her breath, she told him, "You paint a magnificent picture. I could see it all in my mind's eye, but…"

"But you're scared," he interrupted, his face bright and animated. Most of the time only his eyes expressed his feelings, and she had to force herself not to comment on the change. He regarded her carefully, and his demeanor told her that her words were important to him, but the effect of his rapt concentration was lessened by the gentle strumming of his dark fingers on the white linen cloth.

"Of all the things I may have been called in my life," she said, "I doubt that scared was one of them. But you'll have to admit that only a foolish woman would fail to question the words of a man whose tongue is as smooth as yours."

His eyebrows arched sharply, and he rested his fork.

"And the woman who does not recognize a man's truth when she hears it is to be pitied."

She didn't want him to know what his words had done to her, but the loud swish of air into her lips was all he needed. Her eyelids dropped and she cringed at the prints that her nails had dug in the palms of her hands.

He must have seen her agitation, for he shook his head and told her, "A person's first duty to himself is to know who he is. I'm working hard at that, and you'd better start. Why can't you do what you'd like to do?"

"And what's that?" she asked, her tone less than friendly. He reached in his pocket for his credit card, placed it on the table and signaled for their waiter.

"Jeannetta, I promised myself three years ago that I would tell myself the truth no matter how much I hated to hear it. Although some inner sense—call it intuition—tells me I may regret it, you attract me as no other woman has, and I want to spend time with you. A lot of time. If you were as honest with both of us, you'd tell me that you feel the same way. Let's go.

I've got a two-thirty appointment." Her penetrating, disbelieving stare must have gotten to him, because he explained his
rapid change of mood. "I've grieved about two incidents in
my life, and I doubt anything else could move me as deeply.
I'll settle for peace and contentment. What about you?"

"Sounds good to me." She stood and hooked the strap of her
hobo bag over her right shoulder. After their conversation, she
had to start looking for a miracle. His fingers, splayed across
her back as he guided her toward the door, gave her a sense of
security that she hadn't often known. He was there—and he
wouldn't allow anything to shatter her well-being—was the
message that his warm fingers sent to her body. If only that
were true. They stepped out into the early spring sunshine
and she felt his hand through the fabric that covered her arm.

"Headed back to Pilgrim?"

She wished she could figure out what he was thinking.
He managed not to communicate anything but the words he
spoke.

"I'm going over to Columbus Avenue, to find a sidewalk
café and do some people-watching. It's my favorite hobby and
provides me with a lot of material for my books. Have you
ever done it?" She thought he stepped closer, or maybe it was
a sensation. He seemed everywhere.

"A little. What I've done, I've liked." She could swear that
his eyes changed to that brownish-green color with its hot,
come-hither gleam. She couldn't help taking a step backward.
"I like you, too, Jeannetta, and I wish I had time to join you.
I'm sure I'd enjoy it."

"It would be nice to have company." What else could she
say, she asked herself, needing an excuse for having encouraged him. She stepped away, preparing to leave him.

"May I call you?"

Flustered as well as delighted, she ignored the warning of
her conscience. "Y…yes. Well, I…Mason, it's… Well, alright."

"You've got misgivings?"

"Yes, I do, but…I'll be listening for your call." He appeared to mull that over. Then he squeezed her arm lightly and, for a minute, she thought he'd kiss her. Instead, he brushed her cheek with the back of his hand and winked. As she walked off, she knew that he scrutinized every movement of her body.

# Chapter 2

Jeannetta strolled into the Scandinavian Airlines lounge at John F. Kennedy Airport, dropped her bags, sat down and pulled out her writing tablet. Airports afforded wonderful opportunities for people-watching, and she had found several of her most intriguing fictional characters among the sometimes tired, sometimes excited, but always unsuspecting creatures who waited there. Her glance caught the tall, dark man who leaned with the support of his elbows against the airline crew's desk. Loose. Casual. Quickly, she tore her gaze away, but his had already captured her, and she knew he'd seen her admire him.

He straightened up and headed toward her.

"I could have sworn you'd be late."

She couldn't help laughing; she had expected him to say something like that.

"That's why I made it a point to arrive early. Can't afford to let you think you can predict my behavior." His eyes darkened, and his glance swept over her. He nodded, as though putting his seal of approval on what he'd seen.

"A man who's foolish enough to think he can predict *any* woman's behavior shouldn't be allowed out of the house by himself. Woman has perplexed man since the beginning of time."

Her delight in his company had to be obvious, so she didn't try to hide her pleasure in their bantering.

"Then 'man' ought to grow up." She laid the tablet aside, unconsciously inviting him to join her. He didn't accept the invitation.

"We've got nearly an hour before boarding time," he said, after glancing at his Timex watch. "Would you join me for a drink?"

The word *yes* sat on the tip of her tongue, but she remembered her doctor's advice and said, "I'd love to, but I'm not...I mean, I don't drink."

His face framed a set of flawless white teeth when his lips spread in a mesmerizing grin. She knew who'd win that one.

"Then we'll have coffee," he stated. She let him take her arm and usher her over to the bar. Their tour offered first-class accommodations, apart from the business-class seats. She put a few finger sandwiches on a salad plate, and he poured two cups of coffee.

"Let's sit over here where we can see the planes land," he suggested. When she declined cream and sugar, a curious expression that she couldn't fathom spread across his face. He reached for a sandwich.

"Caviar on cream cheese with black coffee, when the world's best champagne sits over there for the taking!" he exclaimed with a frown.

She remained silent while he stretched out his long legs on either side of the tiny table and pinned her with a penetrating stare. *He always seems to want to dig inside of me,* she thought, and put herself on guard.

"Why didn't you return my calls?" She had been expecting that question, but not the twang of bitterness that laced his voice. She'd thought he would shrug it off and forget about a personal relationship between them.

"That ought to be obvious." The blank expression that she now recognized as self-protection covered his face, and he pushed the coffee aside.

"Obvious to you, maybe. You told me I could call you. If you had changed your mind, one word would have been sufficient." She couldn't tell him that the sound of his deep, melodious voice would have drained her of her resolve to avoid an entanglement. That admission would be as good as a confession.

"I should have returned your calls. I apologize."

"Tell me who you are."

Jolted by the low vibrancy of his voice, she repeated her name.

"I know that, and it tells me nothing. What makes you laugh? Cry?"

"Just about anything. It depends."

He nodded. "You're one vague woman. What do you want out of this tour?"

"I told you. I want to see the world."

"So you did." He stood. "Can I get you something?" She shook her head, and he strode to the bar and returned with a glass of club soda. She hoped her discomfort didn't show. She sat back in her chair and dropped her hands in her lap in pretended serenity, but her fingertips clutched the fabric of her green chambray slacks.

"Somehow that Timex doesn't fit the rest of you," she said, in an attempt to shift the conversation to him.

He looked at his wrist. "I've lost at least ten of these things. I always used to lay them aside when I walked into the op…"

Thank God he'd been looking at his watch and not at her, because recognition had to have been plain on her face. She waited for him to continue.

"Once you get in the habit of removing your watch when you're doing something delicate, you should buy the cheapest one you can find."

*Nice cover,* she thought, for the first time experiencing anger at his charade.

"What do you do that's delicate?"

"Wood carving. My favorite pastime."

"What do you carve?"

His deep breath and narrowed left eye told her to ease up, that he disliked personal questions. Tough, she decided; he didn't hesitate to dig into her life.

"Animals, people, whatever strikes my fancy. I like using my hands." He pushed his chair back from the table and looked at his watch. "Boarding in about fifteen minutes. I'd better round up my gang."

*This man's got everything I want,* she admitted to herself, and cautioned herself that if she didn't get her emotions under control, she'd damage her cause beyond salvaging, and she needn't even get on that plane.

He pinned her with a steady gaze. "You haven't told me what you're expecting from this tour."

She resorted to a half-truth. "The experience of a lifetime. We're still strangers. Perhaps if we get to know each other better, I…"

"We will," he interrupted, "put your life on it."

"How can you be so certain?"

He leaned forward. "We'll be spending eight weeks together. By the end of the tour, I'll know every one of my guests better." He leaned back in his chair, tilting it on its back legs and let his gaze sear her with potent intimacy, its sensuality captivating her. Exquisite shivers pummeled her insides.

"You're so sure of yourself."

He raked his right hand over his hair, exposing his strong wrist and long-fingered lover's hands.

"No. I'm not, so you're wrong on that one. But life is short, Jeannetta, and I'm not going to spend it lying to myself or doing what makes me uncomfortable. I'm interested in more than pleasant chitchat with you." He paused as though seeking precise words, and let his chair rest on all four legs. "I don't like stewing over what might have been, so I try to avoid it. You interest me, and I'm probably going to pursue that interest." He stood. "See you in a few minutes."

Jeannetta avoided eye contact with Mason when he checked off her name as she passed him before boarding the plane. She stacked her carry-on luggage and found her seat, pleased that the entire business-class section had been sold to the tour. Minutes later, he touched her arm.

"Ignoring me won't make me go away," he told her. She looked up into his solemn face. "I'll try to make the trip as pleasant as I can but, if you still have doubts, I'll break my rule and refund your money. You have about three minutes to decide."

The investigator's report had described him as a man of honor, and she'd found no reason to disagree. "I'm taking the tour."

His smile, warm and genuine, flooded her heart with joy. His hand grazed her shoulder. "I'm glad."

Some mornings later, shortly after sunrise, Jeannetta strolled along the beach of the Tyrrhenian Sea, knowing a peculiar freedom as the warm May breeze whipped around her thin, wide skirt. Fresh, salty air invigorated her, and she released her cares and enjoyed her first view of the Lido di

Ostia, southwest of Rome. Mason had scheduled one day there for the beach lovers. She had loved every minute of the week they'd stayed in Europe, but she'd gladly have spent most of the time in Italy. No other European country could match it for the sensual experiences it offered: great art; unforgettable food, music and scenery; and, not to be overlooked, the adoration of the handsome Italian men.

She removed her sandals and strolled along the nearly empty shore, occasionally digging her toes in the warm sand, lifting them and watching the sand drift downward through them. The early morning sun cast the shadow of her slim silhouette the length of a city block. She studied it as she did all the things that she found pleasing to her eyes and, in her scrutiny of it, she nearly passed without seeing the figure stretched out before her.

She edged closer, glancing back occasionally to judge her chances of escape. A man lay sprawled supine in the warm sand, his bronze body glistening with beads of sweat as his pores soaked up the sun. She stared down at Mason Fenwick, his flawless physique bare to her eyes but for a tiny red string-bikini swimsuit. His closed eyes and deep breathing suggested that he slept. She gaped at him in open admiration and whispered, "Thank God for my eyes." If she never saw anything else in her life, she had seen human perfection and reveled in it. Her tongue curled into the roof of her mouth, and she swallowed with difficulty. What would he say? What would he do if she fell upon him and took him right then and there? Shocked at her thoughts, she gasped aloud and ran.

His years as a resident had trained him to sleep lightly, and Mason awoke at the sound of Jeannetta's gasp. He sat up quickly, and watched her run down the beach until she reached the bathhouse and disappeared from sight. Josh, the porter whom he'd hired to attend to the luggage, approached.

"That was Miss Rollins, wasn't it?" he said, making certain that it was she.

"Yes, sir," Josh confirmed. "She seemed kinda upset. You know, excited-like, but she spoke to me like she always does."

Mason got up and dusted the sand from his hips and legs.

"Sure hate to leave here," Josh told him.

"Yes, but you'll like Rome," Mason called back to him as he headed for the hotel.

Jeannetta stumbled into the bathhouse, breathless and confused about her reaction to Mason. She couldn't afford to fall for him. From the day she'd met him, she had questioned her ability to carry out her plan. Falling for a man made a woman vulnerable to him and put her at a disadvantage, no matter how you viewed it, and to lust for him as she had—only lust described what she'd felt—made her a pushover.

"Good morning, dear. You're looking fit, as usual," Geoffrey Ames confided to her in a near whisper. He had retired at age seventy-eight and had won the lottery the next day. By now, all of his touring companions knew how he regretted having no one with whom to share it. He'd treated himself to the tour, the first pleasure he'd known.

Jeannetta smiled, relieved that it was Geoffrey who had joined her.

"I didn't swim, but the weather is priceless."

The man appeared flustered, but she understood his embarrassment when he asked her in a tentative voice, "Would a lovely young lady such as yourself care to have dinner with me when we get back to Rome tonight?"

"Oh, Geoffrey, I'd love it. Rome at night. It will be wonderful."

"Then I'll find a place where we can eat under the stars. Would you like that?" She assured him that she would, collected the beach clothes that she had stored there, and trudged off to the hotel for breakfast.

Mason wrapped his beach robe tightly and slid into the booth beside her. Her refusal to look at him while she pretended to read a shaking menu and then attempted to drink the water before the glass reached her lips—with obvious results—told him what he wanted to know. She'd run away to avoid temptation. He hadn't tried to breach the wall she'd raised between them since their plane landed in Copenhagen, but he planned to put an end to the foolishness. Beautiful and statuesque, with an indefinable quality, she had a feminine something that he felt clear to the marrow of his bones every time she came near him. He had made it a point not to impose on his guests, and she'd indicated a desire to have space between them, but she would be his exception.

"Enjoy your morning walk?" He ignored her discomfort and considered himself entitled to do that. After all, she hadn't leveled with him; he was certain of it. Her eyelids closed for a second and furrows marked her brow, but he refused to let her discomfort sidetrack him. He repeated it. Her composure restored, she answered in a tone that belittled the importance of his question.

"Yes, but the sand wasn't as thick as I'd hoped it would be. I love to sink into it halfway to my knees."

"You've been avoiding me," he said, dispensing with preliminaries and small talk.

"Why would I do that? You've been the perfect host."

A muscle tensed his jaw, and he pushed back the irritation he felt. "You don't know what kind of host I've been, because you've managed to stay out of my path."

Her lips twitched, and he thought her breath quickened when he slid closer. "You're imagining that."

He caught the fingers of her delicate left hand in his right one, sensed a quick, involuntary movement of her body and watched her lower her eyes and moisten her glistening bare lips with the tip of her tongue. He squeezed her hand.

"Am I imagining this? Am I?" It didn't surprise him that she jerked her hand from his, but he wouldn't have expected the expression of pain mirrored on her lovely brown face.

She turned fully to face him. "Mason, be satisfied with things as they are. I can't give more." Her luminous eyes belied her words, and her obvious reluctance to say them fueled his hunger.

"You wrote on your application that you are not married. Are you engaged?" She shook her head.

"Alright. I want to know you better, and I think you want that, too, but I won't force myself on you or any other woman. Tell me you don't want anything to do with me, and I'll honor your decision." His fingers skimmed the back of her hand. "But could you walk away not knowing what might have been? Could you?" Encouraged by her silence, he let go of her hand, raised his own to her shoulders and tugged her closer to him. After a minute or two, she looked at him and released a quick breath, and he knew that she'd seen the tenderness he felt and the need simmering in his eyes. He lowered his head and kissed the corner of her mouth and, when her lids flew open to reveal a hot woman's desire, he swore inwardly for not having picked a more appropriate time and place to begin their intimacy.

Jeannetta looked at herself in the long mirror, shrugged, picked up her purse and started toward the door of her hotel room. Satisfied with the way she looked, but not sure why she'd put on that sexy, lemon-yellow silk sheath for dinner with Geoffrey Ames, she considered changing into something less provocative. She hadn't bought it as a fashion statement, but because the color became her and the style suited her figure. Her hand rested on the doorknob. No point in lying to herself; she dressed with Mason Fenwick in mind. He socialized with tour members in the lounge at cocktail time, and she hoped he'd see her leave the hotel with Geoffrey. She leaned against the door, wondering when she had become a schemer. She could have been with Mason right then if she'd been honest and told him that she shared his feelings. She slapped her right cheek as though to knock sense into her head, opened the door and headed for the lounge.

She looked from Geoffrey, bedecked in his dark blue suit, white shirt and blue tie, to Mason, who rested casually against the end of the bar wearing what even a child would identify as a mocking smirk. It was that obvious. Geoffrey greeted her in a manner that belied his modest education and humble background, and his pleasure at being with her shone on his countenance. They got into the waiting taxi for the trip across the Tiber River.

*"Buona sera, Signor, Signore,"* the driver sang in a proud operatic voice.

"Son, I'm lucky I can speak English," Geoffrey told the cabby. "These foreign words give me a headache. We want to go to Trastevere."

"Okay. *Dove in Trastevere?"* the driver asked. Geoffrey told him. The driver took them on a hair-raising ride down the Corso and stopped to give them a view of St. Peter's and the Vatican lit at night. Jeannetta thought his lecture in Italian unforgettable, as he used all but his feet to make them understand. She appreciated his effort, though neither she nor her companion could comprehend a word. Jeannetta couldn't suppress a gasp when they got out of the taxi at the restaurant, Alfredo's in Trastevere.

*"Alfresco?"* the waiter asked.

She nodded. That much Italian she knew, and the environment surrounding the famous restaurant invited them to take a table out of doors. They faced the Church of Santa Maria in Trastevere that had dominated the small square and the Trastevere quarter since ancient times. The tiny white building, one of Rome's true treasures, boasted stained-glass windows and a colorfully tiled roof that gleamed in the clear moonlight. Its aura of unreal, unearthly elegance brought tears to her eyes. Nearby diners rattled their silverware and clinked glasses, but she stared, enraptured, her mind far from the gourmet food and its tantalizing odors of seafood, ripe cheeses, spices and garlic. The setting lacked perfection only because Mason Fenwick didn't have his arms around her. Jeannetta reached over and patted Geoffrey's hand.

"I'll remember this for the rest of my life. If I've ever seen anything more beautiful, I don't recall it." She didn't imagine that the old man preened; her words must have touched him, for he seemed taller by inches.

"I didn't think I'd be so fortunate. I figured you'd be going out tonight with our guide. He's young and handsome and he's got all of his hair. He can't seem to keep his eyes off of you either. I watched him."

"Don't read too much into that, Geoffrey. I can imagine that romances always bloom on these tours, and I expect they die when the plane gets back to JFK Airport. Mason's nice to all of us."

Geoffrey shook his head. "You're wrong about this. I've been around a long time, and I know when a man's got the fever. He may be slow about it, but you've caught his eye real good, and he ain't planning to leave this earth without letting you know exactly what that means."

A part of her wanted that confirmation of Mason's interest, but an inner voice counseled her not to lull herself into forgetting why she knew Mason Fenwick. Her gaze held the lovely little church, and she savored the moment; she didn't need a better reminder.

"I think you're mistaken about Mason. He likes me, but not to that extent."

"Never mind. He'll let you know when he gets ready, and it'll do him good to see you with me. I've got a few years on me, but he'll be thinking about that lottery I hit. He knows money makes short men tall. Yep. It'll do him a lot of good."

To her astonishment, Geoffrey raised her hand to his lips and gave it a pretend kiss just as they stepped into the hotel lobby. She thought he'd overdone his appreciation of her company until she saw Mason sprawled in a leather lounge chair that directly faced the door. He stood at once, and she nearly laughed when Geoffrey patted her shoulder, grasped her hand, smiled and whispered, "It'll come sooner than you expect."

Mason walked to them, a scowl distorting his handsome features, and, ignoring Geoffrey, demanded to know where she'd been. She turned aside and told her escort that she'd enjoyed his company and that she would never forget their evening together.

"It was truly idyllic," she added, intentionally aggravating Mason.

"Miss Rollins, as you know, the first rule of this tour is that whenever members leave the group, I must be told where they're going. Lady, I sat here for three hours wondering whether I should call the police. You strutted out of here in that…that… Walked out of here, got in a taxi and stayed for three solid hours. Three hours in a city you never saw before. You're… That's irresponsible."

"What are you so riled about? I was with Mr. Ames. You saw me leave here with him."

"You were with Ames?" He told himself to calm down,

that she had returned apparently unharmed, and that he ought to forget about her. Then he ignored his advice. "I thought he only helped you get a taxi. You were with him all this time?"

"Sure was," she answered as though he'd find that scenario acceptable.

*Well,* he thought, *she miscalculated.* Ames might be seventy-eight, but he owned the standard male equipment, plus a pile of money.

"Ames told me where he was going, but he neglected to add that he intended to take you with him." He looked at her, standing there wearing that half smile, the picture of innocence, and he wished he could do a few push-ups to cool down his anger. She had a right to do anything she pleased with whomever she liked. He stuck his hand in his right pants pocket and felt the odd-size keys that were forever with him. Damned if he'd let her erase what he'd achieved in years of fighting to control his constant anxiety and trigger temper. He wanted to make her mad, but she just stood there smiling, refusing to budge.

"I hope you remember that we leave tomorrow morning for Paris and that you're to have your bags outside your door at six-thirty."

She took a step toward him. "I remembered. Why are you so angry?"

The balloon inside him burst, scattering his anger as chaff succumbs to the wind.

"I haven't been angry in years." Well, he hadn't until tonight. "I'm annoyed. Please try to be more considerate."

"I'll be ready in time, and so will my bags, so don't get your dander up. Losing your temper at me is bad for your health," she teased.

He stared at the mischievous grin that curled her lips, and he wanted to…

"Are you alright?" he asked, his demeanor having changed quickly to one of concern.

"Oh, I'm fine. Why?" Her smile didn't fool him. She'd experienced a vertigo-like sensation and grabbed the back of the chair. A second-year medical student wouldn't have been fooled by that.

"I'll see you to your room." His hand at her elbow was all the support he knew she'd allow, but he wanted to take her into his arms, carry her to her room and tuck her into bed.

"I can go alone. I'm fine—really, I am."

"It will comfort me to know you're safely in your room. I'm going with you." In the elevator, where the lights shone brighter, a feeling of relief washed over him when he couldn't detect any pallor and she showed no further signs of dizziness.

"Too bad we aren't spending more time in Paris," she said. "I'll only have time to go to the Louvre and the *Jeu de Paume*. I would have loved to visit the Rodin museum and to find some of those new, off-the-beaten-path art galleries that feature folk art from Central Africa. This may be my last… The other members of the tour will be shopping and sipping espresso at the Café de la Paix trying to feel what it's like to be French."

They got off the elevator and strolled to her room nearby.

"I doubt the French ever go to that café. If they want an espresso, they can get it cheaper and better someplace where the waiters only speak French. Sure you don't want to shop?" She shook her head, and he found himself admiring her ability to get that thick, wooly hair into such an elegant twist at the back of her neck. A lot of things about her pleased him.

"Since we're both art lovers, why don't we check out those museums together, all three of them?"

Her quick smile told him that she welcomed his company. "I'd love that. Maybe we can find some of those galleries, too."

"Are you going to shop for African art?"

Why should the light in her eyes dim so quickly? Mason wondered.

"I don't want to buy anything."

He watched her closely. "Not even perfume?"

Her shrug must have been intended to suggest nonchalance, or maybe that perfume didn't interest her. She'd piqued his interest further.

"I don't need anything, and I don't like to own things just for the sake of having them. I only buy what I need. It would be fun, though, to sit on the Avenue de la Paix and watch the world pass." She took a step backward when he moved closer to her.

"You fascinate me. Why do you avoid me?"

She seemed flustered, but immediately covered it with a haughty tilt of her head.

"I haven't done that. Why should I? You seem harmless enough." That smile again. That curve of her lipstick-free mouth that made him want to devour her, to kiss her until she told him he could have whatever he wanted.

"You *are* harmless, aren't you?" she asked him. Well, hell. She was flirting with him.

"Depends on your definition of harmless. I'm your tour manager, and I'm responsible for you, but when the two of us are alone—like right now—my mating instincts are likely to surface. Like now."

Her eyes rounded into two beautiful brown Os.

"You're a very desirable woman, and I haven't forgotten that for one second since the first time I looked at you." The hot energy that shot to his belly must have been reflected in his eyes, because she broke eye contact with him. He wanted to take her and love her until he hadn't an ounce of energy left, but he understood women, and this wasn't the time to press it. Her inability to look at him and her insistent toying with her hands fuelled the heat in him. But he wasn't reckless. Not yet. If ever he'd been suspended over feminine quicksand, this was the time, and he admitted wanting the experience of being sucked into it. All the way. He brushed back the lapels of his jacket and eased his hands into his pants pockets while he stared at her lips. Desire choked him, and he coughed. If she didn't stop fidgeting...

"I'd better say good-night. As you said, I have to rise early."

"Scared?"

"You could say that," she answered, though she didn't look it. He moved closer. "But you could also be wrong." She took the plastic card from her evening purse and would have opened her door had he not taken the card. He placed it in the lock, but didn't open the door. She shifted her glance; her lower lip quivered, and he had to admire her willpower. But when she swallowed hard, he nearly lost his own. A battle of wills, and she'd win if he didn't put some space between them.

"What do you want, Mr. Fenwick?"

"My name is Mason, and I think you know the answer to that. See you in the morning." He sucked in his breath. "Good night."

Mason reflected on their exchange as he rounded the corner to his room. *She's delicate,* he mused, *but she's also strong; warm, but wary.* And she intended to keep him at a distance. It had stunned him to realize how badly he wanted to kiss her, to feel her, soft and submissive, in his arms. He thought of that morning on the beach, still unable to decide why she'd run away. An aura of mystery clung to her, and he sensed an air of transience about her, as though she were only flitting through his life. He'd better watch his step with Jeannetta Rollins, because he'd had his last temporary liaison. Now he wanted a home and a family.

Jeannetta got into her room and locked the door. That had been close. Her thoughts had been filled with the memory of him lying nearly naked in the warm sand, beads of perspiration glistening on his washboard-flat belly. All but inches of him had been a feast for her eyes. The urge she'd had to fall upon him and ravish his body had come back to her. Six more weeks, and it didn't look promising. He hadn't allowed her to create an environment in which he could be approached as a surgeon, and she had avoided him when he socialized with the guests. She couldn't let him believe that she was courting his attention, but, no matter what she did, he steered their relationship toward intimacy. She had to keep it impersonal; if she didn't, she would pay dearly.

After the uneventful flight from Rome to Paris and a routine trip to a hotel near the Champs Elysée, Jeannetta stood on the balcony of her hotel room in the shadow of the Arc de Triomphe, savoring the sights that greeted her eyes. Preparing for the possibility that her ears would someday become her eyes, she relayed descriptions of the French and their antics into her cassette recorder. An old man riding what seemed an even older bicycle fell from his bike in his attempt to prevent his long skinny loaf of bread from falling to the ground. Unharmed, he threaded the baguette through a hole in the basket, looked up and shook his fist at the sky. A woman wearing a yellow, red and purple beret dashed across the wide avenue after her monkey, stopping traffic as she went and leaving her organ grinder to the mercy of two youths, who stood playing with it when she returned with her pet. She promptly left the machine and the monkey and took off after the two pranksters.

Jeannetta rushed inside to answer the telephone and was rewarded with the sound of Mason's deep baritone.

"It's eleven o'clock. We ought to get started if we're going to three museums today. How much time do you need?"

She told him she'd meet him in the lobby in ten minutes.

"I thought I'd stop by for you."

And from the way he'd looked at her after placing her bags on the luggage rack in her room that morning, they'd never reach *one* museum. "Downstairs. Ten minutes."

His chuckle warmed her heart. "Okay, scaredy-cat."

She leaned against the doorjamb, studying a sculpture in the Musée de Rodin. She had to memorize as much as possible so that she could make an accurate recording of it that evening.

"Are you tired?" Mason asked her.

"No. Thank you. I can't rush through this. I want to see these sculptures with every one of my senses, not just my eyes. I want to be able to recall in my mind's eye every line, every bump—feel the cold texture of the bronze. Everything." From his strange, inquiring expression, she wondered what he saw.

"Do I seem odd to you?" she asked, and immediately wished that she hadn't, when he seemed taken aback.

"Why, no. I've just realized that you're a deeply sensual person." Her glance fell on *The Kiss,* Rodin's great masterpiece, and she wished that Mason hadn't witnessed her reaction to it, as he must have, when she sucked in her breath and her lips parted in awe.

"Exquisite, isn't it? A man's homage to his love." Stunned at his unexpected sentimentality, her eyes caressed him as she welcomed this new facet of the man who, with each passing moment, wedged himself more deeply into her being. His diffident smile betrayed his reaction to having exposed himself and, with a shrug, he grasped her hand.

"Come on. We've got a lot more to see." She might have removed her hand if an inner voice hadn't whispered that it belonged in his. The strong, smooth fingers communicated an eagerness to protect, and a need for her woman's tenderness and succor. She tried to ignore the swirling sensation that caught her up as would a dream and incited in her an eagerness for everything he could give a woman. And she couldn't help relishing the comfort of his stroking finger, as a strange, reassuring vibration flowed through her.

He squeezed gently, as though wanting to achieve greater intimacy, and she withdrew her hand.

"Did I hurt you?" The low timbre of his voice communicated a gentleness that she had begun to realize bespoke the true nature of the man. She shook her head, not wanting him to know that his touch had ignited a wild churning in her. She had never felt so close to him. Could now be the time to tell him? She didn't want to make a mistake, because she probably wouldn't get more than one chance.

*"On ferme dans les trente minutes."* Closing in thirty minutes, the loud nasal tones proclaimed, intruding on their intimacy, destroying the opportunity.

"Your fingers are calloused," she said, "and I didn't expect that. I thought they'd be softer, like... Not the hands of a blue-collar man." Her voice quavered and a harsh shudder shook her. She had almost revealed that she knew he'd been a surgeon.

"That's because I carve wooden figures," he said. She could breathe easily; he hadn't caught what could have been a crucial, fatal blunder.

"It's a hobby," he went on. "If I'd known your partiality to soft hands, I might have used some lotion." Laughter lightened his features. "And then again, I might not have." She joined his laughter, remembering her similar remark to him their last night in Rome. He looked down at her for a long time, his gaze, bland and unrevealing, roaming over her features yet obviously seeking some important answer. Abruptly, he smiled, shrugged and took her hand firmly into his. She let him keep it.

Mason paused by one of Rodin's free-forms and ran his hand over it, fondling its lines, stroking it. He didn't hear Jeannetta's footsteps; only the stillness around him interfered with his absorption in the art beneath his hand. He looked up to find her watching him. Engrossed. His heart quickened at the sight of her parted lips, wide eyes and the absence of the serene expression that ordinarily adorned her face. He noticed that she breathed erratically and that her gaze remained glued to the rhythmic movement of his hand. He stopped its stroking, testing her reaction, and she glanced up at him. His breath gurgled in his throat. Stripped bare, exposed, her eyes were windows of her aching, her longing. He didn't have to be told that she imagined his hands on her, stroking and caressing her, that desire had sucked up the coolness she always presented to him and left her emotionally naked.

"Jeannetta!"

She ducked her head and walked swiftly away from him.

"Don't run from me, Jeannetta; don't run from this. There's no point. It will catch up with you, with us."

"I don't know what you're talking about."

He watched her standing with her back against the wall. If she wasn't trembling, his name wasn't Mason Fenwick. He wanted to comfort her, to reassure her that nothing wrong, nothing painful could come of a relationship with him, that he'd as soon hurt himself as damage so vulnerable a woman.

"Denying it won't make it untrue," he told her, as gently as he could. "This is something you and I are going to have to deal with. And soon. We're like moth and flame, and if we put an ocean between us we'd only postpone the inevitable. Because, honey, we'd find each other."

"Think about something else, Mason. We don't have to get entangled."

He raised both eyebrows. "And we don't have to give this up either. We're free, over twenty-one and…"

"You know what would be fun?" she interrupted, and he could see lights dancing in her warm brown eyes. Alright, he'd give in this time; he had learned the value of patience.

"What would be fun?" he asked.

"Let's take the Métro to the opera house, walk over to the Café de la Paix, get a sidewalk table and watch the people."

He stroked his chin, the notion that Jeannetta liked to live outside of herself occurring to him for the first time. He mused over it, certain that he'd discovered something important about her.

"You like that sort of thing, don't you? I seem to recall your having suggested that I sit at a sidewalk café on Columbus Avenue and freeze with you while you gazed at the passersby. What is it about watching strangers that gives you so much satisfaction?"

"I don't know." She waved a hand airily. "People-watching is an art. If I watch a person walking toward me and then away from me, I can tell you a lot of things about him."

The swirling skirts and dancing boots of a group of Gypsies caught his gaze, and he nudged Jeannetta. Immediately, she joined them. The dancers welcomed her, and Mason watched in awe as her feet seemed to take wings. Her head back and arms spread wide in abandon, her whirling skirt became a maze of brown, orange and yellow billowing in the breeze as she gave herself to the music. A glow of ecstasy glistened on her face, and he had the feeling that she tossed off burden after burden as she danced. But for her darker skin and thick, wooly hair, he couldn't have distinguished her from the Gypsies. When at last the music stopped, her new friends applauded her. She waved goodbye to them and, with his finger at her elbow, they continued down the crowded street. She seemed suffused with joy, but the incident depressed him, because he recognized an unwholesome desperation in it, a false *joie de vivre*.

"Gee, what a pretty child. Look, Mason."

He noticed the little dark-haired and rosy-cheeked girl

who stared inquiringly at Jeannetta. She dropped his hand, walked over and hunkered down to the little girl's level. His heart skittered in his chest as the child, wreathed in smiles and delighted with the attention, touched Jeannetta's cheek. The child's mother stood there and watched the exchange, her prideful delight in the beautiful little girl obvious. He had to turn away when a look of longing darkened Jeannetta's face. She's young and so beautiful, he thought. Why did she have that look of longing in her eyes? He stepped to her side, took her hand and helped her to her feet. It occurred to him for the nth time that she needed his protection. But when he offered it, however camouflaged, she made certain he knew that she didn't need it.

At the Café de la Paix, they found a tiny round table at the edge of the café, beside the sidewalk, a prize any time of the year in spite of its cracked marble top, myriad coffee stains and rickety legs, and settled back to observe the changing scene on one of the world's busiest streets. Jeannetta could hardly contain herself.

Mason ordered two cups of espresso. "I was eighteen the last time I sat at this very table," he said, pointing to the initials he'd carved in the marble. "I had the world at my feet—a scholarship to Stanford and this trip to Europe that I'd been awarded for graduating at the top of my high-school class. My horizons had no bounds." He leaned back in his chair and spoke quietly, as though to himself. "Youth is a wondrous thing."

Alert to any clue that might tell her that she could safely broach the subject of her health and whether he'd return to the practice of medicine in order to help her, she cocked an ear. "Do I hear disillusionment behind those words?" she questioned, in an attempt to lead him into a discussion of his past.

"You're hearing the voice of reality. Man proposes and

God disposes." He looked away, strummed his fingers on the tiny table and she could see him detach himself. Well, another time.

"See that couple over there?" she asked him. "The man's wearing a black jogging top."

"Yeah. What about him?"

She cupped her chin with her palms and braced her elbows on her crossed knee. "She wants more from him than he's giving or wants to give." She paused, watching them closely as they passed. "See? She can hardly keep up with him. He's not a bit concerned about her." She pushed her sunglasses higher on the bridge of her nose and waited for his reaction.

"All that with just a glance? All I saw was two people walking past."

"You were looking. I was observing," she said. "That man has a serious problem. Hands in his pockets, gaze on the pavement, hunched over. I'd bet on it." She had his full attention and, deciding that she didn't want to relinquish it, she tossed her head back and looked at him from lowered eyelids. "You're a clever man. You can do as well as I can." Alright, so she was getting fresh with him; he wasn't above a little flirtation himself. His slow smile confirmed it.

"Your passion for people-watching could be a very consuming pastime." He said it so softly that she had to lean toward him, showing more cleavage than she thought prudent. His smile told her he'd done that intentionally. "These characters who flow through your life, do you keep them in mind, forget about them, or what?"

"The ones that I can't forget…" she let her long pause include him in that group "…find their way into my novels."

"You're a writer? A novelist? I thought you wrote jokes and made dolls." His frown reminded her that she hadn't put "novelist" as her occupation on her application to Fenwick Travel Agency. He let it slide.

"Jeannetta, I'm enjoying this, but I have to get back to the hotel and make some overseas calls. Have dinner with me."

He'd take her to a swank restaurant with an idyllic setting; fine wine and elegant food. He was that type. And when he took her back to the hotel, she'd be a pushover. For the snap of his finger, she'd crawl all over him right then; a luscious evening with him would...

"I...I think I'd better turn in early tonight... You...you're marvelous company, but...maybe not." From the lights dancing in his eyes, and the amusement she detected around his twitching lips, she knew he had her number. Those wonderful eyes challenged, teased and coaxed. Oh, how she adored his eyes.

"I haven't bitten any pretty women recently," he bantered. "Besides, I'm responsible for you, so you can trust me. Or does Ames have first dibs on your evenings?"

"Oh, Mason, he's hungry for company," she said with pretended seriousness. "Can he come along with us? You won't mind, will you?"

Streaks of pleasure danced along her limbs when he gave in to his amusement and let his face dissolve into an infectious, devastating grin.

"If Ames is hungry for company, I'll introduce him to Lucy Abernathy. She's practically starving for it. She took this tour last year and the year before, so I'd say she could use some good company."

She thought of dowdy Miss Abernathy and said, "What about Maybeth?"

His smile faded. "Don't tell me you've got a sadistic streak. Maybeth Baxter is a man-eater. In six months, Ames wouldn't have a dime of his lottery millions. Besides, he's too smart to go any place with that woman." He stood and waved for the waiter. *"Garçon. L'addition, s'il vous plâit."* The bill, please. He extended his hand to her.

"This is our only night in Paris. I don't want to eat—I want to dine, and I don't want to look across the table at Geoffrey Ames while I do it." His voice, low, soothing, teased her senses. "I want to look at you while I enjoy my meal." The huskiness of his tone and the soothing strokes of his fingers rattled her will to resist him. *Face it,* she told herself, *you want to go with him; what's the use of being coy about it?*

"Dinner would be nice. I'd like to get back early, though, since we're leaving in the morning." She didn't fool herself; he'd already shown her that she needed all of her wits when, as now, he challenged her, dared her, without so much as one word, with only the mischievous merriment or the smoldering suggestiveness in the extraordinary eyes that gleamed at her from his impassive face.

The man bowed from the waist and taunted, "At your service, ma'am."

She had to stifle a laugh. She wouldn't be outdone; her sense of humor was as good as the next one's.

"Mason, it's easy to forget, sometimes, that you're a mere mortal—but if the rest of us make that mistake, you be sure and keep your head screwed on right. Psychiatrists probably make even more money than surgeons."

She wanted to swallow her tongue. His eyes rounded and, beneath his sharply arched eyebrows, she could see every bit of the white in them. She couldn't let the unfriendliness in his penetrating stare disconcert her. Too much hung on this moment. She put an inquiring look on her face that questioned his change of mood, and prayed that her bluff would cover her slip. After a minute, he relaxed, but he didn't pursue the topic.

"Let's find a cab," he said as they walked out in the warm sun. If he noticed her stumble, he didn't mention it.

"Seven o'clock," he admonished, as a reminder of her tardiness, and she left him and went to her room. She took off her sandals, got her recorder and began to describe all that she'd seen and done since arriving in Paris that morning. But the practice that she had enjoyed in the early days of the tour weighed on her now as an unwanted chore. She put the instrument aside, flipped on the television news program and, minutes later, sat gaping at herself in a frenzied dance, whirling and cavorting on the rue du Chandon with the colorful Gypsies. She remembered the wildness of it, the wonderful feeling of abandon, the… She zapped the channel and soon turned off the television.

Paris was so close to Germany, less than one jet hour away. Maybe she ought to quit the tour, go to Frankfurt and see a specialist. Germans had always been leaders in medicine. She only had the word of two doctors, both of whom could be wrong. For all she knew, they had consulted with one another. Maybe she didn't have a tumor. She hadn't had any dizziness since the first days of the tour, and then only twice, and she hadn't had a headache in several days. Anybody could have a headache. Deciding that she'd think about it later, she undressed and got into bed for a pre-dinner nap.

An hour later, she awakened in the midst of damp, rumpled sheets, her gown clinging to her perspiring body. She hadn't had a nightmare since learning the nature of her illness. But this time, it had ended differently. In Mason's arms, his velvet tongue spreading sweet nectar in her mouth as he lay buried deep within her, powerful waves of sensation had banished the darkness. His hugs and kisses, tender murmuring and total giving of himself, had dissipated her fears, made her a whole, vibrant person again. She struggled out of bed, showered, donned a lavender-pink silk peignoir and walked out on her balcony, hoping to see the sun set. She looked toward the Arc de Triomphe and gasped. Rays of the red setting sun filtered through the leaves of the flowering horse chestnut trees that lined the famous avenue, a humbling vision against the background of dark gray sky. Men and women rushed home, by bicycle, automobile and foot—much as Americans did, though you wouldn't see any Americans carrying a long loaf of unwrapped bread.

Six o'clock. That made it noontime in the northeastern United States, she calculated, going to the telephone. Within minutes, she heard Laura's voice.

"Made any headway with him yet?" Laura's question took the place of a greeting, reminded Jeannetta that she had better treat the matter with the urgency it deserved. She couldn't tell Laura that she'd made headway, but not the kind she needed.

"I'm working on it. What's new?"

"Same old mountains, hon. You soak up all that Paris atmosphere, but you come back with a commitment out of that man, you hear?" Laura's ability to focus the way a racehorse does, with the help of blinders, had always amused Jeannetta, though many found it reason for faulting her intelligence. If she knew your problem, she didn't let you forget it until you solved it.

"Don't you get caught up in that man and forget why you're spending all of that money," Laura went on. "The Lord helps those who help themselves, and if you don't do your part, He'll think you don't care what happens." Jeannetta knew she'd better not tell her sister that Mason had come close to kissing her more than once.

"He hasn't given me the opportunity to bring up the subject, though I've made several openings. From what I've come to know of him, I don't think I'll accomplish anything by jumping in cold and asking him."

"You mean you've been with him for almost three weeks and you haven't even mentioned it? Since when did you get so shy? Something's wrong. You're leaving something out." She could see Laura rest the back of her hand on her hip, and a look of incredulity spread over her face.

"Don't worry, Laura. I'll work hard at it. I don't intend to fail." *I'd better not,* she admonished herself, as Laura blew kisses into the phone, reminded her that she'd have a big bill and hung up.

Jeannetta meandered slowly back to the balcony, pensive, her thoughts weighted with misgivings, thanks to Laura's pessimism. She walked to the edge of the balcony, where she glimpsed a tall man of African descent strolling along the Avenue. He stopped, leaned against a big chestnut tree and looked toward the Arc, seemingly enraptured by the sunset. She had heard it said that one could connect with another person through the mind. Could she compel him to look her way? The force of her concentration produced the first headache she'd had in days. He's strong-willed, she decided, but she wouldn't give up.

"Look at me. Show me your face," she commanded repeatedly. As though in defiance, he straightened up, strolled to the corner, paused, then continued and, finally, as though against his will, Mason Fenwick looked directly into her eyes. She would have liked to evaporate. He stared at her for a long time, didn't smile and turned the corner toward the hotel's entrance.

Cold shivers coursed through her, and she rubbed her arms furiously as she stumbled back into her room. She'd tried that trick dozens of times without having succeeded but, when she would have given anything to fail, she'd finally done it. Maybe the cards were not in her favor; she hadn't done anything right where Mason was concerned. Perhaps she shouldn't have plotted to win his concern, but should have gone to his office, told him her story and accepted the consequences. How could she face him? She laid back her shoulders, went to the closet and took out a scooped-neck sleeveless sheath, a luscious green that shimmered with green crystal beads and stopped four inches above her knee. She covered her long legs with sheer black stockings and slipped her feet into a pair of spike-heeled

black silk evening shoes. A small black beaded bag completed
what she referred to as her masquerade. She'd scrubbed her
face with cold water, buffed it with a terry towel and twisted
her hair on top of her head.

"What you see is what you get," she said, reflecting on her
refusal to wear makeup of any kind or earrings. She dabbed a
bit of *Trésor* behind her ears and between her breasts, glanced
at the mirror and left the room.

Mason pushed back the sleeve of his white evening jacket,
checked his Timex, headed for the elevator and leaned against
the wall facing the door. She'd given him plenty to think about
that day, half a dozen women in the same body. He'd never
known such a changeable woman. He suspected that part of
it was due to the anonymity one gets in a strange place. Her
odd behavior on the balcony of her room. That wild dance,
for instance; she would never have done that in Pilgrim, nor
New York City for that matter. But the longing he'd seen in
her when she talked with that child had been real. And she
took that people-watching thing almost to an extreme. The
writer in her. Maybe. Hard to say. He had no doubt as to the
genuineness of her sensuous nature: art, music and that in-
tuitiveness about lovers. Maybe it was all real. One thing he
didn't question was the fascination she held for him.

The elevator door opened. He supposed he'd have to get
used to the tingling delight that shot through him when she
stepped into the lounge. He could only stare, as a crazy,
schoolboy kind of joy zinged through him when she saw him
and transformed her beautiful brown face into a glowing appreciation of his manliness. He knew that women thought him
handsome, that they especially raved about his eyes, but he'd
long since learned to ignore their shallow adulation.

"Your loveliness, so natural and so beguiling, takes my

breath away. I'll be the envy of every man who sees us tonight."

She tossed her head to the side, in what he'd noticed signaled a flirtatious mood.

"French women aren't slow when it comes to appreciating men either. From what I've heard, they may get fresh with you while I'm holding your hand." Her exaggerated deep breath made him wonder what else to expect. She didn't keep him waiting.

"I've never been in a cat fight, and I'd just as soon my first one happened someplace where nobody knows me. Why not Paris? Ready to go?"

He didn't recall her previously having wrinkled her nose at him in playful flirtation as she did then. *What a female,* he thought, as he offered her his arm. With this woman, he'd have to keep his motor oiled and running. "Slow down, buddy," he cautioned himself.

He'd reserved a table at an elegant restaurant that seated twelve couples or parties of four. Potted palms between the tables guaranteed privacy, and the multicolored lights, reflected off the waterfall in the room's center and in the overhead chandeliers, gave the room a soft allure, a testimonial to the French preoccupation with *l'amour.*

"You like it?" he asked as the waiter seated them.

"Oh, Mason. It's the loveliest restaurant I've ever seen. Thank you for choosing it. I'll add it to the treasure of memories I've stashed away in the archives of my mind."

He couldn't tell whether she noticed his reaction to that revelation. Something wasn't right.

"Oh, you'll see lovelier ones than this," he said.

"Maybe."

It had been on the tip of his tongue to tell her that he'd show her the world, but she lacked the zest of moments earlier, and he thought light banter might unsettle her. He had to get used to her mood changes.

"You're still young." He covered her hand with his own. "You'll visit a few of them with me on this tour. We can have a wonderful time together, Jeannetta." He paused. "If you want it."

"Perhaps." He caressed her hand, and a sensation of sharp, hot darts pounded at his belly when she turned her hand so that her palm embraced his own. He'd better get them interested in another subject, anything to enable him to make it through dinner without an embarrassing show of male want.

"When will you finish your novel?" Uh-oh. Wrong topic, he realized when she placed her fork on her plate, sat back and took a deep breath.

"That depends on a lot of things, some of which are beyond my control." Suddenly, she brightened. "I'd been writing about a woman but, when we were in Rome, I realized that was all wrong. My protagonist is a man and should have been all along."

"Anything to do with anybody you met on the tour?"

Her enigmatic smile curled her lip upward and settled at the corner of her mouth.

He hoped she couldn't hear the wild thumping of his heart. "Well?" he insisted.

"Everything and nothing."

"What kind of an answer is that?"

Her laughter wrapped around him; he could have listened to it forever.

"You inspired the change, but it isn't about you."

"I see. Gonna let me read it?"

"If I finish it, you'll be the first to see it. I promise." He resisted asking why she'd implied that she might not finish it, but they'd gotten out of one dump, and he wanted to see her happy, spirited, normal self, not melancholy and withdrawn. Her hand moved against his, a little caress.

"If I wasn't certain I'd drive these French waiters up the wall, I'd move my chair around this table and sit where I could put my arm around you."

She hid her eyes behind lowered lashes, but trembling fingers nevertheless betrayed her, and he thought his heart had galloped out of control. When she threaded her fingers through his, still avoiding his gaze, he thanked God for the long white tablecloth that covered his lap.

"Some people are big on words," he heard her murmur beneath her breath.

"*What?* We're still in France, lady, so don't tempt me unless you'd like me to show you some wantonness of my own. I probably wouldn't dance in the street with a group of Gypsies, but, take my word for it, I know how to let it all hang out. You want to eat those words?"

She shook her head and corrected her posture, but didn't remove her hand from his. He reached across the table and tickled her chin with the forefinger of his free hand.

"Don't go getting prim on me, sweetheart, too late for that. Look at me."

Her long lashes lifted with snaillike speed. Lord, did this woman know how to flirt!

*"Pour dessert, Monsieur?"* The waiter must have understood his murderous glare, because the man glanced away, then back, as if to say, *sorry, bad timing.* Neither of them wanted dessert, so he ordered two cups of espresso coffee.

He wouldn't press her. Time enough for that when he got her to himself. Her quietness didn't disturb him, because he knew she was feeling something new, just as he was, and that she was trying to deal with it. They left the restaurant holding hands.

"It's only nine o'clock. Would you like to stop by Bongo

Ade's for half an hour or so? It's walking distance. It caters to Francophone Africans, but you don't have to talk to them. How about it?"

"I'd love it. Unless their French is full of local accents, I'll probably be able to understand it."

Rays of yellow, orange, white and blue lights, reminiscent of a Harlem disco, flashed like convoluted rainbows across the dance floor of Ade's home away from home. A low hum of voices melded with the steady rhythm of the drums to which patrons swayed even as they sat at tables or stood talking in groups. With its warm, homey atmosphere, Bongo Ade's needed no welcome sign. Mason found a table, ordered lemonade, which the waitress recommended, and settled in the comfortable rattan chair. He noticed immediately that the West Africans seemed to prefer lemonade and soft drinks, while the Frenchmen and other non-Africans drank wine or spirits. People-watching had a lot to recommend it.

"Excuse me, please."

He looked up as she started to rise, went around to her chair and assisted her. "I'll be right back." He watched her glide away. He had wanted her because…well, a man wanted a woman like her, but he had begun to develop a reason for wanting her that had nothing to do with what he saw when he looked at her. He needed to have a good talk with himself.

Jeannetta closed the door of the ladies' room and leaned against it. She couldn't imagine why she'd teased Mason at the restaurant when she knew he'd exact payment first chance he got. She'd never been so irresolute as now, telling him that he could expect nothing intimate between them and then leading him to believe he had a chance. A woman who did that risked being known as a tease, and the description didn't fit her. At least it hadn't. Mason wasn't a man a woman could ignore, especially if he showed an interest. She had to admit that, with each come-to-me signal he sent her, with each tender gesture, her will to walk away from him weakened more. She rinsed her mouth and glanced up to see two West-African women enter the room.

"Where you from, love?" one of them asked in a most non-African fashion. She told them. The woman switched from French to English. She had spent seven years at the United Nations in New York before transferring to the UNESCO in Paris.

"You and your husband look good together," the woman said.

Surprised at the assumption, Jeannetta replied, "He isn't my husband."

"You'd better fix that," the other woman advised. "If you don't, some other woman will do that for you. He's nice. Real nice."

"He sure is that," the first woman added. "I never could understand how you American women don't see to your men." They talked for a few minutes, and Jeannetta remarked that they seemed less African than she would have expected. They told her, proudly, that they had lived and worked in New York, married Frenchmen, traveled extensively and that they were as uncomfortable in their ancestral villages as she would be. She said goodbye, started back to her table, and stopped. Two women in West-African dress had joined Mason, and his flirtatious smile told her that he enjoyed their company.

She steamed, in what she recognized as a fit of jealousy, strode purposefully to the table and stopped. Seeing her, the smile spread wider over Mason's face and he stood. He introduced Jeannetta and asked them to excuse him.

"I've enjoyed meeting you ladies," he added as they lingered.

Jeannetta could barely control an impulse to flinch when one of the women looked her over, showed a lack of concern for as competition and drawled, "When you leave your man alone in Ade's, you're asking one of us to take him." Jeannetta glanced at Mason from the corner of her eye and wanted to erase that smirk from his grinning lips.

"He isn't that easy to get," she said, running her left hand along his arm possessively and smiling into Mason's eyes. A broad grin animated his elegant features, and she could almost hear her heart sing with delight.

"I am *so* easy to get," he said, grinning as his gaze seared her. "All you have to do is wink."

"I wouldn't have thought you'd be a pushover," she said, her gaze fastened on his tantalizing lips as he bent over to seat her. She could almost touch them with her own.

"Maybe not for some people," he teased. "Go ahead. Push a little bit. See what happens."

The rhythm of the bongos increased, soft and sensual, and the heat in his eyes toyed with her. Desire tugged at her, but she fought it, finally crossing her legs in frustration. She knew the gesture hadn't escaped him but, gentleman that he was, he let it slide.

"Chicken. Don't you want to test your feminine power?"

"Get thee behind me, Satan." He threw his head back and released an attention-getting, happy laugh. A warm glow flowed through her, and his blatant joy drew her into a cocoon of euphoria. His cocoon. What was the point in fighting him?

## Chapter 3

He hadn't taken her hand when they left Ade's, because he couldn't hold any part of her and fight his battle with himself. Her quiet serenity during the ride back had suited him, given him time for reflection. They reached her door, and he held out his hand for her key. Wildfire shot through his veins when she opened her bag, took out the strip of plastic and handed it to him without shifting her gaze from his. *Be careful, man; you don't want any more fly-by-night affairs. No more convenient sex. No more...*

"Here." Her whisper barely reached his ear. He held out his hand for the card and felt it scrape his fingers as her hand shook.

"Jeannetta." He heard the soft rasp of his voice, but did she? Only the rapid quiver of her bottom lip told him that she'd responded to his entreaty. He tugged at the card, but didn't take it. Waited. She glanced up at him with "I need you" blazing in her eyes, and he didn't care about the lecture he'd just given himself, didn't worry about her past insistence that there could be nothing between them. He shoved logic aside.

"I'm waiting for you to wink."

"I never learned how." He took a step closer, testing the water.

"If you can't close one eye at a time, close both of them." His breathing accelerated, and he finally had to shove his hands into his pockets while he wondered if the bottom would drop out of him. Like a slow-moving drawbridge, her eyelids covered her luminous eyes and her hands crept up his lapel.

"Jeannetta. Jeannetta."

Her nerves skittered wildly when the voice that had shaken her before she met its owner produced that urgent, husky sound of need. She knew that her bottom lip quivered, because it always betrayed her nervousness. His large but gentle hands covered her slim shoulders, steadying her. Why didn't he kiss her, take her, love her out of her senses?

"Don't be afraid. I don't wound if I can help it. I'm a healer." She opened her eyes but couldn't move, didn't want to move, as his eyes turned a smoldering dark greenish-brown, and she could feel him inside her as he'd been that afternoon in her dream.

"Oh, Mason. Mason, I..." Goosepimples spread over her flesh and the air swished out of her. His lips touched hers, tentatively, as though he thought she might reject him. Clamoring for him, she parted her lips, slipped her right hand behind his head and pressed his mouth to hers. His tongue swept and swirled in her mouth and she savored the taste of him, sucked it, nibbled it, until he used it to show her how much more they could have together. Wave after wave of vibration pounded her center, and she undulated against him. Hot flames of desire engulfed her and, when she shivered, he tightened his hold on her, slipped his hand between them and swallowed her keening cry. She twisted against his body until he held her away from him.

"We have to think about this, baby. I want to take this key, open that door and lose myself in you but, tomorrow morning, you'd be sorry. You've told me enough times that you don't want an involved relationship with me." Still holding her gently, he sought confirmation that she had changed her thinking about them. "I want you to stand three feet from me and tell me you changed your mind." But she burrowed her face in his shoulder, and he opened her bedroom door, took her in, kissed her cheek and turned to leave.

"Mason." He turned around. "You're… You're…wonderful."

"I'll see you in the morning. Try to be on time."

He had planned to go straight to his room and hit the bed. Instead, when he passed the elevator, he punched the button and headed for the bar.

"Surprised to see you down here tonight," Geoffrey told him as he picked up his bourbon and soda and walked over to join Mason. "If I'm not welcome just nod your head and I'll go on back to my table."

"Why are you surprised to see me?" Mason asked him, hoping that it wouldn't be necessary to tell the man to mind his business.

"Well, you'll be rising with the chickens in the morning, and I figured you'd be turning in."

Mason smiled inwardly. Geoffrey Ames could take a dozen trips around the world, but he'd carry that Georgia country style of speaking wherever he went.

"I'll be turning in shortly. Enjoying the tour so far?"

"Well…yes and no. Accommodations are fine, but I've kind

of set my sights on Miss Lucy, and I'm out of practice. I was
married for well-nigh fifty years, and I guess I just lost track
of how you go about getting a lady's attention."

"You didn't need any help last night in Rome," Mason retorted, referring to Geoffrey's date with Jeannetta.

"It's easy to ask for something if it don't matter whether or
not you get it. I just wanted company, and she's a nice, gra-
cious lady. Now, with Miss Lucy, I've got more than company
on my mind." He sipped first the bourbon and then the soda.
"I was so sure Miss Jeannetta would be going out with you
that I just about fell over when she accepted." He took another
round of sips, raising Mason's curiosity.

"Is that the way Georgians drink bourbon and soda?"

Ames rubbed his chin. "Can't say as they do. It's the way
*I* drink it."

Mason held his gaze for a few minutes. "If you're interested in Lucy Abernathy, I suggest you walk up to her table,
sit down and start talking. She'll be delighted. Trust me." He
downed his cognac. "See you in the morning."

He hadn't wanted company. He had a decision to make.
He'd sworn off relationships that he knew would be temporary. So what was he going to do about Jeannetta? He had
kissed more females than he remembered, but none had responded to him as she had, and none had fired him up as she
did. She alone had made him feel as though he had the key
to her heaven, that only he made the music to which she'd
been born to dance. He knew that, after one night alone
with her, he'd never be the same. If only he could understand his reservations about her. He walked into his room
and swore. He'd tasted her; he'd gone to the bar to get her
taste out of him, but not even the cognac had killed it. She
hadn't been in his room, but he smelled her, not her teasing
perfume, but her aroused woman's scent. He kicked off his

shoes, stripped, dumped his clothes in a suitcase and headed to the bathroom for a cold shower.

Jeannetta checked her room to make certain that she hadn't overlooked anything, closed her suitcase and laid the key on top. She glanced at the uninviting bed, and walked past it to the lone window of her Paris hotel room. The Arc de Triomphe glowed with its brilliant lights, romanticizing the night. She would never forget it, nor Paris, nor that room beside the door of which she had known for the first time the mind-blowing force of desire. She clutched her chest to steady her dancing heart as spasms of excitement rippled through her at the memory of his sweet tongue in her mouth and his aroused sex against her belly. Who could blame her for wanting him? She closed the curtain, turned back the covers and got into bed. She hadn't had much experience with men, but enough to know that her dance with Mason Fenwick hadn't ended. If she let it go any further, her cause would be lost. Tomorrow, she'd ask him.

Resplendent in white pants, long-sleeved yellow silk shirt and green aviator glasses, Mason stood outside car number seven of the Paris-to-Istanbul express, checking off tour passengers as they entered.

"Glad to see you're early, Geoffrey. I've seated you at the table with Lucy Abernathy for meals. You take it from there, man." He grinned at Geoffrey's wink. Winning that lottery must have rejuvenated the old man. Well, bully for him. He looked at his watch: seventeen minutes before departure. Where *was* she?

"Give the baggage one last check," he told Josh, looking over his shoulder in the hope of seeing Jeannetta. A stab of anxiety pummeled his belly when the conductor issued the first call, *"all aboard."* He couldn't abandon his tour, and he couldn't leave not knowing whether she needed him.

"All aboard for Istanbul." Breath hissed out of him when the conductor climbed the steps. In another two minutes, he'd see that door close. An increase in the wind's velocity and the smell of rain alerted him to the possibility of a troubled journey, but he had to shake off that concern; Jeannetta was his only… The wind shifted, and he turned quickly as the scent of her perfume reached him. He rushed to meet her, grabbed her carry-on bag, lifted her onto the coach and sagged against the door.

"I'm so glad you decided to join us." He heard the bite in his voice, but after the scare she'd given him, she deserved it.

"And hello to you, too. What's the problem? You knew I'd be here." He figured that the train's forlorn bellow and the chug of its wheels less than a minute after they'd boarded should set her straight.

She hadn't expected his annoyance, but his glare was nothing short of a reprimand.

"You knew I wouldn't leave here without you," he told her, "and you knew my responsibility to these people. Didn't you consider the dilemma you caused me?" He straightened up and stepped closer to her. "Do you always play it so close to the edge?"

"I'm sorry. I got here as fast as I could. The driver made himself a few extra francs at my expense." Her gaze locked with his, and she had to suppress the urge to reach out to him as the flash of heat in his eyes told her he remembered the night before. That he hadn't forgotten his pleasure in holding her body close to his. But, as quickly as it came, the moment of recognition was gone.

"This tour occupies car seven," he explained, his voice impersonal. "The dining car is at one end and the lavatories are on the other." He reeled off a list of do's and don'ts. She wouldn't allow him to put distance between them, not after the note he'd left her that morning: "My dear Jeannetta, neither of us wanted to become involved, but Providence decreed otherwise. I'm strongly attracted to you, but I'll do my best not to impose it on you nor on our tour members. The next move is yours. Mason."

"Thank you for the note I found under my door this morning. We'll work it out. I know we will. And I wouldn't have upset you this morning if I could have avoided it." His strong fingers gently stroking her cheek encouraged her to smile, stirring anticipation and want in her that must have been mirrored in her eyes, for he leaned forward and brushed her lips with his own.

"Come on. I'll show you to your compartment," he said, taking her bag with one hand and resting his other arm protectively around her shoulder. "You're in L-11."

"Where's yours?" She wanted to know. He placed her bag on the sofa bed, raised an eyebrow and frowned.

"Four doors down. Why? Do you sleepwalk?" Embarrassment flooded her until his frown dissolved into a wicked grin.

"Oh, you!" This man had a streak of devilment in him, but she knew she could hold her own in that department. "I don't think I've done it in the past, but I'm sure I could learn," she teased. "At what point do you think I'd wake up?" His rapt stare both censored her and heated her up and, when his eyes became that greenish-brown that she knew indicated desire, she had the feeling that she'd better not play with him. From his harsh intakes of breath and unsmiling face, she knew he didn't want any more jokes about their relationship.

"Find yourself down there, day or night, sweetheart, and I'll answer any question you can ask, close any door you open and finish anything you start. Come around anytime the spirit moves you. Lunch at noon today. If you need a snack before that, walk down to the dining room. If you need me, dial eight or push the blue button on your intercom. Remember that anything you say on the intercom can be heard by anybody who wants to listen. Have a good rest, and don't come to lunch late. See you."

She figured that by the time she got her mouth closed, he'd be in possession of his equilibrium.

Mason sat at the maître d's desk at the entrance of the dining room. Geoffrey and Lucy lingered over coffee, engrossed in conversation, but most other members of the tour had finished their lunch and either returned to their compartments or gone to the observation lounge. It seemed as though he had looked at his watch more frequently since meeting Jeannetta Rollins than in all his previous thirty-seven years. Didn't she ever go *anywhere* on time? He got up, went to the buffet table and began filling a plate for her. That finished, he laid a few pieces of smoked salmon on black pumpernickel bread and wrapped it in cellophane paper in case she didn't like the cold plate. The woman needed a keeper. He grimaced at the niggling voice of his conscience that proclaimed, "You don't seem averse to looking after her." He refused to glance up when the door opened; he knew who it was.

"Do you always bring up the rear?" he asked, declining to glance her way. "Lunch hour will be over in seven minutes, and the dining room has to be readied for the one o'clock seating. I asked you to be on time." Her soft hand rested on the middle of his back, and he told himself to stay firm, but he couldn't help swinging around after the first soothing stroke.

"I don't mean to upset your schedules, but I've stopped rushing through life. There's so much to see, and so li…so few opportunities. I never used to stop and smell the flowers, as it were, or even to look at them. Nowadays, I savor every precious thing. Back in Pilgrim, the mountains have always been part of my life, and I've taken them for granted. But a couple of days before I left home to join the tour, I stood at my kitchen window late one evening and looked out. That time of year, the mountains are always snowcapped, but that evening, bright red streaked the peaks, and I thought for a moment that there'd been a terrible catastrophe. But I'd only seen the lustrous glow of a setting sun. I couldn't imagine how I had missed that awe-inspiring, majestic sight for so many years."

He knew something about achieving balance in your life, turning corners and taking control of your future, and he knew the feeling of satisfaction it gave. He'd done it. "Haven't you noticed that I don't rush?" he asked her. "I'm never late either, and that's because I budget my time properly. Try it." He motioned toward the buffet table. "I fixed something for you. The dining room will close to our group in about two minutes, so I suggest you take this to your compartment." He watched the smile spread over her face and an uncensored gleam of admiration—or something more…dangerous—shine from her dark eyes. He turned away. *Before I do something foolish,* he cautioned himself.

"Here." He handed her the plate and sandwiches. "Why don't you go in your compartment and eat? I…I've got a few things to do."

"You're not angry because I came in here late, are you?" She put so much weight in that question, he thought, as though his opinion, how he felt about her, mattered more than anything else.

"Nah," he said, as casually as he could. "Now go eat your lunch." Why didn't she move? Why did she stand there sending him vibration after vibration of pure sweet hell, her eyes warm and inviting, smiling at him as if he were a king?

"Thanks for making sure I got something to eat," she said, and blinked both eyes in what he realized was an attempt to wink.

"Get out of here, Jeannetta. Right now." Her eyes widened, and he swore lustily and headed for the adjoining caboose.

* * *

He was sitting in the dining car, reading Colin Powell's autobiography, when she walked in around three-thirty for a can of lemonade.

"Thanks for sending me the *International Herald Tribune*. How'd you know I'd gotten hungry for some news of what's going on in the world?"

He glanced up from his book, vowing not to let her shackle his insides for the second time that day. "My pleasure. It's a courtesy to my guests."

Her mouth drooped in disappointment. "Sure, and I suppose you sent all nineteen of us a red rose to go with it."

He put the book aside and stood.

"You're welcome." Alright. *Let her frown,* he told himself without a trace of guilt. She'd knocked the wind out of him, and he hadn't decided he liked it. Trouble was, she could match him, mood for mood and stance for stance. An inner amusement lightened his thoughts. He never could understand why women felt so much more powerful when they stood akimbo, with their feet wider apart than normal. He grinned down at her. Like a little bantam-weight fighter squaring off against Muhammad Ali. He would have laughed if he hadn't been sure she'd feel hurt.

"Still vexed because I was late for lunch, are we?" she asked in a low don't-battle-with-me voice. "Well, I wandered into car number six and met some Swiss children. A whole car full of them." A glow spread over her face, lifting his spirits, drawing him into the pleasure she recalled. "We had a wonderful time, and I just couldn't leave them. A whole car full of five- and six-year-olds. It was wonderful." He couldn't help staring at her. This mercurial woman, who fascinated him and made him think of a warm fireplace on cold nights. He fingered the keys in his pockets, shook his head and wondered about his sanity. Had he gone so far with her that he couldn't back up? It wasn't possible.

"What's the matter?" she asked, misunderstanding his re-action. "Don't you like children?"

He shook his head in awe.

"You'd be a full-time job for any man," he muttered under his breath.

"What?"

"I hope they'd all had lunch before you descended on them. They won't get another chance to eat until around five-thirty."

She cocked an eyebrow and gnawed her bottom lip.

"You're not overdoing this protective thing, are you?"

He grinned. "Sure I am."

"Well, I appreciate your concern, but don't ladle it out too thickly. Okay?" She turned to go, stopped and reversed her-self. "Thanks for the pretty rose. When I get back to Pilgrim, I'm going to press it and keep it in the family Bible."

He gaped. "You're serious?"

She nodded.

"Why?"

"It's the first thing you gave me, and it may be the only thing. I want to keep it." Long after she left, he stared at the spot where she'd stood.

After dinner, Jeannetta sat in the lounge, sipping ginger ale and doodling on a paper napkin as she surreptitiously ob-served her companions. Leonard Deek, a university professor on a year's sabbatical, seemed to shrink in Maybeth's volup-tuous presence. When she stood, her bosom dwarfed the little man. Chuckling to herself, Jeannetta quickly scribbled three one-line jokes about the decline in breastfeeding and the re-fusal of increasing numbers of men to grow up. Her smile of delight greeted Geoffrey's arrival.

"If you're not expecting anybody, I'd love to join you."

She motioned toward the empty chair.

"I'd love your company, Geoffrey. Where's Lucy?"

"Couldn't say for sure, but I expect she's somewhere primping. Never seen a woman pat and primp like she does. I told her if she was any more perfect she'd have silvery wings, but she just laughed and patted her hair. I hope I'm on her mind when she's doing it."

Jeannetta had to fight a wave of melancholia. Was the need for love so powerful that it ruled one's life regardless of age? And could she live without it? She told herself not to think that way.

"I wouldn't worry, Geoffrey. Miss Abernathy cut you from the pack before our plane left JFK Airport." She thought his shoulders straightened and his chin lifted. She liked his earthy chuckle.

"I must be slower than I thought."

Jeannetta nodded toward the door, warning him to change the subject, as Mason entered with Lucy Abernathy. *That woman is really burning up his ears,* she thought, observing the rapid movements of Lucy's lips. Geoffrey stood and waved them over.

"Sure we're not interrupting anything?" Mason asked.

She'd nearly asked what there was to interrupt, when Geoffrey's cool reply gave her a lesson in the management of men.

"Not a bit sure—we were sitting here in conversation, weren't we? Ya'll sit down while I get us all something to drink." He left the table without waiting for a reply.

Jeannetta nearly giggled as she watched Mason stare at Geoffrey's back. She wondered what Geoffrey had been telling Lucy; her serenity would have been worthy of a queen. It amused Jeannetta that Mason directed his conversation to Lucy, ignoring her. She didn't believe his ego needed bolstering, because no man with his looks, physique and manners could have lacked the adulation of women. Wherever she saw him, he stood out, a belly-twisting example of virile manhood. Geoffrey returned with a loaded tray, and she helped herself to a glass of ginger ale.

With his gaze searing her, Mason raised his glass of cognac, sending dazzling sensations zinging through her body. Applying as much calm as she could muster, she lifted her glass to him and then brought it forward for a sip but, to her amazement the ginger ale poured into her lap. She couldn't control the trembling of her fingers, but she tried nevertheless to smooth over the incident, smiling as though it didn't matter. When she finally glanced up, his dark eyes were fixed on her, but they lacked warmth or sensuality; he had the look of a man deeply concerned. Quickly, she glanced away.

Mason flinched as the liquid streamed into her lap. He'd realized that the glass hadn't touched her lips and, if she'd been drinking wine or any other alcoholic drink, he'd have ascribed it to the liquor, but she didn't drink alcoholic beverages. He'd seen that in his medical practice: the failure to judge distance correctly in relation to one's self. Sometimes that meant missing a step, sitting on the floor rather than in a chair, grasping air when reaching for something. But she didn't have any of the symptoms that accompanied the ailments that came to mind. Still, her fingers had trembled and what seemed like fear had settled in her eyes. He took a slug of cognac. He'd forced himself to quit that kind of fanciful thinking, and not even his concern for her was going to trick him back into it.

"If you'll excuse me, I think I'll turn in." She saw Mason glance at his watch, but where was it written that she couldn't go to bed at eight-thirty if she wanted to?

"I'll see you to your compartment," she heard him say, in a tone that discouraged rejection. At the door, he extended his hand for her key, his gaze sweeping over her. He opened the door and stood there. Waiting. She didn't dare look at him, because she knew he could turn her on with a smile, a wink, and all she could think of was that night in Paris, outside her bedroom door.

"Aren't you going to invite me in?" He said it with reluctance, as though he wished she'd say no, but his posture suggested otherwise. Less than twelve inches separated them; bridge it, and she'd know again the sweet nectar, the pulsing ferment, of his loving. His unsmiling face and purposeful manner jarred her. Had he noticed? Maybe this would be a good time to talk with him and ask him if he'd help her.

"Mason, I...yes...if..."

He interrupted. "Ask me in. You ought to know by now that I don't bite." His unexpected smile sent a flush of heat through her, but she refused to let him see her lose composure.

"What excuse would I give myself?" she asked him, not caring how he took her flirtatiousness. "I can't invite you for coffee and I left my etchings in Pilgrim."

"Then ask me in because you want my company."

She backed in the door, and he followed, closing it with his elbow. He'd expected more feminine surroundings but, except for a jacket thrown across the sofa and the red rose he'd sent her, the compartment bore no testament to femininity. Bare.

He couldn't help showing his surprise. "Didn't you unpack? When you walk out of here, this place might as well have been unoccupied."

"I told you I don't collect things. I'm satisfied with admiring lovely things—I don't have to own them. In fact, I don't like to accumulate stuff. With millions of people hoarding things, more and more must be made, and since everything we have comes from the earth and sea, think what that does to the environment." He leaned against the closet door and observed her beneath half-lowered lids.

"You're a nature lover?" The way she tossed her head back,

and that half smile that curved around her sweet mouth, Lord! He looked toward the writing table, any place but at that voluptuous invitation to forever that glowed before him.

"I love everything that's graceful and beautiful. Everything."

"You love children." He didn't ask himself why his heart pounded while he waited for her answer. She nodded, though he thought her smile forced.

"Don't you?" she asked him in turn. Her delicate hands slid up and down the sides of her hips, rubbing them. *A camouflage for her trembling fingers,* he noticed. He didn't want to torment her; she meant something to him. He didn't know what, but *something.* Yet, the scientist in him had to solve the riddle she represented. Something stood amiss. He'd bet his life on it.

"What are you seeking on this trip?" He swung away from the closet door and closed the space between them. "You want something. What is it?"

"I want to see the world."

He shook his head.

"But you've got plenty of time for that. This is my third year with this tour, and you're the first applicant I've had who was under forty. Young people usually don't have the money and two free months to spend on a tour." He paced a few steps while he waited for her to interrupt him. Nothing. He turned back to her. "My clients are retirees and newly divorced and widowed people who are trying to put order into their lives, to start over. What's your reason?" He hated that he had begun to sound accusing, but he teetered at the edge of caring for her, and he had to have some answers. He needed to know that the wild pounding of his heart that began whenever he saw her wouldn't some day suffocate him.

"Are you running from a broken love affair? Hit the lottery as Ames did? I'm curious."

"I told you—I want to see the world."

He shrugged.

"Sure you do. But why do you feel you have to satisfy this curiosity now? There's a reason, and you aren't giving it."

*He'd have been a successful attorney,* Jeannetta thought. She knew from his turn of mind that the opportunity to bring up the subject of her health had slipped past, if, indeed, it had been there at all.

"Why do you think my wanting to see the world is so unreasonable?" she asked, hoping that he would soon tire of the subject.

"It isn't unreasonable, but if you're twenty-nine years old and have a master's degree, you can't have worked more than five years and, unless college teachers make more than I thought, you've spent a chunk—maybe all—of your savings on this trip. A trip that began two weeks before the end of your school's regular term."

"Some deduction! If your tour had started two weeks later, I wouldn't have had to skip the last two weeks of school." She wanted to tell him that it was none of his business, but it *was* his business. *He* was her reason. When she could force herself to look him in the eye, she saw his skepticism mirrored there. Maybe she could find a way to tell him. She began slowly, fearfully.

"I've never found it easy to talk about myself, especially not with strangers—I mean, not with people I don't know very well. You're asking for personal information, and I'm not…"

He'd moved to within inches of her, and tugged at her hand.

"*Strangers?* Do you kiss strangers?"

"Of course n… Oh, Mason. I'm not sure you've ever been a stranger."

"How about that night in Paris?" His hoarse voice had lost its smoothness, and a rasp of desire greeted her ears. Perspiration beaded on his forehead, and she wondered why he didn't move. Where did he get that awesome control? She stood mesmerized as his eyes lost their blackness and took on the greenish-brown cast that signaled his arousal. Even as her breath shortened almost to a pant, his sexual heat bruised her nostrils. If she didn't get him inside of her, she'd…

"Come here to me, honey."

Somehow, her feet left the floor and the steel-like grip of his powerful arms crushed her to him. His tongue invaded her mouth and she sucked it feverishly. Hungrily. When he cupped her bottom, she let her long legs grip his hips and a spiral of hot darts shot to her feminine center when his bulging arousal pressed between her thighs. He rubbed her erect nipple and, at the sound of her frustrated moan, he set her feet on the floor, reached into her blouse, released her breast and bent his mouth to it. With one hand, she pressed the back of his head, while the other one squeezed his buttocks. His mouth and tongue sucked and tugged at her nipple, sending pulsations to her core. Nearly out of her mind now, she cried out, asking for more. He picked her up and sat on the sofa with her on his lap.

His voice, still minus its natural tone and cadence, washed over her. "I don't want to leave, but I can't remain in here. I've already stayed longer than I should, and I can't break my own rule."

"You mean you've got a rule that says people can't make love on this tour?"

His weak, forced smile tempered her annoyance.

"That isn't the rule, but it amounts to that. Our time will come, Jeannetta. A time when we needn't worry about rules, beepers, intercoms and lack of privacy, and I'd as soon that time came when this tour is behind us and our desire for each other isn't whetted by convenience and close proximity." He shifted her from his lap and stood.

"You're important to me. Don't forget that in the days to

come." He leaned over her, and she tried not to respond when
he brushed her forehead.

"I'll let myself out. Lock your door." With that, he left her.

She'd known before he touched her that he didn't want to
start a raging fire, but she'd ignored the signals, had let her
unappeased desire for him rule her. And she had nearly de-
stroyed any chance she might have of getting his help. And
even if he agreed, out of guilt, to operate, she'd lose him. What
man would forgive a woman for allowing him to care for her,
for making love with him, and then exacting a price? Not this
one. She paced the narrow room, fell on the sofa, sat up and
slammed her newspaper across the room, knocking over the
bud vase. Her anger subsided, and she told herself she'd take
whatever came, but she went to bed knowing that she'd toss
all night, uncertain of the future.

Mason jumped out of bed at the first sound of his beeper,
glancing at his watch as he did so. Twenty minutes past three.
The train had stopped. What the…

"This is Fenwick. What's the problem?" He didn't like
the quiver in the conductor's voice. He grabbed his Bermuda
shorts and jumped into them before the man could get his
voice under control.

"Some soldiers, about eight of them, just boarded the front
of the train. They blocked the track, so the engineer had to
stop. We're only a mile from the Bulgaria border with the former Yugoslavia, so we don't know what's going on. They're
not customs officers. I'm alerting the tour guides and the un-
escorted passengers."

"Are they showing their rifles?"

"Combat-ready, sir."

Mason swore. "Thanks. Keep a cool front, pal. Never let
a man know he's got you down." He flipped off the phone,

hooked it to his belt along with a can of mace, grabbed his keys and raced down the corridor to Jeannetta's compartment.

"Open up, Jeannetta." He hoped she didn't sleep soundly.

"Who is it?"

"Mason. Soldiers on the train. Put on a dress and open this door. *Now!*" While she dressed, he alerted people in other compartments, getting a few surprises as he did so. In different circumstances, he might have found the evidence of bed-switching amusing. Two men and one of the women were sleeping in a bed to which they hadn't been assigned. He dashed back to Jeannetta's door.

"Let's go, Jeannetta. Hide your valuables and money, but bring your passport. Come on, babe."

She opened the door, her eyes wide and unblinking. He didn't have time to allay her fear; later, if there was a later. He pulled her through the door, slammed it and raced with her to his room.

"Wha...what's going on, Mason?"

"We don't know, but we're near the border and, European history being what it is, we may be in disputed territory. If they stop here, don't volunteer information, and don't discuss anybody but yourself. If those soldiers were friends, they wouldn't have their fingers on the trigger."

"We always stop at the borders. What's so different this time?" He wanted to hug her to him, but he needed his wits. He had to keep her safe, and nothing was more dangerous for a beautiful woman than sex-starved soldiers.

"Customs officers don't board these trains with rifles drawn." His glance swept her unsteady form. He shook his head. She'd brought her most valuable possession with her—a little doll. He'd ask her about that later.

"Button up your dress, honey. All the way to the neck. And pull your hair up on your head."

"Why?" He glared at her, partly in frustration and partly in anger at the situation into which he'd unwittingly put her.

"Because those soldiers will see exactly what I see, and they may not be averse to taking it."

Her shaking fingers couldn't manage the buttons, and he fastened her dress, his large fingers innocently brushing her soft mounds and threatening to disconcert him. If he got her safely to Istanbul, he was going to kiss God's good earth. He twisted her hair on top of her head and knotted it. The knock on the door of his compartment was loud and brutish. His lips brushed hers quickly.

"Don't be afraid, honey. If they touch you, they'll have to kill me." With his best nonchalant air, he opened the door, raised an eyebrow and asked, "May I help you?" Only two of them. He hoped the rest weren't busy intimidating the other passengers. They swaggered in without waiting to be asked.

"What country you from?" He told them. The leader of the two examined their passports, and Mason couldn't help expelling a long breath when the man returned them to him. The other man had his gaze fixed on Jeannetta.

"Your husband?" Jeannetta nodded, the leader reminded her that her passport gave her status as single.

"It's over a year old," she told him, referring to her passport. Mason shifted his stance, and icy tingles hurtled along his spine as both men's gazes fastened on Jeannetta, their eyes ablaze with lust. His focus shifted from the can on his belt, and his mind adopted the attitude of the karate master that he was. He hadn't applied those principles since college, but he knew he could depend on them.

The soldiers must have noticed his change of demeanor, because the leader half smiled and told him, "If she was my woman, I'd leave her at home. She is black American?"

Mason nodded. He couldn't let himself be lulled into thinking they were safe, only to have the trial of his life.

"You're the tour leader?"

Mason inclined his head.

"Everybody in this car is American?" the leader asked him. Mason nodded.

The man appeared to have satisfied himself that whatever he sought wouldn't be found in that compartment, but the other continued to drool over Jeannetta. The leader nodded toward the door and spoke in a language that Mason didn't understand, but he didn't doubt the essence of the message: "Leave it. We don't have time for that."

The leader touched the door handle, looked back and asked Mason, "You see any soldiers with this on their sleeve?"

He pulled a small emblem that Mason recognized as the colors of a flag out of his pocket. He hadn't seen any soldiers except them, he said. The door closed behind them.

"Oh, Mason. Do you think they've gone? I'm so scared." He pulled her trembling body to him.

"We'll have to wait until the conductor signals. As sure as they see me alone in that corridor, one or both of them will make a beeline straight to you." She moved closer to him, but he stepped farther back; until he knew the danger had passed, he couldn't allow her nearness and patent vulnerability to scramble his wits. He pushed the buttons on his beeper and held his breath until the conductor answered.

"Motorman, here. All clear."

"Any problems?" Still holding Jeannetta, Mason leaned against the wall. That had been close. The last time he'd been that strung out... He fought back the memory of his scalpel suspended over the lesion in Bianca Norris's exposed brain.

"Just a hundred thirty-three scared passengers. Excluding yourself, of course, sir. They're after terrorists. We'll be on our way shortly."

Mason thanked him and looked down at Jeannetta.

"I'm sorry they frightened you." He sat on the sofa with her cuddled in his lap.

"I wasn't afraid for myself, as much as for you," she whispered. "If anything had happened to you because of me… Oh, Mason, you don't know how scared I got." He set her on her feet.

"I can imagine. I'll walk you to your compartment. You'd better try and get some sleep, because we reach Istanbul later this morning, and you won't be near a bed again until we get to Singapore."

Her hot, welcoming kiss wasn't something a man could easily shrug off. He had to marshal self-control to walk away from the invitation mirrored in her eyes. He wasn't Superman, but if he could turn his back on his profession, work he'd dreamed of enjoying for as long as he'd known himself—if he could make himself do that, he could do anything. He headed back to his compartment, certain that he'd walked away from the loving of a lifetime.


Later that morning, Jeannetta sat in the observation lounge, trying to glimpse the sunrise. A fierce headache, much as her doctor had told her to expect, had kept her awake for the remainder of the night. Geoffrey ambled in, carrying a cup of coffee, and she welcomed his company.

"You're not your usual bright self this morning, Jeannetta." He peered at her as though to verify his words.

"Geoffrey, what holds a man back when he's interested?" She had to wait while he blew the hot coffee until he could bear to sip it.

"Married, engaged, misgivings. Why?"

"Do you think Mason's married?"

His face creased into a half smile. "Nope. I sure don't."

She liked Geoffrey, but his laconic responses sometimes got on her nerves.

"Engaged?" She pressed.

"No. Mason's no cheat."

She took a deep breath and asked the obvious. "Misgivings, huh?"

He let her wait while he finished his coffee.

"I'd say so. A lot of 'em. 'Course it's up to you to rid him of those. I'd best be getting on. Lucy gets spiteful when she sees us talking. Don't you set her at ease, though. Women never act right when they get too sure of a man."

Jeannetta had to laugh. "That's practically the advice you gave me about Mason."

Geoffrey Ames winked at her with his newfound sophistication. "It ain't done you no harm, neither. Has it?"

In a few hours, the train would pull into Istanbul and, seven hours later, he and the tour would be on a plane for Singapore. Mason had dreaded this day as the most precarious of the entire trip; one hitch and he stood to lose a bundle. He headed down to the observation car, hoping to begin the day in the way he most enjoyed—watching the sun break through the clouds, spreading its kaleidoscope of colors across the horizon. He walked into the observation lounge, stuck his hands in his back pockets and gazed at the glorious pinks, purples, reds and blues that shot across the sky. A cup of coffee and ten minutes of this would get his day off and running just right. He whirled around at the sound of a steady, low drone. Jeannetta. She didn't know he'd entered the car. But what…? She sat alone, dictating into an audio cassette a description of the sunrise and what she saw as the train whizzed past villages, farms and endless hills. He started to speak, thought better of it and stood quietly as she related the tiniest of details. Tremors in her voice lent an intimate quality to her dictation. Yes, and an eeriness, too. No one should eavesdrop on another's soul; he left. So much for his visit with the sunrise.

Alone in the dining room, he sipped black coffee and mulled over what he'd witnessed. Why didn't she photograph the scenes? What was the advantage in describing them? Upon reflection, he realized that he hadn't seen her with a camera. Among his tour guests, he'd seen all except her take pictures. He shook his head and his fingers brushed the keys in his right pants pocket. He'd let her have her privacy, but he would rather have begun his day buoyed by that exhilarating sunrise.

A few minutes later Mason stood at the bar, checking the train's Istanbul arrival time with Josh, his porter; Jeannetta strolled by without seeing them, humming a tune that he didn't recognize.

"Miss Rollins is in that lounge every morning at sunup telling that little machine of hers what she did the day before," Josh said. "I've been trying to figure out why she does it if it makes her feel bad. Yesterday morning, she was making her recording and, man, you should have seen the tears. But she kept right on talking, like her eyes were dry. She's strange, that one. Couple of minutes after I sneaked out of there, she came out and greeted me with the biggest smile you ever saw."

"Yeah," Mason replied. "We've got forty-seven pieces of luggage and two crates of supplies to unload here and transfer to Singapore Airlines. I want this stuff at the airport by noon. No later. Got that?" He left the bar without waiting for Josh's reply. He didn't want men discussing Jeannetta. That was one of the problems with romances in groups like this one; you had to listen to things you'd rather not hear.

"Hi. Remember me?"

He whirled around. Lord, would he never get used to her eyes? Eyes that proclaimed the woman as a warm nesting place. He grinned down at her.

"If we'd ever met, honey," he drawled, "I'd remember it.

My five senses are in flawless condition, and I'm a man in the prime of life. You know me from somewhere?"

Her laughter wrapped around him, warming him and unsettling him. Her presence gave him a feeling of contentment, and his fingers automatically went to the keys in his pocket.

"Need something?" he asked her, in his best low, suggestive tone. He could see the laughter starting to boil up in her. Laughter that said his question didn't deserve an answer. As quickly as it started, it stopped.

"Do I need something? How about tall, dark, handsome and male, with a habit of strumming his fingers on any solid surface near him?" she asked with feigned seriousness. Unable to resist touching her, he tweaked her nose.

"All in good time, sweet thing." Her smile—natural and sincere, but so powerfully seductive—reminded him of the lecture Steve had given him when he left for college. If he made low grades, his brother had said, he'd lose his scholarship, be forced to work his way through and probably wouldn't get his medical degree until he reached thirty; but a pretty woman's smile could get him kicked out of college, and he'd never get that degree.

*She is as uncertain about us as I am,* he told himself, watching her enter the dining room. Neither of them behaved consistently. Small children played the game, go-away-come-here; it had no place in his life. He followed Jeannetta to the dining room.

"Remember that the plane leaves at six-forty and, please, for heaven's sake, be there an hour and a half before flight time."

"I'll do my best, but I'd love to see a little of Istanbul. I might not get another…well, I might not come this way again." The childlike lights of eagerness that sparkled in her eyes endeared her to him; at that moment he could have denied her nothing.

"Would you like to see Istanbul with me, Jeannetta?"

"Oh, yes. I would."

He didn't want her to see how much she affected him, so he walked out of the dining room. And nearly knocked Geoffrey to the floor.

"Angry, or in a hurry?" Geoffrey asked him, adjusting his jacket.

"Neither. Where's Lucy? I want everybody in the dining room for briefing." Sometimes he wondered if Geoffrey's professed interest in Lucy might be a screen. The man spent a hell of a lot of time in Jeannetta's company. *Oh, heck, I must be getting paranoid.*

Mason had leased a bus to drive the group around Istanbul before taking them to a hotel. He and Jeannetta struck out on their own.

"I didn't know anybody still mixed cement that way," Jeannetta said as they passed a construction site. "Imagine, mixing that with a hoe. What if it gets hard before it's used?"

"This is a moderately developed country, but it isn't rich, it's… Say, this is the first time you've been outside the Western developed region, isn't it? This one's modern, compared to what you'll find in Africa and most of Asia." He realized that she no longer listened, but stood staring at… What *was* she looking at? A child dived into a large mound of sand, and another made a game of sifting sand through her fingers. In his book, that didn't classify as spellbinding. Yet, she stared, immobile, her face drawn.

"What's wrong, Jeannetta?" He watched, aghast, as her glance shifted in a way that suggested she searched for a way to escape something. He rushed to her.

"What's wrong, honey?" His fingers on her arms absorbed her trembling, and he didn't doubt that something had frightened her. He put an arm around her, drew her to his side and waited for her answer. None came.

Minutes later, she exclaimed, "Oh, Mason, there's a big mosque. Can we go in?"

Relieved that the somber moment had passed, but worried that she hadn't confided in him, he forced a smile. "I don't see why not." They walked toward the mosque, but two young boys stopped them.

"You speak English, mister?" the more forward of the two asked Mason

"Yeah. Why?" Eager smiles spread over the two young faces.

"We practice our English. What you like? We show you." Mason turned to ask Jeannetta if she would like the boys to give them a walking tour. She'd disappeared. His heart surged powerfully in his chest. Where had she gone? He raced into the mosque, smaller than it appeared from the outside, and searched behind every one of the large marble columns, but he neither saw nor heard anyone. Perhaps she had gone out-side…but she would have passed him. Had those boys acted as decoys, distracting his attention while someone spirited her away? He dashed outside, where the two boys waited, spoiling his theory that they had helped someone kidnap Jeannetta. If he ever got her to Pilgrim, he'd take that sol-dier's advice.

If she went to the police, the plane would have left for Sin-gapore long before the officers finished questioning him and filling out forms. He could go to the American Embassy, he reminded himself, but to what end?

"You wait 'til the lady comes back, and then we take you tour? Okay?" one boy asked.

He had to get a plan, and quick. "What's your name?" he asked the talkative one.

"At'ut. We do business? Yes? Very cheap. Three Ameri-

can dollars." Mason sized up both boys as intelligent and re-
sourceful. What choice did he have?

"At'ut, did you see the woman who was with me when I
met you?"

"Sure." The boy gave Mason as accurate a description of
Jeannetta as any warm-blooded adult male might have done.

"I can't find her. I think she went in there," he said, pointing to the mosque, "but she walked away and I've lost her.
I'll stand here until noon. Find her and bring her back here
and I'll give each of you twenty-five American dollars." Both
boys leaned toward him, as though making sure of what they'd
heard, their eyes as round as saucers.

"You wait here," At'ut said. "We bring her back. You don't
lose the American dollars. Wait here." They left at breakneck
speed and, after loosening the collar of his damp shirt and
wiping his neck with a handkerchief, Mason took a position
against a post in the shadow of the mosque. Not an iota of
breeze relieved the sweltering heat.

He could stand the heat; he could take anything, except
losing her. He had to look for her—but if he left there, what
if she came back and panicked when she didn't see him? He
paced the cracked sidewalk, stumping his toe on the loose
rumble. He couldn't leave her fate in the hands of two Turkish urchins whom he might never see again, though there was
some comfort in the fact that twenty-five dollars would buy
nearly one hundred and seventy Turkish lira.

He hated the feeling of helplessness that had begun to per-
vade him, a feeling he hadn't had since his first year of internship, when his team had lost a patient whom he favored.
What if he couldn't find her? A burning sensation on his
arms, neck and face sent him back to the shaded post beside
the mosque. Suppose someone had abducted her. He had no
intention of leaving Istanbul without her but, if he deserted
the tour, he'd get sued for every cent he had and he could kiss

Fenwick Travel Agency goodbye. He squinted at the blazing sun, bowed his head and closed his eyes. He hadn't prayed for such a long time that he doubted he'd get a hearing.

## Chapter 4

"You are looking for the door?" The little man bowed from the waist, the picture of courtesy. Jeannetta glanced around, hoping to see another human being. The man's saintly persona could be a ruse, a trick, but she had despaired of finding her way out. Thick Turkish carpets in a multitude of bright designs covered the floor, the space relieved only by the dozens of silent marble columns scattered about. Each may have had significance for the worshippers, but they only gave her a feeling that she walked in circles. She sighted a paneled-off area and wondered whether it hid a door. The quick glimpse she'd intended to take while Mason talked with the boys had turned into half an hour.

"If you wish to go out, I will show you," the man repeated, though with less patience than previously.

She didn't know the customs, so she bowed her assent. Her rescuer led her to a door so heavy that she could never have opened it. Tentacles of fear streaked through her at the thought that she might be facing a fate worse than the loss of sight. The little man pulled at the door, and bright sunshine enveloped her. She smiled at him and stepped outside.

She stared at her surroundings, looked back at the door through which she had just walked, at the shops across the narrow street. *Where was she?* She took a deep breath and decided to walk to her left. A dump heap. She retraced her steps and walked several blocks, but she saw neither a mosque, a broad avenue, nor, worst of all, any sight of Mason. Her short-sleeved cotton shirt clung to her body; she searched her bag for a tissue, but couldn't find one, and had to use the tail of her long skirt to wipe away the perspiration that bathed her face. Hunger pangs irritated her stomach, but she didn't dare stop for food. She had to find Mason.

Hearing a buzz of traffic, she walked toward it, hoping to find the avenue where she'd left Mason at the entrance to the mosque. Every building that she passed seemed to house an open-front coffee house in which scores of men sat drinking coffee and watching her. Surely she didn't defy custom by walking the street at noon, but she remembered that she hadn't seen a woman. She would never forget the seas of dark eyes—some of them beautiful, but all of them disconcerting—that followed her the way the eyes in Van Gogh's self-portrait follow the viewer. In spite of the blazing heat, she hugged her middle as she walked, as though to protect herself from the unknown, the unseen.

The odor of raw lamb, pungent garlic and a strong, strange pine-like odor bruised her nostrils. She longed to escape it, to breathe a different air. Dank, decaying scents greeted her from an alley as she passed it, and she welcomed the all-pervading aroma of cinnamon, cloves and rose water that soon flowed from several bakeries. Gnawing hunger over her reticence, and she turned into the next bakery. She had discovered that bowing and smiling invited friendship if you didn't have lan-

guage to do the work for you. The old man looked up from
his mound of dough, pointed to a high stool and disappeared
into the rear of the store. She didn't care where he'd gone or
why; she welcomed the respite from the scorching sun and
relief for her tired feet. He soon returned with a young boy,
about eight or nine, she guessed.

"How can we help you, lady?" the boy asked her with a
broad smile. After hearing that she was hungry and lost, he
went in the back and a woman shrouded in black returned
with him. Jeannetta quickly explained that she wanted to *buy*
something to eat and drink and to get instructions back to the
mosque. A rapid translation sent the woman scurrying away,
only to return with three soft drinks and assorted breads,
cakes and baklava. The mosque, the boy happily informed
her, was right around the corner. Replenished, rested and relieved, she struck out for the mosque, carrying a sack of pastries that the woman had handed her. Around the corner stood
the great Hagia Sophia, a fifth-century architectural miracle
that she recognized from travel posters. She brushed away
the tears, raised her head and walked on. She tried to remain
calm, to think, but the strange noises and peculiar and often
unpleasant smells disconcerted her. She had to take comfort
in knowing that he wouldn't leave her alone in Istanbul, that
he'd find her, that he cared enough to search the city for her.
Lord, let her see him before dark.

Mason looked at his watch for the nth time. Four o'clock,
and not a word from the two boys. His feet had covered every
inch of the pavement within a block of the mosque, because
he hadn't been able to stand still. The pangs of hunger had
long since become a painful ache, but he refused to leave the
place long enough to eat. In another thirty minutes, he'd have
to go to the United States Embassy and report her missing;
he'd also have to phone Josh and tell him to take the tour on
without him.

\* \* \*

"Hey, mister! Hey, mister!" Mason whirled around and ran to meet the exuberant youth.

"You come. We find her." He grabbed the boy by the collar of his jacket and tugged him upward, nearly to eye level.

"Where is she? Where is your friend? You tell me something right here." He had to calm himself; the boy bore no responsibility for his state of near madness.

"She with my friend in Ataturk Square. I ask her to come with me, but she refuse. So my friend stay and I come. You still have American dollars?"

Mason nodded. "Let's go. If you're not telling me the truth, I'll take you to the police." The boy grinned, unconcerned about the threat.

"Police my uncle. You come now." Mason had to restrain the anxious youth, who couldn't wait for his prized American dollars; he had barely enough energy to walk, to say nothing of running. He wondered that he hadn't suffered sunstroke; poor hydration had stopped his profuse perspiring and his stomach cramped. Renewed strength flowed through him, however, at the thought that he'd soon see her, verify with his eyes that nothing untoward had happened to her. They reached the edge of the square and stopped for the traffic. He had to swallow hard to stave off the sorrows that welled up in him. Where was she?

"Come. Over there," At'ut urged. Mason searched the distance until his gaze fell on the blob of yellow at the edge of the monument. His heart surged in his chest and he had to run.

"No. Wait. Come back, mister. The traffic, she kill you." Buses loaded with passengers lumbered by; automobiles raced past him; he dodged motorcycles, bicycles, vans and a hearse. But none of them slowed his pace. He had to get to her, touch her, feel her, know for himself that nothing had harmed her. Horns blared, words that must have been curses fell against his deaf ears; a stunned traffic officer whirled around as Mason whizzed past.

He saw the smile break out on her face as she glimpsed him, jumped up and started toward him, and he silently thanked the boy for yanking her back, away from the rushing traffic. He jumped the curb and swept her trembling body into his arms. The hell with custom. He didn't give a damn if the Turks didn't embrace publicly. Her lips parted in a joyous greeting, and he filled her with himself, emptying his relief, longing, need, hunger for her and, yes, fear, into his powerful and explosive kiss. He ignored the tugging at his shirt.

"I've never been so scared in my life, not even when... I was on my way out of my mind when At'ut came back for me. Don't you ever do this to me again." His lips dried the tears that streamed down her cheeks.

"Say, mister, what about the American dollars?" He reached into his pocket and paid them each the twenty-five dollars he'd promised them.

"Thanks. You two were great." Joyous laughter erupted from them as they counted the money.

"When you lose her again," At'ut the entrepreneur of the two, assured him, "you come to mosque. We find her again, quick like today." He thanked the boys and told them goodbye.

"Where were you?"

She recounted her adventures, adding, "About an hour ago, I decided to get a taxi to the airport, thinking maybe you'd gone there, but the cabs didn't stop. There must be a thousand mosques in this city, and I'm sure I've seen most of them today. Oh, Mason, if you think you were scared—I've been terrified that I'd miss the plane, never get back home, never see you again." Her slender body moved closer, and a sense of well-being pervaded him.

"I would have let the tour go on without me, Jeannetta.

There's no way I'd have left you here." He kissed each of her eyelids.

"Good Lord, Mason, we're the local attraction."

He looked over his shoulder and saw that the traffic had stopped and that the passengers leaned from automobiles to watch them. He remembered that kiss and grinned; it had been one hot one, and he hoped they had all enjoyed it half as much as he did.


"If it wasn't so late and I wasn't starved, I'd suggest you show me where you were today. I still haven't had a chance to visit old Istanbul. There's where you find the centuries-old mosques, quaint customs, ancient bazaars, narrow streets and crumbling old buildings—the flavor of Turkey that tourists hope to see. I'm told that many of the inhabitants still cling to the old way of doing things. Too bad you were so concerned about finding your way that you couldn't enjoy the experience." Saliva accumulated in his mouth as he looked down at the pastry she took from a brown paper sack. "I'm so hungry, I think I've forgotten how to eat," he told her when she handed it to him. "I don't know where you got this, but let me tell you, I'm glad to see it." She gave him the bag.

Mason noticed a taxi driver among their audience and negotiated a ride to the airport.

"How do you feel?" he asked Jeannetta when she sagged against him in the cab.

"Stupid. It has just dawned on me that the nice little man who showed me how to get out of the mosque knew I'd get lost, but he didn't care. I had no business in that male sanctuary, or at least not in the place where he found me. What a day!"

"Women use a separate entrance, and you went in the main door." He settled back in the hot, bedraggled car, slid his right arm around her shoulder and his left hand into the bag of pastries. "In other words, if you want to live with Vikings, learn how the Vikings live."

She looked down at his long legs, close to but not touching her, as they sat in the Singapore Airlines business-class lounge. His head lay against the back of the seat, his eyelids covered his eyes and his arms lay folded against his broad chest. She knew he needed those moments alone, to regroup after what must have been an emotionally gruelling day, so she used the time to record her experiences in Istanbul on her cassette.

"I was scared," she said, unable to control the tremors that laced her speech and the unsteadiness of the hand in which she held the recorder. "More scared than I've ever been in my life. It was worse than when they told me..." Startled at what she'd almost said, she glanced over to see his gaze on her, switched off the machine and forced her attention to several of her fellow passengers. She could feel him scrutinize her, but she refused to acknowledge his pulsing hot vibes that stimulated every centimeter of her body, and she shifted her gaze everywhere but to his face. He had questions that she didn't dare answer. After a time, she closed her eyes and was soon deep in thought. Because his refusal to Dr. Farmer had been emphatic, she had procrastinated about asking his help, hadn't gotten the courage to open the subject for fear of hearing that "no" herself, that sentence to darkness. She opened her eyes and smiled at him, hoping to distract him from whatever thoughts he might have about what he'd heard her dictate into the recorder.

His attention was focused on her.

"Didn't you know I'd find you?" he asked. "That I wouldn't leave you behind? Haven't you accepted that I'm going to take care of you, even if you test me to my limits? Even if you insist on being late, getting lost, attracting dangerous men and I don't know what else?"

She wished she knew whether he'd just said he cared for her, or that he always took care of his tour guests. His dispassionate face told her nothing.

A sigh escaped her. "Thanks. I knew you'd try to find me, but I didn't know how you'd succeed without a clue. Of course, I hadn't reckoned on your psychic powers."

He shrugged. "'Psychic powers'? I can't remember the last time I prayed, before today." He flexed his left leg, stood and held out his hand to her.

"I've got to check-in my gang, the flight's boarding. Come with me?" he asked, smiling that warm, intimate smile that she loved.

"Oh, I don't want to get in the way, I'll get in line."

At his incredulous stare, she rose without hesitation.

"If you think I'm letting you out of my sight before you get on that plane, lady, you'd better think again. Not after what I went through today, I'm not."

He grinned—to soften his words, she thought. She tried not to stare at him, to ignore the way in which his mesmeric eyes gleamed whenever he smiled.

"Besides," he went on, "is being with me so unpleasant?"

She wrinkled her nose at him, aware that the day's adventure had augmented their bonds, but she couldn't resist a chiding remark.

"If you thought so, you wouldn't ask the question." But as she stood with him beside the desk while he checked-in the tour passengers, she wondered. Tall. Handsome. Powerfully built. Charismatic. Capable. Intelligent. Could such a man feel the need for praise? She shook her head. Maybe her view of him differed from his own.

Mason led her to her seat and stored her carry-on luggage in the baggage compartment. After all his guests had found their seats, he took the aisle seat beside her. Jeannetta couldn't decide whether his having changed her seat should annoy her. She had originally been assigned 6-D, but he'd changed it to 11-F.

"I didn't realize we'd be sitting together. To where do you think I'll disappear while this plane is in the air?" She appreciated his interest, but she had never tolerated well anyone's attempt to control her. "It's either the lavatory, the cockpit, or out the window. Which do you think I'll choose?" She bit her lip, surprised at her waspishness. Mason stood, rested his hand on the back of his seat and looked at her, his face impassive.

"You don't want me to sit with you?"

"Did I say that?"

"Well, let's get it straight this minute. Do you or don't you?"

She'd boxed herself in, and she didn't doubt that he'd let her take her medicine.

"A gentleman doesn't press his advantage. Besides, I'm not so cruel that I'd want you to stand all the way to Singapore."

"Who says I would?"

"Mason, would you please not make an international crisis out of this, and sit back down?" In his unwavering gaze, she glimpsed a semblance of pain, fleeting though it was. She held out her hand to him.

"If you're sure," he said, seating himself.

"I'm sure."

His mouth softened to reveal glistening white teeth. "I may hold your hand."

With a flash of insight, she knew that his glibness covered the pain she'd seen in him, and she prepared herself to indulge him.

"Okay, if you want to hold my hand."

"I may put my head on your shoulder and go to sleep."

"I guess I can handle that."

"I've been known to snore."

"Not too loudly, I hope."

"Like a buzz saw."

She produced the grimace she knew he hoped to see. "I've heard worse."

"I'll definitely kiss you."

She yanked on the hand he'd rested on the back of his seat.

"Will you please stop trying to bug me?" She found that she loved teasing him. She knew he could take it, that his self-discipline was well-known among his medical peers. A dark shudder passed through her. What if he learned that she'd had him investigated before she took the tour? He'd have two counts on which to cross her off as a scheming woman, and her plans would go for naught, elusive like her dreams.

They dined in companionable silence, causing Mason to marvel at their ability to commune without speaking. Jeannetta didn't babble as many people did when conversation lulled, and it was one of her many admirable traits. Silence didn't make her nervous. He savored the fine cognac, inhaling deeply before rolling a sip on his tongue.

"When we get to Singapore," he advised, "don't go anywhere alone. We'll only be there six hours before we'll have to board the ship. I've arranged for a bus to take us on a two-hour sightseeing tour, with brief stops in Chinatown, the Botanical Gardens, Colonial Singapore and Jurong Bird Park where handlers train birds to sing. If there's time, we'll drive past the Raffles hotel complex. Please stay with the group." He watched her from the corner of his left eye. If his guess was right, the lady would get her dander up. He couldn't help smiling when she turned fully to him and took a deep breath.

"Yes, *sir!* Anything else, *sir?*"

"You're not taking me seriously," he said in an offhand manner, smiling inwardly and pretending not to know he'd riled her.

"And a good thing, too. I don't speak that way to my students but, of course, they're all over eighteen."

He laughed. Nothing pleased him more than the company of a lovely, laid-back, witty woman. He put a couple of pillows on his shoulder. "Lean over here," he whispered.

She hesitated, as though questioning the pleasure she'd get from it.

"Come on," he urged, his voice warm and sugary, as he slid an arm around her shoulder and waited for her to resist. When she didn't, he flipped back the armrest that had separated them, pulled her close and rested his head on her shoulder. No reaction. He let his fingers dance beneath her chin until she could no longer resist and began to laugh uncontrollably. Then he reached down for their blankets, covered them both and felt her curl into him. He hadn't thought she'd get so cozy in the presence of their companions, but he hadn't noticed the lowered lights either.

In those circumstances, a man's options were severely limited. She huddled closer, and he had to struggle to suppress the fire that raged in his blood. His pulse pitched into a gallop when her breathing accelerated. The scent of warm woman began to tantalize his nostrils, and he'd have given a day's income to jog five miles in thirty-two-degree weather. He couldn't tell whether she knew her effect on him right then, and he wasn't about to ask her. She'd caught him on the blind side sometime during the last few days, and he'd as soon she didn't know how vulnerable he'd gotten. When had he begun to need her? He didn't know anything about her, but he wanted her, and didn't want another man near her. She sighed deeply and buried her face in the curve of his neck. If only he could get out of there. He rested his head on the back of the seat and counted sheep, but his passion didn't cool. He imagined himself eating sauerkraut, which he hated, but that didn't lessen the discomfort in his groin, or the pounding of his pulse. A waste of time, he decided, and wrapped his arms around her. What the hell! It wasn't the first time he'd done without, but he couldn't remember having previously enjoyed it.

Let him think her asleep, that she didn't realize the intimacy she'd created between them. She tried to ignore her nagging conscience and its caution that she'd pay dearly for every kiss, each caress, for every minute in his arms. But, even as a young girl, she had dreamed of a man's holding her as though she were precious, his morning sun and evening breeze; she couldn't help savoring this dream come true with a man who in so short a time had wedged himself deep into her heart. She knew she'd eventually have to face the inevitable, that moment when he knew everything and walked away from her. And there was no denying that, if he accused her of dishonesty, she would deserve it; she hadn't led him on, but her attempts to discourage him had been so haphazard that he'd probably seen no reason to take them seriously.

His right arm tightened around her and, in spite of what her head told her, she slid an arm across his chest and accepted his affection. She wanted to raise her head, touch his lips with her own and taste the sweet agony that gripped her from head to toe every time she drank the burning passion of his kisses.

"Jeannetta, do you know you're caressing me? Do you?"

She'd been so absorbed in the feel of him that his low guttural voice reached her ears as if from a great distance.

"Do you?" He stilled her attempt to remove her fingers from the thatch of hair on his chest. "Answer me," he urged, his voice low and thick.

"I... Oh, Mason, I don't know what I'm doing. We're getting so close, and I know that nothing can come of it. I try to keep that in mind, but you're so tempting."

He held her closer when she made a weak and irresolute attempt to move back to her own seat, and she realized that the man in him paid greater attention to her actions than to her words. Who could blame him?

"You don't have anything to fear from me. I'm free, solvent and thirty-seven, and I'm neither married nor engaged. So why can't I hold you in my arms? You're comfortable, aren't you?"

If only it were that simple.

"This is moving too fast, Mason."

"Too fast?" he scoffed. "We've seen more of each other on this tour than we would have managed in six months if we'd been in New York and Pilgrim, unless..." He sat up and gazed down at her, his eyes sparkling with devilment in that way she loved. "Of course, we would have seen a lot, I mean *a lot* more of each other if you'd taken me for a roommate. You still can; I always pick up my socks and, as far as I know, I don't snore."

She sat up abruptly, hitting her head on his chin, which he rubbed reflexively.

"We're getting kind of fanciful, aren't we?"

His hand stroked her back until she succumbed to temptation and moved back into his arms.

"Not in my book. Tell me, are you an only child?"

He hadn't previously asked her personal questions and hadn't given her a chance to ask him any. Maybe this was her chance.

"I have an older sister who lives at our family home in Pilgrim." He'd opened the gate. Maybe this was the time. "What about you? Sometimes I get the feeling that you're a loner."

The muscles tensed in the arm that held her, and she sensed his caution, his withdrawal. "I have an older brother who's like a father to me. He's...well, he's...a great guy."

She already knew that from the investigation, but maybe if she probed...

"How did you decide to start a travel agency? And this tour...it must have been a huge financial risk."

His right hand stilled on her back and the other one covered her own and she knew he intended to take her hand away from his chest where, without thinking how it would appear to him, she'd teased his chest hair as though to coax him into answering her questions. She sat up.

"You like me, as long as I don't invade your privacy, and you'll kiss me with all the urgency and deliberateness of a patriot missile going after a scud…until I get out of my place." She knew that such tactics wouldn't get her what she ultimately wanted, but she couldn't help feeling hostile toward him. He had the power to heal, to sustain life, yet he chose to traipse around the world catering to people who had the means to indulge their selfish whims. Her back stiffened. "What made you choose this line of work?" She almost hoped he'd tell her that it wasn't her business.

He leaned back, ran his hand over his tight curls and breathed deeply.

"I'm not used to answering direct questions about myself, and I've never liked asking them. You took this tour because you wanted to see the world. If I hadn't had something similar in mind, I'd probably have chosen another line of work. Let's get some sleep."

She closed her eyes to hide the pain she knew he'd see there. Bitterness churned inside of her, and she had to muster all her strength to hold back the tears. She'd thought she could face the future, no matter what happened, that she'd learn to accept her fate, but he was handing her a double dose of poison. She thought she could handle life without trees, snow-capped mountains and brilliant sunsets, but a future in which he had no part? Anger surged in her and she glanced up at him, expecting to see annoyance. But his face held no expression. In a flash of intuition, she saw that he cloaked his emotions behind his poker face, that his bland expression served as his shield, his defensive armor. Knowledge, someone had said, was power. She refused to allow him to dismiss her.

She leaned toward him, her voice calm. "You've practically told me to shut up; are you planning to kiss me anymore?"

He laughed, but she didn't place much store by that; she'd learned that this was a man who never surprised himself, and she could only admire his self-discipline.

"Well?" she insisted, but he was saved an answer when a flight attendant rushed to him.

"Mr. Fenwick, Lydia Steward says she's having chest pains, but we're not quite halfway. Should we turn around or keep going?"

He was on his feet in a flash, and Jeannetta knew that the physician had emerged, that it was Dr. Fenwick, and not the tour manager, who moved with such alacrity. She wanted to follow him, to see what he'd do, how he'd handle it. She longed to know how much of his secret he'd expose in such an emergency, but she dared not follow. She'd never forgive herself if she hampered his efforts to help the woman. After some time, he returned, outwardly calm.

"Will she be alright?"

"More than likely, provided she takes her medicine and follows her doctor's advice, but if she has another incident like that one, I'm sending her back to Spokane."

"What happened?" she asked, hoping that he'd respond with a physician's language and manners.

He paused for a while as though gathering his thoughts. "She had a bad case of indigestion, or something similar. I could use a few hours' sleep. How about you?"

She settled in her seat, disappointed.

"Sure. Every living thing has to sleep." If she sounded bitter, she didn't care. She wished she had never heard of him, that she hadn't taken his tour and that she didn't love him to the depths of her soul.

The big business-class seat had wide armrests and a slanted prop on which to rest her feet, but she didn't think she'd ever been more uncomfortable. She tossed about, shifted from one position to another and prayed for the sleep that would take her out of her thoughts. After nearly an hour of it, she felt his strong arm gather her close and fold her to him. He rested her head on his shoulder and drew the blanket across her.

"Now, perhaps we can both get some rest."

She slid her right arm across his chest and cherished the moment.

Mason awoke to the smell of strong coffee and Jeannetta's soft breathing. He glanced down at the delicate brown fingers that clutched the breast pocket of his shirt and covered them with his hand. He had a sense of well-being, of having the world by the tail, and he knew it came from the feel of her stirring in his arms as he awoke.

"Coffee? Orange juice?" the flight attendant asked him. He ordered coffee, remembered Lydia Steward and wanted to check on her, but controlled his urge. He had thought he'd laid to rest the physician in him, but now he wasn't so sure. He'd brought along a medical bag, complete with a stethoscope, that he was glad he hadn't had to use. Finally, unable to resist any longer, he swallowed the last of his coffee, woke Jeannetta, got his toiletries and started back toward the lavatories. Lydia's smiling face reminded him of the feeling of accomplishment he'd always gotten when a grateful patient thanked him, a feeling he realized he'd missed. He paused beside Lydia, and her smiles and words of profuse thanks humbled him, making him want to get away from her, from all of them. Away from the charade he'd carried on for the last three years. He glanced up the aisle toward his seat, where Jeannetta stood, looking directly at him. Perhaps she's getting a much-needed stretch, he mused but, somehow, he didn't believe that.

He returned to his seat, shaved and refreshed, to find Jeannetta dictating into her recorder a description of the plane, the appearance of the flight attendants, the clouds, even the wagons from which the attendants served food and drinks. He couldn't figure out why a writer didn't take photographs of her surroundings, and that bothered him. He cleared his throat and, as he'd expected, she put away the recorder.

"You said you write fiction. Is this a story about travel?"

She hesitated before answering. "No. I'd thought I'd work on it during this tour, but the mood hasn't been right. I can't get into the man's character."

"What kind of man is he? You hinted that I'm not your model and, since I'm not a writer, you don't lose anything by telling me."

Their breakfast arrived, and he thought she'd take advantage of it to change the subject, but she didn't.

"He isn't the main protagonist, though he's central to the theme, and this isn't the story I had in mind when I left home. This is a troubled man who can't come to terms with his feelings, who believes that his strength lies in his ability to stand alone, to need no one, but whose true problem is his inability to give of himself. My problem is that I can't get a handle on his character, how he deals with people, with his surroundings, his adversities."

She talked on, but his ears roared with the hollow echo of his insides. He opened his eyes to shut out the portrait of himself in his white coat, his stethoscope dangling from his pocket as he walked off of that hospital ward for the last time. Cool dampness matted the hairs at his wrist, and he thought he'd strangle from the saliva in his mouth as he opened it to speak.

"How does it end?"

"I don't know. I've just begun to lay it out in my mind, to see how he looks and to understand him."

He forced himself not to cover his ears. Maybe she wasn't

talking about him, but her words rattled around in his mind all the same.

"No, I don't know the end," she went on, "but I expect he'll have his moment of truth."

He sat forward and turned so that he could see her face.

"I've never met anyone who seemed more composed, more at peace, than you, but some kind of aura around you denies it. In these four weeks, you've come to mean something to me and, from what I've learned about you, I welcome that, but you're mysterious. You've got a…a…a quality that's unsettling. I can't help wondering why you're on this tour. Oh, I know you want to see the world. But why *now?*"

She lifted her glass to take a sip of orange juice and tilted it before it reached her mouth. He stared at her and at the juice on her egg and in her lap. She'd done the same thing on the train, only then it had been water.

"Good Heavens! I've gotten to be such an oink-oink. You'd think I could enjoy breakfast with a charming man without getting nervous and spilling everything."

He reached overhead and rang for the flight attendant.

"It's alright, Jeannetta. That can happen to anybody." He didn't believe it. She had tried to distract him, but he hadn't been taken in by her patter. Jeannetta didn't babble; she talked when she had something to say.

Their flight attendant cleaned her dress with club soda and, to his amazement, Jeannetta joked, "Mr. Fenwick didn't enforce his rule against babies on the tour."

He didn't join her laughter, because he could think of half a dozen ailments to which such symptoms could be ascribed—none of them good news.

Jeannetta excused herself to freshen up before the plane landed. She had experienced some of the symptoms her doctor had mentioned, and she couldn't help wondering whether

her time might be running out. She hadn't had her period in months and the headaches occurred with increasing frequency and severity. The thought of flying home from Singapore occurred to her, but she had never been a quitter and she had invested too much in this scheme to throw in the towel without a try. She washed her face, brushed her teeth and combed her hair, looked at herself in the mirror, and thanked God for wrinkle-free fabric.

He stood by their seats when she returned, a deep frown and a quizzical expression on his face. Strange, she thought, since he usually camouflaged his feelings with a poker face. If he'd been as good a doctor as everyone claimed, he might have noticed something about her. Could she pretend she hadn't known what ailed her? She couldn't do it, and the thought nagged her as she left the plane.

Mason checked the passengers through customs and onto the sightseeing bus. He had had their luggage sent directly to the Southern Queen, the boat that would take them on a four-day journey from Singapore to Bangkok, Thailand. He stood by the bus, mopping his forehead and was about to board when Lucy Abernathy grabbed his arm. She panted excitedly, as though she'd run a mile, and her words tumbled over one another, finally making him understand that Geoffrey Ames hadn't arrived.

"I don't know where he is," she yelled. He did his best to ease her fears, but she wouldn't be comforted.

"He said he'd meet me at the bus, and he's not here," she screamed, flexing her knees as though she were jumping.

"I'll find him," he told her, and moved away from the bus but, to his chagrin, she rushed along beside him. When they reached the terminal, she stopped, and a glance at her distorted face told him to expect trouble. He followed her gaze and saw Geoffrey Ames, surrounded by half a dozen Singapore beauties and autographing everything from a magazine to the front of one girl's blouse. And with her tube of lipstick.

Mason threw out his arm to block the irate woman's way, but she brushed past him, and he prayed she wouldn't commit one of the numerous crimes for which hanging was the penalty in the Singapore legal code.

"Don't ever come near me again," she told Geoffrey in a trembling voice, her hands planted firmly on her ample hips.

"Now, Lucy...Lucy, you don't mean that."

"Who doesn't mean it?" she fumed.

"He's so cute," one of the girls exclaimed, amidst a chorus of giggles.

"What?" Lucy glared at the happy old man, who seemed oblivious to her displeasure. "*Cute?* I've got your cute, Mr. Ames."

Mason stared in awe as she pranced off, stepping high as though leading a marching band. He couldn't help laughing at the unrepentant man, whose smile reached from ear to ear.

"We could have left you, Ames."

"I knew Lucy wouldn't let you," he said, still unperturbed. And still smiling. Mason wondered if the man's steps had a more youthful bounce than when he'd gotten off the plane.

"I see you and Miss Jeannetta have been getting pretty close," Geoffrey confided.

"I was thinking the same about you and Miss Lucy," Mason rejoined.

"You planning wedding bells onboard the ship?" Geoffrey wanted to know.

Mason gawked. Had the man lost his mind?

"I just met her in March."

"Time's got nothing to do with it," a confident Geoffrey Ames replied. "When this tour's over, you'll go wherever she goes. Mark my word. Yes, sir. When a woman gets in your blood, she stays there. And there ain't nothing so miserable as having part of you one place and the other part somewhere else. Yep. You've been had."

He warmed up to his lecture, slowing his pace, though Mason had no doubt that the man knew they had a tight schedule.

"Yes, sir," Geoffrey went on. "In my day, romance was the step to marriage. You young people don't seem to understand your feelings, can't make a commitment. That's what a good marriage is—total commitment. The fires burn lower with time, and the hot coals die down. What's left is deep, abiding love. You don't think of yourself without her. She's you. You're happy when she's happy and miserable when she's sad. And if she leaves this world before you do, the best part of you goes with her. In my forty-six years of marriage, I never spent a night away from my Nettie, God rest her soul, and no more of the day than I had to in order to make a living for us—such as it was. And she was always there for me. I lost my job once. It wasn't much to start with—four hours every night cleaning restrooms and floors in a bank building—but it kept us off of welfare. I got home and told her about it and said I didn't have a cent. She smiled and said, 'It's a good thing I made pig's feet and hot potato salad for your supper. You always like that so much.' I never loved her as much as I did that minute. Miss Jeannetta is a simple person. Oh, she's smart and all that, but she don't have any of those airs that those sophisticated women have, otherwise she wouldn't a dressed up to eat dinner with an old man like me. She likes you a whole lot, son. I'd pay good attention to her if I was you."

They climbed on the bus and Mason couldn't help laughing to himself; Lucy had seated herself with another passenger to foil Geoffrey's certain attempts at making amends.

"She's going to make you sweat," Mason told him.

"I can handle her," Geoffrey replied. "You're the one with

the problem." He took the seat behind the driver and motioned Mason to join him.

Mason looked down the aisle. Maybeth had taken the seat beside Jeannetta, so he sat with Geoffrey.

"How're you going to manage? Miss Abernathy is furious with you."

Geoffrey gathered his pants legs up around the knee and made himself comfortable.

"Oh, she'd stay mad if I'd brought one of those beauties on this bus, but I'm not crazy and she knows that. Take my advice and work on things with Miss Jeannetta. She's a diamond waiting to be polished."

"Don't lose any sleep over it," he advised the older man. "I'm dealing with it." He ignored Geoffrey's grunt of disbelief. His fingers wrapped around the keys that were his constant companions, and he leaned back in the seat and closed his eyes. He'd give anything to have a Nettie of his own. A woman who would smile at him when he told her he didn't know how or where he'd get her next meal. He turned to his seat companion.

"How long did you know your wife before you married her?"

Ames fingered his beard and a melancholy smile stole over his face. "Well, I asked her to marry me the first time I took her out. We went to see *Casablanca*. I'd already seen it, but she hadn't. Anyhow, she said yes, but it took two weeks to make the wedding dress. I declare, I thought she'd never finish it. Every time I saw her, she needed another little piece of lace, more beads or something." Mason smiled as images of Jeannetta sewing beads on a lace wedding dress flitted through his mind. He'd bet that, like other modern women, she'd head for a good designer. Of course, professional women rarely had time to sew.

"You're quite a man," he told Geoffrey. "I'm glad I met

you." It wouldn't hurt Ames to get a little of his own medicine, he decided and asked him, "What are you planning to do about Miss Abernathy? You going to cross this off as a vacation romance?"

"'Course not," the man replied, a scowl marring his usually serene face. "I'm going to marry her as soon as I get back to Augusta. That's in Georgia, you know." Mason shut off what would have been a sharp whistle.

"But she's not from Georgia."

Geoffrey Ames's smug smile wasn't lost on Mason, and the man's self-confidence was even more evident when he replied, "No, but she soon will be."

Mason clicked on the mike. "First stop, Jurong Bird Park. Anyone who isn't back on this bus twenty minutes from now, get a taxi to the harbor; we'll be leaving on the Southern Queen at two o'clock." He moved so that Geoffrey could pass. With the tour members gone and the bus empty, he pulled the baseball cap he'd bought at the Istanbul airport over his eyes and slumped down in his seat, hoping for a twenty-minute nap.

"Want some company?" He removed the cap and sat up.

"Everyone else went to the park. Why didn't you go?" he asked Jeannetta. "I thought you'd be happy to see so many colorful birds. First time I went to Jurong, I could hardly believe my eyes." He slid into Geoffrey's seat so that she could sit beside him. He gaped when her hand went to her forehead as though to steady herself, but she smiled and sat down. He might have imagined it, he told himself. Hopefully.

"I would have, but I decided I'd rather use the opportunity to get rid of Maybeth. She's a card. Of course, the possibility of having you all to myself wasn't easily ignored."

He raised both eyebrows. "Are you flirting with me?"

He thought her sudden interest in the floor, the top of her shoes and her lap unusual and a smile curled around his lips at the ingenuity she displayed in the art of finger-twiddling.

Might as well have a little fun. He tipped up her chin and held it until she looked at him. He winked.

"You were, weren't you?"

Hot shivers plowed through his chest when she bathed her bottom lip with her tongue and slanted him a sly grin.

"Why not? You're free, thirty-seven and solvent, I believe is the way you put it. So I can have my way with you without getting into trouble with the law. Come here."

He sat forward. "Whoa, there," he cautioned. "Back on that plane, you implied that I ought to leave you alone, that nothing could come of this."

She slid toward him, positioned her head on the back of his seat, gazed up at him and let him see the warm welcome in her almond-shaped eyes.

"That was before I saw you wearing this silly cap."

He tried to ignore the dark, lusty hue of her voice. If he could hold out for another twelve minutes, the tour members would return and they'd have company, but he couldn't help responding to her. He'd sized her up as a woman who could and would hold her own, but he hadn't thought her aggressive. Her jaw muscles twitched, his belly flexed and he knew what would come next. The painful stirring in his groin jolted him, and he stared down at her. Her eyelids fluttered as if weakened by a powerful light, and she licked her lips.

"Come here, Mason." Longing replaced the welcome in her dark eyes.

"Baby, don't play with me."

"I've never played with you. I may change my tune, but I can't change what I feel."

Air swished out of him. She had never asked him for himself. He wrapped her in his arms, and her soft fingers at the back of his head guided his mouth to hers with a force that he wouldn't have dared apply. Her parted lips sucked his tongue into her mouth, and her arched back pressed her breasts to his chest. God, he couldn't stand it. Wave after wave of hot currents tore through him when she released his tongue and plastered kisses over his face, neck and ears, murmuring things that he couldn't understand. She attempted to straddle his lap, but he used what sense she'd left him with, cradled her in his arms and rested her on his knee. She leaned forward, getting closer to him, and her thigh grazed his engorged center. He would have shifted her position, but she caressed his jaw and whispered in his ear: "Maybe I shouldn't have done this, but all of a sudden I needed to know you. Don't move. Please. At least, I can have this much of you."

If only the runaway train in his chest would stop its mad tumble. He took slower, deeper breaths. "What do you mean by that? Are you trying to tell me something?" The clamor of voices reached his ears, and he quickly shifted her to the seat beside him, stepped out of the bus and counted the tour members as they boarded. He didn't feel lighthearted, but he couldn't resist a laugh when Geoffrey arrived holding Lucy's hand.

Jeannetta took a seat midway in the bus. She wanted to sit with Mason, to be close to him, but she didn't dare. *Are you trying to tell me something?* Subconsciously, she had been but, because of the poor timing, she'd been grateful when their companions returned. She couldn't figure out what had prompted her to abandon her self-control as she had done with Mason, but had never done with any other man. Oh, she loved him, but did loving him mean she'd change her personality?

She adored birds and had looked forward to visiting Jurong Bird Park, but when she'd stood to leave the bus, everything in it seemed to swirl around her. She'd managed to steady herself and to walk as far as Mason's seat at the front of the bus, but the sensation hit her again, and she'd sat down beside him, because she'd had no choice. She supposed the experience had made her reckless with him, because she'd thought at first that her time had about run out. His eyes had changed to that greenish-brown she'd come to recognize as his red flag, his signal to stop or be prepared to go all the way, but she hadn't broken it off. One more bill she knew she'd have to pay. He hadn't accused her of being a tease, but he'd warned her not to play with him. She closed her eyes to discourage Leonard Deek's conversation. Had she been right in thinking she should leave the tour and give up? She turned her head toward the window, seeking as much privacy as she could get, wondering whether she loved Mason so much that she'd voluntarily condemn herself to half a life rather than have him know that she'd deceived him. She took a tissue from her purse and blotted away the lone tear on her cheek. If only she hadn't fallen in love with him. *If.* What a useless thought. She sat up, looked at Leonard and smiled.

"Did you enjoy the birds? I wish I'd gone, too," she said to the quiet Latin teacher.

"At least you were spared that hundred-degree heat. If you've seen one of these preserves, you've seen 'em all." He took out his pad and began making notes.

"I haven't seen one." He went back over his sentences, dotting the *i*'s with little round circles, a practice she disliked.

"Really?" he asked, without looking up. "Well, you can always come back to see them next year."

She turned toward the window.

Mason checked the tour through immigration and onto the Southern Queen for the voyage to Bangkok, Thailand. He looked at his faithful Timex. Seven o'clock Saturday morning in New York. He found a telephone station and placed a call.

"Hello, Skip, this is Mason. I'm about to leave Singapore."

"Wait. Let me get up and get my map you gave me. Where's Singapore?" Mason couldn't help smiling. He found immense satisfaction in the boy's eagerness to learn, to succeed, and he'd vowed that he'd befriend him as long as he showed promise. He'd awakened the boy on a morning when he didn't have to get up early, and he hadn't objected.

"It's in Asia, Skip, and I don't have time for a geography lesson. How's your aunt Mabel doing?"

"What part of Asia?"

Mason laughed. Tenacity was as much a part of Skip as his dark skin and wooly hair.

"Southeast Asia. I said, how is Mabel?" He held his breath. Skip disliked talking about anything unpleasant. "Well?"

"She's in the hospital right now, but…"

"In the…*what?* Who's looking after you?"

"I've been with Steve, but she's coming home this afternoon, so I stayed overnight to clean up the place. Steve was here 'til ten last night. You having a good time?"

"I'm working, Skip, although it's pleasant work. I have to hang up, because I want to talk with Steve. Be sure and do as he tells you, and give my regards to Mabel." He hung up. What a thing to happen with twenty-five hundred miles separating them. Even so exceptional a boy as Skip shouldn't have such responsibility at age twelve. He'd been lucky to have his brother, Steve. He'd resisted becoming involved with Skip, but the boy had adopted him and followed him around until he became a leech on his conscience. He didn't regret his decision to look after Skip and his struggling great-aunt, and he'd developed a deep fondness for the boy. He wrote Steve's number on a pad and handed it to the operator.

"Sorry to get you up so early on Saturday, Steve, but I'm just shoving off to Thailand. What's wrong with Mabel?" He listened, a plan forming in his mind. "That's serious. Do you have time to look for a bachelor apartment in one of those nursing-care complexes? Ask my receptionist to help you."

"Mason, I know their apartment wouldn't win a prize, but it's theirs and, if she leaves that, they'll have nothing."

"From what you told me, I know she won't recover and, unless I do something, Skip will spend the next couple of years taking care of her. I don't want to see his potential wasted."

"What'll you do with him?"

Mason didn't hesitate, because he knew it was right. "He can live with me. That's what he wants to do, anyway. Check the hospital. Get an ambulance to take Mabel home, and give her enough money to last them until I get back. Thanks for looking after Skip."

"He's taken to calling me Uncle Steve. You wouldn't expect me to neglect my nephew, would you?" Steve had said it jokingly, but the thought stayed with Mason.

He looked over the list of boarded passengers once more to make certain none of his tour members had stayed behind. Maybeth had been the first onboard, followed by Deek. The woman toyed with the little man, but he tailed her wherever she went. He'd said he was on sabbatical, a year's leave for research, but what kind of research would a professor of Latin do on this tour? He wondered how many of them had lied about their reasons for taking the trip. He walked up the gangplank and looked back at the soaring buildings in Asia's most modern city. He'd left something of himself in that city, on that bus, something he knew he'd never regain. His ability to walk away from her had died there.

## Chapter 5

Jeannetta looked around her comfortable stateroom, pleased with the soft, feminine decor and glad the decorator hadn't liked wild colors. She had decided not to splurge on first class and was glad; her cabin-class quarters offered as much elegance as she needed. Light filtered through the windows, and she moved a chair in order to look out of one. Passengers strolled the deck, and large gray birds dived off the thick wooden planks at the edge of the water, caught unlucky fish and flew away. Was everything on earth a predator, including herself? She unpacked, found an iron and ironing board in a closet and pressed a few items of clothing. Restlessness hung on her like a heavy weight, and she knew its source. Pretending an airiness she didn't feel, she donned a pair of white slacks, a yellow T-shirt, socks and white canvas shoes, but got only as far as the door before turning around. She had to do something about Mason, had to find a way to talk with him about herself. Four weeks, and she hadn't found an ap-

propriate occasion. Pricked by her conscience, she admitted
that he'd given her a good chance on the bus, and that she'd
used a handy excuse to forfeit the opportunity. Though she
knew she was responsible for her predicament with Mason,
anger seethed within her, and she couldn't help feeling hostile toward him for withholding his precious skills from desperate people.

Determined to find a way, she left the room and strolled
down the deck. The fresh, salty air enlivened her as she
walked along, greeting tour members and other passengers.
She stretched out in a deck chair and watched the Singapore
skyline, waiting for the ship to pull anchor and head out to sea.
A tall man of indeterminate age and race walked over to her.

"I'm Rolfe Merchinson." He extended his hand and waited
for an invitation to sit with her. "Would you join me for a
drink?"

She shook hands; not to have done so would have been out
of character for her, but she refused his offer.

"Thank you, but I rarely drink."

"Why not make this one of your exceptions?" he asked
with the practiced smoothness of a worldly sophisticate. She
picked up the magazine that she'd brought along for the purpose of discouraging unwanted acquaintances, glanced at it
and replied.

"I'm alone here, but I'm not by myself on this ship."

"You're with someone?"

She nodded.

Rolfe Merchinson straightened up, bowed briefly and told
her, "That is a pity. The gentleman is a lucky man, indeed."

She glanced up as Mason approached, slowed his steps,
nodded and kept walking.

"Excuse me."

She reached the bottom of the wide curving staircase just
as Mason stopped and looked back as though to confirm what

he'd seen. *Not a smart move,* she told herself. But she hadn't wanted Mason to think that, forty minutes after boarding ship, she'd struck up an acquaintance with a strange man. Rolfe Whatever-His-Name might have been nice enough, but she didn't play games with men and she didn't want Mason to think her easy pickings. She slowed her steps in the hope that she wouldn't catch him, but he waited.

"Settled in okay?"

She nodded. "My stateroom's super. Couldn't ask for better."

A smile enveloped his whole face and the warmth in his eyes seemed to caress her. Even his stern top lip had relaxed. She detected a difference in him, a softness, a strange tenderness. Maybe now was a good time to lead him to thoughts of medicine.

"How's your patient?"

"She's…" His eyes widened, his lower lip dropped for a second and, as though he'd programmed himself to do it, he looked over his shoulder. Something akin to anger flashed in his eyes. She'd have to brazen it out.

"Is she alright? I wondered why you had to stay with her so long last night if she only had indigestion."

"Jeannetta, Lydia isn't my patient. I don't have patients. She's a senior citizen and I was concerned about her health. Still am, for that matter." His gaze bore into her. Searching. Judging.

"What on earth did I say to bring on this furor?" she asked as she struggled to present him with a bland, innocent face.

"Nothing. But try to remember that travel managers don't have patients, we have customers. I've got a few things to attend to. Please excuse me."

She watched his long, broad back as he strode toward his stateroom.

*That sure didn't work,* she told herself. *You're in trouble, kiddo. The longer you wait, the worse it'll be.* He stopped before turning the corner and looked back at her, and she remembered that late, sun-shrouded afternoon in Paris when he'd wanted to turn the corner and, by the sheer power of her mind, she hadn't allowed it. His gaze sliced through her until she did the only thing that she could; she smiled and held out her hand to him. She half expected him to walk on, but he stood there. She took several steps toward him, his own pain searing her, for she at last knew that he lived with discomfort and unhappiness for having disclaimed his true self.

*Just like I'm pretending to be an ordinary tourist.* She moved another three or four steps in his direction. She wasn't guiltless; *who was she to judge him?*

She took another step toward him, and his gaze didn't waver. For the first time, she could see vulnerability in him. She walked closer, and he took a short step toward her. Encouraged, she took another. His smile was a brilliant lamp, a symbolic beacon in the darkness, and she opened her arms wide and sped to him. Mason met her three-quarters of the way, swept her into his strong arms and twirled around with her before setting her on her feet.

"It wasn't my intention to be short with you. I don't know what got into me," he said.

She had to steady herself when his eyes, a black sea of adoration, caressed her, and his gentle fingers grasped hers in a wordless entreaty that she follow him. He led them to his stateroom nearby, entered and, before his portfolio hit the floor, he had her in his arms. She raised her lips but, even in her frantic eagerness to drown in him, she had the sense that he deliberately prolonged the tension, as though starving himself before a feast. His voice, strangely dark, dusty and littered with the cobwebs of his unhappiness, penetrated her understanding, and tendrils of fear shot through her as she realized the responsibility of sharing his vulnerability. Open honesty had replaced his poker face.

"Look at me, Jeannetta. We're alone now. We're not in a public place, a bus. Put your arms around me and kiss me."

Her wide-eyed gaze searched his face for an answer to the change in him.

He stroked her cheek. "Kiss me. I...I need you."

A bolt of heady sensation shot through her, and she curled into him, wanting, needing to heal him. Desperate to belong to him. Her right hand grasped the back of his head, and she raised parted lips to his. It seemed light-years before his mouth sent flames of passion roaring through her body. She felt the tremors that shook his big frame when she pulled his tongue into her mouth and sucked it. Emboldened, she slid her leg between his, and shuddered at the force of his arousal against her thigh. His hoarse groan stripped her of what reticence she had left, and her hand went to his buttocks and pulled his arousal tighter against her thigh. Frustrated with longing to hold him inside of her, she tugged at his belt buckle, but he pulled his mouth from hers and whispered, his voice harsh.

"Honey, do you know what you're doing?"

She couldn't hear his words for the thundering desire that roared in her head, numbing her to everything but her ravenous craving for him. Her hips rolled wildly, out of control, and his fingers grasped them and held her still.

"I need you worse than I need to breathe, but I have to know where this is go—"

The sharp buzz of his beeper brought them both to the reality of what they were about to do. He released her body and answered, though he continued to possess her with his fiery gaze.

"Fenwick speaking." He listened for a second and flipped off the beeper. "That was the first mate," he explained. "The ship's about to leave harbor, and cocktails will be served immediately."

The ship's bellow confirmed their departure. Mason moved back a step, though he held her hand firmly in his own. He hadn't known himself capable of such burning passion, such a powerful, humbling need. He had to go somewhere and deal with his feelings. Was this the woman with whom he'd share his life? How could he know? She hadn't levelled with him. *Nor you with her,* his conscience needled.

"I guess we can be glad you're wearing that beeper."

"Speak for yourself, honey. As far as I'm concerned, that was the same as being awakened from a deep sleep and routed out of your house in the dead of winter because the place is on fire." She leaned her head against his chest, and he locked her in his arms.

"I want you to sit quietly and decide what you want from me. Whatever it is, be honest with yourself. I've had my last take-care-of-your-needs kind of relationship. I deserve more, and I'm prepared to wait until I find it. I don't doubt that if we hadn't been interrupted we'd be lovers right now, and I'm also sure that both of us would have had second thoughts afterward." He glanced at his watch. "I have to check on Lydia. I didn't like the look of her when she boarded. When we get to Bangkok, I may send her home. It would be a pity, though, because she wanted so badly to make this trip."

"Has she told you the truth about her health?"

He looked closely at her, certain that her voice had wavered.

"I doubt it. Truth isn't too popular these days." The tightening of her fingers in his hand told him more than she knew. "But we'll settle it in Bangkok, if not before." His words held an ominous ring for him, a dark prophesy reverberating in his head. He gazed down at her in wonder that she could induce such a mood in him.

"I hope you don't have to send her home."

He shook his head. He'd told her to face what was happening between them, and she'd managed to skirt the issue. Did she think he didn't know that? She had discouraged him, but she'd also set him on fire and, on at least two occasions, she'd been deliberate about it. He grinned down at her, though he took pains to shut off his emotions.

"When we were on the plane to Singapore, you asked me if I planned to kiss you anymore. You may or may not have been serious, but, I assure you, if you get your ducks in a straight row, I'll kiss you every time I get the chance."

Her eyelids fluttered downward, and he tipped up her chin with his left index finger.

"What's the matter, you don't like the idea?"

She gave him a quick peck on the cheek and started for the door. "Don't we have to dress for dinner?"

He nodded, and she blew him a kiss and walked out. He smiled, a satisfied male reflex at the shakiness of her steps after their passionate exchange, until the doctor in him doubted kisses could make a person stagger.

He showered quickly, and changed into a white shirt, white linen jacket and navy slacks. Black shoes, a red tie and a handkerchief completed his outfit. He left his room thinking how much simpler a surgeon's green cotton garb was than the stylish clothes he had to wear as a travel manager. He strolled along the deck, letting the fresh salty wind invigorate him, but an unsettled feeling stirred in him. He paused and propped his foot against the rail, stared out at the dark sky above him and the South China Sea all around him, black but for the whitecaps of the rough water. So much like his life. He'd opened his soul to her, shamelessly let her see into him, into his heart. She had responded with a passion that he hadn't previously known, but she hadn't offered her trust, her truth, the person inside of her. Could he turn back? He didn't think so, but she didn't have to know that.

He shook off the mood, walked into the cocktail lounge, ordered a vodka and tonic and leaned against the grand piano, his gaze glued to the door. She stopped in the doorway of the lounge and looked around, a vision in a red sleeveless sheath that defined a perfect feminine silhouette. Breath hissed out of his lungs when she saw him and a smile claimed her face. His passion steamed as though hot coals simmered in his blood, and the innocent undulations of her rhythmic movements triggered his desire as she glided to him. Damn. He tossed his drink to the back of his throat, and his fingers squeezed his parents' door keys that were always in his pants pocket. He didn't go to meet her. He waited.

"Hi. I hope you haven't waited long."

He shrugged. "Hi. I've accepted that you have a problem with time."

"I know. I'm sorry."

He couldn't help smiling. She didn't ask to be forgiven, because she knew she'd do it again. He let his gaze roam over her lovely form.

"My pleasure. You were well worth the wait. What would you like?" He touched her elbow and headed them toward the bar.

"Some of those stone-crab claws," she said, pointing to one of the many small tables laden with finger food.

"I meant, to drink."

"Mason, I don't drink anymore." Immediately she wished she hadn't said those telltale words, for both of his eyebrows shot upward.

"Anymore? Why did you stop?" Here was her chance, the perfect opportunity, and she couldn't summon the courage to tell him.

"Prudence."

He lifted another glass of vodka and tonic from the tray of a passing waiter and raised it to her in a salute.

"Prudence, eh?" A cynical smile flashed over his handsome face. "Well, here's to Prudence, whoever the hell she is."

Stunned, she gaped when he tossed the drink to the back of his throat. He grasped her hand, and her heart thudded beneath her breast as he stared down at her with mocking eyes.

"Beautiful. Innocent. Vulnerable. When such a woman lies, it's as though she's smeared grease paint on pristine snow. My table is number twenty. Care to join me?"

She wanted to be with him, but his mood gave her a sense of imminent trouble. She tried unsuccessfully to push back the dark feeling, to banish the intuitive notion that the piper wanted his due. She walked beside him to his table.

"I don't think I like you when you're drinking," she told him.

"Oh, you probably like me as much then as I like you when you lie." She stopped walking, laid back her shoulders and glared at him.

"If you'd rather have someone else's company…"

He guided her along, an enigmatic smile playing around his lips.

"On the contrary, my darling, you've pinpointed my problem. I've discovered that I don't want anyone's company but yours, and that's bad news."

"For whom?"

She couldn't say he'd been rude, but he'd certainly set aside his usual politeness. He looked deeply into her eyes until she shifted her gaze.

"Since you won't level with me, it's bad news for me, wouldn't you say?'

Mason stared, horrified, as she took a glass of tonic from a waiter's tray, only to have it slip through her fingers, as though she lacked the ability to grasp it. After the waiter cleaned the liquid from her shoes and off the floor, Mason led her to his table, held her chair and seated himself beside her. He'd lost his taste for food, but he knew that if he didn't eat she'd know that her accident worried him. He smiled at their dinner companions, reached in her lap and gathered her right hand in his left one, but he couldn't banish the ache in the pit of his stomach. Gloom hovered around him when he let himself think of the horror that her syndrome of ailments suggested. It couldn't be true.

"How's your stateroom?" he asked Lucy Abernathy. Geoffrey had had it changed from tourist class to first class. She smiled up at him and told Mason it was the most beautiful room she'd ever seen.

"You come have breakfast with me tomorrow morning, you hear?"

At Mason's raised eyebrow, she informed her companions that her suite had a dinette as well as a living room.

"She's scared of the water," Geoffrey explained, "and I wanted her to enjoy this trip."

"I'm afraid of the water, too," Maybeth chimed in, "and I'm sure I saw a shark swim past my porthole." She and Lucy were the two tour members who had paid tourist-class rates for the sea portion of the tour.

"Keep the window closed," Leonard Deek advised her, to everyone's amazement.

Maybeth gave him a withering look. "Do you think the people who made this ship were crazy? There's no window down there. I'd have to break open that porthole, and this ship might sink. Tourist class is below water level."

The laugher that followed lightened Mason's mood a little, and he glanced at Jeannetta.

"What about you? You scared of water, too?"

Several in the group twittered softly. He leaned over and whispered in Jeannetta's ear.

"What?" she asked.

"I said Leonard Deek must sit on his brains. Of course, he isn't the first bottom-heavy professor I've met. My freshman English prof fit that description, but her ancestors were probably Hottentots." Her hearty giggle was what he'd hoped his exaggeration would accomplish, and he managed to eat the remainder of what would ordinarily have been a wonderful meal, though his anxiety about Jeannetta had ruined any chance of his enjoying it. He looked around the table.

"I apologize for whispering, but I couldn't resist needling Jeannetta."

Geoffrey eyed him carefully, and he'd have given a few Thailand bahts to read the man's mind. For an uneducated person, he possessed a store of knowledge and wisdom. He hoped they would remain friends. He leaned toward Jeannetta.

"Walk with me a little?"

She smiled, but it bore no relation to the hearty laughter and happy grins that he'd grown to love. He held her hand as they left the dining room and, when they passed a florist, he tugged at her hand.

"I want to go in here."

She looked at him inquiringly, but didn't ask his motive. He hoped the starch hadn't gone out of her. If it had, he reflected, though he'd rather the thought hadn't arisen, it would mean that she'd known all along that she had a problem and what it was. If so, her condition could be more serious than he thought. He bought a red-tipped yellow rose and handed it to her, testing her. She reached for it, but failed to touch it. He pretended not to notice, but he no longer doubted that she had a problem with her peripheral vision.

"Would you like to see the floor show?" he asked her.

"Should be fun. Why not? I don't care to go to the casino, and I'm not a good bridge player."

He splayed his fingers at her waist and guided her back to their table. The floor show held little interest for him, but it would give him an opportunity to observe her closely without her knowing it. He helped himself to a snifter of fine VSOP cognac when the waiter offered it, and watched anxiously as she eyed it longingly, shook her head and settled for a cran-berry rickey.

Jeannetta tried to concentrate on the show and to ignore Mason's intense scrutiny. Her furtive glances didn't tell her whether his gazes were of admiration or curiosity. Maybe she'd fooled him but, if she had, he couldn't be much of a specialist; she'd shown every symptom in his presence ex-cept fainting, and she'd nearly done that twice. She wanted to direct some inquiries toward his profession, to prompt the right questions from him so she could give him the answer that she must. She'd had the chance twice, but the timing had been wrong. If she asked him about himself, he'd take that opportunity to begin delving into her life, and he'd tell her nothing about Mason Fenwick.

Billowing smoke and the reverberation of ancient brass striking brass gongs got her attention, and she watched a young belly dancer swish onto the stage and begin her mo-notonous, twirling undulations. Most of the crowd, particu-larly the men, found it entertaining for the first five minutes, but when minutes became half an hour, she noted with satis-faction that the Western men became bored. The Asian men sat in rapt attention.

"Are you enjoying this?" Mason asked her.

"Not as much as the different reactions, especially those of the men." She nodded toward an Asian at the next table. "He's really having a bang out of this. I don't get it."

Mason's smile, tender and intimate, warmed her heart. "He's not going home to a woman like you. If he were, he'd be as bored as I am."

The words had barely left his tongue when the belly dancer plopped into his lap. His gawk brought a laugh from Jeannetta, and she marveled that he sat without touching the woman, without showing a smile or a grimace or indicating in any other way his reaction to her impertinence. The dancer managed to move, after her cool reception, but Jeannetta noticed her smile became real when she saw the tip he gave her.

An orchestra reminiscent of 1940s bands began to play, and couples flocked to the dance floor. She felt cherished when he held her hand and adored her with his mesmerizing black eyes, and she didn't know whether to feel hurt when he didn't ask her to dance.

"Mason, I hope you don't mind if I take this lady for a spin around the floor," Geoffrey said, though he didn't wait for a reply before extending his hand to Jeannetta.

Mason grinned, shrugged elaborately and replied, "A man doesn't have the right to give another permission to put his arms around a woman and dance with her, not even if that woman is his wife."

Geoffrey, who by then held her hand, retorted, "Sorry, I must've thought I was talking to a man of my own age. I forgot chivalry's expiring with my generation."

Mason glared at him, but whatever he'd planned to say would probably have been an anticlimax, Jeannetta decided, when Lucy Abernathy walked over to her and bowed.

"Jeannetta," the woman said in a soft voice, "do you mind if I have this dance with Mr. Fenwick?"

She'd never danced with Mason, but that didn't matter. Lucy had provided the brightest spot of the evening, and she intended to enjoy it.

"Of course I don't mind, Miss Abernathy, but I wouldn't

get into those fast dances with him if I were you. You'd have to watch your toes, and he wears a size eleven." The sounds of Mason clearing his throat and of Geoffrey's down-home laugh emboldened her, and she risked a glance at Mason. He'd taken Lucy's hand, but she could all but feel the hot sparks that blazed in his eyes. She nudged Geoffrey onto the dance floor; she hadn't seen Mason lose his temper, but she suspected he soon would.

"Now, Miss Jeannetta, something tells me you went a mite too far with your teasing. 'Course I aim to speak to Lucy about her manners, too."

"You dance a mean fox-trot," she complimented, and added, "Miss Abernathy showed the two of you the ridiculousness of the whole business. She carved a permanent place in my heart when she did that."

"It's no use trying to understand women," he huffed. "They want you to love 'em and cherish 'em, but if you try to protect 'em, they throw a fit. Don't y'all know it's one and the same to a man?" The fox-trot ended, but the band started a rhumba, and Geoffrey hardly missed a beat before he swung into it.

"You're a wonderful dancer," she told him.

"Thanks. My Nettie loved to dance, and she taught me. That's what we did on Saturday nights. This is the first chance I've had to dance since she left me. Now, she was some dancer, but you're a fine dance partner yourself." They walked back to the table, and Mason stood as they approached. He nodded to Geoffrey, and Jeannetta felt herself flush warmly at his intimate look.

"I expected to get drenched from these sprinklers," he told her, gesturing to the red cylinders lodged high above in the ceiling. "You and Geoffrey put on quite a show out there with that rhumba. I'll have to stop by some of those nightclubs next time I'm in Augusta." He glanced upward again.

"Out where I lived, we didn't go to clubs," Geoffrey corrected. "We went to dance halls."

"And I don't remember having set a boat or any other place afire," Jeannetta told them, "although I may have steamed up a few rooms." They sat down, and she shifted her gaze from Mason's rapt stare to his long, thin fingers, dark brown against the starched white linen cloth on which he strummed rhythmically. He leaned back in his chair and looked at Lucy Abernathy.

"I thought we were talking about dancing, didn't you?" Mason asked Lucy.

Jeannetta couldn't help marveling at the changes in the woman in one month. Maybe love wrought miracles.

"They're both of them showing off," she heard Lucy say, and it occurred to Jeannetta that she wouldn't have had the courage to utter such a remark as recently as a month earlier.

"Not me. I don't show off. I do what comes naturally," Jeannetta said as she dared him with her eyes to take it any further.

"We're still talking about dancing, I presume," Mason said, mainly to Jeannetta. A slow smile played around his lips. "What comes naturally is what I do best," he parroted her.

"Stick to claims that can be verified," she challenged, and her pulse accelerated as she watched his eye color change in seconds from black to that brownish-green that made saliva pool in her mouth. He stuck his hands in his pants pockets, rocked back in his chair and fixed her with his hot gaze, desire vibrating from him like atomic waves. She glanced nervously toward their two companions, a part of her wanting to be rescued, and the other part wanting to test him. Lucy and Geoffrey had left. Embarrassment suffused her when she thought of what they might have witnessed. She made herself look at Mason, and saw that the heat hadn't diminished—that, if anything, it had intensified.

"Do you want to eat those words now? Or later?" he asked,

accepting the dare. With so many people around, what did she have to fear? She leaned back, as he did, and refused to hide the effect that his drugging masculinity had on her. If he could singe her with part of a table between them and a room full of people all around them, how soon would he have her rocketing to heaven once he got her clothes off? What a man! He brought his chair upright and leaned forward, his chiseled brown face harsh and unsmiling.

"Well?"

She decided to bluff. "Can't say offhand. I'll have to think about it. I don't remember having tasted my words."

"Jeannetta. You're playing with fire. You're... What the devil?"

The slight sensation passed, and she managed a smile. "I got a headache all of a sudden. I'm not trying to get out of anything. I really did." She tried to avoid pressing her hand to her forehead. Immediately, he came to her.

"Come on. I'll walk with you to your room." He draped an arm around her, and his fingers lovingly cradled her to his side.

"Where're we going?" she asked, when he walked them past the staircase.

"We'll take the elevator." She had intended to discourage intimacy when they reached her room, but he didn't offer it. Instead, he opened her door, brushed her forehead with his lips and admonished her. "Call me, if you need me. Don't hesitate. You understand?" She wondered at the expression of deep concern that marred his handsome face.

"I will. I promise." She let her hand dust his cheek, forced a smile and closed the door.

She tossed her evening bag on the bed, kicked off the red satin shoes and sat down. Geoffrey had nearly worn her out with his fast, sexy rhumba; she'd have to avoid spinning around like that, but it had been such fun. Thoughts of the heat in Mason's eyes when she'd returned to their table sent her blood racing, and she hugged herself. After taking a couple of aspirin, she unzipped her dress and stepped out of it.

*His fingers feathered down her arms, eased over her back, unsnapped her bra and freed her round, tight breasts for his pleasure. She threw back her head as his lips possessed first one and then the other until her knees buckled, and she cried out, "Oh, Mason. I need you so. If only you knew!"*

She looked around, almost expecting to see him there beside her. The experience, the pleasure had seemed so real. She sat on the edge of the bed and let the steady sloshing of the waves calm her. Her headache eased, and she walked to her window and looked down at the deck. The moon had drifted from behind the clouds, and she could see a woman, her chiffon dress billowing in the southern wind, reach up to the man beside her as he gathered her in his arms and kissed her.

A dull ache of longing coiled in her breast when the man lifted the woman and carried her until she could see them no longer. She walked back to the bed and looked at her tape recorder. Suddenly, she kicked her shoes across the room and slammed her fist against the mattress. Why her? Why, now that she knew at last what it was to love a man, to want him and to yearn for his children beneath her breast…why this? Why couldn't she be open with him, share her dreams and fears with him? Why couldn't she reveal herself and level with this strong, caring man? The telephone interrupted her reverie.

"Hello?"

"Hi. You alright now?" His low, husky voice wrapped around her, settling her.

"I'm fine. I looked out a minute ago. It's so beautiful out there—nothing but moonlight, sky and waves as far as I could see, and not a man-made thing in sight. It's unbelievable."

His silence unnerved her.

"I take it your headache's gone."

"No, but it eased. Where are you?" Did he want to come to her? Still raw and vulnerable after that spooky experience a few minutes earlier with what she'd only imagined, she didn't know how she'd feel about that.

"In my room. I wanted to know how you were before I turned in. Would you care to join me tomorrow morning around six-thirty to see the sunrise? A view from this boat in this part of the world can't be matched. How about it?"

"Six-thirty?" She knew he could hear her groan. "Okay."

His laugh, warm, deep, and rich, floated to her through the wires, thrilling her. "Who'd have thought you were mush-brained in the mornings? Six o'clock air is good for you. I'll call you at five-fifteen and knock on your door at five minutes to six."

"You're a cruel, heartless man. You'll do that, and I'll have no way to get even."

"Sure you have. Tomorrow evening, you'll tell me good-night and close your door."

"What?"

"That's exactly what you'll do," he said dryly, "instead of kissing me good-night, reaching over and turning out the light. Hmm?"

"I was way ahead of you, if you remember an evening somewhere between Vienna and Istanbul, Mr. Fenwick. Don't tell me you've changed your tour rules," she baited.

"You and I are the only tour members on this corridor."

"What does that have to do with your rules? I accommodated myself to them, because I figured a man of lofty principles such as you wouldn't demand more of his charges than of himself. And I'm right, aren't I?" She didn't want to vex him, but she didn't want him in her room. If he crossed that threshold tonight, she wouldn't let him out of her sight until she'd drained him of every bit of energy. And she'd have the rest of her life to pay for it.

"I see. So what kind of relationship do you think we should have? Before you answer, keep in mind everything that's happened between us since we met, and include what you wanted to happen that didn't."

*Keep it light,* she told herself, wishing she could see the wickedness in his wonderful obsidian eyes.

"Let's see," she stalled. "How about a nice warm friendship?"

"That's it?"

"Yes. Good friends. That's what I want for us."

"Hmm. I'll bet. See you in the morning. Sleep well."

She remembered that she hadn't spoken with her sister in several days, and telephoned her. It amazed her that, in seconds, she could speak with someone half a world away and hear that person as clearly as though she were in the next room.

"Rollins Hideaway. Laura speaking."

"Hi, sis. How's everything there?"

"Jeanny. Bless you, honey. I've been worried about you, since you didn't call. Where are you now?" Jeannetta brought her up to date.

"What about him? Have you mentioned it to him yet? What did he say?"

She expected the questions, and she had no choice but to tell Laura the truth.

"I'm having a hard time with this, Laura, because I've fallen in love with him, and I don't know how to bring it up without his thinking I've been leading him on just to obligate him." She was glad of the distance between them. When Laura got comfortable on her soapbox, she could preach for hours, nonstop.

"You're not serious. Do you know what you're risking?

You give me his name and phone number. I can ask him. You watch what you do off there in the middle of nowhere, and for heaven's sake keep that man out of your room. You girls nowadays don't have a crumb of sense. If it was me, I'd have asked him before that plane left JFK."

"If you're worried about my getting pregnant, forget it," Jeannetta told her. "One of my symptoms is amenorrhea—"

"What's that?"

"No monthly period."

"Well, there're other reasons for you to stay away from him. I sometimes wonder if there's a thirty-year-old single woman in this country who's still a virgin."

Jeannetta laughed. "I sure hope not."

"Jeannetta Rollins, shame on you. It's a pity what this world's come to."

"I'll call you in a couple of days. Go out and have some fun."

"You grab that man and tell him your problem, you hear? Take care of yourself, now."

Jeannetta mused over their conversation. In some respects, her sister took conservatism to the extreme. How could a normal woman be content to live a whole life and die without having loved a man? It occurred to her that her sister might be smarter than she. Laura wouldn't have gotten into the mess she'd made with Mason.

The sloshing of the waves had a bluesy rhythm, and she hummed along. Her good mood partly restored, she took out her recorder and began describing the evening's events. Recalling Mason's phone call and their conversation made her choke up, but she pushed back the tears. She tossed the recorder into a chair, slapped her fist into her right palm and got up. Just standing felt good. She'd do something; she *had* to. She'd never been one to passively accept whatever came her way, and she wouldn't do it now. She grimaced as she passed the mirror. With her life depending on Mason's help, why had she chosen this occasion to behave as though she was merely doing research for one of her novels? "This is your life, girl," she repeated to herself, "and you'd better shape up." She'd tell him, and she'd do it before the ship docked in Thailand.

She stopped pacing the floor, crawled into bed, and turned out the light. Darkness flooded the room, and the vision of him all over her, around her, caressing her, making passionate love to her assaulted her senses. She sat up. When she told him everything, he wouldn't believe that she loved him, and even if she got her life back, she'd lose her heart's desire.

For the nth time, Mason looked at his watch and wrestled with sleep, longing for daylight. Disgusted, he stripped the sheet from his body, walked over to the window, and gazed out at the clouds that raced over the full moon. He found no comfort in it. If he had the answer to one question, he'd know the nature of Jeannetta's problem. But if he asked her anything so intimate, he'd have to give a reason and, unless he told her that his concern was professional, she'd have every right to consider him audacious. But if he told her that, he'd have to tell her everything, and he wasn't prepared to do it. That life was behind him, and he intended to leave it there.

He showered, dressed in white slacks and a white T-shirt, slipped on white sneakers and went down to the ship's galley, where he got two large containers of coffee and some doughnuts. Then he bought a red rose from the florist and returned to his room. He stashed the coffee in a thermal bag and phoned Jeannetta.

"Who's this?"

"Mason. We've got a date in half an hour, remember?"

"You're making this up. What time is it?"

"Five-sixteen."

"In the afternoon?"

He laughed. One of these days he was going to roll her over on her back and love her until she was fully awake.

"You promised to see the sunrise with me, so get up, unless you want everybody on this ship to hear me banging on your door."

"You wouldn't."

"You don't have any proof of that, so you'd better play it safe and get up. Want me to get a passkey and join you?"

"Alright. Alright. I'm getting up. You're a hard man, Fenwick."

He wondered at her wistful manner when she opened the door, until she asked him, "Would the captain really have given you the key to my room?"

"Not in a million years, but I figured you were too sleepy to question it. Come on, let's get a good spot on deck." He let his gaze roam quickly over her and breathed deeply when he didn't detect outward signs of illness. She had her normal color, clear eyes, and steady gait.

"How're you feeling?"

"I'm fine. A couple of aspirin took care of my headache."

He relaxed. Maybe he'd been concerned without cause. "In that case, I could have kissed you good morning." He shoved two chairs close together, and they sat facing the sea. He removed the lids from the containers of coffee and gave her one, and she closed her eyes, sniffed the familiar aroma, and smiled her delight. He didn't remember deriving so much joy from giving a woman a simple pleasure. He reached into the thermal bag, took out the rose and handed it to her. She'd never know how he prayed that she wouldn't drop it.

"Lean over here," she commanded. "This level of sweetness deserves a hug."

He accepted her quick caress, and held his tongue when he wanted to tell her that he'd like to have more, that he needed a steady diet of her. Instead, he said, "I was hoping for something more substantial." But he didn't look at her, because he knew she'd see in his eyes what his lips had wanted to say. He passed her one of the doughnuts.

"Here. Try this." For two cents, he'd take her in his arms and...

"Oh, Mason, look!" He let his gaze follow her line of vision. Red, gray, pink, and purple images greeted him from above, like multi-hued mountains resting amid the clouds. Red-and-blue shadows hovered over the sea, painting the shallow waves, and the sun began its slow, upward climb.

"It's breathtaking," she exclaimed. He stopped looking at the awesome display and turned to watch her, stunned by the longing that he'd heard in her voice. Something wasn't right. Half an hour later, with the spectacle over and nature busy clouding up the sky, he walked her back to her room.

"I wouldn't have missed that sight for anything, but if you hadn't dragged me out, I'd never have seen it. I can't thank you enough."

"The pleasure was mine. Coming down for breakfast?"

She shook her head. "I'd better work on my book."

He nodded.

"Lunch, then. I have to check on Lydia, and keep the rest of the gang happy. If you need me, here's my beeper number." He wrote it on the back of his business card, brushed her cheek with his lips and left her at her door, certain that she'd get her recorder the minute she walked in that room.

Seven-thirty. That made it about eight o'clock in the evening back home. He dialed Skip's number.

"I'm glad to see you're home," he said, when he heard the boy's voice. The possibility of losing the child to the streets was never far from his thoughts, because the boy's surroundings offered every opportunity for criminal behavior.

"Hi, Mason. 'Course I'm here. I do like you said. Besides,

Uncle Steve's already ringing me when I get in from school. Man, he don't give me breathing room."

Mason didn't bother to hide his amusement.

"*Uncle* Steve?"

"Yeah. He said he's old enough to be my father, and he wants some respect. It was that, or call him mister." Mason laughed.

"What's wrong with calling him mister?"

"No, man. It's real second-grade stuff. I'm almost thirteen. You know that."

"Hmmm." He fingered the keys in his right pants pocket. He'd have to put some bricks under Skip while he could still make a difference. "How's Mabel?"

"Doing pretty good. She's sitting up watching television, and she can get to the bathroom. I don't know what I'd do, Mason, if she couldn't bathe herself. Uncle Steve brought me a big pan of his lasagna, a gang of baked sweet potatoes, half of a ham and a pot of collards for the next three or four days. I didn't tell you he put a freezer chest in here, did I? He's real cool. Wait a minute, and I'll let you speak to Aunt Mabel."

"How are you, Mabel?" He'd barely heard her weak hello.

"I'm better, and I feel pretty good. I don't know how to thank you and…" He cut her off.

"Don't thank us, Mabel. Skip adopted us, and we look after our family. Simple as that. If you have any problems before I get back, tell Skip to call Steve. How's the boy doing?"

"Wonderful. I couldn't ask for more of him, and I have you to thank for that, too."

"Put him on. How many classes are you taking this summer, Skip?"

"Three. Geography, something called Chaucer, and English. You know anything about a guy named Booker T. Washington? I have to read his biography."

"Of course I know about him." He thought for a minute.

"Skip, why are you in summer school? Your grades are out-
standing."

"I didn't want to hang out, so I figured if I was in school,
the guys around here wouldn't expect me to."

"Good thinking. When I get back, we'll see some Broadway shows, maybe even go up to Stratford to the Shakespeare
Theater."

"Wow! Broadway? Cool! But Shakespeare, man. I think
I'd rather take cod liver oil."

Mason laughed. "Cod liver oil's good for you. I'll call you
in a few days."

"Say, don't hang up. You didn't tell me where you are right
now."

"I'm on a boat in the South China Sea headed for Thailand.
That's in Southeast Asia. Okay?"

"Yeah. Gee whiz. I think I'll be a travel manager."


Jeannetta skipped breakfast and, on an impulse, ordered
lunch in her room. The handsome Thai waiter, who seemed
little more than a boy, served her lemon-grass soup, shrimp
salad, and assorted tropical fruits, bowed, and asked, "Madam,
why you not on deck? All Americans want suntan. Everybody
out but you. I bring ship doctor if you sick."

She smiled her thanks and showed him the door. No use
explaining if his eyes didn't tell him that she didn't need a
suntan. She answered the phone. At least she wouldn't have to
explain to any of her tour-mates why she hadn't oiled her body
and stretched out practically nude to get a suntan. Most of
them wouldn't be as dark as she if they sunbathed for a month.

"You okay?" She wondered if he could hear his voice. Low,
husky, and sexy. Her temperature climbed up several degrees
every time she heard it.

"I'm fine. Please go back to your sunbath."

"My what? Sunbath? You sure you're alright? I'm a moon

person. I got enough sun one day recently in Istanbul to last a lifetime, while I waited for a missing female. What gave you that idea?"

She told him.

"Ignorance has its advantages," he said, when he could stop laughing. Her insides turned somersaults at the sound of his melodious merriment. Thank God, he didn't know how he got to her.

"Sure does," she managed to say. "Isn't it great that people in these countries look at you and don't think only of race?"

"Yeah. That's why I've been toying with the notion of bringing a young friend along next year. He'll be thirteen, a good age at which to learn this. Join me for happy hour?"

"Thanks, but I...I'd rather not. May run into you later."

"I don't like what I'm hearing. You began this tour spirited, eager to do and see everything, but, during the last couple of days, you've begun to fold up. I'm telling you again, that if you need me, I'm here for you. Meet me down in the green lounge or, if you don't feel up to dressing, throw on something and I'll go there. You're not alone. If you want to go home, my associate can fly to Bangkok and complete the tour, and I'll personally take you back to Pilgrim. Jeannetta, let me help you."

"You don't know what you're saying. If I thought you meant it... If I dared believe you..."

"Why shouldn't you believe me? And why can't you trust me?"

"Because I know you don't know what you're promising."

"Why do you insist in being mysterious? I've thought since we met that you were misrepresenting yourself." His voice had lost its gentleness. He spoke more rapidly, and his tone carried a harsh edge. She didn't feel the empathy he'd sent to her through the wires. She wanted him to hang up.

"Mason, I've been writing almost nonstop since you left me

this morning, and I'm tired. For your information, I ordered lunch here in my stateroom. I have your beeper number and your room number. I'll be in touch."

But he persisted. "Why are you taking this tour? If you refuse to tell me, I may ask you to leave it."

"I've been as honest with you as you've been with me, so get off your high horse. Seconds earlier, you assured me that you're here for me, that I should trust you. Now, you're threatening to dump me in a strange country that doesn't even use the Roman alphabet, where I won't be able to read a word."

"My God, Jeannetta, you know I wouldn't. I only wanted to build a fire under you. I…I care about you, and I don't know who you are."

She suspected that he heard her deep sigh, for he added, "Alright, I'll stop pressuring you. I'll be in my room around six, if you'd like to have a drink then. Get some rest." He hung up, and she stretched out on the bed.

He didn't know who she was, but *she knew who he was,* and therein lay their problem. His threat had clarified for her both his dilemma and the measure of his frustration. She could see that he didn't tolerate well any disturbance of his scheme of things, of the way in which he'd ordered his life. She'd wanted to blurt it all out, but she wouldn't. She didn't doubt his strength; only a man capable of toughening himself to the dark potential of the unknown could walk away from success, wealth, and glamour as he had. But if she leaned on him, that brand-new castle he'd built could collapse all around him. If you loved a man, would you wreck his life? She didn't phone him.

A grand ball had been scheduled for their last evening onboard ship. Jeannetta dressed in a peach-colored chiffon evening dress, swept her hair up and secured it with an ivory comb, slipped into black satin slippers, picked up her black beaded bag, and paused before the mirror. A lot of décolletage, she thought, but since she wore no makeup, the effect ought to be prim enough. She grinned. Nothing prim about half of a size thirty-six C in full view. She found Lucy and Geoffrey leaning against the rail of the ship's leeward moonlit deck.

"Mr. Fenwick's in the lounge," the radiant woman informed Jeannetta.

"I expect they'll find each other when they get ready," Geoffrey said. "Trouble is they can't seem to focus on what counts."

Jeannetta laid her head to one side and looked at Geoffrey Ames. The casual observer would see a simple man and, in a sense, that's what he was. But he had depth and character and, at times, he could be intriguing. Like now.

"What do you mean, Geoffrey?" Jeannetta asked him. He rubbed his chin and looked skyward.

"It ain't something you can teach people. You and Mason got everything you need to be happy together, except what'll keep you that way. Even if I tell you, you won't understand. You'll have to experience it. If it comes, it comes; if it don't, it don't."

Jeannetta glanced toward the entrance to the lounge. Mason stood in the doorway, his gaze fixed on her. Light smoldered in his greenish-brown eyes, betraying his desire, and the hungered look of a starving man replaced his poker face. Even the tilt of his shoulders emphasized his vulnerability to her. Her left hand sprung toward him involuntarily, and she had to force herself to stand there and not run to him. He must have realized from her reaction that he had exposed more than he'd wanted, because he hooded his eyes, straightened up, and strolled toward them almost nonchalantly.

When he reached them, he smiled and nodded to her companions and stood silent, staring down at her. Uncertain or displeased: she couldn't figure out which. She hadn't called him as he'd asked, and she'd avoided the Green Lounge where he'd suggested they meet. She didn't want to encourage him more, because if he touched her they'd be lovers, and she had no idea what course she would eventually take. Ask him to repair her life and wreck his own? Risk his finding her deceitful and leaving her with a broken heart? Maybe… Could she have him for a little while? She lowered her gaze.

"You're a knockout."

She jerked her head up.

"You are. So lovely. Beautiful. And it's all you." His gaze roamed over her, as though cataloguing her virtues, until she shivered in awareness. "I waited for you."

"I know. But we're getting too involved."

"You say that from time to time, Jeannetta, and then you forget about it. I thought the same, but now, I'm not so sure. Have dinner with me."

She turned. "Geoffrey, do you and… Where'd they go?"

"At least I had your attention. They walked off as soon as I greeted them." He looked out toward the sea. "Geoffrey's so certain that he and Lucy are right for each other. Wish I knew his formula for that."

She smiled. "Don't waste your time asking him. He'll tell you either you have it or you don't." The flashing lights announced the dinner hour, and he took her hand.

"Nothing's going to happen unless we both want it, Jeannetta, so let's relax and enjoy each other. You look wonderful, but how do you feel? Headache?"

"It didn't come back."


They sat at the captain's table along with Geoffrey, Lucy, and several people whom they didn't know. Mason passed the lobster Marnier through his teeth, tasted the real turtle bisque, the duck l'orange, saddle of veal, buttered parsley potatoes, steamed mélange of baby vegetables, and barely took his glance from her. He couldn't have remembered the selection of French cheeses, or the mixed-greens salad that followed, if he'd stood to lose a million. And he couldn't pretend an interest in the crème Courvoisier that the chef personally brought to the table. He finally had to admit to himself that the vision in peach who daintily tasted everything put before her was the woman he needed in his life. He had tired of worrying about the mystery that he sensed around her; he loved her, and he'd deal with whatever he faced because of it.

Soft. Elegant. Unassuming. How could she grow more beautiful right before his eyes? He hooded them and let himself enjoy watching her. Still so many unanswered questions, he thought, strumming his fingers on his knee. The dinner ended, and the orchestra members took their seats on the bandstand. He could barely contain himself when he heard the exchange between Lucy and Geoffrey.

"This was truly wonderful," the woman said to Geoffrey, who had donned his Sunday best for the occasion.

"Well, you could say that, and I'm glad you enjoyed it," Geoffrey replied. "'Course, now, if I'm gonna take in this much cholesterol, I'd as soon have it in Southern fried chicken, candied yams, and some good old coconut cake."

A deep, throaty chuckle floated up from Mason's throat. He winked at his new friend, got up, and held out his hand to Jeannetta.

"Dance with me?" A saxophone wailed a love song from the 1930s, and he whispered the words, synchronizing them with the tune: "If I didn't care…more than words can say…" She missed a step, and he pulled her closer.

"Loosen up," he taunted, "and let it hang out the way you did in Paris with the Gypsies. There's no use pretending anything anymore. It's you and me, baby. Forget about the past, all your reasons for not getting involved, our doubts—they don't matter. It's where we go from here that counts."

"Mason, let's…let's sit down. You…don't know what you're saying."

"I hope I've heard that line for the last time."

The orchestra leader announced a request, and a seductive saxophone swung into "Body and Soul."

"That's how I need you," he whispered, "just like that song says." He didn't intend to give her breathing space until she let him know what she felt for him—words or actions, he didn't care which—but he had to know something. A guitar whipped into a duet with the sax, and he wrapped her to him and brought her head to the curve of his shoulder.

"You'll regret this. We both will," she told him with such certainty that, for a second, he sensed defeat. Only briefly, however, because her supple body snaked around him, molded itself to him. Her knee moved with his knee, her hips swung when his did, and her pelvis tilted forward when his dipped to receive her. They danced as one person, and his blood ran hot and fast.

Her breathing accelerated and, with a deep sigh, she gave in to him and did as he'd asked. Her arms tightened around his neck, her breasts warmed his chest, and she seemed to let her body have its way. He tried to ignore the sweat that beaded on his forehead, the thundering of his heart, and the sensuous movement of her hips as she followed his steps. He swung her out in a two-step, intent upon getting some space between them, but the sultry expression in her eyes and the movement of her belly as she glided back to him accelerated his pulse, and awareness slammed into him. He thought he'd explode.

She slid her fingers around his neck and whispered, "You're warm and…and everything. Everything." He stopped dancing. Did she want him to make love with her? Hang his rules. Did she? She had closed her eyes and her lips brushed his jaw.

He wanted to pick her up, run with her to his room, and lose himself in her.

"Let's go, sweetheart. Let's get out of here."

She nodded, although her luminous smile seemed shaky. He splayed his fingers across the small of her back and led her back to their table. She grasped his hand, smiled, then slumped against him in a dead faint.

## Chapter 6

Mason paced the narrow corridor outside the ship's infirmary. A nurse smiled at him, pausing briefly for what he didn't doubt was more feminine than medical concern. On a different occasion, she might have inspired a second glance, but his thoughts were on the woman in that room. He hadn't been allowed inside, because his answer, when the doctor had asked his relationship to Jeannetta, had been "friend." The doctor had shrugged and said, "Wait out there." He'd wanted to say, *but I'm a doctor, and I have as much right as you to be in there.* He'd said nothing and had watched the door close in his face. He'd given that up voluntarily almost three years ago, and he hadn't regretted it. Oh, there had been little twinges once in a while, when he read of a new medicine, ground-breaking test, or special equipment. He'd think how wonderful, how exciting or safer his work would be because of it, only to remember that he headed Fenwick Travel Agency and had no connection with medicine. Then he'd take consolation in getting a full night's undisturbed sleep on a regular basis, not having to deal with anxiety and stress about his patients every waking minute, and in not being the target of every long-lashed socialite whom he encountered. At one point he had fantasized about buying all present and future rights to the manufacture of false eyelashes and sending them to the moon with the next team of astronauts headed that way.

The nurse emerged, still smiling. "Can you tell me what the situation is with Miss Rollins?" he asked her.

"Nothing serious. The doctor will be out in a few minutes." At that, Mason stuck his hands in his pants pockets, propped himself against the wall, and tried to relax. If he'd been away from medicine thirty years instead of two years and nine months, he wouldn't believe that—unless Jeannetta was a closet drinker, and he didn't believe that either. He fingered the old keys and, in his frustration, knew an unfamiliar urge to slam them against the wall. So many years of longing. An hour ago, what he'd wanted for so long had seemed within his reach.

"Well, I see we're still here."

Mason bristled at the doctor's patronizing manner. "She'll be fine," the doctor said. "This rough sea doesn't agree with a lot of people, and she's just seasick. I've given her some Dramamine. That ought to take care of it."

Mason stared at the man, wondering what Jeannetta could have said or done to mislead him.

"Thanks, Doctor." He had to work hard at containing himself, because he wouldn't gain a thing by questioning the man.

"You're still here? I thought you'd gone."

He offered the best smile he could muster.

"You gotta be kidding," he said. "I aim to see you safely in…well, I don't suppose I dare to tuck you in, although that's what I had in mind an hour ago, but I want to walk you to your room." He took her cool fingers in his hand and clutched them to his chest. "I told you that I'm here for you, and I want you to believe it." He refused to comment on her skeptical look. He had to decide whether to send her back to New York and, if so, what kind of advice he ought to give her.

Jeannetta awakened early after sleeping fitfully. She couldn't help regretting that the last night onboard ship hadn't been what it could have, and certainly would have, if she'd been more fortunate. She pushed the thought of the consequences out of her mind, though she conceded that Providence had no doubt rescued her from herself. More than once during the night, she had wondered whether it was Mason or her ailment that had made her knees buckle and caused her to faint. She swung her feet to the floor, showered and dressed hurriedly. She knew where to find him; he wouldn't miss the last opportunity to see that spectacular sunrise.

As she'd expected, he was leaning against the rail watching the awesome sight of the sun climbing out of the sea, its halo of colors straddling the sky.

"I knew I'd find you here." She joined him at the rail to watch the sight.

"And I hoped you'd come. This is so extraordinary. I wanted to share it with you." He took her hand in his, and she shifted her gaze from the spectacle before them to glance at the strong man at her side. He stared deeply into her eyes and gently squeezed her fingers, and she gloried in the shared moment. Still holding her hand, he let his gaze drift back to the brilliant hues surrounding the rising sun.

She continued to look at him. "Not even the sunrise can compare to you," she whispered beneath her breath.

"Let's walk," he urged, when the sun had fully emerged.

She didn't miss the envious glances that women sent her way, nor the covetous manner in which they eyed Mason.

And she couldn't help thinking that her time with him would soon be over and that, if she didn't watch out, she'd blow this one opportunity to gain his help. She noticed the tall, beautiful, and expensively dressed blonde long before the woman reached them. To her surprise, the woman stopped before them and her heavily lashed eyes widened in astonishment.

"Why, Dr. Fenwick," she gushed. "I'm so delighted to see you. I had no idea you were onboard." Before Mason could respond, she turned to her companion. "Brad, darling, this is *the* Dr. Mason Fenwick that I've told you so much about. I owe my life to this brilliant man. But for him, I'd be blind, maybe even dead. He's a marvelous surgeon. Believe me, I always want to know where this man is. You're still on East Seventy-second Street?"

Jeannetta stared at him when he smiled diffidently, and she couldn't help gritting her teeth.

"No. That's all behind me now. I'm happy to see that you're well, with no aftereffects."

Bile formed on Jeannetta's tongue, and she snatched her hand from his as fury roared through her.

"Jeannetta!"

She glared at him, her eyes brimming with tears. *All behind him.* Never mind who needed him; he could stand there and calmly imply that it didn't matter. She bolted for the stairs and ran to her stateroom.

If he didn't catch her before she got in that room and locked that door, he wouldn't have a chance. He didn't expect her to understand; his own brother didn't comprehend or accept his decision to leave his profession behind, though Steve had walked the floor with him while he'd agonized over it. She spun around and raced up the steep, winding stairs and down the heavily carpeted corridor. His hand shot out above her head as she pulled the key from the door and pushed at it. She leaned into the door, but he didn't allow it to budge.

"May I come in? I have to talk with you."

"There's nothing for you to say at this point. *It's all behind you,* you said. The devil with the people who need you. You could stand there and calmly consign human beings to a life of hell and not give a fig. Talent, education, and opportunity, and all of it wasted." She wasn't without guilt, but she didn't let her mind dwell on that; black terror had swept through her when she'd heard from his own lips that he'd finished with medicine. If he thought she trembled from anger, she didn't care, but she'd never been so scared in her life. He pushed the door open, walked in with her and closed it.

"You've condemned me, and you'd hang me without a hearing. All that's gone between us means nothing to you? Do you know what it's like to play God day after day and know you're doing it, to risk lives for your own glory, to do routinely what other surgeons regard as perilous? Do you? And then one day your arrogance almost kills a woman. You make a mistake that puts her in a coma, and if you had moved that knife one iota of a centimeter further, she'd be dead. You don't know what terror is until you have a narrow escape like that. When that doctor told Steve and me that he couldn't save our parents after their accident, I vowed to be a surgeon and to be the best. I gave up my childhood, went without friends, and sacrificed my dreams for a family of my own, because I wanted to be a doctor more than anything. And I walked away from nothing." She'd turned her back, and as he walked around to look at her, he recalled something that had hung on the edge of his mind.

"You didn't seem surprised to learn that I'm a doctor. Have you known all along?" He wondered whether her lips trembled from anger or from a pain around her heart that equaled what he felt. He had to lean forward to hear her whispered words.

"How could you stand there while that doctor misdiagnosed my ailment? I heard what he told you."

His face must have reflected the icy chill that plowed through him when he recoiled from her words, because her eyes widened. He stepped back from her.

"So you know what's wrong, and you've known from the start. That's why you're here, isn't it?" His voice had dropped several decibels, and he knew his temper would rise. "You went to all this trouble to get me back into the harness, back into that operating room. What about your torrid responses to me every time I put my hands on you? And your kisses that promised me the heavens? What else had you planned to offer as part of your little scheme?" He ignored her loud gasp. "Well, I got a taste for you, Jeannetta, and I want you, but your price is too high."

"Would you please leave? Now. I… You've said enough."

Enough? He'd said too much, but the last time he'd hurt like this, he'd been seven years old. He gazed down at her and at his dream of a woman to cherish, one who'd give him the family he'd wanted for so long. His anger dissipated, and his hand went toward his right pants pocket, but he forced himself not to reach for those keys. Home. He could forget about that. He opened the door, walked out, and didn't look back.

She wanted to hate him, but how could she when she loved him so? She could hardly blame him for reacting as he had. He was right that she'd schemed to get him to help her, but her reaction to him hadn't been part of it. She tried to see it all from his vantage point. She hadn't been in his shoes in that operating room, and maybe she would have reacted to his trauma just as he did. But she couldn't help resenting him and her circumstances. He had with three words sentenced her to a life without everything that she loved most, including herself. She closed her eyes and started to the vanity for a facial tissue. When she stumbled over the edge of the bed, she straightened up and walked on. But neither the chair nor the magazine rack were where they'd been when she closed her eyes, and she bumped into them also. She picked herself up, opened her eyes and looked around. Clenching her teeth, she grabbed the magazine rack, tossed it against the door with all her strength and plopped herself into the chair.

Jeannetta wished for her old guitar; from childhood, she had found peace of mind by strumming or picking her favorite tunes. She hummed softly for a few minutes until she could restore her serenity. "I'm the one who's wrong," she admitted to herself. "I burst into his life and expected him to change it for me. I should have told him at the outset, just as Laura said." She sucked her teeth and leaned back in the deep cushions. "But I dreaded hearing him say no." She sighed and started to the bathroom to wash her face. "And I didn't count on our being attracted to each other, nor on my falling in love with him." She looked skyward. "What will I do?"

The Southern Queen docked an hour before sunset. Mason stood at the edge of the gangplank checking off the passengers, but Jeannetta avoided looking at him when she passed. The few branches in view stood still. Within seconds, it seemed, her cotton T-shirt clung to her body, and she thought the heavy, wet air would burst her lungs. She wiped away the moisture that dripped down her face and beaded on her lashes, and would have run to the waiting bus if she'd had enough energy. She caught a strong whiff of the shellfish that fishermen heaped into huge vats, and needed a noseguard when she passed the pile of unfamiliar, decaying tropical fruits that a laborer appeared to haul away. Lucy wouldn't like it, but she sat beside Geoffrey on the bus anyway in order to avoid Mason.

"You two spatting again? I noticed he spent his whole lunchtime watching the dining-room door. And what were you doing? In your room trying to punish him?"

She had to laugh at the man's blunt words.

"Oh, Geoffrey. You know true love never runs smooth," she said, attempting to make a joke of it.

"Garbage. Who told you that?" She ran her hands over her hair and verified what she figured the sweltering humidity had done to it.

"It's over between us, Geoffrey."

The old man rolled his eyes and pursed his lips in disdain.

"There's just about as much chance of that as there is of me walking from Bangkok back to Augusta. Fenwick will be on your tombstone sure as Ames will be on Lucy's."

She looked at the passing scene, but didn't see it, as she pulled at her thumb, pensive. After a few minutes of silence and self-searching, she turned to him.

"Geoffrey, I didn't level with Mason about something important, and I don't think he'll forgive me." Geoffrey patted the back of her hand but, from his expression, he could have been miles away. She wondered if his long silence meant that he agreed with her.

"I don't suppose he's leveled with you either, otherwise you wouldn't be sitting back here with me, snubbing him. The two of you have wasted near 'bout a whole day of your lives being foolish. If I upset Lucy, I tell her I'm sorry, that I'll try not to do it anymore and ask her forgiveness. Why can't you do that?"

Along with the others, Jeannetta checked into the luxurious Oriental Hotel, said by some to be the world's finest, recorded the day's events, had her dinner in her room, and repacked her bags. Then she called Kenyan Airlines and booked a flight to Nairobi, Kenya, for the next afternoon. She chose East Africa because the tour would visit West African countries, and she wanted to avoid him.

"You wouldn't be checking out, would you?" Geoffrey asked when he met her as she walked out of the Oriental early the next morning.

"Yes, I'm leaving the tour." She reached into her handbag and gave him her card.

"I take it Mason doesn't know you're skipping out, does he?" She thought she saw sadness reflected in his eyes. "I guess he doesn't," Geoffrey continued, answering his own question. "You can't love him much, Jeannetta, if you're treating him like this. Even a condemned man gets to speak his piece before they hang him. No use saying I hope you won't regret this, 'cause you will sure as night follows day."

"That's the problem, Geoffrey—I love him so much that I can't risk destroying him." She rubbed her cheek where he'd kissed it before he walked off. She looked at the letter in her hand a long time before she dropped it in the hotel's mailbox. Within an hour, she had a visitor's visa and a ticket to Kenya.

She'd never been in an airport designed for passenger comfort, and this one was no exception. So, after lying awkwardly across two chairs for several hours, she sat up. "I'd better finish this doll," she reminded herself, and took her crocheting from her carry-on bag. She couldn't work up an enthusiasm for it, so she put it away and made notes for her novel. Just before five o'clock that afternoon, she boarded a plane that, minutes later, took off for Nairobi.

Well past midnight, Mason sat at the hotel's bar, out-of-doors along the Klong, the major waterway that teemed with commerce and houseboats day and night. He could have done without the strange, sour odor of the thick, brown waterway, but he didn't want to go to his room, though he'd had to discourage dozens of the elegantly dressed Thai girls who worked

the hotels. He didn't doubt that he could cure Jeannetta because, even without assurance that she didn't have her periods,
he knew she had a brain lesion and suspected the implications. But he didn't want to believe that she had deliberately
set out to seduce him, making him fall for her, and ensure her
chances of getting him back into the operating room. He'd
spent almost six weeks with her, and he'd seen nothing about
her that was less than admirable, so how could she... He let
the thought die, pulled the damp T-shirt away from his skin,
slapped at a mosquito that dive-bombed toward him and decided to call it a night. He thought of his brother, Steve, and
the terrible sacrifices he'd made so that Mason could be a doctor. And he thought of Jeannetta and what her life would be
like a couple of months or less from then. Tomorrow, he'd get
together with her and try to salvage their relationship. He'd
do what he had to do; he always had.

"I'm Clayton Miles. How do you do?"

Jeannetta let her gaze move casually over her business-
class seatmate, allowed him a half smile and replied, "I'm
Jeannetta Rollins." That accomplished, she returned to crocheting a doll that she'd give to the Edwin Gould Foundation
for distribution to homeless and other needy children. She
hoped to have completed about twenty of them by Christmas.

"Is this your first visit to Kenya?"

It wouldn't hurt to talk with him, and it wouldn't interfere
with her crocheting. She might even manage to stop thinking
of Mason, at least for a while.

"Yes. I've never been to Africa, and I'm looking forward
to being there. I've always wondered what it's like to be in
a country where I'd be one of the majority and where black
people governed."

He accepted a drink from the stewardess, and she got a
good look at his hands. Neat. The hands of a cultured man.

"Depends on the country. It can be pleasant, and it can be downright awful. Over here, people care about their family and their tribe, and if you're not a member of either, don't look for compassion."

Curious about the handsome black man, who had the bearing of a university professor, she asked if he was on a business trip.

"I'm afraid those days of dashing around the world on business are over. I marketed a wrinkle-reducing product for a chemist who claimed to have tested it, but, after women used it for a while, their skin tended to get leathery. The lawsuits ruined my company. Up to that time, I had a real good business producing and marketing all kinds of chemicals. Fortunately, I managed my affairs so that I'm personally all right, but my reputation as a businessman is shot. The company went bankrupt, and it depressed me for months. Then I said, the hell with it—and decided to see the world while I figure out what to do with my life. I'm fifty-two and I've no intention of taking a powder. But that's enough about me—what about you?"

To her astonishment, she heard herself telling him about her health, Mason, the scheme she'd concocted to gain his help, and the way her hopes had shattered.

He downed his drink and ate a few Brazil nuts, all the while seeming to dissect what she'd told him.

"Sure you didn't overreact? If I were facing what's before you, I expect I'd have gotten on my knees and begged him." She wrapped the crochet thread around the doll and put it in the little bag beside her.

"Maybe that's because you're not in love with him." Heads turned when he whistled.

"That's a mean complication. If he cares about you, he's dealing with a shrunken ego."

*That's nothing compared to what I'm trying to handle,* she

thought. With dinner over and the lights lowered, she tried to sleep, but whenever she closed her eyes, she saw the sadness that marred Mason's face when he walked out of her room. She feared she'd carry it with her always.

"She skipped lunch and dinner yesterday, and she hasn't come down for breakfast this morning, and doesn't answer her phone," Mason told Geoffrey. "I think I'll scout the shopping mall next door." He said it casually so that Geoffrey wouldn't know how deeply concerned he was about her. He walked outside and, within minutes, his clothes began to cling to his body. Unmuffled sam lams—three-wheeled motorized taxis—roared through the streets, as did old trucks, poorly maintained cars, and more brand-new Mercedes-Benz cars than he'd ever seen. He clasped his hands over his ears when a big jet thundered low overhead and irate drivers honked their horns at the red light. The din nearly deafened him. He searched the mall without luck, figured she might have gone to one of the temples, looked at his map, and struck out for the nearest one. Babies cried, women cooked on the streets over primitive utensils; the smell of assorted strange foods tormented his nostrils, and he looked around for an escape. More of the same. Every place. He crossed the wide street, thinking that he risked his life, dodging among mad motorists hell-bent on winning some imaginary race, walked into the Temple of the Emerald Buddha, a cool, quiet oasis, empty but for himself, and sat on the marble floor. He couldn't help reminiscing about his life, one that seemed so much longer than it had been. He wasn't afraid or nervous, but how would he feel when he went back there? He got up and walked toward the exit, the echo of his clicking heels shouting at him from every pillar and nook.

"May I help you?" a monk in saffron-colored robes asked in a soft voice. Mason thanked him and walked on.

"I think you are worried," the man said, quickening his steps in order to keep up with Mason, who stopped and looked at the short priest.

"Yeah. You might say that," he replied. They stood at the door of the temple, and Mason dabbed at the perspiration running down his face. How could the man not sweat in this heat? The priest bowed.

"Do what you have to do. Everything you possess is on loan to you, even your intelligence. Whether your life has any value depends on what you do with it." He bowed and went away.

Deeply moved by the man's concern and his words, Mason failed to pay attention to his surroundings. During his lapse, he felt a hand in his pocket, turned, and saw the thief making off with his wallet. With legs nearly three times as long as the thief's, catching him proved easy. He retrieved his wallet and headed back to the Oriental.

"Miss Rollins checked out at eight o'clock this morning."

The telephone operator's words battered his eardrums like the toll of a funeral bell. He phoned Geoffrey.

"Jeannetta has left the tour. Do you know where she went?"

"Can't say as I do. She left around eight this morning, and the reason I didn't tell you before is 'cause I just couldn't bring myself to give you that news. I know what she means to you."

Mason didn't want any philosophy and definitely not any sympathy. "I'm going back to New York as soon as Lincoln, my assistant, can fly out here." Lincoln wouldn't want to leave his new bride, but Mason didn't plan to give him a choice. He hadn't remembered that option until he said the words. He felt almost dizzy as plans and possibilities took shape in his mind. He had to hurry. She hadn't seen the last of him.

After lunch, Geoffrey and Lucy joined him in the lounge. Lucy's sudden motherly behavior with him brightened his mood, and he considered the likelihood that approaching marriage automatically made women think of motherhood. But Lucy Abernathy? The woman had long since kissed sixty goodbye.

"I'll leave for New York as soon as I can get a flight. Josh can handle things until my assistant gets here day after tomorrow. So don't worry."

"I won't," Geoffrey assured him, then he cocked his head to one side and studied Mason. "How're you going to find her? She won't be leaving you any clues."

"You think I'll be looking?"

A deep frown creased the old man's face, and then a smile slowly erased it. Geoffrey laughed aloud.

"Why should you?" Geoffrey asked. "This ain't the end of the world."

Mason didn't hide his irritation at his friend's sarcasm. "Don't tell me it isn't. Speak for yourself," Mason muttered.

Geoffrey laughed louder. "My question was as good as your answer. I've been watching people a lot of years, and I know when a man cares for a woman. You go ahead—everybody'll understand."

Mason packed, called Skip and his brother, got a seat on Scandinavian Airlines, and left Bangkok that night.

Jeannetta watched the sunrise from the plane's window and had to fight a wave of melancholy, until she closed the shade and vowed not to get upset every time something reminded her of Mason. She rode into town with Clayton Miles, and discovered that they'd chosen the same hotel.

"It isn't such a coincidence," he said when she commented on it. "There were only two choices. I'm going to sleep for a few hours. How about meeting me in the dining room about one?" She nodded agreement. He'd be in Nairobi for a week, and he'd never know how grateful she was for his company.

* * *

Mason walked into his apartment building after a twenty-two-hour flight, and found Skip waiting in the lobby. The boy rushed forward and threw his arms around him. He marveled at his feelings of contentment as he held the child. When had he developed this deep, paternal feeling for the boy, this sense that he'd come home to Skip? Inside his apartment, the boy didn't waste time reporting his news.

"I'm going to be a doctor, Mason. I made up my mind, because Aunt Mabel is so sick and the stupid doctors can't cure her. I'm gonna cure all of my patients."

Mason sat in the nearest chair. "What did you say?"

Skip repeated it, bubbling with excitement and oblivious to Mason's incredulity.

"I saved up three hundred and twenty-nine dollars toward it, and I want you to help me open a bank account. I have to put away a lot of money, and I wouldn't trust anybody but you." Mason listened as the boy poured out his dreams at a rapid rate, unaware of the pain he caused. How could he encourage Skip, when the boy would someday learn that he'd realized his own dream—and walked away from it?

"You've thought this over and you're sure? You're not going to change your mind?"

"I'm sure. It's all I can think about. I'm gonna work hard, Mason. I just want you to open my account for me." He recognized the gleam in the boy's eyes as the child's vision of his future, and remembered his own dreams. He shook off the inner voice warning him that destiny stalked his heels. To go back…

"Alright, son. Be over here at eight-thirty tomorrow morning. What bank do you want to use?"

Skip's face glowed, his lips curved upward to expose even white teeth and, Mason realized for the first time, a dazzling personality. He stroked the boy's shoulder.

"Can't I use yours?"

Mason nodded. "Now, get going—I've got a million things to do."

"Why'd you come back so early?"

"I have an emergency, and I'll be leaving as soon as I get it straightened out. A couple of days, I'd say. Run along, and tell Mabel I'll get to see her before I leave."

"Steve, how are you?" He listened for a minute. "In my apartment. I got back this morning, but I'm leaving as soon as I straighten out a few things. How about lunch?"

"Fine, we can lunch here in my apartment, all right?"

Mason agreed, hung up, and called the chief of ophthalmology at New York Hospital. Sweat poured off of him and he paced the floor, to the extent the phone cord would allow, as he listened to the familiar voice. He loosened his tie, ran his fingernails over the back of his neck, and tried to control his breathing. The thudding of his heart reminded him of the surge of adrenaline he used to get when he'd donned his greens and walked into an operating room.

"Alright. Eleven o'clock tomorrow morning." He hung up. He'd done it, and there was no going back.

"What brought you back here in the middle of a tour, Mason? It isn't like you."

"I'm going back to medicine. It was inevitable, I guess."

Steve's fork fell to his plate, his lower lip drooped, and he reached for his glass and gulped down some water.

"You're going back to… Are you serious?"

Mason nodded, and continued chewing his hamburger.

"Something must have happened on this trip?"

Mason pushed his plate aside and looked at his benefactor, the man who had sacrificed his own future to help him become a doctor, and who hadn't shown bitterness when he'd walked away from it.

"Yeah. Plenty." He told Steve about Jeannetta.

"A lot of people must have needed you these past couple of years or so. You love her, I take it. Suppose you can't find her?"

"I'll find her, but I don't have much time. When that tumor gets a grip, it can be horrendous. I've got a date tomorrow morning with the chief. Wish me luck."

Steve cleared away their plates and returned with two slices of chocolate icebox pie. "I can't tell you how happy this makes me, Mason. But I'm sorry you're starting again in these circumstances, because loving her will make it doubly stressful."

Mason put a forkful of the pie in his mouth and wrinkled his nose.

"Man, how can you eat this stuff?" He made himself swallow it. "It was always stressful, but I was so cocky, I didn't let it bother me."

He could sense from Steve's manner that his brother meant to air what had long been a contention between them.

"Mason." He cleared his throat a couple of times. "Mason, Bianca Norris is in good health, and she was out of danger when you called it quits. I've tried all this time to understand how you got so upset that you'd give up your lifelong dream just because you made one mistake. Did you think you were infallible?"

Mason shrugged and strummed his fingers on the table. "You have to understand that people, even my peers and my chief, treated me as if I could do no wrong. If a case was difficult or out of the ordinary, they'd send for Fenwick. And Fenwick always did it, never questioning his ability or the danger involved. But that morning, right in front of everybody... Well, you know the rest. I realized, right along with them, that I was just a man, one who could make mistakes like the rest of them. I couldn't sleep that night and, when I woke up the next morning, the thought of going in there made me sweat. I didn't trust myself. In operations that delicate, self-confidence is just as important as knowledge and skill. And those weeks of waiting—the lessons I learned. I had to turn myself around."

"And now?"

"If I don't try, I can't live with myself."

"I remember thinking, back when you were a small boy, that nothing would stop you—you showed guts and brilliance before you went to the first grade. You'll do fine in there, like you'd never left."

Mason spent the next two days at the hospital witnessing surgeries, operating on dummies, and reacquainting himself with his true profession. His fourth day back in New York, he stopped at his travel agency to check on the tour.

"A letter from Bangkok arrived for you this morning," his secretary told him.

He looked at the return address. Oriental Hotel. His pulse raced, his heart galloped, and his fingers trembled as he tore open the envelope on his way to his private office. He stood with his back to the door and read:

My dearest Mason, I'm leaving the tour, and don't worry; I'll be alright. I know that I hurt you, and I'm sorry. I knew who you were, and I tried many times to tell you my problem and to ask your help, but I always got cold feet because, if you said no, it would be so final. When our attraction for each other grew strong, I feared that if I asked you, you'd think I had manipulated you. In the end, that's precisely what you thought. I have unshakeable faith in you, but I know that if you took my case and weren't successful, you'd persecute yourself forever. I care too deeply for you to wreck your life. Love, Jeannetta.

He walked to his desk, sat down, and reread the letter. He had to... Where was his mind? He punched the intercom.

"Viv, get me Jeannetta Rollins's file." He noted her address, phone number, and next of kin. When her phone went unanswered, he got Laura's number from information.

"Rollins Hideaway. Laura speaking."

Mason breathed a sigh of relief.

"Miss Rollins, this is Mason Fenwick, head of..."

"I know who you are. And if my sister can't ask you to look after her case, I sure can."

"Slow down, will you? She left the tour. Do you know where she is? She shouldn't be alone in a strange place, for one thing, and for another, she needs treatment. I have to find her."

"She called from Nairobi day before yesterday, but she didn't say where she was staying. You can't find her in a place that big."

"I can if you don't tell her I'm looking for her." He had been in enough developing countries to be able to trace an upper-middle-class American; in most, only a handful of hotels would appeal to them.

"Viv, get me a flight to Nairobi, Kenya, and call Sidu Adede and tell him I need a visa right now." He made a mental list of what he needed to take with him, called Mabel and Steve, and locked his desk. Twenty-six hours later, he stepped off the plane in Nairobi, went to a telephone, and began checking off hotels.

"Suppose this thing runs out of gas?" a young boy sitting behind Jeannetta in the six-seat Land Rover asked his father, as their guide drove them through the game preserve not far from Nairobi. "How would we get past all these lions to get out of here?"

Clayton Miles turned to Jeannetta. "If I were as pessimistic as that boy, I'd probably end up selling used cars. I lost millions because I trusted a man, but I aim to make a few more millions before I check out of here. Never take adversity lying down, Jeannetta. Get hold of that doctor, and give yourself a chance at a normal life. My guess is he'll be waiting for you."

"I don't see how I can do that, Clayton. I can't ask him to mortgage his life for mine. I intend to put him out of my mind and enjoy this vacation." Her gaze swept the vast plain, and she looked with awe at the endless varieties of birds perched on the tall grasses that waved in the breeze. Her senses were heightened by the sight of the birds enjoying a free ride, while nature protected them from the small animals hidden among the grasses, waiting to prey upon them.

"When you do leave Kenya, where will you go?"

She heard his unasked question: How long would she run?

"Further south. Home. I don't know."

He didn't speak for a long time, and when she looked at him, she wondered why he'd closed his eyes when they were supposed to be sightseeing. When he spoke at last, she thought she detected a tremor in his voice.

"Come to Egypt with me? You'll love the pyramids, the Sphinx, Luxor, the desert. They're something marvelous to behold. Come with me?" Though the loneliness in his voice gave her a deepening sense of kinship with him, she declined.

"Thank you, but I want to see more of this part of Africa, to know more about life here. I want to meet some people and talk with them." Her eyes widened at the sight before her. Giraffes that had to be a couple of stories tall drank from a spring, all the while keeping watch for lions. Their guide drove up a narrow lane and stopped in the middle of the wildlife preserve. Nearby, a herd of elephants drank from a muddy stream, while some of them rolled in it.

"No danger," the guide assured them, "elephants down-wind, we upwind." Jeannetta breathed deeply in relief, reached for her cassette, and recorded the sight.

"Clayton, isn't it strange that the elephants don't mind all those birds on their backs?"

"Not really," he replied. "According to my guidebook, those birds pick off the insects that infest the elephants' hides. The poor beasts probably love those birds."

She closed her eyes and pasted in her memory all that she'd seen that day. As she opened them, a thousand gazelles swarmed by.

"You can bet there's a hungry lion right behind them," their guide explained.

"If you're determined to put Mason Fenwick in your past and to brave what you know is going to be a hard life, why don't you cast your lot with me? Marry me, Jeannetta, and I'll take care of you. I guarantee you'll never want for anything."

Her eyes widened, losing their almond shape, and she worked at the lump in her throat. Had she heard him correctly? He gazed steadily at her, and she frowned deeply, squinting in an effort to understand.

"You couldn't be serious. You've only known me for five days. If I accepted your offer, you'd probably spend the rest of your life berating yourself and hating me."

She felt his fingers lightly on her arm and looked at him. His solemn gaze pierced her.

"Why do you think I'm a frivolous man? Let me tell you that I am not. I think before I speak or act, and I've given this some thought. I enjoy your company, and I've been more at ease when I'm with you than at any time since I locked Miles Chemicals and walked away from it for the last time. When my business went belly-up, my so-called friends had more important things to do when I called. Until we met, I'd been alone, in the truest sense, for the past eighteen months. You've changed that. And I'll be honest. Because of me, a lot of women lost their beauty and aged prematurely. Their class-action suit drained my business, but no amount of money can compensate for what happened to them. If I make your life a little easier, a little brighter, maybe I can ease my conscience. Now, what do you say?"

"But you did nothing wrong, and you have no reason to feel guilty."

He shrugged, looked out of the window, and spoke as though to himself.

"I should have carried out my own investigation before I packaged that cream under my logo and put it on the market. But that's beside the point. We get on well, and we could have a good life together if you'd marry me. Your presence, your carriage, and the way you're dealing with your problem uplift me."

She had vowed that she wouldn't cry about her condition anymore, so she sniffled and calmed herself. "You're a terrific guy, Clayton, and I've enjoyed these past few days with you, but I have to find my own way." She tried to hide her astonishment at his somber, almost sad expression. Even if he had meant that noble gesture, she wouldn't accept it. If she couldn't lose herself in Mason Fenwick, if she couldn't have the essence of him, she wouldn't share herself with any man.

She barely heard the guide's warning of the dangers of being in the preserve after dark, for she had been enjoying the prospects of soon having a few moments alone in which to contemplate all that had transpired that day and to think about her life. Clayton grasped her hand, detaining her as they left the Land Rover, and she couldn't help being conscious of the difference between the feel of his hands and what she felt when Mason's fingers so much as brushed her flesh. Darts of electricity shot through her at the thought of how he made her feel.

"Look, Jeannetta. Don't you feel as though our seeing this beauty together foretells something wonderful for us?"

She gazed up at the purple, red, and orange hues that blazed across the darkening sky as the sun neared its goal. Her free hand went involuntarily to Clayton's arm, and he looked at her inquiringly.

"At times such as these," she whispered, "I thank God for my eyes."

She felt his arm encircle her waist in a gesture of comfort, and his warm smile made her wonder how many women would reject the proposal of such a man. Distinguished, well-mannered, a wonderful conversationalist, wealthy, and handsome.

"Until you tell me you'll never marry me," she heard him say, "I'm not available to anyone else."

"Clayton, I'm sorry, but I…"

"Hush. You haven't thought it over. Give me your address in Pilgrim, so I won't lose touch with you."

She did as he asked. "Better give me your sister's name and address, too."

She did, though she knew Laura would be scandalized at the thought that she had spent so much time in the company of a strange man of whom she knew nothing.

"Meet me for dinner," he coaxed.

"I'll call you," she hedged. She liked Clayton Miles, but she hadn't forgotten that a lapse in judgment had complicated her relationship with Mason—though she doubted she could have staved off the fire that had roared inside her from the moment she met Mason.

Mason found the foreign-exchange booth at the airport, changed dollars for Kenyan shillings, and phoned the Nairobi Hilton. Jeannetta Rollins was not a guest there. That left the InterContinental. If she hadn't registered, he had some work to do. He phoned the hotel and, half an hour later, he'd registered there.

"Miss Rollins went on a tour of the wildlife preserve," a bellboy told him, obviously fishing for a tip. A check with the tour agency enabled him to plan his day, and, after sleeping for the next eight hours, he showered, dressed, went down to the lobby, and sat facing the door.

Mason rose slowly, his heart slamming against the walls of his chest, when she walked through the door. He let his gaze sweep over her, searching every visible inch of her for evidence that she was no worse than when he'd last seen her. Her hair seemed longer, blown forward to frame her ebony cheeks. Nothing more. He relaxed for a minute, and then tensed. She had a man with her, but he'd deal with that later. Right then, his only concern was her health. He ignored the man and walked directly to her.

"Jeannetta, why did you leave? Didn't you remember my telling you that I'd always be here for you? Didn't you?"

Her obvious astonishment at seeing him—her audible gasp, dropped lower lip and widened eyes—held little surprise; she should have known he'd find her.

"Did you get my letter?"

He took it from the vest pocket of his linen jacket and showed it to her.

"You shouldn't have come."

Her hand went to her throat, and he stepped closer, ready to support her if necessary. Mason glanced at the man who remained beside her, and who cleared his throat—a bit insistently, Mason thought. He put a hand on each of Jeannetta's shoulders and looked the man in the eye.

Clayton Miles smiled wanly and introduced himself. But

the man's smile lacked warmth. "I assume you're Dr. Mason Fenwick."

Mason nodded, but he didn't move his hands from Jeannetta's body.

"Am I to assume you're not free for dinner?" Clayton asked Jeannetta.

Mason looked from one to the other. They hadn't had time to develop close ties…or had she known him before she left the tour? When Jeannetta half turned to face Clayton, Mason released her shoulder and stepped back.

"I enjoyed sightseeing with you, Clayton. Perhaps we'll meet tomorrow."

He nodded. "Don't forget what I said. Good night, Dr. Fenwick. Good night, Jeannetta."

Mason stared at the man's departing back, trying to recall why he seemed familiar.

"Will you have dinner with me?" he asked Jeannetta, when he could no longer see Clayton. She agreed.

"I'll be here in the lobby. Perhaps we can go to one of the French or Italian restaurants a few blocks away." He tried to shove his emotions aside, but couldn't. Butterflies darted around in his stomach, and need twisted through him as she stood there gazing at him with warmth and want blazing in her eyes.

"Can you imagine how I felt when I realized you'd gone? You could have left the note for me with the hotel's concierge, but you mailed it to New York, expecting that I wouldn't get there for another three weeks. It might have been too late then. Oh, Jeannetta, why couldn't you trust me? Don't you know that I couldn't live with myself if I didn't help you?"

Her bottom lip worked; she pulled at her hair and swallowed.

"You're returning to medicine?"

He nodded. "I'm back at my old job, and I'm ready whenever you are. But you'd better hurry." Her hand went to her collarbone, and her eyes widened before she lowered her lids, and a soft, dreamlike expression drifted over her beautiful face. He couldn't deal with what he felt for her right then; first thing first. And his priority was restoring her health. A man shouldn't operate on a woman with whom he was deeply involved. Nobody could argue with the reason but, in this case, neither of them had other options.

"I'll wait here," he said, and turned her to face the elevator. If she didn't leave there, he couldn't guarantee that he wouldn't follow her straight to her bed.

Jeannetta showered and changed into a pink strapless dress and jacket, slipped into white sandals, picked up her straw bag, and raced down the stairs, too excited to wait for the elevator. She'd thought she'd faced a mirage when she saw him standing in the lobby. *I'm going to enjoy this evening with him,* she told herself, *and I won't worry about a thing.* The bellboy grinned and bowed when she passed him on the stairs. She took her key to the desk, and the receptionist grinned knowingly. *What is it with these people,* she wondered. Since when did staff take such delight in getting into the guest's private business? When they left the hotel, she wanted to scream to the doorman that she wasn't spending the night in Mason's room. The man had actually winked at Mason. They walked to the restaurant, and she mentioned her mild annoyance.

"Jeannetta," he said, his voice filled with amusement, "they think you were playing around with that guy and that I came unexpectedly and caught you two together. These are boring jobs, and the guests are the only diversion."

She couldn't help laughing with him. "That explanation suggests that you've got a pretty healthy imagination, yourself."

They chose the Italian restaurant, because Jeannetta found

its soft lights and elegant decor enchanting. He seated her, motioned to the waiter, and sat facing her.

"Why did you leave without telling me?" he asked for the second time. He took her letter from his pocket and pointed to it. "You said here that you don't want to wreck my life. Do you believe I could go on with my life as it was knowing what you faced? Didn't you have any faith in what has happened between us? Surely, you don't think a man can hold you as I have done and not care about you."

"I left because I didn't want to risk your having a failure with me, a tragedy that would haunt you forever. If a near-miss was enough to make you walk away, failure would destroy you. I believe in you, but I'm not sure that you do. After all, you said that medicine was behind you, a thing of the past. I don't plan to waste time feeling sorry for myself—I'll do and see all that I can, while I can."

"You didn't reply to the most important part of my question, but I don't suppose dinner is the place to discuss something this serious." His fingers strummed the table a couple of times. "Who is Clayton Miles?"

"I don't know." At his raised eyebrow, she explained, "I mean, I met him on the plane. He's interesting, has good manners, and he's very pleasant company." She watched Mason carefully to gauge his mood, to determine whether he might be jealous. If so, she decided, he knew how to hide it.

"His name's familiar. What does he do?"

"He's a chemist." She knew from the set of his jaw and the way he ground his teeth that she wouldn't like his next remark.

"Why is he staying here?"

She glared at him. "This is where he had reservations."

She realized that her glare didn't carry much weight when he said, "Is that why you're staying here?"

"My last name is Rollins and yours is Fenwick," she told

him, "and that should tell you what I think of your imperti-
nent question."

He didn't give in. "I didn't suggest anything. I asked you
a question."

"It will be a great loss if you hold your breath until you
get an answer."

They finished the succulent shrimp brought up from Mom-
basa, Kenya's second city, and the waiter served their main
course, which consisted of fried tilapia—a fish common to
East Africa—overcooked zucchini, and broiled locally grown
mushrooms. Jeannetta couldn't figure out how the fish and
mushrooms could be so tasteful and the zucchini, the only
Italian dish on the menu, so awful. She said as much to Mason.

"Anybody can open a restaurant, decorate it in red, white,
and green, and call it Italian. I wouldn't be surprised from the
taste of this fish if the chef hadn't been working on a Hundred and Twenty-Fifth Street in Harlem. This stuff is good."

She nodded. "Kenya is famous for its fruits. I'm going to
have an assortment. Some of every kind on the menu."

He finished chewing his mouthful of fish, put his fork
down, and assumed the posture of a man preparing to run.
"Where are you planning to put it? You couldn't possibly have
any more space in there." He pointed to her stomach.

"Alright. So I love to eat. Be a gentleman, and don't rib
me about it."

He laughed, reached over, and tweaked her nose. "I like
women who have a lusty appetite and aren't ashamed of it.
What I can't stand is the woman who orders food, pushes it
around on her plate and leaves it—as though that's supposed
to be feminine—then goes home and wolfs down a couple of
peanut-butter sandwiches."

"Not me. What you see is what you get."

He leaned back in his chair, and she could only guess at
the reason for his sudden seriousness.

"Yes. I've known that from our first meeting. And I like that about you. I like it a lot."

Excitement ploughed through her as his voice dropped a few decibels, and grew dark and suggestive.

"I like everything about you. Everything. Right now I want to…"

She felt her eyes widen and her lip drop, and he must have noticed her impatience to hear what he wanted, for he suddenly clammed up, stood, and held his hand out to her. He walked with her halfway to the door, turned, and laid a bill on the table. When he rejoined her, he joked, "You've got me so damned befuddled that I forgot I'm supposed to ask for the check. Wait here while I go over to the cash register."

They walked down Muindi Mbingu Street, crossed Kenyatta Avenue, turned into City Hall Way, and walked on to the corner of Uhuru Highway without speaking.

"Tomorrow, we ought to check out the Conference Center and some of the government buildings," Mason suggested. "The first time I came here, it surprised me that Nairobi is such a modern city, at its center especially. What do you say we meet for breakfast around nine and walk through the city, huh?"

"It wasn't what I expected either," she said. "It's well laid out, with broad, paved streets and avenues, traffic lights, and modern stores. Our guide said that you have to go to the city market to find traditional wares."

He squeezed her hand and urged her closer to him as they walked along. The clear bright moon cast their shadows before them as they turned off Uhuru and walked across the park toward the hotel. Jeannetta looked up at the sky that was bright as early morning, at the white swirls that played hide-and-seek with the moon, and she missed a step.

Mason dropped her hand and wrapped his arm around her.

"It will be yours again, everything. All of it. I promise you. So don't let this depress you."

She looked up at him and smiled, the only response she could give him. Their brisk strides slackened into a stroll, and she knew that, like herself, he was reluctant to let go of these precious moments.

Kenyans went to bed early and got up early, so the streets were deserted except for the few tourists who walked back to their hotels after dinner, a movie or local entertainment. She felt his fingers tighten on hers as two strangers staggered toward them. He switched sides, putting himself between her and the men, who appeared to be foreigners, and they staggered on their way.

"How about an aperitif? It's early yet," he said, heading them toward the bar. "Jeannetta, I want you to go back to New York with me as soon as we can get a flight out. I don't want to waste any more time."

She rested her glass of tonic on the counter and made herself say those fatal words. "I'm not going with you, Mason. I've decided to take whatever comes. I don't want to be on your conscience, and I won't let you ruin your life for me. I have faith in you, but I don't believe you're sure. And even if you are, it's as risky as it ever was, and if your reasons for walking away were valid once, they're valid today. I won't let you do it."

He jumped up, knocking over his glass of cognac, and rubbed the back of his neck with his left hand, wet and smelling of the high-priced brandy. He shook his head as though to clear it, and she'd have sworn that he had difficulty focussing on her. He walked away from the bar, then went back and stood over her.

"Run that past me again. Slow and clear so I can understand it." He spoke in a low, strained voice that shook from frustration or anger, she didn't know which. When she reached out to touch his arm, he moved beyond her reach.

"Well?"

"I'm not going back with you." She took a bill from her purse and would have laid it on the counter, had he not stopped her.

"You're my guest. I invited you to have a drink with me. Remember?"

Breath hissed from her lungs when she saw the sadness, the distress, mirrored in his obsidian eyes. "Mason... Oh, Mason..."

"Come on," he interrupted in barely audible tones, "I'll walk you to your room."

They neared her door, and he stopped. "How can you deliberately do such a thing? You think you're brave, but not even Hercules would have volunteered for what you're choosing. Why, when it's unnecessary?"

How many times did she have to tell him that, with a 50 percent chance of failure, she wouldn't let him ruin his life on account of her?

"What changed your mind, Mason? Pity? You told that woman who'd been your patient that you were no longer a doctor, that you'd put it all behind you. And you knew right then what was wrong with me. I'm not the only person who's needed your services these past two or three years. What about them?"

"That's unfair. I went through hell after that last operation, reliving those times that I had heedlessly tweaked the devil's nose, and acknowledging for the first time how lucky I'd been. What scared me was the thought that I'd been playing God. My chief told me last Monday that he never enters that operating room without praying first. That never even occurred to me."

"But you did it successfully so many times. Did you lose your nerve?"

He shrugged his left shoulder and tilted his head to one side.

"I don't know. I don't think so, but I know I can help you, and I want to. I have to. Let me help you."

"I'm out of sorts. Seeing you here unexpectedly, and realizing what you've done… Let's talk at breakfast."

He walked her to her door and stood looking down at her. His wistful expression tugged at her heart, and she reached out to him.

"Jeannetta. Honey, come here to me."

She had told herself that she wouldn't let him wrap himself around her heart with his loving. *But I need him,* she thought, as she went mindlessly into the powerful arms that enfolded her in his adoring embrace. Her right hand caressed the side of his face, and he pulled back enough to gauge her feelings. He must have seen her hunger, for he pulled her to him with trembling, unsteady hands, covered her open mouth with his own, and let her feel the force of his longing. His tongue, bold and hot, swept every crevice of her welcoming mouth as if to learn it all over again. Her moans seemed to elevate the heat in him, because his left hand went to her hip, and he molded her to him, letting her feel his virile strength. She raised her arms to him, wanting to give him full access to her person, to let him have his way. Her hands slid to the back of his head, holding his mouth to hers while she sucked his tongue; she felt the shudders that raced through him when he grabbed her buttocks and rose heavy and strong against her. Blood pounded in her brain, and hot currents of desire stormed through her trembling body.

Should she drag him into her room or…? She loved him all the way to her soul. How could she make love with him and then carry out the plan that she knew would hurt him?

She pulled his tongue into her mouth, held him as tight as she could, and loved him with every ounce of her strength. He stepped back, held her off, and gazed into her eyes.

"What is it? There's no reason to feel desperate, honey," he soothed. "We're in this together, and we'll come through it all right. Together." She relaxed in his arms, exhausted by her emotions.

"I think I'd better tell you good night," he said with obvious reluctance. "I'd rather not, and you know it, but I... You said you're exhausted, and I won't want to risk a mishap." He brushed his lips over her cheek. "Nine o'clock in the dining room."

Jeannetta sat on the side of the bed, her head in her hands. She'd made the right decision; any other would cripple Mason for life, and she refused to do that. She packed, phoned the airport, and went to bed. The next morning, she phoned Clayton Miles, thanked him for his kindness, and hung up before he could answer her. She left her note to Mason with the desk clerk. At a quarter past nine, she was on her way to Harare, the capital of Zimbabwe.

## Chapter 7

He had spent the night scrambling the sheets, tossing and dreaming. At dawn, he dragged himself out of bed, more tired than he could remember, dressed, and decided to watch the sun rise in Kenya before meeting Jeannetta for breakfast. He strolled along Uhuru Highway for a couple of blocks until the changing sky announced the coming sun, and leaned against the trunk of an old coconut tree to witness its rise. How could he make her understand the horrifying experience of having the certainty that a person's life can be snatched away by your error? She didn't want to accept that, prior to that near-fatal incident, he'd never thought of it in that way, because he'd never considered his fallibility where his work was concerned. He'd been cocky. All-powerful. But he'd gotten a dose of the humility that every surgeon must eventually drink. The sun was up in full, and he'd hardly noticed it. He walked back to City Hall Way, past the elegant government buildings, hardly aware of his surroundings.

"Got a couple of shillings, rich mister?" a boy of no more than seven asked him. Mason fished around in his pockets, careful not to expose any bills in the event the boy had accomplices, and gave the child some coins. To his amazement, the boy handed him a used toothbrush and, when he questioned him, explained that it was fair exchange; he didn't beg.

"I can show you around the town for some more shillings," the boy told him. Mason thought about it for a minute.

"What are you doing out here in the street so early?"

"Best time to find tourist. Make money. First bird gets biggest worms. I show you around." They walked along City Hall Way, and Mason had to admit that the boy knew the town and its buildings and monuments.

"How old are you, and what's your name?"

"Jomo. Almost eight."

Mason couldn't associate an American boy of that age with such sophistication.

"Do you go to school?" He was curious about the boy, but he had a hunch that if he got too close, he'd lose his shirt.

"Second grade. We go to marketplace now." Here was the Kenya of the common man. Hundreds of traders prepared their wares for the day's sales. Women hung colorful baskets, woven mats, wood carvings of animals, eating and cooking utensils, ornaments, hides, and an assortment of other goods. Jomo stopped at a stall and grinned.

"This is my grandmother, rich mister. You buy something from her?" Mason bowed to the woman and bought several wooden bracelets on which were carved heads of giraffes, lions, and other animals.

"I can take you to see the Masai for a hundred shillings," the boy urged. "For some more, my cousin will take you to see Kilimanjaro."

"What do you do with your money?" Mason had no intention of going miles away from Nairobi into Masailand with the boy, but he didn't doubt that Jomo could get him there and back.

"I save to buy a wife. I need many shillings." After questioning Jomo, Mason learned that the boy was a member of the Kikuyu tribe. He flinched as his gaze locked with Jomo's grandmother's piercing, unnerving eyes.

"Go back to your hotel," she said. A tremor of apprehension skipped down his spine, and he couldn't doubt that behind her gaze lay special knowledge.

"Why?"

"Go back." He forced a smile, thanked her, and asked Jomo to walk with him to the InterContinental. He gave the boy the equivalent of ten dollars and watched the happy youngster accost another tourist. Skip saved to become a doctor, and Jomo saved to buy a wife. He could imagine the life that the enterprising little boy would have if he'd been born in the United States. He decided to leave his purchases in his room and to freshen up before meeting Jeannetta for breakfast. When he stopped at the desk for his key, the receptionist handed him an envelope. His heart plummeted when he saw her handwriting, and he didn't open it until he'd closed the door of his room. *Déjà vu!*

Dear Mason, because I love you with every fiber of my being, I won't let you do it. Nothing that you have revealed to me will make me believe that you're willingly going back to medicine. I'm not happy with my decision, because I know I'm letting myself in for a bad time. But as I see it, I've got a fifty-fifty chance of losing my life either totally or partially and, if either happens, you'll lose yours altogether. I'm not convinced that you're ready for it; I know I'm not. Thanks for wanting to help. This is final. Jeannetta.

He crushed the note into a ball and slammed it across his bed. *Now what?* He sat down and reached for the phone, and his gaze fell upon the crushed note. He picked it up, pocketed it, took it out and reread it. She loved him. He had thought she did, but she had at last told him. He needed that love, needed it desperately. But if he didn't find her and get her back to New York in a hurry, she'd never be his, her pride wouldn't let her go to him unless she was a whole person. He packed, ordered a car, and went to the dining room. To his surprise, Clayton Miles joined him.

"I tried to find you," Clayton said. "I wanted to tell you that she was about to leave."

"Thanks. Any idea where she went?"

"Your guess is as good as mine, but it shouldn't be too difficult to check out. Around here, money buys more than goods and services."

"Tell me about it." He extended his hand. "I hope to meet you again." He stopped the chambermaid in the hallway.

"I'm trying to find out where Miss Rollins went," he said, holding a ten-dollar bill in his hand. "Did she leave anything behind? Any papers? Maps?" The maid opened the door.

"I haven't cleaned in there yet. You look around."

He found travel folders in the waste basket, and the phone numbers of the Zimbabwe Embassy, Kenya Airways, and the Princess and Sheraton hotels in Harare. She'd bought a ticket to Harare, Zimbabwe. At six-thirty that afternoon, he boarded a flight to Harare and, this time, he vowed, she wouldn't get away from him.

He called the Sheraton first and hung up before the operator connected him to her room. No point in tipping her off. He got to the hotel after midnight, slept fitfully, and rose early the next morning. He wanted to call New York, check on his business, Mabel, and Skip, but he had to give priority to Jeannetta. Steve would take care of Skip and, if necessary, Viv could handle the business while Lincoln guided the tour. He headed for the dining room and stopped. She stood in the lobby at the tour desk with her back to him, inquiring about a trip to Victoria Falls on the Zambezi River.

He walked rapidly to where she stood. "Jeannetta!"

She whirled around. Her bottom lip dropped and her hand went to her chest.

"Mason! How did…?" He took her in his arms and swallowed her words as his mouth covered her trembling lips. He didn't care if they had an audience, or whether the culture frowned on public expressions of affection. When she attempted to resist him, he deepened the kiss, holding her closer. Her groan of capitulation sent rivulets of heat cascading throughout his tall frame, and he had to struggle for control of himself. He eased their passion with light kisses on her eyes, cheeks, and forehead. And with his arm around her, he walked her to a cove near the elevators, away from the gaping onlookers.

"You ran away from me again. Didn't you know I'd find you? I'll always find you, Jeannetta. You can't tell a man you love him so deeply and kiss him off in the next sentence. At least, not this man. Come back with me and let me help you. We're losing precious time." His gaze swept her features, caressing, adoring.

"If you're going to talk about that, please go back where you came from. I want to enjoy my vacation, and I don't want to spend it worrying about the future."

"There's no use denying the truth. When the curtain falls, and—believe me—that could happen any day, it may be too late, and I may not be able to help you."

She attempted to move, but he'd placed her between himself and the wall. He felt her soft, sweet hands on his chest and had to stifle the urge to crush her to him.

"You didn't follow me this far to depress me, did you?" So she was in the denial phase, a problem he'd had with many of his patients. He'd use another tactic.

"Then let's spend the day together, enjoying being with each other. What tour are you taking?"

She told him.

"Sounds interesting. Mind if I join you?"

Jeannetta longed to get out of the minivan and touch the giant rock formations. Reddish, sandlike rocks of various shapes and sizes clung together, as though created by a master mason, to form massive, eerie shapes—some as high as thirty feet. The rocks sat in a wide area of reddish-colored sand. She dug the toe of her shoe into it, scooped up a handful, and watched it sift slowly through her fingers. Mason fingered the keys in his pockets. She'd done the same thing when they passed a building site in Istanbul, and he wondered at its fascination for her.

"These rocks are thousands of years old," the guide explained, but their rough appearance denied it. Jeannetta pulled Mason's sleeve.

"Look." They gazed at a male monkey meticulously grooming his mate, and Jeannetta turned away when the female expressed her loving gratitude. But the experience made her feel as if she'd been cheated, and she welcomed Mason's arm tight around her, stopped and turned to him. She sucked in her breath at the message of deep caring in his eyes and let him take her weight for a minute. He held her steadily, and she knew she could trust him; she had never doubted that, but she didn't want to expose what she feared might have become his Achilles' heel. And she didn't want him to tempt fate again because, this time, he might not win. They walked on behind others on the tour, arm in arm.

"I didn't bring a camera," Mason said when a flock of black

birds with red beaks and red-and-yellow combs flew over-head. She wished for her recorder but had to settle for what she would remember. His arm slid around her waist and, as she nestled against him, it occurred to her that he might have begun to read her thoughts.

"Close your eyes, imprint them on your brain, and tell your-self to remember them," she said and she could have bitten her tongue when she saw his startled look; she was glad that he didn't comment on it. Instead, he squeezed her shoulder and advised her to think pleasant thoughts.

She grinned, glad for his light mood. "Now we're cooking together for a change. Look over there." She pointed to several cheetahs prowling behind a high fence. "They'd be handsome if they didn't have such small heads," she said.

"Yes," he agreed, "but with a large head, they probably wouldn't be the world's fastest animal."

The guide announced lunch, and shepherded them to a nearby restaurant with outdoor seating, that featured grilled meats, fresh fruits, and iced coconut milk.

"We'll have an hour at Victoria Falls before sundown, when it's most spectacular," the guide promised. "It's only a half-hour flight, so we have plenty of time."

Jeannetta stood with her back to Mason, enjoying the feel of his arms around her and experiencing the mile-wide Vic-toria Falls as they exploded into the Zambezi River. Hun-dreds of rainbows in every conceivable combination of colors straddled the river, a halo for the falls. She turned her face to his chest and wept.

"You alright?" he asked as the little plane headed back to Harare.

She nodded. "I hope I didn't upset you back there, but it was so beautiful, so breathtaking, that I couldn't stand it."

"I've never seen a more riveting sight either. The urge to

sink to my knees and pay homage to it was almost irrepressible."

Mason disliked lying, but he figured that, in this case, the truth would do more damage. When she had wet the front of his shirt with her tears, the bottom had dropped out of him. He looked down at her, asleep with her head resting on his shoulder, and placed a protective arm about her. If only he could make her understand what she'd pay for her stubbornness. She stirred against him, and he leaned over and traced her forehead with his lips. He admitted to himself that she'd found a niche deep inside of him, and he wished he knew how their story would end. The plane circled the airfield to land, and he checked her seat belt, accidentally rousing her.

"You make a great pillow." She tried unsuccessfully to stifle a yawn, and sputtered out her next words. "That's the best sleep I've had in ages."

He looked at her and, since he didn't much feel like joking, he let his eyes answer her. She looked away.

"I can guarantee you an even better sleep, one you're not likely to forget soon," he boasted.

"But first…"

He didn't object to her needling him. She had backed away from their passionate exchanges as often as he.

"Yes. But first…if you're guilty, don't accuse," he admonished her.

"Humph. The only thing I'm guilty of is being sensible."

He released a mirthless laugh and followed her down the short aisle and off the plane. The hotel van awaited them and, as they drove past one of the famous jacaranda trees blooming with purple flowers, Mason asked the driver to stop.

"It was planted ninety-nine years ago," he said. "Would you believe it? And still blooming." She slid her arm through his, and he gazed down at her. "It's nearly as beautiful as you are."

"Meet you in the dining room in forty-five minutes," he told her as they collected their keys from the hotel reception.

"Okay."

"Can I take you at your word?" he asked her, and smiled, as though to soften it. "Don't tell me you have the nerve to be affronted by my remark. Sweetheart, we're down here almost to the end of Africa because you've skipped out on me twice. But not anymore, so don't even try it."

"I said I'd meet you for dinner," she huffed, "and I will."

Jeannetta took a leisurely bubble bath, dried off and applied *Trésor* body lotion to her skin. She sat on the edge of the bed, filing her toenails, and decided to call Laura.

"What're you doing way down there, girl?" Laura asked in a pleading tone when Jeannetta told her where she was.

"Laura, try to understand. I have to do this. If you knew what I've seen today, you wouldn't scold me."

"I don't care what you saw. You're out there denying what's happening, and I want you to come on home. You get the next plane back. You hear?"

"I can't promise you I'll do that." Jeannetta didn't want to upset her sister, but Laura could be difficult when she didn't get her way.

"What about Fenwick? Have you gotten in touch with him? Have you? I gotta see that man so I can figure out what he's got that made you lose your head. If you're not gonna speak with him, you'd better come on back here so I can look after you. You hear?" Jeannetta hung up. She had long thought that Laura would smash her ego if she let her.

She got out a pair of sheer stockings, a rose-colored garter belt, and matching bra and panties. "What am I doing?" she asked aloud. She sat down and thought over their relationship, all that they had experienced together. "I love him as I love my life, and this is my last chance to show him what he means to me. Maybe when he wakes up tomorrow, he'll understand what I've been trying to tell him." She slipped into a dusty-rose sleeveless sheath that ended two inches above her knee, and looked at herself in the mirror. She put on a pair of three-inch sandals, let her hair hang around her shoulders, and left the room, taking only her plastic door key.

Mason paced in the lobby near the front door, his hands locked behind him so that he wouldn't look at his watch every two minutes. He had every other exit covered with the help of twenty-dollar bills so, unless she had climbed out of her sixth-floor window, she was in her room. He'd learned that she had a weak regard for time, but this bordered on...

"Guess who." She had approached him from behind and covered his eyes with her hands.

"The most beautiful woman in the world," he answered, his good humor restored.

"Methinks you exaggerate, sir."

He looked down at her, drinking in her loveliness, that ephemeral something about her that drew him as ants to sugar, nails to a magnet.

"Arguing with you usually gets me nowhere," he said, unable to hold back the grin that he knew had spread over his face. "What do you say to your being the second most beautiful?"

He couldn't help laughing aloud when she tilted her head to one side and looked at him inquiringly before asking, "Who's number one? You never told me whether you have a girl back in New York. Do you?"

He looked toward the heavens in a gesture of feigned exasperation.

"If you had been satisfied with being the most beautiful, that question wouldn't arise. Let's go out. I want to show you off."

* * *

Jeannetta tried without success to gauge Mason's mood. He vacillated between playful and serious, but his facial expression didn't alter.

"I hope you're enjoying this," he said at one point. "French food is all sauce and no substance, and that endless talk about *l'amour* is so much babble. Outward manifestations of it end with marriage."

"You know this firsthand?" she asked, needling him. He sipped the wine.

"About the food, yes. But where that love business is concerned, I only know what I've observed in my French friends. Those guys can woo an alligator out of its hide, but as soon as they say those vows, they forget how to do it."

She couldn't imagine that he would. "I'll bet nobody would ever be able to say that about you."

"Not in this life."

Shivers skittered from her breast to her belly when he lowered his voice and promised her everything with just a look. She wet her lips and swallowed, and she had to clutch her middle as sparks shot from his hot gaze.

"You sound as though you've got a notarized certification of it," she dared to say.

His look turned somber. "You like to play with fire, it seems."

She gazed steadily at him. "When I'm cold, Mason, really cold, I get as close to it as I can."

He stopped eating. "What would you say the temperature is in here right now?"

She knew what he was asking, and she wasn't backing down. She rubbed her bare arms. "Feels like the left side of thirty-two degrees Fahrenheit."

He reached in his pocket for his wallet and glanced at their waiter, who held two dessert menus.

"What would you like for dessert?" he asked her.

"Nothing, thank you."

"Coffee?"

She shook her head. He held his hand out to the waiter for the bill, never moving his gaze from her eyes. She wouldn't have believed herself capable of such a fit of nerves, though she knew that her demeanor belied what she felt. He stood and held out his hand, and she looked at him for a long minute before placing her right hand in his. They walked the two short blocks back to their hotel. He didn't speak, and she was glad for that, because she didn't trust herself to say anything. He walked straight to the elevator, punched his floor, and looked at her. She said nothing, and he pushed the button that closed the door and then released her hand. The elevator stopped, the doors opened, and butterflies flitted around in her stomach while he stood there looking down at her.

"Come with me?"

She gave him her right hand, and he held it until they reached his room; he paused and he let her read the question in his eyes. She squeezed his hand, and he opened the door.

"What happened to your misgivings, Jeannetta?" He tried to control his anxiety, his fear that she'd overcome her need as she had so many time times in the past.

She looked him in the eye and didn't evade his question.

"I still have them, but I…" She shook her head slowly and diverted her gaze.

He tipped up her chin with his left forefinger.

"You said you love me." Fine tremors wafted through him at the new lights in her eyes and the smile that curved her sweet lips.

"Yes. Oh, yes, I love you. But what about your misgivings?"

"I still have them, too, but they're no longer strong enough to keep me out of your arms. I've never held a woman who confessed to love me and made me believe her, and I've longed for that. When I met you, I knew I wanted you, but I resisted because I'm tired of casual relationships. I'm convinced now that what's between us isn't casual, Jeannetta, and that it won't ever be." He stepped toward her. "I've never needed anyone or anything the way I need you. Let me love you." He didn't want to pressure her, but he was desperate to bind them so tightly that she'd stop pushing him away. If she let him love her, the way he knew he could, she'd go back with him.

He hadn't known her to be so quiet, softer than flower petals, yet the answer in her eyes didn't include submissiveness. A bolt of sensation shot through him, hardening him, when she wet her lips, rimmed them with the tip of her tongue, and gazed up at him. He watched her swallow the damp heat of desire and run her hands from her hip bone down her thighs. Her lower lip dropped, and he had her in his arms. He covered her mouth with his and showed her with his marauding tongue what he intended to do to her. Her hips moved against him, and he stilled her with his hand firmly on her buttocks. Her groan of frustration heated him to the boiling point, and he rose firm and powerful against her belly. His senses whirled dizzily when she took over the kiss, sucking on his tongue, caressing his hips, holding his head while she took her pleasure.

"Slow down, sweetheart. I don't want this to get away from us." He could have been speaking to the moon. She sucked on his bottom lip and rubbed her body against his leg. He had to set her away from him; another minute of that, and he'd be over the hill. He slipped her shoulder straps down her arms, watched her dress pool around her feet, picked her up, and carried her to his bed. She clung to him while he turned back the covers and lay her on the white sheets.

"Trust me?"

She nodded, and he leaned over and dropped a quick kiss on her lips. He stood close to the bed and stripped off his shirt, never taking his gaze from her desire-filled eyes and welcoming smile. He took in her scantily clad body, peeled off her garter belt, the sheer hose, and reached for her skimpy panties. When he glanced at her for permission, she lifted her hips and, a second later, his mouth watered, and he stiffened as he stared at her beautiful, thickly tufted love nest. Her hand went to his belt buckle, freed him of the pressure around his waist, and he gazed down at her and waited. When she unzipped him, he sprang free and ready into her hand, as his shorts and trousers dropped to the floor.

He leaned over, gathered her in his arms, unhooked her bra, and buried his face between her full breasts. She shifted to give him access to her nipple, and he pulled it into his hungry mouth, and nourished himself.

The full power of his virility loomed before her, and she wet her lips in anticipation. Hot darts danced inside her and then zoomed straight to her petals of love, and she couldn't help spreading her legs and raising her arms to him. He seemed to hesitate, and she thought she'd die right that minute if he didn't get inside of her.

"Mason. Please, I need you. I need you."

He positioned his knee on the bed, and his gaze swept her nude body. Her hips moved upward to him of their own volition, and she felt a gush of love liquid when he groaned and tumbled into her waiting arms.

"Not so fast, honey," she thought she heard him say, when she fastened her lips on one of his flat pectorals. His hips moved and she caressed the little nub with her tongue while she rubbed the other one with her fingers.

"Slow down, baby," he crooned. "Ah, Jeannetta. *Jeannetta!*"

She reached down, found him thick and ready, and stroked him lovingly. She sighed impatiently, adoring the feel of his mouth on her neck, ears, and shoulders. His lips found her nipple again. She jerked upward, because nothing had prepared her for the feel of his strong, talented fingers as he separated her secret folds and stroked her. Tremors shook her, and her heart slammed in her chest.

"Mason, darling. I can't stand any more." She threw her leg across his hip, and he leaned over her.

"This is important to me—you're important to me. Forget everything, and let's love each other. Look at me now. I want to see your face when I lock us together." His rough, smoky voice sent shivers of desire through her.

"Yes. Yes. Please." She pulled him over her, and looked into his desire-filled, greenish-brown eyes.

"Now!" She lifted her body to meet him and, when she felt him at her portal, she cried out.

"Mason, please." Oh, the wonder of it, as he slid into her depths. He was iron-hard, hot, velvety smooth, and big. He let her adjust to him and then began to move. Immediately, she felt the tension build within her as he whispered encouragement, told her that she was wonderful, all he could ever need or want. She caught his rhythm, but lost it when her body disobeyed her and went wild. Spirals of unbearable tension coiled upward from her feet to the nest of love that he masterfully stroked, and she felt herself begin to grip him rhythmically, until her spasms clutched him. He increased his pace then, and she tumbled out of control, screaming his name.

*"Mason! Oh, I love you. I love you so."* She wrapped her legs around his hips as that heaven-and-hell pleasure took control of her, and then relaxed, replete and exhausted. Restored, she gripped his thigh and held him to her as she drove for his pleasure and, in seconds, his arms tightened around her and, with a shout of joy, he splintered in her arms.

He let his elbow take his weight as he rested in the circle of her arms. "I ought to move over. I'm too heavy for you."

The feel of her hands on his shoulder muscles, gently stroking, gave him a sense of belonging that he couldn't remember having had before.

"You aren't too heavy," she corrected. "You aren't too anything for me. You're perfect for me."

"I hope you mean you're happy right now."

"It was wonderful. I didn't know I could feel as I did with
you."

He raised up and looked into her face. Sated. No other word
would describe her. Well, if he wanted to go for absolute truth,
he could say she looked like the gal who'd just been elected
campus queen. Or the cat who'd just finished off the canary.
Pleased with herself. He dropped a kiss on her flaccid nipple
and watched it harden. He attempted to move away from her
but, even as he shifted, he reached full readiness.

"Don't move," she protested. "You belong right where you
are."

He gathered her closer. "Don't you know what's happening? I want you."

Her eyes widened, and he kissed the tip of her nose.

"You started this. I was resting, teasing a little bit maybe,
and this nipple of yours acted up and, well...what's a man supposed to do?" She wrapped her legs around him and shifted
her hips, sending waves of current all through his body.

"A man's supposed to do what a man's supposed to do,"
she answered and parted her lips for his kiss.

The ride was short and sweet. They knew each other now.
She opened herself to him, holding back nothing, and she
gave. And gave. Whatever he asked, she gave fourfold, and
then she took, drawing his inhibitions out of him until he
could withhold nothing of himself. Shaken, trembling, he
knew himself for the first time in his life and, in triumphant
submission to her, he filled her with his essence. He collapsed
upon her, strung out, glad she hadn't asked him for his soul,

because she'd taken the rest of him. He separated them, fell over on his back, and pulled her close. In seconds, she slept. He looked at her, as beautiful in the grip of orgasm as she was in a long flowing gown, and his pulse quickened. It was best that she slept; her tender loving had loosened his tongue. He flipped off the light. An unaccountable eeriness crept over him as he dozed drowsily, and the blackness of the darkened room seemed to thicken. "I don't want to live without her, and I couldn't bear to see her suffer. I…"

He slept.

Jeannetta stretched languorously and curled into the warm man who cuddled her to him. His soft murmurings lulled her, and she nuzzled his shoulder and dozed off. Awakened by his restlessness and the low drone of his words, she sat up and gazed down at him. She felt the moisture on her right side, noticed the dampness of his body and the sheet that half covered them, and leaned over him to hear his words more clearly. His hand went out, brushing her shoulder.

*"I can't fail. I…can't botch this. I won't. I can't make a mistake with her. I can't…I…mustn't let my finger slip. My finger is slipping…I'll fix it. I have to. She needs me…I can't fail."* She patted his hand, awakening him as gently as she could. Drawing in quick, heavy breaths, he turned on his right side and slept.

What had she been thinking? She'd made up her mind to go wherever he took her. Anywhere. The sweet, tender way in which he'd loved her, giving her what she had reached for and longed for, but never achieved—a thorough and powerful completeness—had given her a lapse in judgment, she decided. She had gone to sleep looking forward to his reaction when she told him she'd go back with him and do as he suggested. But not after what she'd just witnessed. She stole out of bed, dressed, and slipped down the hall. She wouldn't be on his conscience; you couldn't love a man as she loved Mason Fenwick and knowingly ruin his life. This time, she wouldn't leave a note.

The Oxford Hotel sat on West Queen Street about eight blocks from the Sheraton, and one-third its size.

"If a man asks where you took me, tell him the airport."

The taxi driver looked at the twenty-dollar bill and smiled.

"Yes, mum. He won't get it from me."

She checked in, amused when asked to pay for the previous night because it was seven o'clock, five hours before check-in time. The small hotel had its advantages, she decided, when she walked out on the balcony and saw that it overlooked a well-tended garden and a small waterfall that served as a bath for the birds. She called her sister.

"I wanted you to know where I am."

"Why don't you come home?"

It was no use trying to explain. "There's one more place I want to go, and then I'll call it quits. If I had the opportunity, I'd go to South America and take a ride down the Amazon, but I don't suppose I'll get to that."

"Jeannetta Rollins, don't you dare do anything like that. Have you lost your mind?"

"Stop worrying, Laura. You'll send your blood pressure sky-high."

"A Mr. Miles has called here a few times asking about you. Seems like a real nice gentleman. Who is he?"

"A friend. Someone I met in my travels. If he calls again, tell him I'm fine." It occurred to her after she hung up that Laura hadn't asked about Mason, and that didn't ring right.

Jeannetta smiled when she saw that the hotel served breakfast on a terrace facing the garden. She relished the cool crisp air, the smell of perfume from the rose garden, and the flitting and chirping of birds, and she wished she'd brought her cassette recorder. A matronly woman approached.

"Mind if I join you? I used to live here years ago, but I live in London now. I'm on vacation."

Jeannetta put the local morning paper aside and gestured to the chair facing her.

"Please. I'd love some company," she told the woman, wondering where she and her family had stood politically when the former Rhodesian government ceded power to the African majority.

"How does it feel being back?" she asked the English woman.

"It's easier than I thought it would be. I do miss the old days here with my family and all that." She spread her arms in an all-encompassing gesture. "But time marches on, and it's good to see that the blacks have done a good job of preserving the country. Salisbury—I mean Harare. It's hard to keep up with these name changes—is still clean and beautiful, and so many new buildings, new schools and such. That's progress, I suppose."

"That's because you people gave it up graciously and didn't tear it up fighting to stay in power."

"Yes. I've thought about that a lot, but look at what's happening in Liberia. You can't blame that on colonialism. And look at some of these other countries that are torn apart by tribal conflict." Jeannetta took a deep breath. She had heard this argument before. Which was best? Colonial control or tribal conflict and devastation?

"Don't forget that the colonial powers cut across tribal lands and boundaries when they carved out these countries, establishing nations without regard to tribal affinity. Arch-enemies under one flag? In this region, one's tribe is more important than country will ever be. You know that. What can you expect?" The woman heaved a deep sigh of resignation and sipped her morning tea.

"What we're getting, I suppose. But it's such a waste of human life and resources. Kids ought to be able to play without dodging gunshots. Thank God, the children here can grow up normal."

Jeannetta wondered about the woman's sad expression until she heard her say, "The whole world needs to clean up its act."

She told her breakfast companion good-bye and went to her room, but she couldn't fit her key in the lock, and had to try repeatedly before her shaking fingers found the keyhole. She went in and lay down with her eyes closed. A few minutes later, she opened them and said a prayer of thanks. She walked out to the balcony, and her eyes widened as she exclaimed with pleasure, "Let me get my recorder."

Dozens of colorful birds perched on the banister of her balcony, and she spread cookie crumbs to keep them there while she described each one. She went back inside and attempted to write in her novel, but didn't like the story line and couldn't think of a way to change it. Mason crowded her mind, but she pushed thoughts of him aside. She'd sell her house in Pilgrim and buy a small bachelor apartment in New York City, one in which she could easily maneuver.

"No, I won't," she swore, as the bile of it seeped into her mouth. Why should she give up everything she loved? Her little house? Her work? Her mountains? *And Mason!* She answered the phone.

"Grace Tilden here. We took our morning tea together."

*Did we?* Jeannetta, who wouldn't taste tea before noon, smiled inwardly at the British manners.

"I have a friend who would take us for a spin around the city, out to the zoo and back to her house for dinner, if you'd like."

Jeannetta thanked her, but declined. "I've got to get back home, and put my life in order." No more running from the inevitable. She threw her suitcases on the bed and started repacking.

## Chapter 8

Mason woke up with a start and patted the rumpled sheet beside him. He hadn't been dreaming; the musky scent of their lovemaking confirmed what his body remembered. Their night of loving had lifted him to heights he'd never known. And still she'd left his side. He had sensed her desperation that second time but, after what they'd shared, he wouldn't have thought she'd leave him. He phoned the desk.

"Miss Rollins checked out, sir, and I don't think she used a hotel taxi, because none of the hotel drivers logged in a trip for her."

He thanked the clerk, and called Laura.

"She checked out," he said, "and I don't know where she is. Think she'll go back home?"

"I don't know, Dr. Fenwick, but, when we talked, I got the feeling she was getting tired of running from place to place. What will you do now?"

"Find her." Telephone calls to the local hotels yielded no

clues. He headed for the airport and bought a ticket to New York. When he found her, he wouldn't let her out of his sight until he had her under anesthesia. But that had better be soon.

Two days later, wearing a thick beard, his body weary from the loss of sleep during forty-eight hours of flights and lay-overs, he got off the train in Pilgrim, New York. At the local post office, he telephoned Steve.

"What in Job's name are you doing in Pilgrim? Viv hasn't heard from you in days, and she wants your okay on over a dozen appointments. Some of the cases are urgent." Mason put his right hand in his pocket and fingered the keys. Wasn't this what he'd left? This stress, race after race against time? A lot of people wanting immediate and undivided attention? Steve would have to understand.

"Tell Viv not to make any firm appointments. Man, I haven't even announced that I'm reopening my office, and I'm not available to anybody until I take care of one thing. Someone needs me, and she comes first. After that, we'll see. How's Skip doing?"

"I suppose you'll get around to telling me who *she* is. Skip's fine. He got a scholarship from his choral group, and he's anxious about when you're coming back. He's real proud of that scholarship."

"Me, too. I'll call him tonight." Mason went to the postal clerk's window.

"Can you tell me where I'll find the Rollins family?"

"Sure can," the pretty woman replied. Part Native American and part Caucasian, he judged. He wrote the directions to Rollins Hideaway, put the note in his pocket, and turned to leave. He had to call Skip.

"Mason!" the boy shrieked. "Where are you? Can I come over right now?"

"Calm down, son. I'm upstate, and I may be here for a few

days, but I wanted you to know that I'm back in the States, and I'll see you soon. Congratulations on that scholarship. I'm proud of you."

"You are? Gee. Thanks."

"How's Mabel?" He sensed from Skip's diminished buoyancy that his aunt might have deteriorated.

"Not so hot. She wants see you."

He had to look into that situation as soon as he got Jeannetta to see reason and treated her.

"I'll call her tonight. And don't worry, I'll take care of things there."

He hung up, got into a taxi and headed for Rollins Hideaway. The woman who greeted him bore no resemblance to Jeannetta, so he assumed she wasn't Laura.

"Don't ever come up here in winter without a reservation," the woman said. "You want something on the first floor or the second? Second's quieter."

"I'll take one on the second. Is Miss Rollins here?" He hoped she'd say no, because he wanted Jeannetta's sister to be friendlier and more...

"She's at the market. I'll tell her you want to see her." He got a shower and lay down for a few minutes, only to be awakened by the ringing phone seven hours later at six o'clock in the evening.

"Dr. Fenwick, this is Laura. Nice to have you with us. We start supper at six-thirty, but if you don't want to come down, you may eat in your room."

"Thanks, but I'll be down in a couple of minutes." He pulled on jeans, a T-shirt and sneakers, and walked down to the lobby. Laura met him, but he noticed she didn't offer to shake until he extended his hand. After an exchange of greetings, he watched her size him up. *And frank about it, too,* he mused.

"She's not as foolish as I was beginning to think," Laura said dryly as she motioned him to sit down.

"Any idea where she is?" he asked.

"She's been wrong all through this," Laura said, "but she didn't plan for it to happen like it did. I hope you can talk sense into her."

*But what about answering my question,* he wanted to ask her. Instead, he told himself to have patience.

"Tell me where you stand in this. I have to know precisely what I'm dealing with."

"Do whatever you can for her. She thinks she's strong, that she can face anything, but she hasn't dealt with blindness. Except for music, everything she loves comes to her through her eyes."

He nodded. "I've noticed that." He stretched his legs out in front of him and strummed his fingers on the arm of the chair. "I have to find her, because she doesn't have that much time left, and I don't want to be faced with the impossible. Where do you think she'll go?" Laura looked intently at him, and he didn't doubt that she judged him.

"You want to put another trophy on your mantelpiece, or do you care about her? Which is it?"

He tilted his head and weighed his answer. Her audacity didn't bother him, but what he felt for Jeannetta was private.

"Because of her, I'm returning to a profession that I gave up when it began to bring me more pain than pleasure. Going back will not be easy, but I'd walk off a cliff blindfolded before I'd refuse to help her. I *have* to do this, as much for myself as for her, and I hope I have your blessing."

"And my prayers. Her train pulls in tomorrow afternoon, but I wouldn't meet it, if I were you. You'll be more successful if you wait until around six-thirty, when she's home." She looked squarely into his eyes. "Do you love my sister?"

"She's everything to me."

Her deep sigh told him that his answer wasn't what she wanted, but that she accepted it.

"Alright. I'll let you know when she gets home."

The following evening when the sun hovered low, near the time of day that Jeannetta loved most, he covered the few blocks from the Hideaway to her house, with his heart hammering in his chest. He couldn't force Jeannetta to do what was best for her, and if she refused help, he didn't know what he'd do. He took the neat brick walkway to her door in three long strides, his eagerness to see her overcoming his anxiety. The door cracked open, but the chain separated them.

"Who is it?"

His stomach muscles tightened, moisture beaded his forehead and he could hear the thudding of his heart. She stared directly at him and asked who he was.

"Open the door, Jeannetta." A painful knot clutched his insides when she squinted in an effort to bring him into focus.

Her whole body came alive when she heard his beloved voice, but immediately she tensed. He had outmaneuvered her and, now, she wasn't able to get away from him. She'd talk with him, but she wouldn't budge from her position.

"Why did you come? Haven't I made it clear that I don't want your help?"

"Open the door, sweetheart, or I'll break it down, chain and all."

A warm glow enlivened her, raising her spirits. Did he care that much?

"Why?" She kept her voice cool, a part of the armor she'd have to wear in order to stand her ground. She heard the tired exasperation in his voice and felt herself softening.

"You ought to know by now that I will not give up. You don't know what you're facing, but I do."

"Please go away." She would have closed the door, but he prevented that with his foot.

"I need you, Jeannetta. You let me make love to you, and you held me in your body and loved me until I lost touch with myself. And now you tell me to please get lost. Just go to hell and leave you alone. Haven't you thought about what I felt with you that night and what I went through the next morning, when I reached for you and you weren't there?"

"Don't make this more difficult than it already is. Please, I..."

He interrupted her, and she wished she could see his eyes more clearly; she'd always depended on his eyes rather than his words to tell her what he felt.

"How did you think I'd react to your leaving like that after you pulled out the stops and showed me what loving you could be? Did you lie when you told me you'd love me as long as you had breath in your body, or were you just caught up in the moment, in getting what you wanted?"

Her hand reached out involuntarily, but she let it drop to her side. She couldn't let him think she'd used him to satisfy her physical needs, but she couldn't let him risk performing that operation.

"Please, Mason. You don't believe any of that—you couldn't. So, let it rest. I'm glad you've gone back to your profession, because I know that's where your heart is, but you can't jeopardize your chances of succeeding by making me your first case. I won't let you." She wished he'd leave, because she wouldn't hurt him by closing the door and, if he stayed there—his presence more palpable than when she'd been able to read his mesmeric eyes, and her need to feel his arms around her overwhelming her—she knew she'd give in. He shifted his stance then, and the low hum of excitement that had teased her since she'd cracked open the door and heard his voice suddenly galloped through her nervous system. His male aura curled around her, and she sucked in her breath.

"I nearly went out of my mind when I realized you'd disappeared again, and you didn't leave me a clue as to where you'd gone. Don't you care that I need you? Don't you? Open this door, baby, and let me get you in my arms."

She lifted the chain.

A groan tore from him as his hands encircled her body, and he crushed her to his big frame. She had no shame about the desperation and passion that he must have heard in her answering cry. Her pulse leaped, and her heart nearly burst when at last she could clasp his head with her hands and feel his mouth possess hers in a plundering kiss. She savored his tongue swirling in her mouth as though he had to relearn every crevice, and an unearthly sensation heated her blood as his arms tightened around her, fitting her to his body. She moved against him. It wasn't enough. She needed more. All of him. Everything. But he broke the kiss and held her away.

His fingers traced her eyes, opening the lids as his fingers moved from side to side, and she realized that he examined them.

"Thank God," she heard him whisper, and he seemed to release a gush of air.

"What? What is it?" she asked, as he pulled her back to him and rested his head in the curve of her shoulder.

"I don't think I'm too late. I read your tests last week, thanks to Dr. Farmer's help. You've lost your peripheral vision, and there's more, but I can handle it. Oh, honey, why don't you trust me?"

"I do. Oh, Mason, I do. But you're human, and I don't want to be on your conscience."

He didn't move, but she could detect the restlessness in him from the muscle that twitched in his jaw where her fingers rested.

"You're worried about me?"

She shook her head, unwilling to burden him or to give him ammunition with which to persuade her to do as he asked.

"Then, you do love me. That's what this is all about, isn't it? You were willing to let me take the chance. In fact, you wanted me to take the chance until you loved me. Isn't that right? *Tell me!*"

She couldn't lie to him; the words wouldn't come. She nodded.

"Jeannetta. Sweetheart." His arms went around her and brought her into the protection of his warmth and caring.

"Mason. Oh, Mason," she sobbed. So near to her, and yet so far. It was more than she could bear. She leaned away from him, and her hands traced his face until his skin warmed her palms. Her fingers caressed his closed eyes, roamed over his lips, nose and ears, and her palms grazed lightly over his cheeks and forehead until tremors shook her body. She hadn't wanted him to know that she only saw his shadow, but she couldn't help herself; she had to see him, really *see* him. He must have realized why she'd done that, because he beseeched her.

"Sweetheart, don't. It will be alright, if you just trust me." His arms brought her closer, and she relaxed in their loving circle.

"I do. I trust you implicitly. I have from the moment we met." She sensed the quickening of his breath and the easing away of his tension, and she raised her lips to his. The deep and rapid thrusts of his tongue sent the fire of desire shooting through her. She needed to feel him against her, inside of her, and her right leg raised to grip his hip as her groan of passion echoed through the foyer. Her need became a flame burning out of control. He rose against her, pressing into her belly, and her fingers caressed him, encouraging, urging until his cries pierced the silence, and the powerful man shuddered against her. She undulated wildly, all control dissipated.

"Jeannetta. Stop it, baby. Give us a chance to make this memorable. Let me love you the way I want to. The way I need to." He carried her up the stairs, strode unerringly to her bedroom and set her on her feet.

Mason knew he couldn't communicate with her with his eyes, so he asked her, "Do you want this, Jeannetta?"

"Yes. Yes. Oh, yes." All woman and all his. His blood quickened when his hands met the thin sheen of moisture on her arms, and he knew he'd find more where it counted most. She grasped him eagerly, and he drew the snug-fitting T-shirt over her head, gripped her shorts and heard the button hit the bedpost. Her fingers fumbled with his tie and the buttons of his shirt, and it saddened him that he had to still her hands and do it himself. His blood began to simmer when her fingers grazed his pectorals, and he grabbed her bra, pulled it up over her head and bent to her swollen nipples. With unsteady hands, she unbuckled his belt, eased her fingers past his navel, groped for him and found him. Her busy hands made him want to relax and take it, but his heart wouldn't let him do it. He thought he'd blow up before he could finish undressing them both and lie her in bed. He looked down at her, arms raised to him in a gesture as old as woman, and sprang to full readiness. Her nostrils flared and perspiration beaded on her forehead as he knelt to her embrace.

His senses whirled dizzily as she guided him to her lover's portal, and he sank into her sweet heaven. He felt her relax, stop driving for what she needed, and give way to his lead, and he had to push back the tears. Home. She tightened her grip on him, and he thrust gently, careful not to let her push him too far too soon. Even so, when she caught his rhythm and joined his dance in perfect harmony, giving him everything as she'd done in Zimbabwe, he had to think of something other than the passionately hot lover beneath him. Her long legs wound around him, and the sound of his name on her lips nearly sent him over the edge. He murmured to her.

"You're mine, and I'm yours. You do whatever you want with me. Let it go. Give in to me, baby." He put his hand between them, caressed her as he accelerated his movements, and she rewarded him with a keening cry and the beginning ripples of completion that clutched at him until he shouted his release and she yelled his name in ecstasy.

"Oh, Mason. My love. I love you so."

He wanted to tell her what he felt, to open his heart to her, but the words didn't come. He kissed her eyes and her lips and laid his head on her shoulder.

"You… I've never known anyone like you. You're the only woman who's given me this feeling of completeness. Wholeness." His lips brushed her shoulder, and he looked down at her breasts, their smooth olive skin and dark aureoles, hard with desire. She moved beneath him, exciting him, making him proud that she wanted him when he knew he'd satisfied her thoroughly only minutes earlier. This time, she exhibited no submissiveness, but demanded what she knew he could give her, and he gloried in her womanliness.

*She's what I need,* he thought, as her hands grasped his buttocks and she lifted herself to his loving, drawing him deeper until she pitched over the edge, draining his essence and tearing at the shield in which he'd shrouded himself for thirty-seven years.

He lay awake in the darkened room, glad that he'd slept during the day, because he didn't intend to go to sleep nor to leave her side until she gave him her word. She stirred beside him, and he drew her closer.

"Are you awake?" For an answer, she kissed his shoulder.

"Be prepared, Jeannetta. I am not going back to New York

City until I can take you with me. I intend to stay with you until you give me your word." He felt her tense, but he plowed on. "Nothing and no one will make me leave here until you come with me."

"What about your business?"

He turned on his side, propped himself up with his elbow and gazed down at her.

"My next tour is ten months from now and, in the meantime, my secretary and my assistant can run the business. If they need my advice or opinion, you've got a telephone."

She looked away from him. "Are you accepting any patients yet? What about them?"

"Not to worry. You're my only patient right now." He couldn't understand her stubbornness nor what she thought she'd gain with it, so he punctuated his words. "You. *Only you.* And it'll be that way until you give up this notion of being a martyr." He could see that she bristled at the remark.

"What are you saying? If I don't let you operate, what will you do—go back to surgery or keep your travel agency?"

"Honey, I own Fenwick Travel Agency. I've been hoping that my brother would operate it but, if he won't, my assistant can do it. I'm a surgeon. I know that now, and that's what I'll be no matter what. A dozen people have asked their doctors to try and persuade me to help them, and the guilt of ignoring that far outweighs any concerns I have about performing that surgery." He fell over on his back and encouraged her to relax on top of him. She slid into his open arms.

"I suppose this crisis in my life has forced me to develop some humility," he went on. "I hadn't had much of that since I completed my internship. To tell the truth, I doubt I was ever humble, but it's been brought home to me with hurricane force that I'm not all-powerful, and I needed to learn that." *I won't push her right now,* he told himself, reasoning that their lovemaking had probably exhausted her.

"Can you sleep in that position?" he asked, hoping she wouldn't move and he'd have the upper hand if she attempted to leave him. He breathed more deeply when she nodded, wrapped her arms around his shoulders, and closed her eyes.

She rolled off of him and burrowed into her pillow.

"You've been awake for at least half an hour, and I'll bet you've been lying there plotting. Your mental wheels are already preparing you for flight," he said, his tone light as though her behavior didn't concern him.

"G...go back to s...sleep," she slurred.

"Not this time. I'm a morning man, remember? If you'd planned to move on, you've missed your chance. You're my woman, Jeannetta, and I'm sticking with you. No man could do what you're asking of me. If you don't give me your word that you'll go to New York City with me as soon as I can make arrangements—Tuesday at the latest—then I'll just stay here."

"You make the alternative sound like a threat. Believe me, I've never heard of such delicious punishment." She yawned, raised her arms above her head, stretched and purred. "It's like giving a kid an allowance for misbehaving. Will you stay forever?"

"Stop playing with me, woman." He looked down at her, watching her breasts jut forward when she twisted and stretched, and his voice lacked sincerity. She couldn't see them well, but she knew from his hoarseness that his eyes had become greenish-brown. And it didn't surprise her when his fingers skimmed her thigh and his hot breath teased her skin seconds before she felt him suck her nipple into his mouth. She squirmed, and he couldn't doubt that she liked it, but he raised his head.

"You want me to make breakfast, or..."

"Ooh," she gasped, as his lips encircled the little brown au-

reole, pulling and sucking, while his fingers danced wickedly
and wantonly inches away from where she wanted them to be.

"What do you want for breakfast?" he teased, his voice dark
and lusty. She swallowed hard; damned if she'd beg him. His
fingers inched closer to their prize.

"What do you want?"

She buttoned her lip and swallowed more. If he wanted to
play games, she'd do her best to accommodate him.

"Won't talk, eh? Okay by me." He bent to her breast. Exasperated at his teasing, she reached for him and lovingly encircled his velvet steel. A groan erupted from his throat, but
he wouldn't give in to her. Suddenly she remembered what
she'd wanted to do to him when she found him lying on the
Lido beach, and she led him to his back, straddled him and
took him mercilessly, wantonly, withholding nothing, until he
surrendered. Until they both surrendered. Spent. She gazed
down at him, but when she couldn't make out his expression,
she let her fingers graze lightly over his face. Yes, he smiled.
She thought her heart would burst.

Mason held her against him while the fingers of his left
hand played in her wooly curls. Contentment permeated his
whole being. Her lovemaking hadn't been desperate; he was
sure of that, but he'd give a lot to know why she'd gotten aggressive with him. He couldn't think of anything more alien
to her character. Or was it, he asked himself, remembering
their tryst in the tour bus. Her arms encircled his neck, and
she stretched out on top of him. Then it came to him. *Jeannetta hadn't been able to see him clearly, and she hadn't been
able to judge from his eyes his reactions to what she did, so
she had let her inhibitions fly.* Great for their lovemaking, but
that was as far as it went.

He got up, walked downstairs, got the reports on her clin-
ical tests that Dr. Farmer had sent him, and reviewed them

briefly. Then he went back to bed and pulled Jeannetta close. "Trust me?"

She nodded. "You know I do."

He reached for the phone on the night table beside the bed, placed it on her back, picked up the receiver and dialed.

"This is Dr. Fenwick. Schedule surgery for tomorrow morning. The patient's name is Jeannetta Rollins, and I'm checking her in this afternoon. Thanks." He hung up and held his breath while he waited for her to protest or to accuse him of seducing her in order to get his way. But she said nothing, and the muscles of his belly tightened while he awaited her next move.

Wet drops splashed on his chest. He raised her from where she lay prone on top of him, and the sight of tears bathing her face tore at his insides.

"What is it, baby? Have I gone too far? I only want to help you before it's too late. You have to know that I'd rather hurt myself than you. Talk to me, honey." He listened to words that came haltingly, but firmly.

"No. You haven't hurt me, and I know you won't if you can prevent it. You've made me feel special. Please promise me that if it doesn't work out the way you want it to, you'll be satisfied that you gave it your best shot, and you'll understand that I'm content no matter the outcome. Promise me that, and I'll go with you this afternoon." He stared at her, his emotions so near the surface that, for seconds, he couldn't trust himself to utter a word. Had his month of gruelling torture and guilt ended at last, and could he find the words to let her know what her trust meant to him? He held her face and he kissed her, because no words could tell her what he felt.

"I promise. And all I ask of you is that you trust me. My chief told me last week that we doctors don't perform miracles, but that miracles are often performed *through* us. If I remembered that, he added, everything would fall in place."

She'd been quiet while he spoke.

"You alright?"

Her answer was a kiss on his neck.

"Can you be ready to go to New York with me this afternoon?" He held his breath for fear she'd procrastinate.

"I'll go with you." Air gushed out of him, and he gave silent thanks.


"I don't have much time to get things together here," Jeannetta told Mason, who watched her fumble her way around the house.

"Just pack a gown, robe, slippers, and your toothbrush, honey. We're not going on vacation."

She wrinkled her nose at him, and his hand went to his chest as if he could steady the fluttering of his heart from the simple gesture. He could see the pieces of his life marching toward each other and fitting themselves together in a perfect whole. Only six weeks earlier, he wouldn't dared have imagined it. "Aren't you going to tell Laura?"

Jeannetta turned toward the direction of his voice. She didn't mind the haze in which she had awakened the previous morning, because he was with her, though she knew now that she would have hated experiencing it alone. She groped for the phone, but failed to touch it.

"Where's the phone?" She didn't even care if he knew how bad things had gotten. He handed it to her.

"Laura, I'm going to New York with Mason this afternoon. The surgery is tomorrow morning."

"Thank God. I didn't want to see you ruin your life for some supposed altruistic reason. I've never been in love, but if it makes you do unreasonable things, I don't want any part of it. Mason looked capable to me." Jeannetta sat down, because, once Laura got going, she preached a sermon.

"You always did attract men, and some were good ones,

too. I used to envy you, because you had the beauty, smarts, height, and all that. And I never could see why you couldn't accept one of those nice men and settle down. Maybe now, you will. Honey, I sure hope so. I can't close the Hideaway and go with you to New York, but, I'll be praying for you."

"Thanks, Laura, and don't worry. I'm in good hands." Laura envious of her? She couldn't believe it.

"By the way," Laura added, "that Mr. Miles called here this morning, and I told him you're back. He is one persistent man, and you know I don't lie." She paused for a second, and Jeannetta knew she was about to get some unsolicited advice. "Don't you think you should rent out your house and stay here at the Hideaway 'til you get healed up?"

"Thanks for the offer, but it'll be time enough to think about that when I start recovery. I have to get over this next step before I worry about the future. Mason will let you know how I am. And Laura, for once, I appreciate your meddling and telling him where to find me."

Mason waited with Jeannetta in the admitting office and, later, accompanied her to her room. She placed her recorder on the little night table, sat on the edge of the bed, and Mason took a chair beside her and held both of her hands.

"Have you so little faith in me that you brought the recorder with you?"

She removed her hand and tugged at his arm. "I believe in you with all my heart, but this gives me something to do. I can't sustain an interest in my novel, and that hasn't happened to me before, so I think I'm going to scratch it. A different story plays around in my mind, and I'm going to have to write that one as soon as I recover. That's why I need the recorder, so I can put down these ideas."

The phone rang, and Mason handed it to her.

"This is Clayton."

"Oh, Clayton. I'm so glad to hear your voice. I've decided to do it, and now that I've made up my mind, I can't wait to put it behind me."

"You have company?" He must have deduced that from the stiltedness of her conversation. She told him that she did.

"Fenwick, no doubt."

It embarrassed her to admit that Mason hadn't left the room when she got a personal call.

"Yes."

It probably didn't make sense, but she could suddenly sympathize with the filling in a sandwich, and she didn't like the feeling. "Mason is my surgeon, Clayton, though he's with me right now as a friend."

"Alright. Good luck. I'll see you in a day or so. And don't forget that I asked you to marry me, and that you haven't answered yes or no. So you're half engaged."

"We'll discuss that some other time." She hadn't thought she would ever be glad that she couldn't see Mason's eyes, but she was.

Mason reminded himself that he'd long ago mastered his temper. "A friend, huh? I can't wait to know how you'll act with me when you decide I'm your lover." He took the old keys out and looked at them; the night before, with her in his arms, he'd thought she might be his home. He tossed them about a foot high, caught them, and put them back in his pocket. Miles was after her, but what was *he* after, his conscience prodded. He had no answer; one step at a time, he told himself.

"There's nothing between Clayton and me. Surely, you don't think I could…"

He cut her off. "Of course I don't think you'd make love with me if you had an intimate relationship with another man. But Clayton Miles wants you."

"Okay, I'll print a sign telling men it's illegal to want me and stick it in my hair where everybody can see it." The laughter that rang in her words warmed his heart and eased his concern that she might get a pre-op case of nerves.

He moved closer and took her hand. "You'll have to add in big letters, 'except for Mason Fenwick,' otherwise I might find myself behind a grilled fence dressed in regulation drab blue."

She pooh-poohed the remark. "Not even a barbed-wire fence could hold you."

He draped his arm lightly around her and asked her, "Do you remember that morning on the Lido beach?" She nodded.

"Why did you run away? I know you did, because I saw that wide gauzy shirt you wore trailing behind you as you ran. I was half asleep, but I knew someone stood there watching me. The first thing a doctor learns when he begins residency is not to sleep soundly. What happened?"

Her left hand grazed his chest, and he held her closer.

"You'd be shocked. You should have seen yourself lying there at my mercy, almost completely nude with sweat beaded on your body."

He heard her swallow and told his libido to get lost.

"I almost gave in to an impulse to strip that little G-string off of you and make love to you then and there. My hand had actually reached toward you when I came to myself. If you'd felt what I did, you'd have run, too. The violation of your person would have been against the law."

He couldn't suppress the mirth that boiled up in his throat and came forth in peals of laughter.

"Baby, believe me, you wouldn't have done anything illegal, because you would have had my complete and eager cooperation. I can't think of anything that could have excited me more."

She gasped in astonishment. "On a public beach?"

He grinned as the picture of it flashed through his mind.

"Well, hell, honey. You were barely speaking to me in those days, so I'd have taken what I could get when I could get it."

"I can just see the salacious newspaper headlines for which the Italian paparazzi are famous—'African-American man and woman heat up the Lido.' Or maybe 'American blacks show how it's done.'"

"Alright. Let's not get carried away. Anyhow, I think you ought to get some rest, because you and I have an early appointment in the morning. I'll stay with you until you're asleep."

"They gave me sleeping pills, but I don't want them."

He tried to concentrate on *Essence* magazine while she prepared for bed.

"I'd sleep here in the room with you, but hospital regulations don't permit it." He kissed her with a gentle brush of his lips over hers, and his anxiety for her dissipated when she kissed him without a hint of desperation. He lowered the light and sat opposite her in a chair. Twenty minutes later, he gazed down at her, brushed her forehead with his lips, and left.

Jeannetta fought the clutches of sleep; she'd wanted to tell him something. Oh, yes. That business about having a private investigator dig into his life and give her a report on him. She shouldn't have done it, and she had to tell him so she'd have a clean slate with him. The sound of his light footsteps receded... She had to tell him...

At six o'clock the next morning, scrubbed and ready, Mason looked down at his gloved hands and remembered his chief's admonishment that miracles were performed not by doctors, but through them. He had decided not to see Jeannetta before she'd been anesthetized, because he wasn't sure how he'd react if she seemed afraid. He didn't deserve to be heard, but he said a prayer nonetheless. Then he put the past and the future out of his mind and concentrated on the now. He knew that the group assembled in the operating theater was unusually large, that the interns, residents, nurses, and surgeons not in attendance had come to watch him make it or lose it. He smiled inwardly. They were entitled to their skepticism but, by damn, he'd show them. He looked down at her sleeping peacefully, her trust evident even in unconsciousness. He extended his right hand to the head nurse, looked at the instrument she handed him, winked at her as he'd always done in earlier times, and went to work.

Four hours later, he found a telephone and called Laura.

"It went well," he told her. "She's resting in the intensive-care room. It was a neat job, my best, Laura, but I won't know for weeks, maybe longer, whether I've been completely successful."

"Well, if you did your best, I couldn't expect more. Thank you isn't much at times like this," she said, her voice breaking, "and I know all this has been hard on you. But I do thank you, Dr. Fenwick, and I have to tell you that I admire you. You get some rest and come on back soon as you can. You hear?"

"Thanks. And Laura, call me Mason." He stopped by ICU to check on Jeannetta and, as he stood there, his fingers automatically went to the pocket in which he kept his keys but, instead of them, he grasped the note that an attendant had handed him after he completed the surgery.

"'My love,'" he read. "'You've done your best, and I'm happy. I shall always be happy, and I shall always love you. This is your true calling, so, no matter what happens, stay with it. Love, Jeannetta.'" His lips brushed her cool forehead, and he turned quickly away, blowing his nose to camouflage his emotions as he strode swiftly down the hallway.

He got coffee at a take-out shop on the way home, savored it, took a quick shower, and fell into bed. "I'm not tired," he marveled, sitting up. He flipped on the radio and turned it off as soon as he heard the country music. No use going to the other stations, because he couldn't stand rock or rap either, and he didn't feel like concentrating on classical music. He needed to see Steve and Skip. He'd turned a corner, found his stride, and he had to share it with them. A call to the hospital satisfied his concern about Jeannetta, and he struck out for Steve's apartment.

His brother opened the door, and contentment washed over him as Steve welcomed him with open arms. He couldn't remember the last time they had embraced so heartily.

"Well, how did it go?"

Mason shrugged his right shoulder and brushed his fingers over his tight curls. "So far, so good."

Steve walked off a few paces, turned around, and looked at him. "That's all? What did you feel going back in there?"

Mason hadn't let himself think much about that. "I can't say, truthfully, because I tried not to think about anything except the job."

"How bad was it?" They walked to Steve's study, two men of commanding height and presence. Regarding Steve from the corner of his right eye, Mason had to wonder what his brother might have become had he been selfish and ignored his younger brother's needs.

"Another month or so and it might have been too late," he said, adding that, "it's difficult to reverse the disease after the patient loses sight. I won't know for a while whether we have a complete cure." When Steve raised an eyebrow, he amended it. "I mean I can't be certain yet that I've corrected the problem and that she's good as new. I don't expect she'll get any worse." But the operation had been a success, he reminded himself, and released a long breath.

"Want a drink?"

A half smile played around Mason's lips. His conservative brother considered daytime drinking to be a form of debauchery.

"Not until I've done an examination. She has to have an MRI, a skull X-ray, a thorough ophthalmoscopic exam. Everything. I need my wits. Jeannetta's my priority."

"You can't focus entirely on her," Steve said, clearly aghast. "You'll be a nervous wreck. Take on some other patients—they're waiting in line."

Mason watched as his brother's eyes narrowed, warning him to expect a drilling.

"You planning to quit if you don't cure her?"

Mason leaned against the edge of their father's old roll-top desk and folded his arms across his chest.

"I know you're not proud of some of my decisions, but every one of them expressed the truth as I saw it. My integrity is intact, and I take pride in that."

"Yeah. Me, too. I didn't mean to lecture, but you're getting on with your life, so it's time you forgot about that one almost-error." He grinned, and Mason thought of their father; Steve's likeness to him had made it easy for both of them to remember the man whom they had loved so much.

"Now that they all know you're human, how did they act this morning?"

"Funny," Mason said, a laugh lacing his words. "This morning, I had a room full of 'em, and they all looked as though they expected me to tear it. Man, that was a good feeling—no place to go but up. None of that idolatry I thought I loved."

"Maybe it's a good thing you slid on your rear. I can't remember the last time you came over here after surgery. I've missed these times we had when you couldn't contain your excitement after you'd taken a difficult case and succeeded. Sometimes, I wondered if I'd have to tie a lodestone on you to get you back to earth. Then, women discovered you. A physician shouldn't allow himself to become a socialite." He walked over, patted Mason on the shoulder, and must have seen the emotion mirrored in his brother's eyes, for he turned quickly away.

"I'm glad you made it back. Come on, how about some hamburgers and a beer?"

"Hamburgers sound good to me, but save the beer." In the kitchen, Mason pulled a straight-back chair from the table, straddled it, and rested his chin on his forearms.

"How about taking over my travel business? You can do it. I'd be a silent partner, and knowing you were in charge would free me to concentrate on my patients."

Steve looked him in the eye. "I've told you a hundred times that you don't owe me anything. You're my brother. Whatever I did, I'd gladly do all over again." And he would, too, Mason realized.

"There's a woman who takes that tour every year. A high-school teacher. She once asked me if I had a brother and, when I told her about you, she said the two of you were cut from the same cloth. At least, take the tour. You'll like her." Interesting. Steve's hamburgers needed a lot of attention all of a sudden.

"Why do I have to wait until next May to meet her?"

Mason tried not to show his astonishment. "Good point," was all he said, but he made a mental note to get in touch with Darlene Jones when the tour returned.

"What are you planning to do about Skip? He wants to be a doctor?" Mason meant to bite his hamburger and nicked his tongue.

"This is good stuff, and it would be even better if you'd left some of this onion in that bin. Skip's a great example of what some care and a little help can do. If he makes good grades, I'll send him to school."

Steve pushed his plate aside and leaned back in his chair.

Now what? "Skip wants you to adopt him, and he says his aunt wouldn't mind."

Mason coughed up the crumbs that stuck in his windpipe and reached for water. "This is a day for surprises. What else did he say?"

Steve reached for a pickle, pointed it toward Mason and grinned. "Well, if you want to know, he said he tricked you when he asked you to be his big brother because, from the outset, what he wanted was to be your son. You might say he wormed his way in."

Mason couldn't suppress an outright laugh. "Slick little devil." He glanced at Steve, who watched him closely.

"He's very special to me, Steve, and he needs me. He needs you, too. I'm going to listen to what he has to say." He washed his hands, stretched out on the sofa, and went to sleep.

Several hours later, he jumped up, startled. He'd have to get used to that beeper again; it was one of the things he hadn't missed during his hiatus from medicine.

"Dr. Fenwick." That sounded strange, too, as he'd gotten accustomed to referring to himself as "Fenwick."

"An ICU nurse at the hospital called to say that Miss Rollins is awake and asking for you," Viv said. His stomach unknotted, and he breathed deeply. Mention of a nurse had sent his heart racing and twisted his belly.

"Should I start looking for another job, Mr. Fen…I mean, Dr. Fenwick?"

"Viv, for pete's sake. I'm not closing the travel agency. In fact, you'll probably get a raise, because you're going to have more work. Anything I need to do there?" Assured that there wasn't, he headed for the hospital. He'd done it. He hailed a taxi that seemed to stand still even as it moved and, as he walked through the hospital door, he strove for professional decorum, but when he got off the elevator, he chucked it and ran.

## Chapter 9

Jeannetta shifted in bed, reaching for the elusive sun rays as she tripped through the beautiful forest. Great elms, oaks, and pines, heavy with branches, bowed as she drifted among them; hyacinths and roses showered her with perfume; and the squirrels, raccoons, foxes, and bears smiled at her with greenish-brown eyes as she passed. She wandered out of the forest and down to the beach and dug up a handful of sand but, when she tried to sift it through her fingers, it wouldn't leave her palm. Four little black dolls that she had crocheted for the Edwin Gould Foundation to distribute to poor children at Christmas danced around her. And from somewhere far away, Mason called her. But his voice was such a lovely masculine velvet that she didn't want to answer for fear he'd stop. She smiled in joyful appreciation. The animals ran away, the dolls disappeared, and the forest, beach, and ocean dissolved into a lovely white cloud.

"Darling, talk to me. Let me hear your voice. Answer me,

sweetheart. How do you feel?" The blur slowly disappeared, and he was there, close. His own masculine scent, his special aura, enveloped her, and she knew that the hand holding hers belonged to him. His lips brushed her forehead, and she had to struggle not to slide back into the Heaven from which she'd just come.

"Come on, baby, say something to me. Anything." She squeezed his hand, and her face dissolved into that luminous smile that always thrilled him to his soul. Thank God, they'd passed the first and worst hurdle.

"Hi." He needed to hear a few more words so that he could judge her speech, but that one was worth a gold mine.

"Hi," he said, as casually as he could. "How do you feel?"

"It is over? What time is it?"

"About seven-thirty." He did a few simple tests and, satisfied with the results, sat beside her bed.

"Did you leave me with any hair?" she asked, as though reluctant to know the answer. The strength of her voice pleased him.

"Plenty. When the bandage comes off, you'll be able to comb your hair so that it hides that bare spot. In a few months, you won't know it was shaved." She patted his hand, and her smile tugged at his heart.

"Where were you just now, honey?" He listened to her tale and almost wished he'd been there with her.

"I'm glad you had such a pleasant adventure. It means things are going well."

She reached toward him.

"Could I give you a kiss?" she asked him, her voice low and sultry. The woman had a penchant for testing his self-control at the most inconvenient times. He grimaced at the thought of what a hot kiss would do to him right then and stood, removing himself from temptation.

"Don't you think we'd better wait a while for that? Wouldn't want to raise your blood pressure," he joked, though there was little likelihood of it. She mumbled a few incoherent words, which he recognized as evidence of grogginess.

"You always jack up my blood pressure," she said, her words distinct and husky. "I only have to think about you, and it shoots up."

"Really?" He sat down beside her bed again. "I'd like to hear some more of this."

She smiled, shakily, he thought.

"That's because you know you're sexy and…hmmm. Men like you should be banned. We females don't stand a chance around you." She nodded sleepily, and he settled back, enjoying himself.

"I thought you'd gotten your revenge for yourself and half the other women in this country, considering what you've laid on me." He didn't want to overtax her, so he brushed her cheek lightly with his finger and rose to leave. This little touch wasn't the kind of contact he needed with her, but she smiled in return, and his heart fluttered in gratitude. He glanced at the IV that sent life-sustaining fluid into her body, checked her vital signs, and started toward the door.

"Mason…" He'd never get enough of the sweet sound of her voice, trusting, soft, and seductive. He turned to face her.

"There's something about your hands. Long tapered fingers. Smooth and perfect as though you'd never worked. Beautiful hands. First time I…saw…looked at them, I imagined… wondered how they'd feel on my naked body. Hmmm."

He walked back and leaned over her. "And how do they feel?" he asked, keeping his voice low.

"Hmmm. Hot. They make me want to scream for you to get all…all…" Her voice trailed off.

He should be ashamed of himself for taking advantage of her, but he wasn't. He'd been through hell in the last fifteen hours, and he deserved a boost. He watched her as she slept, kissed her cheek again and left, fingering the keys in his pocket. In about two months, he'd have some decisions to make.

Jeannetta gazed out of the same window that had framed her dreams as a child. Yellow leaves peppered the green mountainside, signaling the approach of autumn, though the heat of mid-August still nourished the garden and the little animals that munched on its produce. She wondered about Laura's strange behavior. Her sister couldn't have cared for her more faithfully since they'd decided she would recuperate at the Hideaway, but Jeannetta knew she hadn't mistaken her sister's coolness. She busied herself by dictating notes for her novel, since Mason had urged her not to strain her eyes with reading or writing, limiting her options for whiling away the time. She had begun a new novel, fully cognizant of Mason's role in her decision to drop the other one; he'd shown her how special a man could be, that he could care deeply for you and still not let you inside of him. She picked up her old standby, the guitar that her father had given her on her seventeenth birthday, and began to strum and sing, but a headache and the needlelike sensations around her wound reduced the pleasure that the music usually gave her.

She wondered how much hair she had; a thick bandage covered most of her head, and she had to sleep on her left side. She didn't care how it looked, though, because what it symbolized meant more to her than her thick crop of wooly hair. Mason had promised her that the wound would heal in a few weeks and that, if she wanted to, she could wear a wig. She didn't think she would.

She wrapped a yellow scarf around her head and ambled into the breakfast room with the intention of serving herself from the luncheon buffet table, and what she saw made her

think her heart had tumbled to the pit of her stomach. She
muffled a gasp and blinked her eyes, wondering whether she
had lost her sanity. Surely she wasn't looking at Clayton Miles
perched on a stool at the breakfast counter and staring, as
though lost, into the eyes of her enraptured sister. She opened
her mouth to announce her presence and stopped herself as
Clayton spoke.

"I'm not free to say what I feel, Laura, because I'm committed. I don't have to tell you that I'm sorry. You have to
know it. Never in my fifty-two years have I felt anything so
strongly. Forgive me." She watched Laura, a woman without
guile or feminine ego, and understood for the first time the
true meaning of loneliness.

"Nothing to forgive," she heard Laura say. "I've been a
wallflower all of my life, and I don't expect that to change.
I'm average, maybe even less, and that's the way people have
always treated me. So don't worry—I'm used to it." Jeannetta
flinched at Laura's self-derision.

"If I had the right, I'd make you see that you're talking nonsense, that you're precious. You're the most…" Jeannetta spun
around and left; she didn't want to hear it, and she didn't want
them to see her. Clayton married? Then how had he planned
to marry her? Had he deliberately set out to mislead her sister? And why? She walked back to her room, taking care not
to hurry and make herself dizzy. But she did that automatically, because she didn't think of herself, but of Clayton. She'd
considered him a man of principle; now she wasn't so sure.
She turned the curve at the top of the stairs and bumped into
Connie, the chambermaid.

"Connie, is Mr. Miles a guest here?"

"Yes, ma'am. Since yesterday. He must have come yesterday afternoon, I think, 'cause he had dinner here last night
and I sure made his bed up this morning."

Jeannetta wished she could check his arrival and departure dates on the office computer, but Mason had forbade her to use one until he gave her the okay. She walked on toward her room and, on a hunch, turned and called Connie. Better not to ask the woman if Clayton had been there before, because Connie had perfected gossip to a fine art. She chose her words carefully.

"When was the last time Mr. Miles was a guest?"

"A little over a week ago, but he only stayed a couple of days."

Jeannetta nodded. Maybe he'd visited her in the hospital while she slept, or when she'd still been under anesthesia. How peculiar. When had Clayton gotten to know Laura well enough to speak to her as he had? She couldn't figure it out. With his money, a twelve-room, low-profit ski lodge couldn't be the reason. She sat down at the little desk in her room, picked up the phone, and ordered her lunch.

Jeannetta had never known Laura to be the object of a man's affection; maybe it was better for her to have the experience, even with a man committed to someone else than to spend her life without it. She didn't know, and didn't think she had the right to judge. She and Laura had always been so close, but lately… Maybe she'd better not mention it. The phone rang.

"How's my favorite patient?"

She grasped her chest to stop her runaway heart. "Feeling fine. She'd like to see her favorite doctor."

"Really? I promised Skip I'd help him apply to the YWHA for a music tutor. It'll be late before I can get up to Pilgrim, but if you want to see me, count on it. Any vacant rooms in the Hideaway?"

"I don't know, but you may sleep on the sofa in my sitting room if you don't want to sleep with me."

You could almost see him bristle. "What kind of remark is that? You think I'm a piece of deadwood? Woman, don't you

remember what happened the last time I was in your bed?"
Fear rioted through her body. Had she been in bed with him?
She had or he wouldn't have asked her that question. Dear
Lord, what else had she forgotten? She'd be cool about it, as
though it didn't matter.

"Uh…"

"Don't you?" he interrupted. "Well, sweetheart, that doesn't
compare to what I need with you now. Not by a mile."

Jeannetta had to force back a swell of apprehension and
tell herself to stay calm. Maybe he hadn't meant that they'd
actually made love with each other. After all, they had shared
some sizzling kisses, and some of their petting had taken them
right to the brink. She'd play it safe.

"You've pulled out the stops more than once, so I'm not
sure which one of those heady sessions you're talking about.
You want to be more specific and refresh my memory a little bit?"

"Don't tease me, Jeannetta."

Tension gripped her as the seriousness of his voice warned
her that she had a problem. Her fingers clutched the bed sheet.

"We made love in my room in a Zimbabwe hotel," he went
on in a dry, hollow voice, "and in your bed in your house up
there in Pilgrim. Do you remember, or don't you? This is your
doctor speaking now. Do you?"

Dumfounded, she struggled to remember, and her delay
in answering must have increased his suspicion, because his
tone lost its lover's groove and assumed the determined pro-
fessionalism of the doctor.

"What plane did you take from Zimbabwe to New York?"

"Mason, I'm…I…"

"What happened after you left Nairobi?" She knew from
the huskiness in his voice that he was anxious about her condition, that the man warred with the doctor for expression of
feelings. She fudged the truth.

"That escapes me right now, 'cause you're pressuring me. Anyway, I was teasing…or I think I was. I remember us talking about your hands and me in a forest. Look…I think I'm mixing things up. I don't remember Zimbabwe, or you in my house down the street. I… Oh, Mason, is that bad?" She paused. "Mason, did Clayton Miles come to see me while I was in the hospital?"

Mason had begun to think that she wouldn't have a problem with short-term memory.

"Miles? Yeah, he did. On consecutive days. Are you asking me about that because you don't remember?"

Her answer was too long coming, and he knew she was denying the truth.

"Uh… Oh, Mason, I don't remember. Will it ever come back?"

"Usually. And soon. Don't try to remember things, and don't upset yourself about it."

"Are you coming up here tonight?"

"I'll be there, but don't wait up. If you're asleep, and if it isn't too late, I'll wake you." She could bet he'd be up there, because he didn't like what he'd heard. To think that she didn't remember the powerful, gut-searing way in which she'd pitched her inhibitions and loved him until she'd taken everything from him but his soul. And he'd bound her to him as securely as flesh could cement itself to flesh. But she didn't remember, and that made her vulnerable to the ubiquitous Clayton Miles.

"Okay."

She sounded reluctant. He'd learned that he wasted time when he tried to anticipate Jeannetta's thoughts. So he waited.

"I'll connect you to the desk," she continued, as though her mind were elsewhere. "Ask for a double room and, if they have one, bring Skip. I'd love to meet him, and he'd enjoy this environment."

He hadn't expected that one. "Skip's looking for a job for the next month. He had one delivering homemade bread, but his employer took a month's vacation, and he needs work." He didn't want Skip sidetracked from his goal of saving a hundred dollars each summer month toward his education, but a short stay out of the city wouldn't hurt him.

"Bring him, Mason. You can never tell what might happen."

Mason smiled inwardly. "You've got that right. Once Skip enters your life, I can promise you it's never the same. See you later."

Laura brought up her lunch. Jeannetta had thought she'd have sent it up by one of the help.

"Thanks, hon," Jeannetta said. "I didn't expect you to bring it, because I know how busy you are. You work from the time you get up until you hit the sheets at night, and I'm just adding to your workload."

"Nonsense. Gives me a chance to see how you are." Her words lacked conviction, and Jeannetta could see that she'd forced the smile.

"Laura, what's the matter?"

"Nothing. Maybe I'm just tired." It wasn't like Laura to avoid looking at the person to whom she spoke, but she did just that. Jeannetta stared at her sister, who turned to leave without a semblance of a conversation. Laura, who never missed an opportunity to delve into your private affairs, hadn't mentioned Mason's name.

"Sit down a minute, Laura." Jeannetta didn't believe in procrastinating, especially when it came to Laura, who could hold a grudge or nourish a misunderstanding until clearing up the matter became impossible.

"Something's happened to us, Laura, and it's not good. What is it and what brought it on?"

"Has anything changed?" Laura asked with an unlikely look of innocence.

"You're not talking to me, Laura. You're fencing. Have I done something?" She watched, disbelieving, as her sister sighed deeply and curled up her thin lips at the edges in an expression that Jeannetta hadn't previously observed.

"No. You haven't done anything, Jeanny, except be yourself. You never had to do anything. You only had to *be*."

Stunned, Jeannetta asked her, "Whatever are you talking about?"

"Haven't you ever noticed how different we are? No, I guess you haven't, because you've had it all. You're beautiful, with your flawless, ebony complexion, perfect face and figure, lovely hands, and soft voice. And you didn't do one thing to deserve it—just an accident of birth. But it's brought you so much. Everything. My hair is straight, but it's thin and stringy, while yours is long and thick, and you can do whatever you want with it. I'm forgettable, short and dumpy, but you've got a model's height and a siren's figure. I've worked so hard to make this Hideaway a four-star lodge that my hands look as if they belong to an old woman. Mom and Dad left me the controlling interest in it, because you were too precious for this kind of work. I love you, but I resent you. I always have."

Her cup clattered in its saucer, spilling tea in her lap, as Jeannetta tried to steady her hand and place the saucer on her lunch tray. With trembling fingers she clutched at her throat. Dr. Farmer's revelation that she had a brain lesion hadn't given her a bigger or more alarming jolt than Laura's words.

"Laura! You don't mean…" The thought trailed off when she looked into her older sister's implacable gaze. "I'm sorry. I never guessed. I always looked up to you, loved and admired you as my older sister, never dreaming how you felt. Does this have anything to do with your not telling me that Clayton is here?"

Her sister was the old Laura again, and she didn't allow an expression to cross her face.

"Did he come here to see you, or me?" Jeannetta persisted.

"Both of us. You might as well know that if it weren't for you, I'd have a man of my own at last. After all these years of watching you and all the other women I know with their men, I'd have my own."

Jeannetta stared at her in astonishment, unable to suppress an audible release of breath.

"Why don't you tell him about Mason?" Laura went on. "That the two of you are lovers. Why do you keep him dangling like you do Jethro? No wonder Alma's upset."

Jeannetta jumped up from the bed, stood over Laura, and shook her finger.

"Don't be cruel, Laura. You know I don't dangle Jethro, that I avoid him. And you also know Alma's paranoid about that man. She's welcome to him. Where did you get the idea that Mason and I are lovers and that I'm dangling Clayton?" She bit her tongue when she remembered Mason's words earlier that day. "From what I heard him say to you this morning, you'd better be careful. He's a married man."

It was Laura's turn to bristle. "Who told you that? It's not true. He said he's committed to someone, and when I asked him a few minutes ago who it was, he said he asked you to marry him so he could take care of you. He's trying to make up for his past mistakes. Either marry him or tell him you can't because you love Mason. You're playing your cards pretty close to your chest, anyhow. When the illustrious Dr. Fenwick finds out that you had him investigated and that you plotted to meet him so you could get him to operate on you, he may decide you had an ulterior motive for going to bed with him."

"*Laura!* For God's sake, what's gotten into you? Yes, I schemed to get to meet him, but all that happened before I ever saw him." She stopped speaking, and her gaze bore into Laura's steady stare.

"What gives you the right to say I've been intimate with Mason? I haven't but, if I had, it wouldn't be anybody's business but ours. We're both free, and I love him."

"Maybe you do, but if he finds out all of this, you'll be in the same boat as I'm in." Her face must have reflected the alarm she felt, because Laura's belligerence suddenly faded. "Don't worry, he won't know it from me, but you remember that old saying, 'Birds don't go north in winter.'"

"No, they don't," Jeannetta replied after musing over her sister's words. "I gave Clayton my card so he'd know where to find me, but it looks like he found you." Laura's breath quickened and a deep crimson brought a youthful glow to her round face. Jeannetta reached out to her. She didn't want to hurt her sister, and especially not about herself and Clayton Miles.

"You're telling me that you and Clayton care for each other?" The older woman fidgeted nervously, but she looked Jeannetta in the eye and nodded.

"Then I misunderstood what I heard. He's free, Laura. I never intended to marry him, and I told him his offer was too generous. I've never hidden from him my feelings for Mason. I'll straighten it out." Laura's face brightened so quickly and so luminously that Jeannetta's lower lip dropped.

"Clayton is a wonderful man," Laura said, barely above a whisper. "If he'd wanted you, I would have understood. He hasn't told me exactly what he feels, but he's made me know he cares."

"When did he get here?"

"Last night. You had gone to bed. He… Oh, Jeanny, when I knew he'd be here, I almost went out of my mind, waiting. The feeling… It's like something's consuming me. Like something burst wide open in me and is just waiting for him to close it." Jeannetta pulled Laura into her arms and hugged her for a long time, stroking her back, healing their wound.

With wisdom she hadn't applied to herself, she held Laura at arm's length. "You're in the wrong place, hon. When Mason gets here tonight, I won't leave him alone while I chat with you."

Laura stood there, letting her know that their chasm hadn't been breached, that their slate wasn't yet clean. "Are you going to…to talk with Clayton?" So that was it. Laura wanted Clayton freed of his presumed obligations.

"Ask him to come up here in about half an hour. I'll talk with him. And you get out of that apron and those green slacks and put on something pretty. Make it bright-colored and, preferably, knit fabric. Something feminine and clinging. Put on some perfume and go up to his room and wait for him."

"I couldn't do *that!*"

Jeannetta laughed aloud as Laura gaped at her. "It's time you got over being so straight-laced and gave in to your feelings. I remember a time when I probably wouldn't have said that, but I wasn't in love then. Now, go on. You're in for something special."

Laura whirled around with more speed than Jeannetta associated with her sister. "You're not saying that I…I mean that we…I…" She let the thought die, but Jeannetta was now the wiser, the more experienced.

"I'm suggesting that you loosen up and enjoy him, that you do whatever feels right. Now, go on."

Jeannetta remade her bed, slipped into a simple green coat-dress, and went into her sitting room. If Clayton Miles was misleading her sister, he'd pay for it.

Mason looked over his new medical office, checking it against his specifications. He'd gotten what he wanted, a large suite at Ninety-sixth Street and Fifth Avenue—the dividing line of wealth and poverty, because he intended to serve both. He'd have office hours from twelve noon to six-thirty weekdays, leaving mornings free for surgery. He'd see the wealthy on Tuesdays and Thursdays, those less able to pay on Mondays and Wednesdays, and those who couldn't afford to pay on Fridays. Some rich people were uncomfortable around people who weren't like themselves, and he needed their patronage in order to serve those who couldn't afford to pay. But when patients had an emergency, he'd scotch that schedule.

He liked the restful colors, sand and a soft, yellowish-green. He'd hung two landscapes, silkscreen prints by the painter Louis Mailou Jones in his waiting room, and a nearly life-size photo of the dancer Judith Jamison dressed as Josephine Baker hung in his private office. He could still remember how she'd held him spellbound on the Broadway stage in *Sophisticated Ladies*. Limited-edition prints by Selma Glass decorated each of his examining rooms. He loved the great painters, from Michelangelo and Rembrandt to Miró and Catlett, but he'd hung some originals by less expensive contemporary African-Americans in his office. He meant to put captions under each, so that his patients would know about the painters' lives.

Mason looked at his watch as Skip bounded into the waiting room. "Skip. I've told you a dozen times that a man is worth no more than his word. If you say you'll be here at two o'clock, I don't expect you to walk in here at twenty minutes past. And I don't ever want to have to repeat this. Got it?"

"Yeah. Sorry, but I…"

"Skip. Yes, sir. I'm old enough to be your father." The boy's sheepish expression belied his character. Now what?

"Yes, sir. That's what I've been getting at. Sort of. Why can't you adopt me and be my real…?"

"What the…? Say, man, what is this?" The boy's eyes rounded, then he narrowed his eyes and took in his surroundings. Mason observed him closely; Skip never bothered to pretend what he didn't feel, and hostility flared from his piercing eyes.

"Ain't this a doctor's office?"

Mason stared right back at him. If he didn't deal with it openly and honestly, he'd lose the trust he'd so carefully built.

"*Isn't* this a doctor's office? Yes, it is." Skip moved around jerkily. Prowl was more like it, Mason decided.

"But I thought you said meet you at your office. You ain't no doctor. What *is* this, man?" He ran his hand over his hair and pierced Mason with a hostile stare. "You been acting strange lately." He paused, less certain, and asked, "Are you a doctor?"

"Don't say 'ain't,' and yes, I'm a neuro-ophthalmologist. I…"

"Can the lessons, man. What about your travel agency?" Mason explained as succinctly as he could, and ended with, "And you are not to address me as 'man' anymore." Mason could see the boy's gathering rage, as his jaw worked involuntarily and he began to clench and unclench his fists. He sought quickly to dispel it.

"You don't have to like everything I do, but if you're going to hang out with me, you'd better learn to respect my decisions, and fast."

Confusion replaced the boy's rage.

"How come you didn't say nothin' about it when I told you I wanted to be a doctor?"

"I didn't see it as relevant."

"You didn't see…" The boy resumed his catlike prowling around the room, slapping his fist against his palm. "Let me get this straight. If it hadn't been for this…this bird of yours, you'd still be a travel manager?"

At that, Mason conceded himself the right to a show of temper.

"You've got a problem with that?"

Skip didn't yield.

"I don't know, man. I mean, Mason. Like I'm dying to be just like you, but if I get to be a doctor, I sure as h— I sure ain't gonna check out and go around the world. I don't think I like this."

In for a penny, in for a pound.

"Sit down, Skip." He related his story in detail, beginning with his near-accident while operating, sparing nothing. "Being a doctor is more than glamour, more than ego and self-importance. It's healing sick people, but when you take chances with their lives and do it for self-aggrandizement, there comes a time when you have to stop and take stock of what you're doing and why. I reached that point the morning my hand slipped and my patient almost paid for it with her life. I realized at that moment that some force beyond me, greater than I, had saved the woman's life, that I wasn't infallible and that I was capable of irreversible damage to my patients. I didn't quit because I got scared, but because I had dared to play God and I found out that I'm not all-powerful."

He didn't have to be told that he had deeply impressed Skip. The boy sat watching him as though mesmerized.

"I wasn't accusing you. I just couldn't understand how you could give up what I want so badly. You were A-one, right?"

Mason nodded. "Yes, but I got cocky, and that's dangerous."

"So what about Jeanny? Is she your patient or your bird?"

"Jeanny?"

"Jeannetta's too long a word."

Mason laughed. His hours with Skip gave him so much pleasure that he sometimes wondered if he could ever repay the boy.

"She's my girl and my patient, but that's an accident, and it's not a good thing."

"Is she okay? Nothing went wrong?"

Chills danced down his spine as the possible scenarios flashed through his mind.

"She's okay and nothing went wrong. I expect she'll be good as new in a couple of months." He watched Skip rub his chin, run his hand over his tight curls, and shake his head.

"Gee, man, weren't you scared walking in there after three years and picking something outta somebody's head? Especially when she was your bird?"

Mason smiled to himself at Skip's choice of words.

"I didn't let myself think of anything but what I had to do. I wasn't scared, but I had a good talk with God when I'd finished. We'd better get moving."

"Like wow, man… I mean, Mason. How big is this place we're going?" Mason laughed at the boy's enthusiasm and patted him on the head.

"Bigger than you are. Did you bring your biology books?"

"I brought all of my books," Skip said, and patted the school bag that had been a present from Mason.

"Okay, let's get started." He glanced around, admiring what he saw, glad to be back where he knew he belonged.

"Who's this trip for, Mason? Me or you?" Mason raised an eyebrow at the boy's astute question.

"Both of us. This is your big chance to get some polish." *And mine to find out where I'm going,* he added to himself.

"Come in." Jeannetta looked at her watch. Nearly four hours had elapsed since Laura had left her room. Had a dread of seeing her detained him? "Hello, Clayton."

"Hello." He rushed to kiss her cheek, but she sensed a new reserve in him, and emotional distance where previously none had existed.

"How are you, my dear?" Banalities. Forced conversation. He meant to stick to his promise to marry her until she voluntarily released him, though he had to know that that kind of gallantry had made a lot of people miserable.

"I'm glad to see you, Clayton. How long have you been here?" Maybe she shouldn't put him on the spot, but she meant to find out as best she could and as quickly as possible whether he intended to hurt Laura. He looked her straight in the eye and she had the uneasy feeling that he'd judged her. Then he raised his head and looked toward the ceiling.

"I asked you to marry me, Jeannetta. More than once I've told you that I'd be honored to have you as my wife. I'll be happy knowing that you're well-cared for. What is your answer?"

"I'm honored, Clayton." He paled visibly—dark though he was—his eyes widened and his breath quickened. She couldn't help marveling when his left hand jerked voluntarily toward his chest, only to have him force it into his pants pocket. She put him at ease.

"I appreciate your gesture more than you can know, but I'm sure you'll understand that I can't marry you when I love another man."

Air flowed out of him with such force that he released it through his lips, and his entire upper body sagged as the tension eased out of him.

"Are you going to marry Fenwick?"

She shook her head. "That's irrelevant. The point is that he's the one, and I can't marry anybody else. So don't worry. I'm going to be fine."

"Has he told you that the operation succeeded?" he asked doggedly, causing her to wonder whether she'd been unfair to him.

"He won't know for a few weeks or maybe months. Are you in love with my sister?"

Both of his eyebrows arched sharply. "She told you?"

Annoyance pricked at her. How else would she know?

"She told me that you wanted to declare yourself but couldn't, because you were committed." Jeannetta couldn't help remembering how she had allowed Alma to think that she encouraged Jethro's advances in revenge for Alma's having seduced Jethro and tricked him into marriage, although Jethro had been engaged to Jeannetta. She had tried several times to set it right, but Alma's vicious gossip and supercilious behavior had discouraged decency on Jeannetta's part. So she had let the woman worry. But that lesson was all the motivation she needed to avoid future tangled relationships. She stared hard at Clayton, scrutinizing him in a way that must have surprised him.

"You and I are friends, or so you said. But you'd been here twenty-four hours and hadn't greeted me. Surely you wouldn't marry a woman if you felt that way about her."

He's a fighter, she realized, when he straightened his shoulders, tilted his head and wordlessly dared her to question his integrity.

"I didn't want to hurt Laura by going to you, and, though I would have honored my proposal, I dreaded knowing I'd have to—feeling as I do about your sister."

"Laura looks and acts tough," she told him, "but she isn't. People think I'm fragile, but they're invariably surprised to learn otherwise. If anybody hurts my sister, they'll hear from me. You get the message?"

His wan smile and cold eyes told her that he wouldn't take much more, but his mild words denied it.

"Too bad you think you have to warn me, though that was more of a threat. You'll learn that I'm honorable."

"I'll be watching for it, too," she replied, refusing to weaken her stance. He grasped her hand before she could move away.

"This isn't the way friends should talk to each other. I'd prefer to have your blessing."

She tried to release her hand, but he held it firmly.

* * *

"What are you doing up here? I want you to move around." At the sound of Mason's voice, her glance shot toward the door. "You're not to stay in…wh…what's going on here? What the hell *is* this?"

"Mason!" She smiled, her heart bursting with joy at the sight of him, as Clayton released her hand, but her smile evaporated when she noticed the scalding fury reflected in Mason's dark eyes.

"What is it? Oh," she exclaimed, when she followed his gaze to Clayton. "You remember Clayton Miles, don't you?"

"Bad pennies don't *let* you forget them. So give it to me straight, Jeannetta. What is this man to you?"

You'd think a man of his brilliance wouldn't need her public declaration.

"He's a man who wants my sister, Laura," she said, mainly for Clayton's benefit.

"If he can't see how you feel about him, you ought to let him sweat!" Clayton said as he left the room, but if Mason heard that, his next words didn't indicate it.

"If he's nothing to you, why were you holding his hand?"

Her joy at seeing him didn't mean he couldn't make her mad, and she bristled.

"How did you get the temerity to walk into my room without knocking or having yourself announced?" He folded his arms across his chest, accentuating his maleness and teasing her with his provocative posture.

"'Scuse me, baby. I wanted to surprise you." The natural seductiveness of his low, husky voice addled her, and she rubbed her arms and swallowed while his gaze pierced her. She watched, mesmerized, while his eyes changed to greenish-brown, and she got a whiff of his man's scent and felt moisture on her skin. Like a hawk, he watched her, and she took a few steps backward, knowing that he'd come after

her. She sprang to him when he held out his arms and lost
herself in his drugging kiss. His lips, his skin, his smell be-
sotted her, and she had to hide her face in the curve of his
neck while she fought for composure.

"I didn't mean what I said," she murmured. If he'd thought
she did, he wouldn't be holding her. He had wanted to see her
face light up when he walked into her room, but conceded
that he shouldn't have done it. He held her away and gave her
what he hoped was a stern look.

"We have to avoid these hot scenes, honey, because I don't
want you to get overly upset. Anger is just as detrimental as
passion. Try not to get excited." He had to laugh at her raised
eyebrow and rueful expression.

"Where's Skip?" Jeannetta asked.

"Downstairs in the office at the computer. He was as happy
sitting there as a worm in a barrel of apples."

"I want to meet him." He walked them to a floor lamp and
removed the shade.

"Time enough. I want to examine your eyes." He dressed
the wound.

The cool early morning breeze of late August drifted into
the room, and Mason grabbed a fistful of it and stretched his
long body, his arms extended toward the ceiling. He glanced
toward the other bed and had to laugh, though he was barely
awake. Skip sat up in bed waiting for Mason to open his eyes.
"I'll go back to New York the day before school starts," the
boy said at the end of a long and rapid discourse. "Since you're
going to get a place for my aunt Mabel, and I won't have to
worry about her, I can stay up here. Can't I?"

He heard the worry and anxiety in the boy's voice.

"You really want to stay up here for the next six weeks?
This room's expensive."

"Laura said I can have the maid's room, since she lives at home with her folks. And she said I can mow the grass, wash all the windows, polish all the floors, dry-clean the carpets, wax her car, and a couple of other things she named. I'll get the place ready for winter, and she'll pay me eight bucks an hour, room and board. Man...I mean, Mason, that's money." Mason wanted Skip to stay at the Hideaway, but he didn't like the idea of his doing such heavy work.

"Skip, that's hard work for a twelve-year-old. Whose idea was it?"

The boy grinned cockily. "Mine. If there's any work around, I find it. Okay?" That's what he'd thought.

"We'll see."

"*Merde,* man. I work that hard at my aunt's place and don't get a cent. Just think, I can put fifty dollars a day in the bank. That's twenty-one hundred bucks." Skip jumped off the bed. "You're not going to make me give that up, are you?"

Mason yawned. He'd gotten accustomed to Skip's bursts of energy, and he'd handle this one with some words to Laura.

"I'll think about it, and watch your language. You aren't the only one who's studied French."

"Okay. So how come you didn't stay with your bird last night?"

Mason had to stifle a laugh; the boy was incorrigible.

"Skip, do not refer to Jeannetta as my bird, and try being your age. This is not a subject for children, of which, believe it or not, you are one." He grinned broadly at Skip's expression of amazement. "And, son, men mind their business when it comes to such things. You shower first, and make it snappy. I'm ready for breakfast."

He watched the boy dash into the bathroom, and the memory of Steve's sacrifices for his own well-being settled in his mind. Was he about to take on an even greater responsibility? And what if Jeannetta didn't want to mother someone else's twelve-year-old?

## Chapter 10

Jeannetta had never thought she'd have occasion to envy Laura her relationship with a man, but when she walked into the kitchen and saw the glow on her sister's face she could only stare at the transformation and know that Clayton had brought it about. Feminine softness radiated from Laura, her movements and gestures had taken on a new daintiness, and her fair complexion reddened whenever she risked a glance at Clayton, who seemed unable to look at anything or anyone but Laura. If she'd made love with Mason, wouldn't she know it, and wouldn't she react to him as Laura did to Clayton? She knew she loved Mason, but she sensed a peculiar gap in their relationship. She turned and went to find him.

The handsome young boy was talking animatedly to Mason, as though pleading his case for something important, and she saw that he had the man's rapt attention.

"You must be Skip," Jeannetta said as she walked toward him with her right hand extended.

The boy started to meet her, turned back, and asked Mason, "This is your...I mean, is this Jeanny?"

"Yes. I'm Jeannetta."

"Wow, man." A grin spread across his face, and his whole visage brightened as though a floodlight had been turned on him, and Jeannetta knew she would like him. Still, her raised eyebrow bespoke her astonishment when he declared, with a hefty shot of confidence, "It's time I met you, 'cause me and you are gonna be seeing a lot of each other."

She glanced at Mason for an explanation, but he limited his visible reaction to a dry smile.

"Skip has problems trying to be a child and keeping his imagination in check." The boy whirled around.

"But me and her are gonna be tight. Right?" Jeannetta saw the boy's desperate need for love and, when Mason walked to him and slung an arm loosely around his shoulders, she understood that the man she loved knew how to give it.

"Stop lapsing into that street language, and speak the way I've taught you. If you behave yourself, I'm sure she'll want you to be her friend," Mason told him, adding, "Now stop worrying and go talk with Laura. You may work five hours a day, but not a minute more, and you're not to get on a ladder that's over six feet high. Got it?"

"Yes, sir. But...Mason..."

*"Skip!"*

"Okay, Okay."

Jeannetta couldn't miss the parental pride with which Mason watched Skip as the boy sped from the lounge. "He's very attached to you."

"Yes. He is. He'll keep you busier than an ant, but he's a great kid. If you still want to go fishing, we'd better do it before the sun gets too high."

"Can Skip come along?" Her heart fluttered at the suggestion in his obsidian eyes when they swept slowly over her with half-raised lids.

"What's the matter? I'm boring, or you don't trust your virtue with me out there in the woods?" A flirtatious grin added fuel to his seductive glance and wicked tone.

She laid her head to one side, and rested her right knuckle on her right hip bone. "Are you playing with me? I don't seem to remember your getting this familiar with me. Not that I don't like it—I'm just burning my brain up trying to figure you out. I understand you when you're being the doctor, but when you're somewhere between suitor and lover, I'm lost."

"The doctor told you not to tax yourself trying to remember, but the lover is going mad wanting to hold you to your words and behavior when you spun out of this world in his arms."

She touched the bandage on her head, winced, and smiled with what he knew involved a good deal of effort to ignore the discomfort.

"When I say out of this world, I mean heaven on earth," he emphasized. He watched her swallow hard just before her lips parted and her eyelids dropped, the way they did when desire claimed her, and he told himself that they would recapture what they'd lost, even if her memory of their loving didn't return.

"I can think of at least one way for you to restore my memory of that in a hurry."

"Honey, if you're thinking that, don't mention it to me, because I remember, and I don't need that provocation. When your doctor says you're well, you won't have to ask. Trust me." He tried to soften the words with a smile, but he didn't feel like smiling. He picked up their fishing gear and a folding chair.

"What's that for?" She pointed to the chair.

"Jeannetta, I know you don't like having me coddle you, but cut me some slack here. You are recovering from serious major surgery, and I have to see that you act like it. I can't stop being your doctor just because I've got something going for you. Come on." He settled Jeannetta on the short pier at the edge of the lake, baited her hook, slipped off his fatigues and dived into the water.

Jeannetta forgot about the fish. Mason's long, lean physique with the rippling muscles, slim hips, and broad chest presented a feast to her eyes. Clothed in the tiniest of swimsuits, the vision brought back the memory of him lying in the sand on the Lido beach wearing only his red bikini. Pictures of sea and endless sand forced their way to the fore of her mind and, with it, another experience begged to be recalled. She could feel it thumping against her cerebral walls. Strange; she had forgotten everything of that part of the tour except Mason on that beach. The red, white and yellow ball on her line bobbed in the water, but she ignored it. Powerful strokes brought him past the pier, and she would have loved to strip off her clothes and join him.

"This isn't like me," she told herself, trying to bring to her conscious mind the strange something in her that *knew* him. He'd suggested that they had become more intimate than she'd remembered. If they had, she'd give anything to know how he'd made her feel.

"You've got one terrific kick," she called to him, when he pulled up to the pier.

"I'd better have, big as I am. What did you catch?" She laughed, recalling that she'd ignored the "bite" for the pleasure of swooning over his near-nude body as he flashed through the water.

He had eyed her surreptitiously and watched her hand go repeatedly to her forehead.

"Do you have a headache?"

She nodded, but he saw that she did it reluctantly.

"Are they frequent?"

She smiled that wonderful way in which her face seemed to welcome the opportunity to show pleasure. He hopped up on the pier and observed her closely.

"It's getting too warm. Come on, let's go back to the lodge." Mason grimaced at the scowl on her face; she wasn't thinking what he was thinking. No doubt about it. As they walked back to the lodge, he prayed that she'd remember the powerful and explosive, brain-branding loving they'd had together—not once, but twice. He didn't want to entertain the thought that she'd never remember. He saw her staring down at the ground.

"What do you see there, Jeannetta?" He stroked her shoulder in gentle encouragement. "Tell me."

She let a handful of sand stream through her widespread fingers.

"I remember trying to do that, and the sand stuck in my hand and wouldn't fall out. But when?"

"You were coming out of anesthesia after the operation, and that was a kind of delirium. What else do you remember?"

She shook her head.

"Nothing? Not even the night before I took you to the hospital?" He had to hide his sadness and consternation, so he turned his face away from her.

"Let's take the shortcut through the forest," he suggested. "I don't want you to get too tired." Minutes later, he wished the thought had never occurred to him.

Though the wind was nonexistent, a dank, dusty odor assaulted his nostrils. He stopped. The cracking of dry sticks and leaves hadn't come from their footsteps, so he waited. Almost at once, a brown bear ambled across their path, glimpsed them and stopped.

"Don't move, and don't say a word, honey." He surveyed their surroundings as best he could from the corners of his

eyes, to find out if the bear had cubs, and whether he and
Jeannetta stood between them and the big animal. At least
that posed no problem. He hoped the bear was nearsighted,
but he wasn't about to test it. His belly knotted to a figure
eight when the animal took a single step toward them and
stopped. His fingers gripped Jeannetta's waist. This was one
time when his black belt in karate would be of little help, but
it would take more than that bear to get her away from him.
The animal suddenly turned and bounded into the thicket,
and he breathed again.

"That was close, and we'd better get out of here. Next time,
we'll use the main road." He could be thankful that Skip
hadn't wanted to come with them, because the inquisitive
boy would have wandered around and might have bumped
into the beast. He didn't want to rush her, but he wouldn't be
at ease until they crossed the highway.

"I sure wouldn't want to be within kissing distance of one
of those boys."

Mason squeezed her to him. For the second time, he'd
been willing to give his life for her. "Being that close doesn't
mean you'd get kissed. I'm pretty close to you," he needled,
"but, if kissing me crossed your mind, you did a great job of
keeping it to yourself."

She covered his hand with her own and squeezed his fingers. "Ask, and it shall be given," she said.

Without thinking, he playfully patted her bottom, bringing a gasp of surprise from her, and he had again the painful
reminder that she didn't yet recall their intimacy as lovers.

"I have to ask?"

She raised an eyebrow and glanced at him through half-
lowered lids. "Do you?"

They'd reached the highway, and waited for the traffic to
ease. He cupped her chin, raised her face to his, and covered
her mouth with his own in what he'd meant as a quick ex-

change. But when she parted her lips and stepped closer to
him, he dropped the chair and fishing gear and brought her
into the strength of his body. Her mobile lips asked for his
tongue, and he couldn't, wouldn't, deny her. But he wouldn't
let her drag him into hot, seething passion as she'd done so
many times. He cooled the kiss, gently put her away from
him, and grinned.

"Just checking." He held her hand as they walked on to
the lodge. Maybe he ought to turn her over to another doctor.
But who? He knew many competent physicians, but he didn't
think he'd be able to entrust Jeannetta's well-being to anyone.
Perhaps he should ask her whether she'd accept a change. But
what if she agreed?

"Do you have a friend named Geoffrey Ames?" Laura
asked Jeannetta when she and Mason entered the lodge.

"Yes. What about him?"

Mason's broad smile told her of his delight that she remembered Geoffrey.

"He wants to come here with his new bride for a couple of
weeks. Said you'd vouch for him."

Jeannetta turned to Mason, her heart singing with delight
as she recalled her fondness for Geoffrey, and their shared
good times. "Oh, Mason. Isn't this fantastic? They really did
get married." He stared deeply into her eyes, and she didn't
doubt that he hoped being with Geoffrey and Lucy would trigger in her mind what he wanted her to remember.

"I never doubted Geoffrey's intentions," he told her. "Nor
Lucy's. Wish I could be here with them."

"They'll get here tomorrow," Laura told him. Jeannetta
asked if he could stay for the weekend.

He needed to stay, to be with her as much as possible, because he had to do whatever he could to make her know what
he'd done with her and to her on those nights when she'd

screamed his name in ecstasy and told him she'd love him forever. And he wanted to examine her incision and change the dressing. After thinking about it for a minute, he decided he could do it at Pilgrim's small General Hospital. He'd stay.

"I'll call my offices and see what's going on. Laura, where's Skip?"

"In the back with Clayton learning to clean things with natural ingredients. You know, without chemicals." She looked up from her bread making. "Is he any relation to you?"

"No, but he may be one of these days. He wants me to adopt him, and I just might do that." He pinned his gaze on Jeannetta as he said the words, and when her eyes widened, he could see that she was taken aback.

"Don't you want children of your own?" she asked.

He looked directly at her, but she had found something interesting across the room. He didn't let her off.

"You're not against adoption, are you?"

"No."

That simple answer left him unsatisfied. He called his medical office, learned that he didn't have any urgent business, and decided to take Jeannetta to the local hospital that afternoon. He phoned and made the appointment.

"Laura, you got any snacks? I eat a lot," Skip exclaimed, barrelling into the kitchen with the speed of one fleeing vipers. He glanced around and saw Mason and Jeannetta.

"Oh, hi. Mason, you ought to get into this environment thing. It's a gas, man...I mean, Mason. I already learned that you can do almost as much with vinegar and baking soda as you can with those detergents. I'm gonna learn a lot up here." He glanced over at Jeannetta, and hardly broke his stride. "While you're getting well, Jeanny, you and me can be buddies. I'll take you down to the lake, and we can pick berries. You ought to see the raspberries around here." His grin blessed them all. "Stuff like that. And you can teach me stuff. Mason said you teach college. Wow!" He paused finally to breathe and Jeannetta was able to comment.

"I see you like to learn."

"Yeah. I want to learn everything, and that'll take a lot of time." Apparently unimpressed by the laughter that followed his words, he plowed on.

"Mason's going to adopt me, but maybe he has to get married first. I dunno." The boy looked hopefully at Jeannetta, and Mason knew that she had locked her gaze on him, but he looked into the distance.

Mason pushed his hands into his pockets. Hauling her into his arms wouldn't solve one thing. The tension bounced off of Skip, who seemed suddenly ill at ease.

"Any fish in that lake, Laura? Jeanny didn't catch any," the boy said, as though deliberately breaking the silence.

"Plenty," Laura assured him. "Water's full of 'em. Clayton caught the ones we had for supper last night."

Skip looked hopefully at Jeannetta.

"You know much about fishing, Jeanny? Boy, I sure could use a lesson, and I don't have anything to do right now."

"I want her to rest," Mason intervened. "You two can fish some other time. You're making great progress, Jeannetta, so don't push too hard and ruin it."

"Is she really sick," Skip asked him, "or are you just manning your turf?" Mason couldn't help laughing at Skip's choice of words, though the first thing he'd do if Skip came to live with him would be to clean up the boy's language.

"Skip, I thought we agreed that you don't get into my personal affairs. Right?"

"Kids ask their parents anything they want, don't they? Right, Mason? And I'll be your kid as soon as you sign some papers. Right? That way, when you get old, you'll have me to take care of you." The boy's hopeful expression tore at his heart, and he knew a peculiar and strange new feeling of pride and contentment. It wasn't the satisfaction he'd known after successfully completing a difficult operation, but was more similar to the pleasure he knew as a young boy tending his vegetable garden, nurturing his seedlings and watching them grow. That garden had been his greatest joy, but he hadn't thought of it in years. Until now.

"I'll keep that in mind," he said, and he'd come to a decision. He saw the fires of love dancing in Jeannetta's eyes, walked over to her, and let her read his own.

Jeannetta held his gaze. Warm coils of comfort flowed in wave after wave from him, directly to her heart. The protective heat from his big body enveloped her and strengthened her. Why couldn't he tell her how he felt about her? His eyes said "I adore you," but it wasn't enough. She nodded to him in a mute excuse for herself and walked upstairs to her quarters. Clayton met her on the stairs, turned and walked up with her.

"We haven't had much of a chance to talk. I want you to know that Laura has given me a sense of stability. I can imagine that you've been worried about my rootlessness. I've always known where I was going, but losing my life's work knocked the starch out of me. I have reason now to pull my life together and get moving."

"I'm happy for both of you, Clayton. You must be good for Laura, because anyone can see she's glowing with happiness." Jeannetta kept her other thoughts to herself, though she couldn't suppress a smile when the man reacted with an expression that bordered on cockiness.

"Just wanted you to know that a lot has changed since we first talked on that plane." He turned around and went downstairs.

Jeannetta closed her door and lay down. Laura had to live her own life and, if Clayton made her happy for only a short while, it would be more than her sister had ever known. She removed her jeans and shirt, closed the blinds, and tried to sleep.

An hour later, she awoke with a headache, and with images of green malachite columns, waterfalls, and gray sandstone carvings flashing through her mind. She took a tablet that Mason had prescribed for her, dressed, and went to find him.

Mason watched Jeannetta walk away from him on her way to her room. As a travel manager, his life had been relatively uncomplicated. Cut and dried. Now, Skip wanted to drag him into uncharted waters of parenthood; his dual role of doctor and lover complicated his feelings about Jeannetta; and, in a couple of weeks, he had learned that maintaining businesses as disparate as medicine and travel reduced his fitness for either. He couldn't allow Jeannetta to complicate her recovery by becoming overconfident, but discouraging her and forcing her to slow down brought a stabbing pain to his heart. And his affections for Skip went deep, but...parenting was another matter. He walked out of the kitchen, leaving Skip to trail after Laura, and headed for the back porch where he could get a good stretch. He found Clayton there, cleaning tools.

"Skip's quite a boy, Mason. He says you're going to adopt him."

Mason shrugged. "He seems to want that, and he operates on the principle that wanting it makes it so."

Clayton smiled, as though to indulge the younger man. "Why not? Faith has worked many a miracle. Jeannetta had faith that you'd help her, and she believed that your best would be good enough, but she was also willing to sacrifice her sight and her future so that you wouldn't have it on your conscience if you failed. And you didn't fail."

Mason walked to the end of the porch and looked toward the setting sun.

"Not in the way that I could have, but she isn't out of difficulty yet." Why was he discussing Jeannetta with a man whom he barely liked? he wondered.

"She seems to have confided a lot in you," Mason told Clayton, in a tone devoid of friendliness. "I hadn't realized the two of you had grown so close."

"Slow down, man," Clayton chided. "We were soothing our individual wounds, not each other's. We were strangers, and I suppose you know that sharing your concerns with a stranger whom you never expect to see again can be a powerful healer, because you're totally honest. You ever try it?"

Mason's attitude toward Clayton probably needed some repair work, but he didn't much care. "What do you mean?" He glowered.

"You and I have more in common than you know."

Clayton had done nothing to invite his disrespect, but his behavior hadn't been entirely above question either.

"Let's hear it," he said, his tone harsh and sarcastic.

But Clayton chose not to respond in kind. "That's right. She told me about you. Well, I started Miles Chemicals with a seven-dollar-and-ninety-five-cent beaker and built it into a multi-million-dollar company. Then I made the mistake of trusting another person's research reports on a cream that removed wrinkles, when I should have checked. Money poured in, and then the bottom fell out. After several months' use, the product toughened the skin. The women didn't have wrinkles, they had leather. I lost a class-action suit…and my business."

Mason stared in disbelief. "You're *that* Miles?"

Clayton nodded. "I made financial restitution, but that hasn't restored my reputation nor erased my guilt feelings."

Mason's head snapped up. "Jeannetta isn't part of your absolution. Don't even think it."

"No. But Laura is."

They were talking, so now was as good a time as any to air his reservations, so he looked directly at Clayton. "Few men would have the nerve to go after sisters, especially in such quick succession."

He'd touched a nerve, alright. Clayton stiffened and assumed the posture of an adversary.

"I never went after Jeannetta, as you put it. I offered her an honorable way to a comfortable life, because I didn't believe you'd do that operation. I knew all about your celebrated case, more than she could tell me, and I didn't expect you ever to operate again."

Mason nodded absentmindedly, his thoughts partly in the past. "Neither did I."

"I fell for Laura minutes after I first saw her."

*I'll bet,* Mason said to himself, and then remembered how he'd wondered what hit him when Jeannetta walked into his travel office. He had to admit the possibility. A thought occurred to him, and he found himself advising Clayton to prove that the maker of the wrinkle cream had lied about the tests and to clear his name. Within minutes, they had begun plotting Clayton's course of action.

His conversation with Clayton had disturbed him; Jeannetta knew her diagnosis before she took the tour, but how much did she know of his background as a surgeon? He walked out of the lodge and headed toward the lake, because he needed to be alone, to think. But Skip caught up with him.

"You can go on back to New York City, Mason, and I'll take care of Jeanny for you. I won't let her out of my sight. I swear it. That's another reason why you ought to adopt me. I can keep your bird in line."

Mason laughed aloud and put an arm around the boy's shoulder.

"Stop calling her my bird. And another thing. You don't keep women in line—they're capable of doing that themselves." He stopped at the edge of the lake, and Skip moved closer to him and assumed an identical posture.

"I'll be real good, Mason, and I won't give you any trouble.

Ask Aunt Mabel. She never has to worry about me. The problem is she's going to wind up in a nursing home."

He hurt for Skip. The child hadn't been able to ask what would happen to him when his aunt could no longer live at home. She hunkered down to Skip's level, and looked him in the eye.

"Stop worrying. I won't let anything happen to you." Skip kicked the dirt and looked afar.

"That's not good enough for me. I want you to be my dad. Most of the guys in my school have a dad, but I never had one. I'm gonna be tall, and I could even look like you if I get rid of this Chelsea haircut. Couldn't I?"

"Maybe, but that's not important." The child's burden weighed heavily on him. How did a father act when his son hurt so badly?

"You scared Jeanny won't like me?"

"Forget that. I'll have a talk with Mabel when I get back to New York, and we'll take it from there. Right now, I want you to stop worrying. Where I go, you go." He stood and put his hands in his pockets to prevent his arms from going around the child in a fierce hug.

"If I go everywhere with you, Mason, what're you gonna introduce me as? Just Skip?"

At that, he hunkered down before the boy again, gave in to the powerful urge, and clasped Skip to him. Skip wrapped his arms around the strong man's neck, and clung in an unspoken plea so violent that emotion surged in Mason. He summoned what composure he could manage, pried Skip's fingers loose, took his hand, and started back to the lodge.

Jeannetta saw at once that marriage hadn't changed Geoffrey Ames's demeanor, though Lucy had obviously guided him to a good tailor.

"This here's my bride," he exclaimed to Laura and all

within earshot as he registered at the desk. Jeannetta noticed that Lucy had also adopted a classier style of dress. She dispensed with the banalities of formal greeting and clasped them each in a big hug.

"You're looking good, Jeannetta," Geoffrey announced, "but you're lacking some of that spice you used to have. You ain't been sick or nothin', have you? How's Mason?"

She'd forgotten the man's directness.

"Well, actually, I'm recovering from surgery right now. That's why I'm wearing this African-looking headdress—it covers my bandages. I had a brain tumor, but Mason says I should be good as new within the next couple of months."

"Mason said...? I don't get it." She told him that Mason had performed the surgery, and watched the old man gape in amazement.

Geoffrey rubbed his chin and shook his head. "You mean he's a doctor, too? Well, I always figured him as a smart one. Doctor, huh? Imagine that, Lucy?"

She took his hand and smiled up at him, but didn't say anything. Jeannetta couldn't help wondering what had happened to still the woman's once-verbose tongue.

"Everybody's surprised," Skip ventured. "I'm Skip, and Mason's going to adopt me."

Mason walked in and seized Geoffrey's hand in a warm handshake. "Congratulations. How'd the rest of the tour go?"

"Great," Lucy said, "but I was sure glad when we got out of Bangkok. Those girls don't care whose man they chase." She poked her husband in his ribs. "And *my husband*"—she emphasized the words, savored them and continued—"Geoffrey, here, was a kid in a toy store. He just ate up the way they fussed over him. By the time we got to Nigeria, I was ready to come home. Two months is a long time, and I wanted to get married before it got cold so I couldn't wear my mother's wedding dress." Moisture formed at the corner of her eyes.

"It's seventy years old, and I thought I'd never get a chance to wear it."

Jeannetta shifted her glance to Mason, and tremors raced through her at the sight of so much feeling mirrored in his dark eyes.

"This calls for a celebration," Mason stated. "Drinks are on me."

They seated themselves in the lounge, and Skip helped Mason serve the soft drinks to all but Geoffrey, Clayton, and himself, for whom he set out champagne. Lucy and Laura didn't want any, and alcohol was contraindicated for Jeannetta, whose medicines included an antibiotic. She noticed, with amusement, that Skip took a seat between Mason and herself.

"Don't I get any of that like the rest of the men?" he asked Mason, pointing to the champagne and placing his other hand possessively on Mason's thigh.

"As soon as you're twenty-one, son."

Jeannetta watched from the corner of her eye as Skip moved closer to Mason, settled back in his chair, and sipped his ginger ale.

The newlyweds went upstairs to settle in and Skip went with Laura for a promised lesson in the art of making fudge brownies. Mason sipped the last of his champagne, saluted Clayton, who returned the gesture and left them alone, and cradled Jeannetta in his arms.

"What will you do about Skip?"

"I'll probably adopt him if I find there's no reason why I shouldn't. He wants my word on it, but I can't promise him until I investigate the obstacles. I don't want to disappoint him."

"He's become possessive of you, and he copies your every gesture."

Mason said he hadn't noticed, but his obvious pride in the boy warmed her heart.

When Laura served them a family-style dinner that night in her personal quarters, Geoffrey's keen old eyes took in the state of affairs, and he remarked, "Looks to me like cupid's been pretty busy," as he glanced from one couple to the other. "'Course, I was expecting to see something on your third finger, left hand," he said pointedly to Jeannetta. "If y'all knew what you were missing, you'd tie the knot."

Jeannetta wished he'd change the topic, but he wouldn't, she knew, until he'd made his point.

"This here sure is one fine piece of roast pork, Laura. Nothing like good home cooking to keep a man satisfied and his feet in front of the fire."

"We bought you a bolt of ecru lace for your dolls," Lucy interjected, as though allying herself with Jeannetta's discomfort.

"That'd make nice trimming for a wedding dress, too," Geoffrey put in. "'Course, like I said, it ain't none of my business if y'all want to waste precious days making up your minds."

"Here, Geoffrey, have some more biscuits and some of the greengrocer's fresh-churned butter," Laura said. "No use making Jeannetta miserable. A snake couldn't move her 'til she's ready. Y'all don't let that potato soufflé go to waste, now. You hear?"

If you wanted a fire extinguished, send for Laura, Jeannetta mused.

Clayton assisted Laura in serving the dessert, and Skip bounded into the kitchen to help them. Mason noticed later that, as the boy savored his raspberry cream pie, his gaze swept repeatedly over his surroundings.

"Do you always have flowers, candles, and stuff like this on the table when you eat?" he asked Laura.

She explained that the table settings depended on the occasion.

"Gee, this is great. I'm really gonna learn a lot up here. Say, Laura, are you Clayton's girl?"

Laura frowned, before her face creased into a warm smile. "I sure am, honey. I sure am."

Mason got his linen jacket from the closet, walked over to Jeannetta, and rested his hands lightly on her slim shoulders. "Let's go catch some air."

He walked them along the highway, and when she rubbed her arms to warm them against the night's coolness, he took off his jacket and draped it around her shoulders. Their long shadows preceded them, and a ghostly silence hovered around them in the eerily beautiful and stark moonlight. Mason wondered how he withstood the city's noise and distractions, how he lived without the peace that pervaded him at that moment. The rustling breeze swayed the compliant trees, and somewhere a dog barked. The wind shifted, the smell of pine drifted to his nostrils, and visions of a blazing fireplace, his children, and Jeannetta flashed through his thoughts. And not for the first time. He reached for her hand, stopped, and turned her to face him.

Her gaze seemed to beseech him, to implore him. But for what? She unmasked her vulnerability and, in the midst of the strange, shifting shapes of the trees swaying against the moonlight that filtered through their leaves, he witnessed her naked need of him. Joy suffused him but, in the next minute, his heart pounded with his uncertainty. He put his hands in his pockets and looked steadily into her eyes. If only she remembered what they'd been to each other.

"Marry me, Jeannetta." He hadn't kissed her or even touched her, and he could see that his words had stunned her. They surprised him, too, but he knew at once their rightness.

"Wh…what?"

It hadn't occurred to him that his proposal would take her aback to such an extent.

"I want to marry you." Now that he'd said it, he wanted it badly, more than he had ever wanted anything in his life. He sucked in his breath and waited. Surely...

"You don't mean it. You...you couldn't."

"I've never meant anything more, or been more serious, in my life." A man wanted to see thousands of glittering lights dancing in his woman's eyes after he told her he wanted her for all time, but when she looked up at him, hers held only a strange sadness.

"I...I don't know. Let me think about it."

Ice-cold metal balls vied for space in his belly, and he was glad of his ability to conceal his feelings. He spoke carefully, so that the tremors so near the surface wouldn't control his voice.

"You don't know? I'd have thought you'd already made up your mind about that."

Why wouldn't she look at him?

"In a way, I had. I don't take your proposal lightly, but I can't give you an answer right now."

He opened his mouth to ask her what she had to consider other than that she loved him, but his vocal cords failed to respond. They walked back quietly. He wanted to take her hand, to feel her close to him but, after that rejection, he couldn't make himself do it. He told her good-night in the lounge and went to the room he shared with Skip.

After a restless night, Mason walked slowly down the stairs and into the breakfast room, hoping to see Jeannetta there and, at the same time, fearful that he might. Her place setting was untouched, so he surmised that she hadn't eaten. He was about to look for her in the garden when Clayton walked into the room.

"I'm going to stay around for a while and handle my appeal from here. You gave me sound advice, and I think Laura would be more accepting of me if I straightened out my life. She's very conservative."

Mason refilled his coffee cup and motioned Clayton to sit down.

"If Laura's concerned about that, it's not for herself, but for you. She'd marry you today, if you asked, and I'd bet my last dollar on it. If I can do anything to help you with your appeal, give me a ring. Laura knows how to reach me."

Clayton stood.

"Thanks. I won't forget this."

Mason resisted looking for Jeannetta. She knew he would be leaving early and, if she'd wanted to see him, she would have been in the breakfast room. He wanted to see her, to hold her, to... He looked to the ceiling. He'd had some difficult times in his life, but not one had pulled him under. This wouldn't either. He raced upstairs, awakened Skip, and told him good-bye.

"I'll take good care of your girl," rang in his ears as he headed for the door and New York.

Jeannetta sat in the broad stretch of sand that separated the lake from the glassy slopes that bordered it. She dug her bare feet into the cool yellow grains, raised them and watched the sand drift down between her toes. She picked up a handful of it and sent it into the morning breeze. How slowly time passed when you waited for a man to open his heart to you, to let you inside of him. Let you *know* him. For all his competence, strength, kindness, compassion, and gentleness, Mason didn't know how to love. He couldn't reveal himself to her. She had no idea what hurt him, what angered him, or even at what point you transgressed in an area of importance to him. She couldn't read his facial expressions, because he fixed them at will. Yet she loved him beyond all reason.

His reaction to Geoffrey's remark had showed that he wanted a home and a family. She tossed some crumbs to a starling at the edge of the grass and pondered what she knew of him. Skip needed him, and she surmised that he needed Skip. She got up and started back to the lodge walking slowly as Mason had urged her to do. Why had he asked her to marry him, and why would a man want to marry a woman without ever having told her that he loved or cared for her? Without ever having revealed himself? Protectiveness? Guilt? Those had been Clayton's reasons.

"Mason's gone?" Laura asked when Jeannetta walked into the kitchen. She nodded.

"I have to tell you," Laura began, "I know he did the surgery and all that, and you could say he's a terrific specimen of a man, 'cause he is. But I'm not sold on him yet. It took him too long to get down to business."

Jeannetta pushed back her annoyance. "Don't criticize him for that. He did the surgery as soon as he could get me in the hospital."

"Well, I guess you did give him a hard time. No matter. He did it, and you got a new lease on life." She poured the last of the coffee into her cup. "You told him about that investigation yet?"

"I remember telling him I wanted a clean slate, so I must have. Still, I'm not sure. But not to worry. No P.I. discusses his client's business, so it may be best to let sleeping dogs sleep."

Laura took a long sip of coffee. "If you say, hon, but I wouldn't trust it. When you get caught doing something wrong, Providence is usually sound asleep, and you can't get any help there."

Jeannetta marveled that her sister slipped back into her

pre-Clayton personality whenever her man wasn't near her. Habit could be a curse.

"About time something happened between you and Mason, isn't it?" Laura said. "He doesn't seem to me like the type to let things drag on and on. Don't you think it's out of character?"

"What? Oh. Yes, I suppose so. The P.I.'s report described him as a man of action. Decisive. A take-command person." She felt her face sag. "He was also reported to be very popular with glamorous women. Nobody would call me glamorous."

"You don't show a lot of cleavage, and you don't wear your skirts slit up to your waistline, and you don't layer a lot of junk on your face, but you're as good-looking as any woman I know. You want me to ask him what his intentions are?"

Jeannetta had to laugh. "Hon, that's out of fashion."

"Humph. Fashion never did make sense to me," she snorted. "A bunch of men telling women what to wear? Things are good between you?" she asked, her voice filled with hope.

A deep sigh escaped Jeannetta. "Sometimes, the physical attraction between us has the force, the power, of a hurricane. It almost consumes us."

Laura's eyebrows shot up. "Then how come you haven't made love?"

"Mason says that we have, but…" She tried to still her trembling lips and to stop the flow of moisture from her eyes. "But I can't remember it."

Laura's whistle split the air, and Jeannetta glanced around to identify the other person in the room. Seeing no one, she looked back into her sister's empathetic face.

"If you can't recall it," Laura advised with her newly acquired wisdom, "let him show you what it was like. That's probably what's wrong with the two of you—you're in different stages of your relationship."

Jeannetta stared at her. "You think it happened?"

Laura shrugged. "What would he gain by misleading you? Nothing. Besides, he can prove it. Ask him if you've got any little moles, what they look like, and where they are. He'll tell you."

"I will," Jeannetta said in a subdued voice. "I would already have done that, but he's my doctor, and whenever doctor and man do battle, the doctor wins."

Laura chuckled, shaking her head as though perplexed. "Honey, you always were one to do things in a big way," she reminded Jeannetta. "From the time you were little, if you laid an egg, not even a magician could sweep it under a rug. If it was me, he'd do what I want him to do."

Jeannetta gasped at her. "You're a quick study."

"Clayton's a great teacher," she retorted, as she turned her back and walked out of the kitchen.

Minutes later Skip charged in. "How you doin', Jeanny?"

She glanced up from her writing and smiled at the rambunctious child.

"I'm doing fine, Skip. Want some ginger ale?" He removed his baseball cap and regarded her with a sheepish look.

"You already on to my habits. Thanks. Er…Jeanny. Look, if you wanna go downtown before it gets too late, I'll take you. I promised Mason I'd look after you while he's gone. He'll be my dad soon, and I'll be responsible for everything when he's not around. Mason is a class cat. He got my aunt into a nice place where she can get good care—she's very sick, you know—and he's seeing about getting to be my dad right now. He said so yesterday." He gulped down the ginger ale and wiped his mouth with the back of his hand. "If you get to be my mother, I won't care if you pop my bottom when I do something wrong…you know…like other kids' moms." The pain of his loneliness tore at her. He wanted a response, she knew, and when no words would pass her lips, she stood, opened her arms, and wrapped him in the love that flowed out of her.

"Let's go," she said.

Skip's eyes rounded. "Is it okay?"

She assured him that a walk toward town wouldn't hurt her. They reached a small square still some distance from Pilgrim's center, and Skip suggested they sit on the bench, since he hadn't seen any Pilgrim, but she knew he feared having tired her. Jeannetta sat there enjoying her favorite pastime. A few paces away, she noticed that two women restrained their dogs on leashes while they talked. Only Alma, in all of Pilgrim, owned a French poodle. The little dog turned up his nose and pranced off when the big mutt attempted to establish a friendship. Jeannetta couldn't help laughing.

Later, she told Laura, "You should have seen that little poodle looking down his nose at the low-class mutt. Well, I've heard of dogs taking on the personality of their masters and mistresses, but that's the first time I've seen it. That dog did precisely what Alma would have done."

"I don't suppose you know Jethro called here several times while you were in the hospital."

"What'd you tell him?"

"I told him if he had rocks in his bed, he's the one that put 'em there, and he oughta leave you alone. When he had you, he was sniffin' around Alma, and ever since he married her he's been after you. He gives men a bad name, and I told the scoundrel as much."

Jeannetta curled up on the sofa in Laura's living room, and glanced at Clayton, who sat nearby making a list of the records he needed from his safe-deposit box in a New York City bank. Her straight-laced sister Laura was actually living with a man to whom she wasn't married. She couldn't believe it.

"Maybe I should tell Alma she's mistaken about Jethro and

me; I haven't said a word to that man since he admitted to me that he'd gotten her pregnant."

"Forget it," Laura snorted. "If your best friend sleeps with your fiancé, she deserves what she gets. I never could see what either of you wanted with him. 'Course, this is a small town, and you didn't have a lot to choose from."

"My excuse is that I was twenty-three."

Clayton answered the phone. "She's right here, Mason. Right. I'm getting it together now. And thanks, man." He passed the phone to Jeannetta.

"Hi. Could you call me on my phone in about two minutes?"

"Ten minutes. There's no need for you to rush. Later."

She answered on the first ring. "Hi. I wasn't sure you'd call."

"Why's that? You're still my patient…aren't you?"

Oh, Lord, was it like that now? Well, she was fighting for her happiness, and she wouldn't sell short. "Yes, I'm your patient, Mason." Uncertain of his mood or his reason for calling, she decided to let him lead the conversation.

"Skip called me a few minutes ago." She should have known he would, after his self-proclaimed role of caring for her in Mason's absence.

"He did? I thought he was in the office exploring the Internet."

"He wanted me to know that he'd taken you into town. How do you feel after that walk?"

She winced at his impersonal tone. "I got tired, but I enjoyed it. Mason, I'm not sure I can handle this detached, doctor persona. How can you treat me as though I'm precious, coddling and loving me and then talk to me as though I'm only a case in your files?"

"How can you give me so much of yourself, responding to

me with every nerve in your body—and I'm not talking about making love, which you can't recall—leading me to think I'm the most important person on earth to you, and then calmly tell me I'm not husband material? I'm thirty-seven years old, and it's never occurred to me to ask any other woman to marry me."

"I didn't say you're not husband material; I promised to think about it." She looked down at the telephone wire that had somehow gotten twisted around her arm. *Just like my life,* she thought.

"Well, hell! You think it's flattering to have been as close to a woman as I've been to you, and have her admit she doesn't know whether she'd marry you? Woman, you've practically taken my clothes off of me, and I'm not including the times we made love. We've faced danger together; we've stood waist deep in nature, stripped of all sophistication, and we've laughed together." She heard his harsh release of breath. "Jeannetta, don't you remember sitting with me on the deck of the *Southern Queen* and watching God's paintbrush lift the sun out of the South China Sea? I thought we were as close, that moment, as two people could be."

She groped for a chair and sat down. He'd told her more about himself in that minute than in all the weeks she'd known him. And yet, he'd said nothing personal about himself. How could she explain it without sounding foolish?

"I don't know how much has transpired that I can't recall, Mason, but I do know that I love you, and have for some time. Something's missing between us, something that I need, and it's holding me back."

"What are you saying? What do you need? If I don't know what it is, I can't give it."

She leaned forward in the chair, placed her elbows on her knees, and propped up her chin with her left palm. He wouldn't like it, but he deserved her honesty.

"I don't know what's inside of you. I know what I see, but not who you are. Maybe I didn't make myself clear, but I don't know any other way to say it."

"And yet you love me."

"Yes."

"Where does that leave us?"

She knew that her answer would end the conversation, but she could only speak the truth. "I don't know."

"Well, if and when you do know, share it with me. Will you?"

Was it defeat, or frustration, that she detected in that remark? She couldn't be sure, because it sounded so alien to him. Yet he'd said it.

"Nothing's going to change what's in my heart."

She remembered to tell him about the strange images that had played in her mind. "Mason, do green malachite columns in a huge lobby-like enclosure, a lot of rainbows and waterfalls, say anything to you."

"Did you dream this, or did you envision it while you were awake?"

From the urgency of his voice, she knew he thought it important.

"I was trying to go to sleep, but these images stayed in my mind until I got an awful headache. Why?"

"The lobby of the hotel at which we stayed in Zimbabwe had about six of those big round columns, and on our sight-seeing tour outside Harare, we went to Victoria Falls. It had I don't know how many rainbows forming arcs above it. You're beginning to remember, but your head ached because you pressed too hard. It'll come."

"I hope so. I want to remember…everything."

"Not any more than I want you to recall it."

## Chapter 11

Mason left his lawyer's Wall Street office, took the Lexington train to Ninety-sixth Street, and walked the block to Steve's apartment. At the corner, he stopped at a bank to arrange an income for Mabel, and the aroma of hot coffee greeted him as he entered.

"What's this?" he asked the bank officer with whom he was discussing opening an account for Mabel. His gaze locked on a man, obviously homeless, who filled a bag with muffins and brioches, poured himself a cup of steaming coffee, and left without saying a word or even resting his glance anywhere but the food-laden counter.

"That must be his seventh or eight trip in here today. We asked him what he was doing with it, and he said he had some friends who couldn't get around as well as he, and he wanted to help them."

"How old would you say he is?" Mason asked the woman.

"He looks forty-five or more, but from his sprightliness,

I'd say he's probably in his late thirties. The coffee and breads are for the customers, but the manager told us that he needs it more, and we should let him help himself until it's all gone.

Mason finished his business and followed the man out. When asked where he lived, the man replied, "Under the elevated up by a hundred and eight street."

"I got what was coming to me," the man said in response to the empathy he must have seen in Mason's expression. "I'm supposed to be an engineer, but I wanted to make a fast buck, and I let myself get lured into the brokerage business. The firm engineered some unsavory deals and got kicked off the stock exchange, I was out of a job, lost my apartment, and my wife took a walk. If you can't get cleaned up decently, you can't look for a job. You know the rest."

"I wish I knew of a way out of this for you," Mason said, thinking that he'd been lucky that he hadn't floundered as a travel manager, and that he could still practice his craft.

"Don't sweat it," the man replied. "There's a way up, but I have to decide to take it, and I haven't done that yet. You stay cool, man." Mason walked on, realizing for the first time what a gamble he'd taken with his life, and the measure of his good fortune in not having to pay for what he now saw as a gargantuan error.

When Steve opened the door, Mason regarded his brother carefully. He hadn't gone beyond high school, but he'd made a decent living, enough to support them and to send his younger brother through school.

"Steve, you're forty-two years old, and you could have a much easier and more fulfilling life if you'd come into partnership with me. Managing your emergency office-machine repair service wears you out, because half the time your workers don't show up, or one of them ruins something and you have to do the job, sometimes three jobs in one night. The travel agency is a money-making concern, because I've been there to manage it, and I can't do that when I restart my practice. I won't have time." He explained his plan to open his office two days for the rich, two for those of modest means, and one day for people unable to pay.

Steve nodded. "Pop would be proud of you for that. When are you going to start?"

"I told you that, until I can discharge Jeannetta, I won't take on another patient."

"When do you think that'll be?"

Mason shrugged both shoulders and fingered the keys in his right pants pocket.

"Soon, I hope. She has flashes of recall, and that means she's on the way." He leaned back in the chair and locked his hands behind his head, but his words were barely audible. "I asked her to marry me, and she turned me down."

Steve gawked. "You asked her to… Good Lord. And she…" He released a piercing whistle. "You love her, or you want to protect her?"

"Both." He understood Steve's look of perplexity, because he couldn't figure it out either.

"Did you ask her why?"

"Yeah," he said, shifting his long body into a slouch, "but her reason didn't make sense to me. Look, man, it won't kill me; if I could go back into that operating theater and perform that surgery with that bunch eyeing every move I made and waiting for me to make a mistake, I can take *anything.*"

Steve leaned against the roll-top desk, put his hands in his pockets, crossed his ankles, and looked at his brother.

"I hope you don't think there's any similarity between that and not having the woman you love. Before this gets cleared up, you'll find that you're the problem. You probably know a lot more about women than I do, Mason, but the ones who trailed around after you when you got to be a famous surgeon were pretty shallow. They wanted to be seen with you, to have you escort them to the Jack and Jill gala, the Urban League banquet, or some Delta or AKA shindig. For that, they'd accept whatever you offered and give you anything you asked for. Jeannetta Rollins is different—she's demanding more. I don't know what it is, but I'll bet it's something you've never had to give up. Bring her down here sometime. I want to meet her."

Mason spread his palms on his knee caps and grinned at the picture he'd conjured up. Imagine *bringing* Jeannetta Rollins anywhere.

"I'll ask her nicely."

Steve laughed. "Bully for her. You're not giving up on her, are you?"

Mason pushed himself up to a standing position, stretched luxuriously, and shook his head. "Man, you know me better than that. Problem is, I don't have a clue as to what she wants that I don't give her." He reached down for his briefcase, but straightened up without lifting it. "When she has her full memory, I'll know better where things stand with us." *And I'll know whether she loved me or merely used me,* he said to himself. Steve detained him when he would have left.

"I didn't get to see Mabel over the weekend; how is she?"

"She won't make it," Mason said with a sad shake of his head. "She's used up that extra something that makes people live when medical science says they shouldn't. I'm going to start adoption proceedings. Skip wants it badly, and I'm not turning him over to Family Services and heaven knows what kind of foster home. I want him with me."

"You'd better hurry up and do it while Mabel can help you. Skip's a great kid; if you wouldn't adopt him, I would. Get a lawyer."

"I did that this morning. He's drawing up an affidavit for

Mabel's signature, and he'll take it from there. But I won't feel easy 'til I have those adoption papers in my safe-deposit box."

"Skip will be one happy boy; when he's with me, he can't seem to talk about anything but wanting you to be his dad."

Mason had to laugh. "He says I'll have him to take care of me when I'm old."

"And you will, too, so don't sell him short."

Mason frowned and looked toward the ceiling. "Well, I've cast the die; I'm going to be a father." He took in his brother's broad grin. "What's so amusing?"

Steve laughed. "Don't worry about your approaching fatherhood; Skip will give you all the advice you need."

Approaching fatherhood wasn't his worry; his main problem was the widening chasm between himself and the woman he'd come to love with every fiber of his being. The woman who seemed comfortable knowing that they had slipped away from each other.

Jeannetta wanted to telephone Mason, but what could she say to him? That she'd changed her mind about being his wife? The phone rang. She turned over in bed, struggled to release herself from the tangled sheet and the twisted gown that clutched her tired body. She pulled the coverlet from the floor where she'd kicked it as she wrestled with sleeplessness, knocked the pillow off her head, and tried to sit up. She peeped at the clock as she lifted the receiver.

"Hello."

"Hi. I awakened you, and I'm sorry. I wouldn't have thought you'd turn in so early. Any problems?"

"No, but you said I'm not to read or to write much, though I did write for a few minutes yesterday afternoon, and I'm not to watch TV, so what's left? The bed."

"Don't trash it. The bed's probably been the scene of more

awesome, mind-altering experiences that any other place on this planet. If the company's right…there's no limit. Trust me."

"Hmmm."

"What does that mean? Oh, yes, I said the wrong word."

Jeannetta stood up. "In a game of words, you'd probably win, but I'm after something more meaningful."

"I'd ask what, if I wasn't sure you'd dress it up so much that I wouldn't know what you're talking about."

"Did you call me to pick a fight?" She poked her tongue at the mouth piece. "Because if you did, I'm hanging up and going back to bed."

"That wasn't my intention, but I won't back away from one. In fact, honey, a good fight with you would do me a world of good right now."

"Too bad; I'm not going to accommodate you." She had a sense that he was warming up to a good verbal sparring, but she ached all over from bouncing around in the bed trying to sleep, and she wasn't in the mood for it.

"Don't want to fight, huh? How about making love? Would you do that if I were there right now?"

"And disobey my doctor, who thinks that a little thing, so mild by comparison, as a tongue darting in and out of my mouth, would raise my blood pressure to crisis level?"

"Don't get out of line there," he growled. "I can stay at fever pitch for longer than it takes me to get from here to Pilgrim, and then let's see how brave you'll be."

"You don't scare me. If I stood within thirty yards of a horde of wild elephants and didn't trem…Mason. Mason, when was I that close to elephants? I've got to get dressed and find Clayton. Maybe he was with me."

"I was with you, Jeannetta. We were on a preserve in Zimbabwe outside Harare. You and I." Excitement streaked through at the urgency in his voice. "What else did you see, baby?"

"I don't know…there are some monkeys, a male and a female, and they seem to be intimate…I…do you think it's all coming back?"

"Yeah. You're on your way. I read your last tests, the ones taken in Pilgrim and transferred here electronically. They're very encouraging. Read or write about an hour at a time, no more than four hours per day altogether, and wait a while for TV. Don't walk alone too much, and try to avoid the midday sun."

He could switch from hot to cold faster than a hailstorm. She'd love to cuff him. "Thanks, doctor." If he heard the sarcasm, so much the better.

"Wait a minute there." She knew she'd annoyed him, because he spoke rapidly with no inflection. "Are you saying I'm just your doctor? Nothing more than that?"

"Oh, Mason, how can you ask such a question?" If she hadn't already known that academic degrees didn't give men an understanding of women, he'd have convinced her.

"Why shouldn't I ask? You turned me down."

She took a deep breath and weighed her words carefully. After all, she didn't want to drive him from her, only to help him understand.

"I don't know you, Mason, and I can't marry a man whom I don't truly know. I don't understand what goes on inside of you. I know that you want to protect me, to take care of me, and I appreciate that, but it isn't what I need. I don't need you to be my fail-safe in case I stumble." His silence cut like hot acid, but she had to tell him. "I can take care of myself. I appreciate all that you've done more than I can express it but, unless and until you offer me what I need, my answer is no."

"No? That's it? *No?*"

"I love you but, as things stand, marriage isn't for us."

"I see. Well, thanks for setting me straight."

She wouldn't react to the harshness of his voice, she told herself. "I don't think you see at all. *And how I wish you did.*"

"You're still my patient, I take it."

"Of course."

"Alright, I… Look, Jeannetta, we…we'll be in touch."

Mason replaced the receiver carefully, deep in thought. Needles and pins produced a tingling in his fingers and toes, and lightness claimed his head as though all the fluid had been wrung from his body. He told himself to get a grip on it, but he needed time to digest what had just happened to him. For the first time in his life he had let himself love a woman, a woman who believed that he didn't meet her needs. He swallowed a curse; anger wouldn't solve anything. Maybe he should have given her the details about the two occasions on which she had thrashed beneath him, calling his name as he kept her hanging at a precipice, begging him for ecstasy while he branded her with one powerful thrust after another. Maybe he should have told her all the things he knew about her that would leave no doubt in her mind that she'd made love with him. Like the little red mole beneath one of the chocolate-brown nipples that he'd held between his lips, teasing her, while she begged him to suck them. He could have told her that they tasted like Tia Maria. Just as good and just as heady. Or should he have merely reminded her that a man had to have known a woman intimately to know how many moles she had at the edge of her pubic hair?

Mason paced the floor of his bedroom. What he wanted was to get her back in his bed, and then he'd show her, love her until it all came back to her. He knew that she would eventually remember everything, but would that time come too late? He stopped short. He didn't want to believe it, but maybe she had never loved him—had enticed him, used him to get what she wanted. Pain flowed through him, enervating him.

It couldn't be, he told himself. Not even Ethel Waters was re-puted to have been that great an actress. Maybe he ought to get back up to Pilgrim and have it out with her.

After Mason's call, Jeannetta gave up the idea of sleep, dressed and went down to the lounge, where Geoffrey held Lucy's hand and lectured Clayton about the importance of clearing his name. Jeannetta couldn't help being amused; all was right in Geoffrey's world, and he wanted smooth going for all of his friends. She had turned to leave when he asked why she wasn't in New York with Mason.

"I just spoke with him, Geoffrey. Quit meddling."

Geoffrey cocked his head to one side and peered at her. "He wasn't too happy when I saw him, and you ain't exactly bouncing. So, seems to me that you two need to spend more time together. I don't expect to let Lucy here out of my sight for more than a couple of hours at a time. We don't have mis-understandings when we're together, only when we're sepa-rated and start thinking about things that ain't got nothing to do with what glues a marriage. You don't see Clayton here leaving Laura with all these fellows that come up here to fish, do you?"

Jeannetta looked from Geoffrey to Lucy. She doubted that she had ever seen a happier woman, and she smiled in delight as Lucy inched closer to her husband. Geoffrey leaned back, propped his left foot on his right knee and looked at Jeannetta.

"I knew all the time that you two hadn't leveled with each other." Geoffrey looked up toward the ceiling. "That kind of thing does a lot of damage, and takes a lot of healing." He patted Lucy's hand and stood. "Where's Skip?"

"On the Internet," Clayton responded. "I'll bet my last dol-lar that this visit of Skip's is going to cost Mason a state-of-the-art computer." He glanced at Laura and smiled the secret smile of a lover. *Everybody seems to have that something spe-*

*cial except Mason and me,* Jeannetta thought. Maybe Geoffrey was right; their relationship had been flawed from the outset. She walked over to her sister.

"Laura, I need to write, and I'll have to get away from here to do it. Pleasant company represents too much of a distraction, and Mason said he wants me to be active but quiet. My house is leased for three more months; I don't start school until January—if Mason will let me, I need to begin relying on myself. I have to look for a place where I can work."

Never at a loss for advice, Laura told her, "You shouldn't be in New York City and you shouldn't be too far away from Mason. You're not out of the woods yet."

"You're right; Kay and David Feinberg will be in Europe until mid-October, and I think, maybe I'll ask them to let me baby-sit their house and their dog while they're gone. I think I'll do it. You remember Kay; we shared a room at NYU." She watched Laura put on her worried look.

"Child, that's way past Fire Island. I don't know...doesn't seem right." She looked to Clayton as though seeking support for her argument. "West Tiana is a little inlet, and it's probably safe from storms but, honey, it's so far. What if she needs Mason?" She directed her question to Clayton.

"You're worrying unnecessarily, sweetheart," Clayton replied. "If Jeannetta needs Mason, she can probably signal him by mental telepathy. If I guess right, the man's antenna is pointed straight at her. I'd better see why Skip is so quiet." He headed for the office.

"And other thing," Jeannetta said, hoping to circumvent Laura's open disapproval of her plans. "Mason said the environment out on Long island will be good for me—clean air and a lot of natural scenery." She watched Laura purse her thin lips and knew she wouldn't like the words that were about to pass through them.

"Honey, you sure you don't want Clayton? Is that why

you're content to let things slide with you and Mason? I don't want to see happen to us what happened to you and Alma when she slept with..."

Jeannetta interrupted, her tone harsh. "Laura, I don't want to have to tell you this again. I wouldn't see Clayton if he strolled past me butt naked. Okay?" She watched Laura's lower lip drop and her eyebrows arch sharply.

"Your eyesight couldn't possibly be that bad."

"It isn't. We're not talking eyesight here, Laura; this is a matter of chemistry. You should have had a look at Mason lying on the beach wearing nothing but red G-string bathing trunks. If you'd seen that sight, honey, you'd be fired up for life."

"If you say so. But I didn't see it, and I *am* fired up." She had paused for effect, Jeannetta realized, when she added: "For life. Mason isn't the only hot stuff on this planet; my Clayton can start fires with the best of them."

Who *was* this woman? Jeannetta squelched a laugh as she eyed her newly liberated sister.

"From the looks of you these days, honey, I don't doubt it."

Laura's quick change of manner startled Jeannetta. Now what?

"Now that all of Pilgrim knows a celebrated doctor comes here regularly to see you, Alma's out for revenge. I've been meaning to tell you," Laura said, her mood pensive. "The jealous woman's threatening to take that lie about you and Jethro to the dean of your department at SUNY. She tells everybody that you never denied having an affair with Jethro."

"No, I didn't deny it; the idea was too ludicrous. Besides, that was the only way I could punish her for what she did. My closest friend sleeps with my fiancé and tells him she's pregnant, when she isn't. That hurt. I'm sorry they aren't getting along, but whether I tell her the truth won't matter. She'll believe what she wants to believe. If she used her brain, she'd

know that, as far as I am concerned, Jethro Williams ceased
to exist when she told me they'd gotten a marriage license."

"What about the dean?"

"Alma was once on the dean's staff. Enough said."

"Don't be so smug about it. She tricked him into marrying her, because she was jealous of you; now she knows you
got the better part of the deal and she'll do anything to upset
you. 'Course, if you ask me," Laura went on, warming up to
the subject, "Alma's got a big blob where her head's supposed
to be, and sometimes I think she manages to sit on *that*. You
be careful."

"Okay. Okay."

"And don't go too far from Mason," Laura nagged, following Jeannetta up the stairs. "I know you're going to do whatever you want to, but I don't like this. Anything could happen."

"But nothing will. How about driving me to Payne's Drug
Store first thing tomorrow morning; I don't know what I'll
find out there in West Tiana."

Laura nodded in agreement.

The two sisters were standing at the cashier's station in
Payne's, joshing with the proprietor's daughter, when Laura
nudged Jeannetta.

"Look over there. Darned if it isn't her royal highness."

Jeannetta followed her sister's gaze, knowing that she'd see
Alma Williams; she had already started toward them.

"I heard you'd had a brain operation," she said to Jeannetta. "I suppose that means you have to give up teaching."

"Hello, Alma." Jeannetta had to force a smile, because she
refused Alma the knowledge that she'd been disturbed by the
woman's gossip-mongering. "Actually, I signed a new contract
a couple of days ago." She scrutinized the woman carefully
for her real reaction; anybody who lied with as much finesse
as Alma had to be a consummate actress.

"Well," Alma said, "contracts have been broken. By the way, did you know that that doctor of yours practically killed a woman?"

"You ever been sued for slander, Alma?" Laura asked. "Well, prepare yourself, because you're about to get it, you hear?"

Jeannetta almost admired Alma's arrogant toss of the head as the woman prepared for her parting shot.

"You don't say. The dean said she'd be getting in touch with you, Jeannetta."

They returned to the lodge to find Geoffrey, Lucy, and Skip still at the breakfast table. Jeannetta asked Geoffrey whether he and Lucy would like to spend a few days at West Tiana with her.

"No thanks. We left the Georgia heat and came up here for some cool air. You go ahead. Lucy's fallen in love with Skip and that great big oak out back, and Skip wants to learn everything Lucy knows. They'll have a good time. You're not going to drive, are you?"

"Hadn't planned to."

Skip left his place at the table and rushed to Jeannetta. "You going away someplace?" She told him her plans.

"What about me? Weren't you gonna tell me?"

Her heart skipped several beats as she observed the boy's crushed demeanor; she hadn't considered that he cared for her.

"Yes, of course," she assured him, "and I'd let you go with me if you hadn't agreed to work, and if Mason didn't mind."

Lights danced in Skip's eyes, and a smile beautified his young face. "You going off somewhere with Mason, huh?"

She hated to disappoint him, but she couldn't mislead him. "Don't hope for that, Skip." She watched his enthusiasm fade along with the gleam in his eyes, as he hung his head. His painful need to belong somewhere stabbed at her and she folded him in her arms.

"You'll be special to me, no matter what happens between Mason and me," she tried to assure him but, unappeased, he stared into the distance.

Geoffrey tried. "She'll be back, and while she's gone, you and my Lucy can bake cookies." Skip looked at Geoffrey, and she didn't remember having seen so vacant an expression on a child's face.

"I promised Mason I'd look after Jeanny, but I can't if she's checking out. He'll think I lied."

Jeannetta decided to telephone Mason and let him ease Skip's worries.

"I've decided to stay out at the Hamptons for a few weeks," she told him, "but I'm afraid I've upset Skip, because he's staying here and won't be able to look after me." She bit her lip as she forced herself to sound serious for Skip's sake.

A comforting feeling of security settled within her as she listened to his dark, husky voice, reassuring her, telling her that he'd be there for her when she needed him.

"You need a good rest, though I'd prefer that you were someplace nearby." He listed a number of signs that she should regard as foretelling an emergency. "If you experience any of them, call or beep me. But don't waste time about it. Promise?"

She promised and gave him the address and phone number.

"Let me speak with Skip." His abruptness stunned her, but she later realized he'd had a good reason. She handed the phone to the eager boy. Seconds later, Skip tossed the phone in the air and let out a whoop. Jumping and slapping his fist into his palm, a gesture he'd taken from Mason, he yelled, "Mason is adopting me." Immediately, he became subdued.

"But my aunt's pretty sick and wants to see me, so I have

to go to New York." He looked at Laura as she entered the dining room with fresh muffins.

"Can I still have my job when I come back?"

Laura nodded. "Of course you can. You come right on back to the Hideaway, you hear?"

Making a quick decision, Jeannetta told Skip that he could go with her to New York.

Mason looked at his watch for the nth time since he'd spoken with Skip. Two-thirty. The boy should have been there. His office door opened, and Betty Goins sauntered in, unannounced, as usual.

"Heard you'd come to your senses," she said in greeting, leaned forward, and pressed a kiss on his mouth.

"Yeah, and I bet you heard it less than an hour ago." He needed a lot of self-control to refrain from wiping his mouth with the back of his hand.

"Don't be mean, Mason." She pouted.

He couldn't help laughing and wondering what he'd ever seen in her. "Alright, but don't you be so obvious." He lightened his tone, but he stared directly into her eyes; he wanted her to believe him when he said, *nothing doing.*

"We can still see each other, can't we?" She moved closer to him.

"Sure," he replied, backing his chair away from the desk and her, "but with my present preoccupation, that's all we'll do. I'm involved with someone." He pointed to his temple. "And she's right here thirty-six hours a day. You wouldn't get a rise out of me no matter what you did. Trust me."

She sauntered a step closer. "You're sure of that?"

Mason threw his head back and laughed. "Does water flow downstream? Let's leave it where it is, Betty. We've been friends, and I'd like to remember us that way."

"Oh, Mason, darling don't be like this." He watched her

lower her lashes, drop her head to one side and rim her lips with the tip of her tongue, and he started to lose patience with her.

"If you want it crude, just say so."

Her head snapped up. "Alright. You can't hold it against me for trying. How's your precious patient?"

"Doing great." He paused, remembering Betty's wide contacts. "You remember that class-action suit against Miles Chemicals?" Betty took a seat beside his desk, swung one of her long legs over the other one, and let her red silk skirt rise high above her crossed knees.

He grinned at her. "No dice, Betty. What about Miles Chemicals?"

"Sure, I remember that. One of my friends joined the suit, but her skin is already back to normal. I used it, and nothing happened to me."

Mason leaned forward. "How long did you use it?"

"As long as it was on the market. A year and a half, or two, I'd say. Why?"

Mason strummed his long fingers on his desk and thought for a minute. "The owner of that factory went belly-up because of that suit. He's a good guy, and he doesn't think he deserved what he got. He doesn't want the money returned; he wants to clear his reputation. He'd been assured that that formula had been properly tested."

Betty swung her knee and eyed Mason for effect. Seeing none, she got down to business. "I'd go back to court, if I were in that man's place. The instructions said that, if your skin felt dry, smooth it liberally with olive oil. That's what I did. He ought to make those women get their skin examined. I'll bet there're isn't a one whose skin isn't back to normal."

"Thanks. I'll pass that along."

"Well, if we can't get together, I guess I'd better take off."

He dialed the Hideaway with the intention of speaking to

Clayton, but Betty opened the door to leave, and his heart pounded as though it were a runaway train. She stood facing Jeannetta and Skip. He dropped the receiver in its cradle. She glanced back at him, but his gaze seared the woman who occupied a permanent place in his heart.

Skip raced to him, his arms wide. "Dad! Dad! When will we get the papers? I started to think they wouldn't let you do it." He turned to Jeannetta. "Can you believe it, Jeanny? He's my dad now." Mason didn't bother to correct him, because the only thing lacking was the judge's seal, which would be affixed within a week. He saw the tears of happiness in Jeannetta's smiling face and the lack of understanding in Betty's. Thank God, he'd avoided that pitfall. He let his arms tighten around Skip, stunned at the swell of love that flooded his senses. He reached one arm out to Jeannetta.

"Sweetheart, come here, please." He held them both until the three of them broke apart at the soft sound of Betty closing the door.

"You think Jeanny should be going out to Long Island by herself, Dad? She said it's almost three hours on the train."

Mason looked at her and hoped that his eyes mirrored what he felt, that she knew they reflected the heart of the man, not the doctor. "We can't run another person's life, son. We can only say what we believe to be the truth, wish them well, and let them go." He tried to ignore Skip's startled look. The boy had learned some archaic assumptions about women and their capabilities, and he intended to set him straight. He looked at Jeannetta, and hated the feeling of helplessness that stole over him when tears swam unshed in her beloved eyes. Why did she keep them apart with the cryptic explanation that he didn't meet her needs? He didn't believe a word of it, but she left him with no choice, and he had to accept it. He looked down at her small suitcase.

"You shouldn't be carrying luggage."

"I can carry it, Dad," Skip exclaimed. "I can go to the station with her." Mason smiled at the boy, whose voice caressed the word "dad" as though it had magic properties.

"No, son. You have to come with me to see Mabel. We'll get a taxi for her."

"Can the taxi take her all the way to the Hamptons? Huh?"

Mason rolled his tongue around the left side of his jaw. "It's a thought. A good one."

"No way," Jeannetta interjected. "I know you fellows mean well, but I'm taking the train."

"Call us when you get there. We'll be home," Skip advised.

"Where's home?" Jeannetta wanted to know.

"With my dad," the boy answered proudly.

Jeannetta sat on the terrace facing Shinnecock Bay and the distant Atlantic Ocean, anxiously awaiting her first glimpse of the sunset. Robins, a finch and a few blackbirds serenaded her, and the cool ocean breeze sent her inside for a sweater. She couldn't see the sun, but the sky had become a rainbow of colors, settling slowly into a dark bluish gray with flashes of red and pink, the only sounds the rustling of the birds. Her longing for Mason intensified as darkness closed in, but she worked hard at shoving the yearning aside and concentrating on her work. She couldn't help being amazed at the way in which her fingers had flown across the keyboard of her laptop. She hoped Mason would lengthen her work time. She hadn't written about him; she couldn't bear to commit her thoughts of him to paper. But the hero of her story had closed his heart to everyone, even to himself. Neither the woman he loved and needed nor his precious golden retriever was allowed to sense his sadness and the way in which his soul ached. She saw her task as that of imbuing the hero with such self-knowledge as would bring him to share his inner self and, in so doing, accept himself and let the love of his woman heal him. Close to home, she reasoned, but once begun, she hadn't been able to steer the story in any other direction.

She nibbled absentmindedly on a cold chicken sandwich as darkness settled around her, fireflies rose from the grass, and crickets began their evening song. She sucked in her bottom lip and told herself that she had gambled for high stakes, wanting all of Mason and not that small portion of himself he'd so readily given. The sound of the telephone crashed into her reverie.

"Yes?"

"How're you getting on out there, Jeannetta?"

"F...f...fine." She hadn't expected his call, and she hoped the man and not the doctor was on the other end of the wire. "It's wonderful out here, Mason. Quiet, cool, and a sunset you wouldn't believe."

"Ah, yes. I remember that you have a passion for sunsets. I love the sunrise."

"I know."

"You know?" She wondered at his surprise. "You remember?" he asked.

"I don't know why I know it, but I do." Tendrils of fear sneaked over her nerves at the thought that she might have a permanent disability. "Why are you asking me that? Am I having chronic memory problems?"

"A few problems, but you're getting over them. We've discussed this at least once since your operation. Do you remember that?"

"Well, yes, you said we've made love, and I'd give anything to remember it. You wouldn't fool me, would you?"

"Fool you?" She thought she detected testiness in his voice. "I'll be delighted to prove it, and maybe I'll shake up your memory in the process."

"You sound pretty confident," she replied lamely. She'd

been so certain that he'd been having fun at her expense, but if he could prove it…Laura's words came back to her.

"How can you prove it?"

"Jeannetta, if you're interested in the proof, just say it. Do you want to know?" That impersonal tone, again.

"With whom am I speaking now? The doctor, or the man who kissed me on a road in Pilgrim as though he could eat me alive? Which one?"

"Both," he shot back. "And if you think you can stand another round of that, I'll be in my car in five minutes."

"What'll you do with Skip?" she asked, not sure that she'd done the right thing in challenging him, and certain that he wouldn't come prepared to divest himself of his emotional armor.

"Skip's back at the Hideaway; I can't pry him loose from the place. Well?"

"I…uh…"

"You want to see me or not?" he broke in.

"I want to see you."

"It's six-forty; I'll see you in two and a half hours."

She begged him to drive carefully, and gave him the directions.

"Who else lives at the end of that road?"

"Just me."

"That wasn't what I wanted to hear. I'll be there soon."

Had she lost her mind? Unless he offered more than when he had proposed, what did she stand to gain from an evening with him? She took the menorah that David had inherited from his grandfather off of the mantelpiece to ensure its safety, and lit the fireplace. The evening had cooled and, face it, she thought, dancing flames would drive a man's heartbeat into a trot quicker than warm radiators. She put on a long red cotton shift and shod her feet in gold thongs. As usual, she didn't wear makeup or jewelry; she didn't want props. She wanted him to know exactly what he got—*if* and when she gave herself to him.

Mason called the Hideaway, and Skip answered. "Hiya, Dad?" He had to get used to his new title, but he didn't think he'd find that difficult. As any father would, he had called to tell Skip where he would be if needed.

"You gonna stay with Jeanny for a while?" the boy asked hopefully.

"Skip, you're still twelve, and you don't get into my personal business. Right?"

"No, sir. But you're going to see her?" The boy was incorrigible.

"Yes. Get Mrs. Ames to go over your chemistry and geography with you."

"I don't need that, but I don't guess it could hurt. Say, Dad…" Here it comes.

"What is it, son? I've got to be moving."

"That's just my point, Dad. Hurry up and get going and… and…"

"And what?"

"Stay as long as you want to. That's not meddling, is it?"

"Not really." He had to laugh. Skip was determined to have Jeannetta for his mother and had begun to nag his soon-to-be father about it. The night before, Skip had practically lectured to him on Jeannetta's virtues, though he couldn't imagine how the boy had been able to chronicle them so accurately. He supposed that Skip's difficult life had equipped him to evaluate people; it certainly hadn't left him shy about going after what he wanted. And what he seemed to want and need most was to be a part of a normal family with his own mother and father, something he'd never known.

Mason bought a large vase of red roses, stargazer lilies,

and calla lilies, and two bags of fresh-roasted unshelled peanuts. He slid into his Cougar, strapped his seat belt, turned the
radio to WKCR jazz and headed for Long Island. With rush
hour over and the traffic sparse, he'd see her in less than three
hours. And when he left her, she'd be a different woman. He
caught himself. If she had used him, he'd know it, and if she
had leveled with him, he'd know that, too. He settled back,
flipped on the cruise control, and quit thinking; he intended
to greet her with an open mind.

He followed her perfect instructions, arrived at the end
of Burkes Road, and killed the motor. A dead end. As he sat
there getting his bearings, a bloodcurdling sensation plowed
through him. She walked toward the car shrouded in bright
moonlight with a big German shepherd leashed close to her
side. He released a long harsh breath and gripped the steering
wheel. She could never know what that image had engraved
in his mind, kicking his heart into runaway palpitations. If
he hadn't done the job and done it well, that would have been
her life. She tapped on the window as he sat rooted to the
driver's seat, appalled by that sickening symbol of what might
have been.

"Hi." He relaxed as her brilliant and intimate smile began
to warm his soul. Could she smile at him that way if she didn't
care deep down? He started to unlock his door, but she motioned him to remain inside.

"Hi. Roll down the glass and stick your hand out. I have to
introduce you to Casper." He tensed as the big dog smelled
his fingers, looked up toward their owner, and sniffed again
before wagging his tail.

"Now, pat him gently on the head a couple of times." Mason
complied, and waited for the next ritual. Finally, Casper sat
down and thumped his tail, and Jeannetta told Mason that he
could safely open the door, but that it would be wise to get out
slowly. Out of the car at last, Mason thought he'd better pat

the dog again for insurance's sake, did as much, and was rewarded with a wagging tongue and a thumping tail. He opened the trunk, removed the flowers, nuts, and his medical case.

"I take it he's a guard dog." He watched the animal from the corner of his eye as he stepped closer to Jeannetta. Her smile broadened, and her lips met his in a kiss that was warm and brief, too brief. They walked around the back of the house, and he stopped them at the patio lamp.

"Let me look at you." Stepping back, he let his gaze roam over her face, her slim rounded figure, and he sucked in his breath. He wanted to hold her, love her, and keep her close to him for the rest of his life. Couldn't she see how much he loved her and needed her? She grasped his hand, and he hoped that meant she felt what he felt.

"I have to take Casper to his house, because he won't go in otherwise. He's trained to do as he's told." She patted Casper's head, and the dog went inside his elegant dog house. Mason didn't attempt to guess the implications when she glanced up at him, took his hand and said, "Let's go in."

Inside, she took the flowers, and he watched her hips assert themselves beneath the simple red dress. On some women, it would have been an ungainly sack, but she wore it with sexy, feminine grace. He had expected a beach house but, looking around the living room, he saw a well-appointed place for year-round living. His gaze landed on the menorah.

"Your friends are Jewish, I take it."

"Yes. Kay and I roomed together in undergraduate school, and I was one of her bridesmaids. We've had a lot of fun together."

He nodded. "I had some good times in my college days, too." He tried to figure out her mood. She seemed accepting, but was she?

"It's strange, your being here, but I'm glad you came."

"Me, too." He hoped she hadn't forgotten that he'd come in

response to what amounted to a challenge from her. He opened his medical bag. "Let's get this over with, so we can send the doctor packing." He couldn't help grinning at her skeptical look and raised eyebrow, which he took as a warning that she wouldn't bend easily. How could he have fallen so deeply in love with her without knowing important things about her, essential aspects of her character? This woman had a back-bone of steel. He examined her and, satisfied, closed the bag.

"Where do I put this?"

Her answer should have told him what to expect, but she didn't tip her hand when she suggested the foyer. Not in her bedroom or the guest room. He stuck his hands in his pants pockets, wiped his face of all expression, and gazed at her.

"We're acting like strangers, Jeannetta."

"Our last conversation left me feeling like one," she said. Funny, she had a habit of remembering things one way when he saw them from a different perspective.

"The last time we were together, I hugged you, woman."

"A hug and a conversation are different forms of communication."

He frowned, although he took courage from the fluttering of her long, thick, black lashes, but a smile fought for and won possession of his face. He caught her looking at his mouth and sucking the inside of her lip, and his smile became a broad grin.

"What kind of communication is kissing?" That was what he wanted right then, some mind-boggling loving, not the flirtatious bantering at which she was such a genius. But when she tossed her head back and propped her left fist on her left hipbone, he knew that sexual fencing was what he'd get.

"You should know; you're a master at it." He tried not to show too much pleasure at her remark, but he must not have succeeded, because she frowned and asked him, "What are you up to, Fenwick?"

He spread his hands in a gesture of defenselessness. "Who, me? I'm just trying to make some headway here. And if you'd just take your hand off your hip, I'd feel a lot more comfortable. I had an aunt who used to stand like that, only she usually waved a heavy skillet with her other hand. No offense meant, of course." He ran his hand over his tight curls. So far he hadn't made any progress with her. He looked around for some help, saw the screened-in side porch and took her hand. "Let's sit out here."

She went with him, but protested that the night air chilled her.

"That's why I'm here," he said with a wink. "To warm you up."

He reclined in the chaise lounge with his arms around her. "Can't you imagine us growing old together like this, after our kids are grown and married and we have a gang of grandchildren?" His hand smoothed her thick hair away from her face as he talked, and it excited him when she snuggled closer and wrapped her arms around his waist.

"What do you say? Wouldn't we make terrific grandparents?"

She giggled almost to the point of strangulation.

"Mason do you realize how far out of character you're being?"

"Sure I do, but being myself got me nowhere, so I'm trying to imagine how all those married fellows did it."

"This business is woman-specific, honey," she purred, "and each one of us has…uh…different requirements."

"I'd hoped that when you finally got around to addressing me with an endearment, it would at least have the ring of intimacy."

The clock chimed, and she leaned away from him. Regarding him intently, she spoke softly, almost as though to herself. "Romance is like everything else, you gain by giving."

"Now, we're getting somewhere." He gripped each of her shoulders and stared into her eyes. "What do you want? Name your terms." Her narrowed eyes and the sound of her throat clearing weren't reassuring, but he refused to back down.

"Well?" he urged. "You can be pretty frisky when we're talking on the phone and, come to think of it, you know how to be aggressive when it suits you." He paused and decided to let if fly. "I hope you haven't forgotten the way you nearly seduced me on that tour bus when we were in Singapore, and in broad daylight, too. I knew what you wanted then, because you telegraphed it to my brain, my nervous system, my libido, my whole body. Use a little of that ingenuity right now, and tell me what you want." Her eyes seemed to search for something deep inside of him, and he found himself automatically closing an emotional gate. Her eyes dimmed, and he knew she had discerned it. He'd deal with that later, but right then he had to know what she required of him.

"You told me you love me," he went on, "and I can't find a reason to disbelieve you. Yet, you won't agree to marry me. What do you want that I'm not giving you? You've got a price. Name it."

"You," she answered, boldly meeting his gaze. His eyes widened in astonishment. Hadn't he offered to give himself when he proposed? Perplexed, he shook his head.

*"Me?"*

"You. Your whole self." Her hand caressed his jaw and, with a tenderness that amazed him, he trapped her wrist, but her lips parted in surprise, and he released her.

"Shut-eye time," she announced, standing and suppressing a yawn. He took his time getting to his feet. She walked ahead of him, turned, locked the door after he'd entered the dinette, and faced him, questions mirrored in her face.

Did she know that her body had relaxed, her pelvis tilted toward him, and her nipples were little hard pebbles peeking at him through that dress? He sucked in his breath and gave himself a silent lecture. This night could be the most important one of his life. His gaze settled on her mouth as she absentmindedly licked her lips, and he rubbed his damp palms against the sides of his pants, swallowed, and reached out to her, unable to withstand their fencing, incapable of denying himself any longer.

Jeannetta hurled herself into his waiting arms. Shivers of anticipation crept over her limbs as she waited for the touch of his mouth. Of their own volition, her lips parted for him in her longing for greater intimacy with him, and her body pressed itself to his. He tried to slow it down, to pull away, but she clung to him until he relented, thrust his tongue between her lips and let her feel his virile power. Her body rocked with the awareness that slammed into her, and her control shattered when he trembled against her. She had forced him to that point, but she didn't care; she needed it, needed some evidence that he belonged to her, that she could somehow pierce his emotional shell and know the man whom she loved. With obvious strain, he moved away from her, though his fingers rested lightly on her arms.

"Sweetheart, I wanted a kiss, but you know we can't take this any further until your doctor releases you."

"You don't think my doctor is being overly cautious?"

He pulled her back into his arms, and she welcomed it, loved the feel of his hands stroking her back.

"No, I don't. Hell, he wouldn't approve of the heat you turned on there either." His grin sent her heart into a dizzy trot. "Woman, you pick the damndest times to put me on a rack."

"Are you going to spend the night?"

His rueful smile touched her heart.

"That's right. Turn the knife." His demeanor darkened.

"Jeannetta, I do not claim to be a saint, and I'm starved damned near to death for you."

She sucked on her bottom lip and glanced at him from beneath lowered lashes.

"The guest room?"

He glared at her. "You're pitching hardball, honey; I'm going home."

"Of course you are. Tomorrow morning. Right now, you're going to eat a sandwich, drink a glass of milk, and get some sleep. What's so funny?" she asked when his booming laugh reverberated throughout the house.

"Just the right touch. As soon as you see reason, I'll let you tell me when to get up and when to go to bed; I may even eat oatmeal for you but, tonight, baby, I'm going back to New York."

"You're serious?"

"Does the sun rise in the east?" He got his medical bag, took out the sack of peanuts, and asked her, "Where can I warm these up?"

"You don't want a sandwich," she asked him, walking toward the kitchen.

"We will not discuss what I want, Jeannetta. I haven't had any hot roasted peanuts in ages, and this is a good time for them."

"You won't get to New York until after midnight." He dumped half of the nuts into the pan she gave him and put them in the oven.

"True. But I'll like myself when I get there."

"What about the sunrise?"

"There'll be others, plenty of them."

She watched his face bloom into a smile, as though reflecting a cherished idea.

He had, indeed, been thinking of the two of them, she knew, when he said, "Ever since my parents died, I wanted to live in a big house high on a hill with the world visible from every direction." His smile slowly ebbed. "You could have your sunset, and I, my sunrise." In that second, she had a glimpse of him as the man she needed and wanted for herself, and she wouldn't settle for less. Go on, let it out, she wanted to shout at him when he concentrated on removing the nuts from the oven. She let her right hand cover his left one so he'd know that she understood his need, but he avoided her eyes, took her hand, sat down, and focused on the peanuts.

"What's that?" he whispered. Goose pimples broke out on her bare arms as she caught his tension. "Any wild animals around here? There it is again." He jumped up from the table and raced toward the front door.

"Mason, wait. That sounds like Casper." The low growl grew louder and more ominous.

"My Cougar is the only car out there. What do you think he's after?" He doused the lights in the living room and looked out of the window. The growling intensified and, when a loud yell rang out, she clamped her hand over her mouth.

"Steady, baby. Do you have a gun around here anywhere?" She shook her head.

"I don't know. I c...c...couldn't u...u...use it if th...there was one." She had never had a need for the big dog's protection, and needles pricked her whole body at the sound of his increasingly loud and angry growl.

"I'm going out there; he could kill somebody."

It had never occurred to Mason that Jeannetta could move with such speed. In a second, she was between him and the door, facing him with an expression of defiance that he would not have associated with her.

"You're not going out there. Period." He checked himself when he would have moved her aside and summoned control.

"I can take care of myself, and you, too, if necessary. So please step aside." She didn't budge.

"David said Casper won't mortally wound anybody unless the person tried to get in the house or attacks someone who lives here, but if you go out there…" The growling had ceased, and he thought he heard scratching and whimpering.

"Is that Casper?" She moved quickly, grabbing his hand, and he followed her to the back door. He opened the door, but the dog didn't enter.

"I think he wants us to follow him," he told her. "You stay behind me." They saw a youth dragging himself away from the house, and Casper ran ahead and stopped him.

"What were you up to?" Mason asked the boy.

"I didn't know he'd bite. I…I was going to take him home with me. I thought maybe he was a hunting dog. I wanted a pet."

"How old are you?" Jeannetta asked the boy, who was favoring his arm.

"Sixteen."

Mason looked at Casper to make certain that the dog trusted him. Satisfied, he told the boy, "I'd better look at your arm; come on inside." They started back to the house and Casper blocked the way.

"I can't let him go off like this; he could get an infection, gangrene. Try to get Casper to walk back to his house with you." He could see that Casper wouldn't cooperate, took the little phone hooked to his left side, and dialed nine-one-one.

"We'll stand here until we get help, because this dog has no intention of letting the boy in the house."

"He'll be in trouble," Jeannetta said.

Pity was not what the boy needed, he told her, as he recalled Skip's desperate efforts to avoid getting into trouble; this boy needed discipline. "Better now than later." He looked directly at the young man. "The next time you want a dog or anything

else, find a job, go to work and, get it honestly." When the
police arrived, along with an ambulance, Mason dressed the
boy's shoulder wounds, gave him an antibiotic and a stern
lecture, and stood with Jeannetta and Casper until their in-
truder and the others were out of sight. Casper wagged his
tail, and Mason knew that morning would find him in West
Tiana. Probably sleeping on the porch, he murmured to himself, fighting off the onset of an ill temper.

"It's definitely too late..." Jeannetta began. He looked at
her, shrouded in bright moonlight and her come-hither dress.
Not that the dress made a difference; she would have enticed
him if she'd been draped in a sackcloth.

"Go to bed, Jeannetta," he told her, "that way, we'll both
stay out of trouble."

"But where will...?"

He arched both brows and seared her with a libidinous
stare, exposing his need for her.

"Alright. Alright," she said. "The guest room's upstairs
to your left at the end of the hall. See you in the morning."

He watched as she wasted no time getting up the stairs. He
took a coat from the hall closet, walked out on the screened-in
side porch, pulled off his pants, shirt, and shoes, and stretched
out on the chaise lounge. He threw David's coat over himself
to ward off the cooling air. Not for money would he go up
those stairs; he didn't think he'd ever walked in his sleep, but
there was a first time for everything.

Jeannetta looked down at the dress pooled around her feet.
Did she dare to walk back down those stairs? He'd welcome
her; she didn't doubt that. But she also knew that he wouldn't
hold her in high esteem if she seduced him into violating his
principles. And he had made it clear that, where her health was
concerned, the doctor ruled the man. She walked to the window and looked out at the moonlit garden, its plants already

adjusting to the changing season. She ought to be grateful for what she had, and she was, but the man she loved was bunked downstairs somewhere while she prowled in her bedroom, hot enough to ignite a furnace. What she felt bore no relation to gratitude. She wondered if it would help to scream.

"Girl, you're getting yourself shook up," she muttered aloud, as she sat on the edge of the bed and pulled off the thongs. She stretched out on the coverlet, hoping he'd forget about honor and open her door.

She awoke with the thought that if Mason really had made love with her twice, the experience hadn't exactly blown his mind. She showered, dressed, and went downstairs. When she didn't see him in the den or the living room, she rushed to the window and let out a long breath. Thank God. His car was there. She found him in the kitchen, shirtless, stirring pancake batter. Her eyes rounded and her bottom lip dropped, before she could gather her composure, and she battled a wild urge to run her hands over his naked shoulders, biceps and every inch of flesh not hidden by his undershirt.

"Good morning." She knew he'd caught her ogling him, and ducked her head in embarrassment. "Where did you sleep?"

He looked up at her and grinned. "Hi. I slept on the porch. Do you know that's the first time I ever slept outdoors? The air was wonderful, and after a while all the night creatures went to sleep and you never heard such quiet…" His voice trailed off into a dark whisper. "Like what you see?" He set the cup of batter on the counter and started toward her, but she backed up and put the table between them.

"Oh, no, you don't. The next time you start a fire in this house," she pointed to herself, "you are going to put it out." Her pulse raced as he looked down at her and smiled, the slow, intimate beauty of it dulling her senses.

"You're the one who started that hot scene last night," he said, his smile broadening and lights dancing in his eyes. "All

I was after was a kiss, but you pulled out the stops and, honey, I'm a hungry man."

She nodded toward the stove and the smoking frying pan. "Is that why you're making pancakes?"

He rounded the table, pulled her to him, and covered her lips in a quick, demanding kiss before releasing her and walking back to the stove.

"I'm making these things because I always eat breakfast, and that's all I could find, but pancakes and nothing else that goes in my stomach are going to satisfy the hunger I'm talking about. So be a smart gal and stay away from the subject of my appetite. Where's the butter?"

"Butter? I'd think a doctor would be concerned about cholesterol."

"Absolutely. Where's the butter?" She got it for him, and her eyebrows arched at his practiced performance when he shook the pan and flipped over a cake.

"Where'd you learn how to do that?"

"Working in dozens of greasy spoons. I hope that stuff over there is maple syrup." He pointed toward a bottle.

"It is. Where'd you grow up?"

His head came up sharply. "San Francisco. Would you rather eat in here or on the patio? The sun'll be up in about half an hour, and I'd hoped we could watch the sunrise together."

"I love it out on the patio early in the morning; give me a minute to set the table." She went in the pantry for the linens and flatware and leaned against the doorjamb, certain that all she longed for had slipped through her fingers. Maybe she asked for more than he could give.

He took her hand as they walked down to the beach after breakfast with the early morning breeze whipping around them. Contentment, peace, enveloped him, and he let his right arm circle her waist and bring her closer to him.

"When I didn't see you in the living room or the den, I thought you'd left."

"That isn't my style. No offense meant, of course," he added, stopping and tweaking her nose. "Not like some people I know."

She showed no remorse for it, and he asked her whether she deserved some punishment for putting him through hell with her international escapades.

"I am not going to let you drag us into a fight and ruin this perfect morning."

They reached the beach, deserted but for them, pulled off their shoes, and walked along the water's edge as the sky welcomed the dazzling colors of the rising sun.

"If I wasn't dressed, I'd stretch out here." He pointed to a spot in the sand. "I love the feel of sand and cool breeze on my body."

Jeannetta picked up a handful of yellow grains and let them sift through her fingers, reminding him of other times he'd seen her do it. He wondered at its significance.

"You ought to burn your red bikini swim trunks—if you could call them that; they're indecent."

He stopped and gently turned her to face him. "You still think about that. Maybe you should have followed your instincts."

Her heavy lashes flew upward, and she looked into the distance. "Have you ever been... Has any woman ever...well... just *taken* you?"

"You mean have I ever been raped?" He had to laugh at the idea.

She nodded.

"Well, noooooo. Of course not. I'm rather big for that, don't you think?"

She looked out across the ocean, wet her lips with the tip of her tongue, and then met his gaze. "You came pretty close to it that morning on the Lido beach." He couldn't have moved if disaster had threatened them. If she'd wanted him a full two months before they made love, it was small wonder that she gave herself with such abandon.

"What stopped you?"

"I told you; I came to my senses. I still can't believe I got so close to committing such an awful crime." She stared, tongue-tied, as his laughter reverberated through the trees.

"*A crime?* We won't discuss what my reaction would have been, at least not so long as I'm still dealing with self-imposed celibacy."

Her gape of amazement was followed by a smile so dazzling that he had to believe she prized beyond measure his admission to wanting only her. He glanced at his watch. Seven forty-five, and time he headed back to the city and checked out things in his office. They strolled arm in arm to the house, and as they reached the patio, the ringing of his phone jarred their quiet world.

"I've got to get back. Mabel is worse, and she wants to see Skip and me. Come back with me. After what I saw last night, I don't see how I can leave you here."

"Please understand, Mason. I can't leave the house, Casper, my work. You saw that Casper will protect me, so don't worry."

"I need some tests on you, though that can wait a couple of weeks. But, honey, this place is deserted. Casper is a powerful dog, but could he handle two or three thugs, especially if they had guns?"

"The police were here within minutes after you called them last night. I have to stay, so please don't make me displease you."

"I don't want you out here alone where I can't protect you." What had he said to get her back up? He looked down at the fist propped on her hip and shook his head. If he lived to be a thousand, he'd never understand women.

"Now what?"

"You want to protect me, but it isn't protection that I need; I need you."

He frowned.

"What are you talking about? I've offered myself to you, and you've made it clear that you'll have me as a lover, but not as your husband. What does that make me in your estimation?"

"Oh, Mason, if only I could make you understand." He had to go; Mabel had about used up her resources, and time was of the essence. He phoned Laura and told her to send Skip to New York.

"I've got to go." He turned and looked at her. "You may wear your hair combed over that wound when you go out but, at other times, keep it uncovered." He grasped her hand. "Come on." She walked him to his car and stood on tiptoe for his kiss. She had to sense, to feel the pain that he couldn't hide from her. "I'll call you." As he drove off, he glanced at the rear-view mirror to see her white gauzy dress billowing in the breeze, and Casper standing close to her side, wagging his tail.

## Chapter 12

Jeannetta couldn't work; her mind clung to her tepid parting with Mason. She remembered how her parents had shared everything, had discussed problems, painful and pleasant, with Laura and herself. As far as she knew, they never argued and, with the wisdom of adulthood, she believed that their peace and congeniality sprang as much from knowledge of each other as from love. So she didn't think she had erred in holding out for the best of Mason. If she only knew why he wouldn't share himself with her, she'd know where to begin.

She walked out into the still, cool morning and released Casper. He stood obediently while she hooked a chain to his collar, and wagged his tail in anticipation of his morning frolic on the beach. It amazed her that the big dog didn't use his strength against her to force his will, but always waited patiently for her direction. After twenty minutes of chasing behind him, she brought him back to the house, took off the chain, fed him, and was about to put him in his house when his tail stood. She turned to see a Lincoln Town Car pull into the driveway.

A tall, well-dressed, and obviously furious man rushed from it, but Casper's angry growl brought him to a sudden halt. For the next half hour she dealt with a surly and indulgent parent who automatically took her for a maid. Upon learning that she wasn't, he demanded that she have the charges against his son dropped and his record cleared. It cheered her that Casper's presence tempered the man's belligerence. A bully, that's what he was, but not with Casper. He ranted and bellowed at her but, with each glance at Casper, he took a step backward.

"You ought to be thankful that my visitor was a surgeon who took care of your son's wounds. Your boy got a good lesson for trying to steal a dog. When my friends get back, you may speak to them about the charges; it's their house and their dog. Now, please leave."

"How dare you…"

"Do you intend to leave with or without Casper's help? You've got thirty seconds." After shaking his fist in the air, the man bolted for his car, got in, and rolled down the window.

"I hope I don't find out that you've bought the place because, if I do, you'll be looking for another one, and you'll have a hell of a time selling this." He backed out, and she wouldn't have been surprised if the speed with which he did it had split his tires. She went inside and called Laura.

"I'm sure glad you called, hon, 'cause I was just about to ring you. Skip's shaken about Mabel—she passed away, you know. Mason's on his way here, and we just can't get the child settled down. You want to try calming him?"

"I thought he was supposed to meet Mason in New York. What happened?"

"Mason called back before Skip could leave and gave us the news. Here he is."

"Hi, Jeanny. I guess you know what happened. Aren't you coming up here with my dad?"

She couldn't, and she knew he'd feel as though she had deserted him.

"If I leave here, Skip, there won't be anyone to take care of the dog, and he's too big for me to take with me."

"He is?"

She told him about Casper and promised that, if Mason didn't mind, he could visit her and the dog.

"Have you got a computer?" She offered to let him use hers when he visited.

He responded proudly. "That's okay; I can borrow my dad's laptop. Aunt Laura and Mrs. Ames have been teaching me a lot of things."

"*Aunt* Laura?" She couldn't believe Laura let him call her that; if so, she didn't need any more evidence of Clayton's powers as a miracle worker.

"Yeah. She said I couldn't call her by her first name, and since she's going to be my aunt…you know, she's your sister…and all. Well, you know…"

She wondered at his sudden silence.

"You're gonna marry my dad, aren't you?" This wasn't the time to disappoint him, but how could she lie?

"Skip, I'm so sorry about your aunt. It hurts, I know, but now you have Mason and he'll look after you." She thought she heard a sniffle.

"I know, but I didn't have time to get there. When Dad gets here, do you mind if I ask him to let me stay with you one weekend? He'd been complaining that you shouldn't be out there by yourself."

This wasn't the time to give him the impression that he wasn't needed, so she let it slide, but she'd get around to divesting him of the notion that she couldn't look after herself. She hung up and wandered around the house, out of sorts and aware that the feeling enveloped her whenever Mason left her. She slapped her knee. *Something had to give!*

Working with her needles always gave her a sense of peace, so she took some materials out to the patio and began crocheting dolls. Lost in the rhythm of the needles, images of another scene in which she had sat on a veranda and gazed at a garden of flowers, butterflies, and bees swirled around in her mind. She knew it was real, but couldn't place it. Frustrated, she called Mason's travel office and left a request that he telephone her.

"Are you alright? I'm on my way to Pilgrim, and I just got your message."

Everything settled inside of her with the sound of his voice.

"Hi. I'm okay. But I just had a vision of a garden of flowers in some far-off place, and I can't figure out where it was. Were we together in a garden?"

"I don't think so, but nearly every private home and most hotels in Zimbabwe have flower gardens. What else did you recall?" She told him about the butterflies and bees.

"Where did you go when you left my room the morning after we made love that first time? In Zimbabwe."

She couldn't contain a gasp. "You're so insistent about this, Mason. You must have some proof, and I want to know what it is. Please tell me. I'm trying to remember, and if what you say is true, it must have been wonderful, and I don't want it to remain a mystery to me."

"It *was* wonderful. Both times. Since you ask, you've got two little red moles on the lower part of your left breast, one just above your belly button, and three almost where your left thigh joins your hip, pretty close to your venus mound. Right? And remember, as an ophthalmologist, I didn't look below your neck, when you were under anesthesia."

"Oh, Mason, I'm so sorry I don't remember."

"With your permission, madam, I should be honoured and pleased to joggle your memory."

Shivers danced all through her at the promise she heard in his low chuckle.

"I'll bet," she told him dryly.

"Don't push it; it will come back, and my considerable experience tells me it won't be long. Everything else there alright?"

With his uncanny ability to sense problems where she was concerned, she wouldn't be surprised if he suspected her morning encounter with the irate stranger.

"Casper and I are fine, thanks." Well, it wasn't a lie, and he didn't have to know everything, she told herself.

"I could use a kiss."

She couldn't help laughing. "Sure you could; you've got these wires for protection."

His laughter warmed her. Oh, what she wouldn't give to be with him.

"Go ahead, tease me. I'll haul you in here and get those tests and prove my suspicions."

Her heart skidded down a foot and into her belly. "What suspicions?"

"My suspicion that Dr. Fenwick can discharge you and leave you to the mercy of Fenwick the man."

"Really?" she blustered. "In that case, place the order with the hospital out here, and I'll get the test tomorrow."

"You're pretty anxious," he growled. "Challenging me again, are you? Alright. Call Dr. Betz there in about two hours, and be prepared to take the test tomorrow. No food or drink after seven this evening. I'll call you late tomorrow with your test results. Meantime, from the minute you leave the hospital, fill up on protein and carbohydrates; you're going to need them."

"You look after yourself, too, dear," she advised sweetly,

"and if you have any doubts about what to do, get in touch with Michael Jordan, Carl Lewis, or one of those other sports fellows, and find out what keeps them going." The sound was that of tires screeching. But it couldn't have been; Mason was a level-headed man.

"Are you okay?" she asked him.

"Just wait 'til I get my hands on you."

Warming up to their bantering, she baited him with, "Tell me what you'll do," and held her breath for his response.

"Have you ever been hot and cold, wet and dry, crazy and sane, dying and bursting with life all at the same time?"

Shivers of anticipation raced down her spine, and goose pimples covered her arms.

"Not that I recall."

"I know you don't, but I intend to remind you; and I doubt it will ever slip your mind again, no matter what happens."

"Hmmm. Pretty big talk for a guy whose principles *always* rule his libido and who's never tempted to waver."

"Where'd you get that idea? Why do you think I slept on that chaise lounge on your back porch with my feet and half of my legs hanging off of it? If I'd gone to that guest room, I'd have taken you with me. That was willpower, and, if you want to test it, I'll keep you busy 'til you scream for mercy."

"Ho hum. Talk's easy done. I always heard that a man boasts of his feats because nobody else sees things his way." She couldn't help hugging herself when his deep warm laughter teased her ears.

"I've forgotten how we got into this conversation, but you have a habit of giving me a hard time when I'm not around to make you eat your words. I'll see you in a few days. Meanwhile, get plenty of rest, eat wholesome food, and conserve your energy." The dial tone terminated his joyous laughter.

"Oh, boy! I can't wait," she said aloud, and returned to her needlework, hoping for more revelations.

* * *

Mason pulled up in front of Rollins Hideaway and killed the motor. What would he say to Skip? The boy raced out of the building, ran up to him and stopped as though uncertain how to greet him. He put an arm around the child's shoulder and received a powerful hug; he wouldn't have thought Skip strong enough to embrace him so tightly.

"I know it hurts, son, but this is life. You have me now, and you are not alone. You understand that?" Skip nodded. "You and I have some business to attend to, and then we're going home."

"But my job still has a week to run, and Aunt Laura's depending on me. I can't leave her in a mess." They entered the Hideaway, and Geoffrey walked toward them.

"Lucy and I will be more than happy if Skip could visit with us for a few days before school starts. She says he can learn advanced math, and she wants to teach him." Mason fingered the keys in his pants pocket and made a decision.

"Thanks. I appreciate that, but Skip and I have to learn how to be a family, and the sooner we start, the better. I'll have less time next month when I resume my medical practice full time; after that, we won't see much of each other. He and I will be down to see you, though, and we'll always be in touch, Geoffrey."

The old man cocked his head to one side and looked Mason in the eye.

"Only a fool throws away a diamond, son, and Jeannetta Rollins is a rare one. Don't forget that. Give her our love."

Mason watched them get into the waiting taxi.

"Why didn't Laura or Clayton take them to the station?" he asked Skip.

"They offered, but Mrs. Ames said she wanted to ride around the lake and look at the mountains before she leaves Pilgrim. What kind of business do we have, Dad?"

"We have to get you relieved of your duties, and then we're going home." He explained to the boy while they walked up the stairs to their room that, in a few days, they'd have services for Mabel. He closed the door, kicked off his shoes and sat down, and, to his surprise, Skip brought him his house slippers. He looked at the boy and grinned.

"I see fatherhood has its rewards. Thanks."

"I told you," Skip said. "I'm going to take good care of you." Both of his eyebrows arched.

"Son, I'm only thirty-seven years old. You can take care of me when I'm eighty."

"Gee. Do I have to wait that long?" He couldn't help laughing; he didn't yet have Jeannetta, but this wonderful boy was his. His son. He gave silent thanks that they'd found each other.

Three days later, he and Skip began a new life. He took the boy to his office at the travel agency and introduced him to his staff, then to his medical office to meet his secretary and technician.

Edna had gone for the day, but he found her notes: Steve wants you to call him, and Dr. Betz said the tests are great and he's sending them by FedEx. He phoned Steve. He'd tell Jeannetta about the tests when he'd read them for himself.

"Mason, can you stop by here? I need to talk with you."

"Okay, but Skip is with me."

Steve's silence told him that the conversation would be personal.

"Uh…okay. He can surf the Internet, and we'll talk in the living room."

"What's up, Steve?"

"Hi, Uncle Steve. Is it alright if I check out the Internet?" Steve nodded.

"What's this all about, man?"

Steve motioned to a big overstuffed chair. "Take a load off your feet." He went in the kitchen and returned with two cans of Pilsner. "Mason, a private investigator in one of the buildings that I service left a manila folder in the men's room, and when I opened it to see whose it was, I saw your name. So I stopped and read it. The next evening, I took it to the private investigator who'd left it there and confronted him. I refused to return it to him until he told me why he was investigating you. He had no choice but to level with me, because the folder also contained records of several of his current cases. Jeannetta Rollins ordered the report when she was considering taking the tour, so she knew everything about you. That guy is so good that he has his name on his door in brass, and he sits two doors from the company president. I'm sorry, Mason, but, from where I sit, this isn't squeaky clean."

Mason pushed his beer aside, and his right hand automatically went to the keys in his pocket. Another left hook to the belly. He looked up to see his brother's gaze locked firmly on him, but he didn't reply. He didn't want to react right then, because he needed to deal with his feelings in private. He loved his brother, but he couldn't help feeling some hostility toward the man who had pricked his balloon. With her test probably clean, he had planned to release her the next day and to see her within forty-eight hours. He rested his head against the back of the chair and told himself to be fair. Steve was doing as he always had; he put his brother's interests above everything else. Still, it wasn't Steve's place to judge her.

"I have to let this set a while; then, if you want to talk about it, okay. But not now." Steve nodded, but Mason knew that his brother wasn't remorseful for having told him; he'd thought it over well.

"How long have you known about this, Steve?"

"A couple of days. I did a lot of thinking about it, and you do the same. Our daddy used to say 'haste makes waste,' so don't do anything rash." At Mason's raised eyebrow, Steve corrected himself.

"I know that last comment was unnecessary; I'd trust your judgment any day."

"You said you wanted to meet her; I'm going to arrange that." Steve's head turned sharply toward Mason, and he looked hard at his brother, seemingly unable to utter a word. "By the way," Mason went on, ignoring his brother's state of mild shock. "I met a guy, a homeless fellow I'd like you to try out. I'm not certain, but you might be his one chance."

"What's special about this one?"

"He's an engineer who lost his business, his home, and his wife, in that order. He's only been on the street for about seven months, so there's hope for him. What do you say?"

"Okay, I'll give him a shot…if he wants it."

"I'm not sure he does, but he ought to have a chance. Thanks. I'll get in touch with him as soon as I can." A smile played around the corner of Steve's mouth, almost unwillingly, it seemed to Mason.

"I get a bang out of the way you tell a person to butt out of your business," Steve said, as much to himself as to Mason. "Not a single unpleasant word," he went on, as though bemused. "You merely change the topic. I can't help wondering what you'd do if some unfortunate guy insisted on pulling your strings. What *would* you do?"

"No telling. I need to think about what you said. Okay?"

"Sure. How you deal with it is your business; I thought you should know."

Mason got out of bed, turned off the air conditioner, opened a window, and let the cool night air soothe his body. She'd known him for over five months now, six if you counted their first meeting in March, and she'd had numerous opportunities to tell him about it, to apologize, to say she wished she hadn't done it. Nothing. And how many times had he asked her why she'd decided to take the tour? Her answer each time was that she wanted to see the world. Granted that thirty thousand dollars was a lot of money, even for a two-month, first-class world tour, and a smart person would make certain of the sponsoring agency's integrity. But she investigated *him,* not the agency, and she did it because her sole reason for taking that tour was to get him to operate on her. He couldn't even blame her for that. But when she let him care for her, before she let him love her, she should have told him.

He threw on a robe and headed for Skip's room, needing the assurance that, at least, all was well with his boy. He blinked at the bright light.

"Why aren't you asleep?"

"I couldn't." He pointed his finger around the room. "I got my own room, my own closet and bathroom, even my own radio and computer. You're used to all this, but I always had to go out in the hall to the bathroom. I can't get over it. How do you expect me to sleep?"

He sat on the edge of the bed. "You'll get used to it, just as I did." He told him of the way in which he and Steve had struggled after losing their parents, and of his debt to his brother. "For a few months, a while back, I forgot where I came from but, once I remembered, I started to straighten out my life. Don't forget your roots, son; they're a part of who you are."

"Yes sir, Mas...Dad, you gonna marry Jeanny, aren't you?"

He thought for a bit and couldn't help being amazed that Skip could show so much patience, when the matter had become important to him.

"You and I aren't going to lie to each other, Skip. To be honest, I don't know." The boy sat forward in bed, his face crumpled with worry.

"But don't you want to?"

"Yes, I want to, but we have things to work out, and we don't seem to be getting anywhere."

"Want me to talk to her, tell her what a great guy you are?"

He couldn't help smiling. Innocence had its virtues; if nothing else, it allowed you to have hope.

"I'll take care of it, son. It's something that I, alone, can do. Now go to sleep, because you're getting up at seven o'clock." He went back to his room, got in bed, and stared at the ceiling.

Jeannetta raced to the phone, wondering who would call her so early in the morning. She'd just returned from a walk along the beach and had taken Casper with her. The ringing stopped about the time she picked it up, so she went back outside, fed the dog, gathered some orange and yellow marigolds, put them in the dining room, and sat down to work. Half an hour later, the phone's ring jarred the silence.

"Hi."

At the sound of his voice, her whole body came to life, and tiny needlelike pricks danced along her nerves. "Hi, yourself," she said, trying to sound casual.

"I thought I'd have to take a ride out there. I rang half a dozen times and, when you didn't answer…well, I didn't know what to think."

"Casper and I were on the beach."

"Oh, yes; let us not forget Casper."

She didn't see the need for sarcasm, and she wondered at it, because he didn't usually resort to that. "Have you seen my test?"

"I got a preliminary report. So far, so good. But that isn't why I'm calling. I'd prefer to discuss this face to face, but that isn't possible, and I need to talk about it right now."

She flinched at his cool and impersonal tone. "What is this about, Mason?"

His brief silence did nothing to allay her anxiety. "I can understand why you would have investigated the agency, and even why you hired a private detective investigator to scour my record and dig up whatever dirt he could find, but I do not understand and cannot accept your letting the relationship between us get to this point without telling me you did it. You didn't know me last March; I could have been a larcenous crook, so you were entitled to satisfaction that you were making a good investment. But that wasn't your purpose. You claimed that you only wanted to see the world, but what you wanted was certainty that I could do your operation and that I hadn't left medicine in disgrace. Fine. Suppose I say that, too, was your right. But you had no right to tell me you loved me, to make love with me, and to encourage my caring for you, without telling me you'd done this."

She released a deep sigh as she recalled Laura's prophesy. The piper had come to collect. "I can't deny what you're saying because all of it's true. My excuse for not telling you is that I was afraid of hearing you say no when I asked you to operate. I kept putting it off. Then, as I got to know you and learned to love you, I didn't want to hurt you by telling you about the investigation, so I kept quiet about it and prayed you'd never find out."

"As I think back, it's clear to me that I gave you plenty of chances to tell me about this *and* about your scheme to get me back into medicine. I've been sifting through this, and I don't much like what I see. I can't accept it, Jeannetta. I'm sorry."

Sheer black fright swept through her and pinion-like darts of panic knotted her belly. "What are you saying?"

"You said we're not suited to each other, that I don't meet your needs. Maybe some of your reasoning is subconsciously based on my humble background. Some of it could be more personal. Whatever. I'm accepting your judgment. I'll call tomorrow with a final report on your health. Take care."

She gazed at the phone, horrified. *"That's it?"*

"'Fraid so. Good-bye, Jeannetta."

She'd gambled and lost. Would he have reacted in this way if she had agreed to marry him? She supposed she'd never know. Calmly, she opened her computer, began chapter eighteen of her novel, typed five or six lines, and wiped the water from her face with the back of her hand. She typed faster and faster, then she looked at the screen and saw rows of nonsensical phrases, half-spelled words, sentences in which "Mason" appeared a dozen times. The water of her pain pooled in her lap, and some of it settled like brine on her tongue. She got up, washed her face, and went back to work but, within minutes, the tears that poured from her eyes obscured her vision. She wanted to ignore the phone, but the persistent caller won out. She moved slowly toward it; it could be anyone. Anyone but Mason.

"Yes," She spoke softly to hide the trembling she knew her voice would display.

"Jeanny, this is Laura. You alright?"

"I'm fine," she lied.

"Well, you won't be for long. Alma Williams has told everybody in town that Jethro left her for you. She says he's spent the last month with you."

Jeannetta imagined that her shriek could be heard for miles.

"I needed this. I've been leading a dull life out here with not a thing to occupy my mind. This is just the ticket."

"Jeannetta Rollins, you sure you're alright?" Jeannetta rolled her eyes toward the ceiling.

"Fine as French perfume. Anything else?" She looked around her at the house that wasn't hers, the furniture that wasn't her taste, the paintings she would not have chosen. If she had her car, she'd get in it and drive until it needed repair, no matter what Mason said. Laura's scolding got her attention.

"This isn't like you, Jeanny. You get on that train and come on back home. You hear?"

"I'll be back when Kay and David get here. Not before. Now for heaven's sake, calm down. I've had as much as I want to handle today." She regretted the words as they were leaving her mouth.

"What do you mean by that? Something's gone wrong between you and Mason. I just know it. I told Clayton that if you didn't stop stringing him along, you'd regret it."

"Laura," she began patiently, "does Mason strike you as a man anybody can dangle? Does he?"

"Oh, he can dangle, alright, but not the way you've been doing it. If you want the fish to bite, you got to know how to cast."

Her mouth dropped open; this new Laura became more amazing with the passing days.

"This fish bit."

"He sure did, but is he still on the line? Or was your reeling so fancy that he got loose? You come on home and deal with Alma. You hear? For all you know, that foolish Jethro will show up at your front door. Then what'll you do?"

"Let him. Casper could use a little exercise."

They said good-bye and she dropped the receiver into its cradle. One more hassle. Feeling miserable, and fighting a slowly rising tide of anger, she turned back to her computer, erased what she'd written after Mason's unsettling call and began the culmination of her novel. Anger, she realized, could be energizing. She had pitied Alma for her marriage to a man who didn't love her, though the woman had gone into it fraudulently, but she would have to put a stop to that vicious tongue. Pilgrim was as puritanical a town as its name, and she couldn't risk being the subject of every sermon preached there for the next month. And gossip was the fuel that kept the town's motor running.

She let the phone ring, but when she heard Skip's voice on the answering machine, she picked up.

"Hello, Skip, what a pleasant surprise."

"Hi, Jeanny. How you doing? My dad told me last night he's not sure you're going to marry him. It's not because of me, is it?"

"Darling, I'd love to have you for a son, but this is between your dad and me." She understood his longing to be a part of a real family, to have a mother and father to love and who loved him, and she would have loved to help make his dream come true. But that gift was no longer hers to bestow.

"I don't think my dad wanted me to call you, so I better not say anything else. I'll ask him when I can go see you, okay?"

"Of course. I'd love to see you." Absentmindedly, she dropped the receiver toward its cradle and heard it bounce on the table top. She had put it in place and had started to the terrace when she heard Casper's growl and then the wheels of a car crunching the gravel. Her heart skipped wildly in her chest and then slowed. The postman. She should have known it wouldn't be Mason, because he was not a wishy-washy man; if he said good-bye, he meant it. She talked aloud to herself, reaching deep inside for inner peace.

# Chapter 13

Jeannetta's fragile peace of mind deserted her the next day at noon when she heard the urgency and anger in Laura's voice. "Mason and Skip just got here, and Mason brought the *Morning Herald*. I told you to put a stop to Alma. You know Ed Wiggins; he publishes the paper. Well, she told him she's suing you for alienation of affection. I called him up and told him to get out of here with that nineteenth-century stuff, but he says she can do that. Honey, Mason is pacing the floor like a caged tiger. You want to talk to him?"

She did. Oh, how she wanted to hear his voice utter a loving sound, but she declined.

"If he wants to talk, Laura, he'll call."

"There you go being clever again. Sometimes I'm glad I don't have your degrees; my uneducated way of doing things makes a lot of more sense. What are you going to do about Alma Williams?"

"I'll take care of it. Save me a copy of that paper, please, and don't worry about it."

* * *

Mason sat in the coffee shop with Laura and Clayton, while Skip broadened his mind on the Internet.

"Who is this Alma Williams?" Mason asked Laura. He listened to the story, strumming his fingers on his knee while Laura related it. "That's ridiculous."

Clayton sipped his cappuccino and leaned back in his chair. "You don't believe it?"

Mason knew he was releasing his own frustration when he eyed Clayton with a steel-like, unfriendly gaze. "Anybody who has spent any time with Jeannetta ought to know that such behavior is beneath her."

Clayton's loud laugher, unusual for him, told Mason that he'd just been tested. "How are you planning to help her?"

"Leave it to me, man; I'll think of something."

"Aren't you at least going to ask her whether it's true before you stick your hand in the fire?" Laura asked. "You know, let her know you're there for her."

The temptation to laugh at Clayton's stern glare at Laura was too great. Mason dropped his head in his hand and his shoulders shook. He had a mind to ask them if they knew how much like a long-married couple they appeared. Skip bounded into the room, ending that conversation.

"Dad, there's a hurricane watch for the East Coast, and it's supposed to hit Long Island. Jeanny's on Long Island. I found the place with my web crawler. Shouldn't you call her and tell her to come home or something?"

Apprehension gnawed at him, but he kept his expression neutral; Skip adored Jeannetta, and he didn't want to worry him.

"I'll call her; I was planning to do that anyway." He didn't bother to explain that his call wouldn't be a professional one. He hadn't wanted to come to the Hideaway; the sooner he got some distance between Jeannetta and himself, the quicker he'd get his life in order. But he had promised Skip that they would visit Laura and, if he did nothing else, he would keep his word to his son. He went up to their room and telephoned her.

"Hello." The soft, unsteady voice crept into him, shook him, its ability to clobber his senses taking him unaware.

"Hello, Jeannetta." His hand reached voluntarily for his chest as though to still his galloping heart. He was too old to be experiencing the kind of ache that tore through him. *He needed her.*

"Mason. How are you?" He couldn't let himself hurt her by using a professional tone, because no matter what she'd done, he loved her.

"Well enough. Skip tells me a storm's headed your way. Are you planning to come in?"

"I hadn't heard of it, but I'm in a protected cover, and Kay said this house never gets storm damage. I'll be alright."

"Don't be too sure; Skip said it's being projected to move right over you." He paused, unwilling to give her his news, because that would end their conversation, and he'd have to hang up. He made himself do it.

"You're free of me, Jeannetta. Your tests showed excellent results, and if you avoid stress, limit reading, writing, and TV hours to four hours a day for the next two weeks, you're home free."

"I see… I mean, thanks. Thank you for everything, Mason." She didn't want to hang up and neither did he. He switched the phone to his left hand, stuck his right one in his pocket and fingered the old keys. How on earth was he going to give her up? Her and all of his dreams.

"Don't forget to take care of yourself, Jeannetta," he managed, when the silence roared in his ears, broadcasting the extent to which their once warm and loving relationship had skidded.

"I… You, too, Mason. Mason, you may send your bill to me at Hideaway."

Sputtering wasn't something he did, but words nearly failed him. "Jeannetta, I hope that's the last time I hear you mention compensation to me. I should pay you for having led me back to my true calling, the life I love most. Consider us even. All the best."

"Good-bye, Mason." He looked out of the window at the autumn-hued mountain and wondered what his life would be like a year hence. Well, standing there wouldn't give him the answer, and he could at least get the rest of his life in order. He had to get back home and get ready to open his office after Labor Day. He called Skip as he ambled down the stairs.

"I'm ready to go. You stay with Laura for a few days and let Clayton help you finish building that chemistry lab."

"Okay. But you sure you won't need me for something?"

Mason ran his fingers over the boy's tight curls.

"I probably will, but I think it's best you stay here for two or three days. You'll know where I am." He looked down at Skip's hand tugging at his wrist.

"Are you going to West Tiana to look after Jeanny?"

Mason had promised never to lie to Skip, but he didn't know the answer to that himself.

"I don't know, Skip. I…I just can't say."

"She's real nice, Dad."

"I know, son. Believe me, I know."

He made it back to New York in an hour and a half.

"Any messages, Viv?" He wished he could have Viv at his medical office when he opened up in a couple of weeks, but she'd become indispensable to the travel agency and, if he persuaded Steve to manage it, his brother would need her.

"Steve called, and we had a nice long talk, but I couldn't get him to say he'd be my new boss. He did promise to stop by here, though." She winked at him. "How'm I doing?"

"Great. What about that storm? Heard anything?" She confirmed Skip's information that the storm would pass directly over Long Island. He twirled two pencils. No way could he leave her out there alone in a storm on that dead-end street; if anything happened to her, he would never get over it. He picked up the phone and dialed Skip.

"You leave that place right now, you hear?"

Jeannetta wanted to cover her ears, but instead, she said, "Laura, you mean well, but even if I wanted to leave here, I'd have to take Casper with me, and I can't. The place is secure, so stop worrying."

"Well, if you won't listen to me, maybe you'll pay attention to Clayton," Laura told her.

Exasperated, Jeannetta released a sally. "Laura, I know Clayton has replaced the King James version of the Bible as your source of Gospel, but what he says isn't sacred to me, so give me a break. I can't use any of Clayton's wisdom right now. I have to get back to work. Good-bye." She finished taping the window panes and went outside to look at the clouds. Casper's whimpers alerted her to his precarious situation, and she decided to put him on the screened back porch. She remembered having seen a piece of oilcloth in the pantry, got it and nailed it over a section of the porch-screen to provide dry shelter for Casper. Then, she gathered as many candles as she could, found a portable radio, a flash light and some matches, made some sandwiches, and settled back to await whatever came. The black clouds soon released torrents of rain that pelted the house in an ominous rhythm. As she lighted the woodburning fireplace, Casper's low growl brought her upright. The growling increased, and she glanced toward the window just as the headlights illumined the driveway.

"Who on earth…?" She thought her heart slammed into her belly when she saw Mason's white Cougar. She had thought he was at the Hideaway. Casper growled furiously and she rushed to the porch to pat him and reassure him. She got an umbrella and opened the front door, but the rain and wind nearly knocked her backward, and drenched the marble foyer floor. She braced herself, stepped out, and attempted to open the umbrella, but within seconds she had no idea where the wind had taken it. Mason stepped into the foyer, drenched from the short run in the rain, pulled her from the door, and managed to close it.

She took his wet hand and walked them into the living room, pulled his jacket off of him and laid it in front of the fire. Then she brought several bath towels and wrapped one around his shoulders. She stood behind him trying to dry his trousers with a towel, and he turned and looked at her, seared her with the hot longing in his eyes. Her breathing quickened and deepened, and she knew he couldn't help noticing the sharp rise and fall of her bosom, and the way she longed for him.

"You're wet, too," he said, the first words spoken since he'd stopped the car in front of the house.

She shook her head vigorously. "It's okay. I don't care."

"I do."

She lost her battle to stop the trembling of her lips. "Do you?"

"Oh, sweetheart."

She was in his arms, and his mouth moved over her, plundering hungrily until she parted her lips and took his tongue into her mouth. He hadn't forgiven her, and she still needed something that he hadn't given her, but their bodies gave the lie to it as they clung to each other. She wanted to wrap herself around him, to know the limits of his virile power, and she held him as tightly as she could until he groaned and stepped away from her.

He answered her inquiring look with a rueful smile. "Walking away is easier said than done."

She didn't want to hope in vain, but she began to believe they had a chance. Maybe Laura was right about her fishing theory.

"I missed you, Mason. Oh, I know, all this happened yesterday, but it seems like years to me."

"Don't I know it. By the way, where's Casper?"

She was not going to let that hurt her. She'd try instead to understand him. "Do you want to change the subject?"

His half laugh was that of a person caught out. "Actually, no. I just wondered." His attention seemed to shift to the sounds of the storm, the rain that pelted the house, and the noise of the wind, giving the impression of someone anticipating danger. And she knew his thoughts focussed on the storm and their safety.

"I put Casper on the back porch. He's quiet, because he knows you." She went to the closet and got a robe. "I'm sure David wouldn't mind your borrowing this. I can put your clothes in the drier, and you won't catch a cold."

"Don't tempt me with that thing. If I pull off my clothes, it'll happen after I've taken yours off of you. I'll dry standing here, thanks."

She laughed. If he knew how good that sounded to her, he might regret having said it. She decided to test the water.

"You don't honestly think I have to lure you with a man's robe, do you? I always thought I had more beguiling assets. 'Course, if that's what lights your fuse, by all means put your arms in it." The lights flickered. Suddenly, she hoped they'd go out, hoped the storm would isolate them from the world until they'd resolved their differences. His steady, humorless gaze nearly unnerved her.

"*You* light my fuse."

Emboldened by the hunger in his eyes, she took recourse to daring. "Not recently, I haven't."

His hands gripped her forearms, and her body burned from the intensity of his hot gaze.

Rain pelted the roof, fire crackled in the big stone fireplace, the flames danced like frenzied sex partners, and the scent of half-green pine logs filled her nostrils. He was there. Big, masculine, handsome, and virile, the only man she had ever loved. Sparks shot through the grill that separated them from the roaring blaze, and another kind of spark shot through her body, lighting her passion.

She met him with raised arms and parted lips, and thrilled as his strong arms held her still for his plundering kiss. The evidence of his desire, strong, virile, and nestled near the portal of her womanhood, telegraphed a message to her brain, startling her. She knew what he'd do next, his lover's technique. The picture of his perfect body supine in yellow sand, almost every inch of him exposed to her in early morning sun rays, floated back to her, and the movement of her hips begged for his entrance. Dizzying sensations of long-awaited release streaked through her when his hand covered her breast, and damp warmth settled in her core. He stepped back and gazed intently into her eyes.

"Have you forgotten that you're no longer my patient?"

She didn't flinch from his stare.

"No. And neither have I forgotten that my doctor discharged me." Excitement hurtled through her when the telltale greenish-brown colored his irises and his lips parted. She tried to move closer to him, but he kept a safe foot of space between them.

"Nothing has changed; we're right where we were yesterday morning."

The wind howled, rain pelted the windows and roof, but things weren't the same, no matter what he said.

"It's changed for me, not completely maybe, but you're here

because you needed to protect me in this storm when, yesterday morning, you'd told me good-bye and hung up."

"And you'll take me as I am? Offering nothing more than before?"

She sucked in her breath and willed her fingers to the buttons on her blouse.

"Aren't you doing the same?"

Her blouse hung open, exposing her bare breasts to him, and hot lights glittered in his eyes.

"Answer me, Jeannetta."

The urgency of his low guttural tones sent the heat of desire coursing through her. "No strings. I want you. I need you..."

He pulled the blouse from her shoulders, hooked his thumbs in the waistband of her skirt and panties, and peeled them from her body. Her busy fingers worked at his shirt until she could open it and touch her breasts to his hard chest. Frenzied with passion, she loosened his belt, unzipped him, and pressed herself to him as the remainder of his clothes dropped to his feet. He stepped out of them, fitted her to his body and held her there. Her whole self was a flaming torch as his lips claimed her mouth, his tongue dabbed at the pulse of her throat, and his hands alerted her body to its God-given potential.

He lifted her, and eased them to the floor, and carefully placed her on the thick brown carpet before the fire. Her arms opened to him as he knelt above her, and spread her legs for his loving entrance.

"Tell me, honey, can you remember being with me like this? Close your eyes and let it happen."

Her body twisted beneath him, inviting, urging.

"I don't and, right now, all I want is for you to love me, to show me what I don't remember, what I'm like with you." She brought him fully into her arms and lifted her body to him, but he took control. His fiery possession of her mouth erased thoughts of all but him, and she hooked her legs around his hips. When she couldn't hold back the need to move beneath him, he locked her hands above her head and pulled her hard nipple into his mouth.

"Mason, please…I…I can't stand this." He suckled her more vigorously until she cried out, "Honey, I'm going to explode." She didn't know whether rain and wind crashed through the window, if the door banged open, or if the storm only raged with intensity inside her, as his masterful strokes hurled her into ecstasy.

Mason looked down at Jeannetta asleep in his arms. The hurt from her lack of trust remained, and he didn't know how to rid himself of it. He did know that by making love with her again, he'd eliminated any chance of being happy without her. She suited him in every way that mattered. Her soft, sated purr sent frissons of heat through him and he felt the hunger grip him again. The wind had died down, but sheets of rain pelted the windows, and the storm in him raged anew. He reached for a towel, covered her with it, and let his eyes feast on her beloved face. Her lashes lifted and frowns creased her forehead. Then a smile spread over her face, and she raised herself up and kissed his mouth.

"Are you sorry, Mason?"

His heartbeat accelerated at the sight of the naked anxiety in her eyes. "I couldn't regret what I just experienced with you. No. I'm not sorry, and I'll never be."

"But does it change anything?"

He let his fingers trace her spine and tried not to let his mind dwell on how much he wanted her right that minute. "I don't know. I haven't begun to sort it out, so I'm as puzzled as you are that we could unite as we did with so much between us that isn't right. Excuse me, but if I don't put some wood on this fire, we'll freeze."

\* \* \*

She wrapped a bath towel around her and, as she stood, her glance took in the ceiling-high window and the sheets of rain that cascaded down its length.

"Mason! *Mason!* Look at that. Look!"

"What? What is it?"

"That water. I've seen it in my dreams, falling down a mountain into a river. And that hotel lobby with the malachite columns, the jacaranda tree, the…the veranda of that hotel with the flowers and butterflies…the morning I…you had a nightmare…you were afraid your knife would slip when you operated on me…you were talking in your sleep, thrashing in bed and I…" Her bottom lip dropped and her eyes widened as she stared into his anxious face.

"I remember…I remember that night, everything, and at my house in Pilgrim, when I could hardly make out your image. Thank God, I remember it all."

His arms went around her, and he smothered his face in the curve of her shoulder.

"Imagine not being able to remember something so wonderful as what we shared; I'd never had such feelings."

He raised his head and looked at her. "Why did you leave?"

"I had decided to go back with you and do whatever you recommended, but after I listened to you struggling with your subconscious, I couldn't be responsible for your turmoil if you failed."

"But you risked certain blindness, though it might have been reversible. Why?"

She tightened her arms around her body, walked to the window, turned, and faced him. "No matter what you believe, I loved you then. I love you now."

He looked down into the flames, and her pulse raced with her fear of rejection.

"It's best I don't respond. I won't say there's no hope for

us, because I try to be honest about what I feel. But I have to come to terms with my reservations about you; if I don't, this resentment will harden, and that's no basis for a lasting relationship. I expect the same goes for you."

Her breath lodged in her throat, and she could only nod. He was saying that they had a chance.

"Can we still see each other? I mean, I need to know how you are, how Skip is."

"Alright. I'll touch base with you, and you can call me while we try to get a handle on this thing. We have to accept that we may not be able to work it out, and be ready to get on with our lives." She got the robe and handed it to him.

"That dark gray color doesn't do a thing for you, but then you're not a blue-eyed blond like David."

"Tell me what turns you on, and I'll stop by a store and order some of it." If he was serious, his sly grin and teasing tone belied it.

"Red string bikinis," she threw over her shoulder, as she headed up the stairs, to her bedroom. The other two times when they'd made love, he had drowned her in a vortex of ecstatic passion, but when he'd held her in his arms at the end of it, she had ached with unbelievable pain. The same deadening emptiness began to invade her.

When she had given Casper his morning run and finished her chores, Mason had already been driving for an hour. The south shore had been spared the brunt of the storm, and West Tiana hadn't sustained any damage. She had no inclination to work, but was tempted to daydream of her night and morning with him. He'd awakened her with loving that was tender, gentle, and caring, but he had been almost demonic in his drive to wring every semblance of passion from her, draw gesture after gesture of total submission from her, and to thrust her into orgasmic ecstasy time and time again. But she couldn't fault him; he'd been as honest as he was determined, and when he'd been lost in his own vortex of passion, he had let her see and feel his complete surrender. But he hadn't repeated his marriage proposal, and she didn't know what her response would have been if he had.

She got a rake and combed the debris from the lawn and hedges, well aware that if she didn't stop procrastinating, she wouldn't complete her novel by the Labor Day deadline. Nevertheless, she found other excuses. When his call finally came, late that evening, she understood the reason for her day-long mental vacation.

"Hi. This is Mason."

She fell backward across the bed, kicked off her shoes and rolled over on her belly.

"Hi."

"None the worse for your overnight activities, I trust?"

She glared at the phone and told herself to let only sweet words come out of her mouth if he started talking like a doctor.

"What activities, honey?" Excitement pervaded her, and she swung over on her back, as his rumbling laughter worked its magic on her.

"That's right, play dumb. You were there right along with me, sweetheart."

She rested both feet on the head of the four-poster bedstead and looked up at the ceiling.

"You must be talking about some other girl. I was here in this house all last evening."

He laughed aloud, and she wished she could see his face.

"Yeah, but whose boots were under your bed, baby?"

Laughter bubbled up in her, and she gave it full rein. "Search me."

"You don't know?" he growled.

"Well, from the look of this bite on my neck, it must have been Count Dracula, but he's supposed to be a myth, isn't he?"

"I'd laugh, but I'm not sure that's funny. Apply an antibiotic cream and a Band-Aid. That ought…"

"Cut it out." She yelled it, and she didn't care. "What would you do if you didn't have a cent?"

"Well, I don't know," he said, after obviously having thought about it. "I've never been flat broke. What would you do?"

"Me? I'd write Avon and tell them how much I love their toilet articles and inveigle them into sending me some free samples."

"Alright. I forgot you write jokes for comedians. Don't tell me anybody bought that one."

"I haven't tried to sell it, because I just made it up, but it already served the purpose of getting you off of your medical soap box. I didn't want Mason, the man, to get away from me."

"I'm not going any place. Sleep well." She blew him a kiss and waited.

"I kiss you, too. Good night, and be careful out there."

She sat up and tried to think. His mood had been intimate, but not his conversation. The job ahead of her would challenge any mortal woman: she had to teach him what it meant to love, and she had to earn his forgiveness.

Mason washed his pizza down with tomato juice, rinsed his plate and glass, and put them in the dishwasher. Skip usually rushed to do that. How could he miss the boy so badly when they'd been living together less than a month? He called him.

"Hi, Dad. Did you know Aunt Laura's worried about Jeanny? You want to talk to her?"

"Not right now. What's the problem?"

"Gee, I don't know. Uncle Clayton said it's just gossip. I'm ready to go home. When you coming up?"

"Tomorrow morning." He had to do something about getting Skip in Sunday school, but that would have to wait another week. He'd postponed it, because churchgoing wasn't one of his habits. Being a parent changed a lot of things; you not only had to know what was right, you had to do it. He hung up and took Steve's call.

"Thought I'd drop by for a minute, if you're not busy." Half an hour later Steve arrived with a quart of peach ice cream and a small coconut cake.

"I figured you'd already eaten dinner," he explained. They served themselves generous helpings of the desserts.

"Say, how'd you and Darlene Jones make out?"

Steve rested his spoon and seemed to pick his words. "So-so. I liked her alright, and I probably could've liked her a lot better, if I'd ever had a chance to say anything."

"What do you mean?" He watched Steve for signs of irritation, but saw none, and probed further. "She wouldn't talk with you? She always seemed pretty gregarious to me."

"The problem was that she talked *to* me. All the damned time. I couldn't get a word in edgewise. She acted as if I expected her to entertain me, and I couldn't get it across to her that I wanted a companion, someone to talk *with,* to share things with. I quit calling her; I didn't need the frustration."

"I'm sorry, Steve. I'd hoped the two of you would make it."

Steve helped himself to another slice of cake.

"How is it you never introduced me to Viv?"

Mason jerked forward. "Viv? I…it never occurred to me. You want to meet her?"

"Well," Steve began with uncustomary diffidence, "we've talked on the phone a lot since you got back from the tour; I'm either calling your travel office, or she's calling me trying to trace you, so she said to me one day that we'd been talking for ages but we'd never met, and maybe we ought to introduce ourselves. I told her I'd been thinking the same thing, so we agreed that I'd pick her up at the office after work and we'd get a drink, or go to dinner or the movies or something, whatever we felt like."

Mason stopped eating and stared at his brother. "What happened, man?"

"Well...I walked through the door, and this pretty woman sitting there looked up and saw me. Man, I stopped dead in my tracks; I couldn't have moved, if you'd pushed me."

Mason didn't bother to hide his disbelief; of all the scenarios he could have imagined, this wasn't one. "Are you serious?"

"Am I ever! She smiled like pure sunshine, got up from that desk, and came to meet me with her arms wide open. 'You're Steve,' was all she said, and I walked right into those arms." He shook his head as if he couldn't believe it. "Man, I haven't been the same since." Mason knew his mouth hung open but, in the circumstances, not even Steve would consider that bad manners.

He stared at Steve. "You fell for Viv?"

"Hook, line and sinker, and if that makes me stupid, it's too late to tell me."

"Stupid? Man, that's a stroke of brilliance. Viv's wonderful. Is it working?"

"It's working."

What would Steve say to the idea forming in his mind? "You two would make a great business team."

"That's what she says, but it's...I don't want to louse this up by working with her."

He had never discussed Steve's personal life with him, and he wasn't sure how far to go, but he'd had his share of lectures, so he was entitled. "Some of the best partnerships are husband-wife teams."

"You think so? I haven't gone quite that far."

"You headed that way?"

"Looks like it."

Mason got up and slapped Steve's back. "Right on man."

Steve cut his third slice of cake, put a forkful of it in his mouth and allowed Mason to wait until he chewed and swallowed it. "I've been aiming to ask what's going on with you and Jeannetta."

"We're in limbo. I'm not what she needs, or so she says, and I've wondered whether that's a ruse, a cover to hide the fact that all she ever wanted from me was…"

"Don't finish it, Mason. Don't say it."

Mason shook his head in wonder. Nothing and no one had perplexed him so much as Jeannetta.

"Yeah. I know. When I start to think, to remember some things about her, I know I'm being unfair."

Steve finished the cake, stashed their dishes in the sink, and leaned against a wall, facing his brother. "You mind if I meet her?" At Mason's startled look, he added, "Skip's crazy about her and, when it comes to people, kids have good antennas. What do you say?"

Mason shrugged both shoulders and resisted reaching for his old keys.

"Alright with me. I'll arrange it."

Steve shook his head as though displeased. "Mason, I'm asking you to bring her to my apartment to see me." Their gazes locked, and Mason understood that Steve was demanding respect.

"Okay. I'll speak to her."

He parked a few feet from the Hideaway's front door, because he intended to stay just long enough to get Skip, but Laura rushed to him waving a subpoena and clutching a legal-size envelope in her other hand.

"I got a court summons to witness against my own sister, and I know this letter contains one for Jeannetta. Alma Wil-

liams has gone too far with her lies. This will be the talk of
Pilgrim."

He couldn't believe it. "Let me see that." He looked at the
claim that Jethro Williams currently resided with Jeannetta
Rollins in West Tiana, Long Island, and that the claimant demanded restitution from Jeannetta and a divorce from Jethro.

"What are we going to do?" wailed a distraught Laura.

Mason examined the document closely and shrugged. "Forget it. Didn't you notice the dates between which they're supposed to have been living there? According to this, it began
before I put Jeannetta in the hospital. Do you want me to stop
it now, or do you think Jeannetta would like to see Alma Williams eat crow?" He walked to the phone as the last words
fell from his lips.

"Hello, Jeannetta." He told her of the court orders.

"Would you like me to call the judge, have the hospital send
the record, or what? It would serve her plenty if you let the
town know what she's like." He listened to Jeannetta's story
of how it had begun and her culpability in not having denied
it, for the sake of vengeance.

"Alright. I'll speak with the judge." He did, and received
the judge's agreement that Alma would be penalized if she
mentioned the accusation again. That done, he stopped by the
Hideaway, collected his son, and headed for home.

Jeannetta sat on the porch in the late afternoon autumn sun
reading through her novel and making minor corrections. She
loved the story and what she'd done with it, but it saddened
her. She was glad for the telephone interruption.

"Hello."

"Hi, Jeanny. Whatcha doing?" A smile eclipsed her face
at the sound of Skip's eager voice, and she told him she'd
been working.

"I think you ought to come here with me and Dad, Jeanny. I don't like this woman who keeps calling Dad."

She didn't know what to say. "How's your father?" seemed a safe thing.

"He's okay, Jeanny, but some woman named Betty calls here every day, sometime three or four times. I'm not saying she's Dad's bird. That's you. But, like, I don't want this chick to be my mother." She couldn't help smiling, though twinges of anxiety stole through her.

"Skip. I'm not sure you should be telling me this. Your father is entitled to privacy, and…"

"Yeah. I know. I'm squealing on him, but she ain't no good for him. She don't even like me, Jeanny. And I sure as…I don't like her."

"I'm sorry, Skip, but if your father wants to see her and talk with her, there's nothing I can do." His words hit her like sharp darts in her chest, but she controlled her voice. If she cried, Mason would hear of it. She managed to conclude the conversation. What she wanted most right then was to hear Mason's voice, but she couldn't make herself call him. She had to talk with *someone,* so she called Laura. And wished she hadn't.

"I was just going to call you, hon," Laura began. "I suppose you know one of Mason's old flames is helping Clayton with his lawsuit. Clayton says she's given him some useful information, but I tell you I'm not sold on her. She's calling him all the time, and now she's taken to coming up here, claiming it's 'such a relief from New York.'"

Jeannetta laughed at her sister mimicking the woman. "Don't think of her as competition, Laura; Clayton has eyes only for you."

"Humph," Laura snorted. "You know that, and I know that, but I'm not sure about this hussy, walking around here all day dressed up with her pants so tight I think they'll split, and a

pound of makeup. I can take care of her, though," she seemed
to assure herself. "Clayton said she used to be Mason's girl,
and maybe she's really after *him*. Clayton said she's typical
of those New York women."

"Laura, I'm sorry, but my pot's boiling over. I have to go."
Jeannetta hung up, looked toward the ceiling and sucked her
teeth.

"Clayton said. Clayton said." Didn't the man ever do anything but talk? She hadn't lied to Laura; she'd used an apt figure of speech. And she liked Clayton, even admired him in
many respects but, for heaven's sake, he wasn't *the* latter-day
oracle of truth, no matter how hard Laura tried to make him
into one. She returned to her reading, but couldn't muster an
interest in it. Had she been foolish in rejecting Mason's proposal? Could she have taught him the meaning of love once
they'd married? Too late now, she reminded herself; he has
grievances of his own.

## Chapter 14

Mason walked into Skip's room. "I didn't hear the phone ring; who were you calling?" The boy gazed at him, eyeball to eyeball, and refused to back down. Without being told, he knew Skip had called Jeannetta, and that he wouldn't apologize for having done it.

"Well?"

"I called Jeanny. You're not planning to marry Betty, are you?"

"*What?* What gives you that idea?"

The boy's belligerence had vanished, to be replaced by a sad, worried look. "'Cause she's always calling you, and you always talk to her."

Mason sat down, because he didn't want to seem threatening. "I'm your father. You look at me when you speak, but you don't stare me down as you would a roughneck kid. Don't ever do that again."

"I'm sorry, sir."

"Alright. Now, Skip, I won't always run my personal life to suit you, but you can be sure that I'll take your interests into account. You do not have to worry about my marrying Betty. Okay?"

"Okay." From the boy's release of breath, he imagined that he'd been deeply worried.

"But what about Jeanny, Dad? She…I like her so much, and she likes me a lot. I know she does." He looked at Skip's worried face, at the moisture pooling in his eyes. He didn't want to see him cry, and he knew that, if one drop fell, Skip would be mortified. He walked over to him and knelt in front of him.

"I love her, Skip, and I'm trying to straighten things out; I can't promise more. I have some errands to do, and I've decided it'll do you good to go with me."

They walked down to Bloomingdale's and Mason bought two pair of jeans, three dress shirts, two ties, two crew-neck sweaters, and overcoat, and a pair of leather gloves, all in medium size. He and Skip took the bus to One Hundred and Eight Street and Third Avenue and walked over to Park. Mason found the homeless engineer at once and called him aside.

"This is my son, Benjamin Fenwick; you didn't tell me your name."

The man didn't bother to contain his surprise; with eyebrows raised, he cocked his head to one side and rubbed his chin.

"Ralph Harper." He looked at Skip. "How do you do?" To Mason's amazement Skip replied, "Cool, how 'bout you?" and extended his hand.

Mason handed the man the package of clothing. "I'm Mason Fenwick. My brother has a job for you repairing office machines. Don't worry, he'll teach you. It's night work in office buildings around the city. Here's his phone number, and fifty dollars for whatever you need that isn't in this package. You said you couldn't look for work because you couldn't make yourself presentable. Now you can."

The speechless man managed to mutter his thanks, turned to his friends, and waved.

"Where're you going now, Mr. Harper?" Skip asked him.

Ralph Harper's startled glance at Skip telegraphed his surprise at being addressed in such a manner. "To the shelter, man. This time when I get a shower, I can put on clean clothes. Make sure you don't ever need one of those places. They're the pits."

"You think he'll do it, Dad?"

Mason was making up his mind about some other unfinished business.

"I don't know, son. I gave him his chance, and he has to do the rest. What did you learn today?"

"Not to get homeless and to help the ones I see." Mason knew a sense of joy that came from loving his son, and he had no doubt that he would give his life for the boy. He grasped Skip's hand.

"Let's go out on Long Island to see Jeannetta."

The smile on Skip's face and the added bounce to his step confirmed the boy's excitement and eagerness to see her. Mason stopped short. In his happiness, he had momentarily forgotten that a deep chasm separated the woman he loved from himself. He didn't want to disappoint Skip, but he doubted the wisdom of an impromptu visit to Jeannetta.

"I think we'd better call first, son; she may not be home."

Mason closed his bedroom door and phoned Jeannetta. His pulse pounded when he heard her voice. Soft. Feminine.

"Jeannetta, this is Mason. How are you?"

"Fine. Which Mason is this?"

In spite of the annoyance that he wanted to summon, he

laughed. "Which one do you want?" He hoped the noise he heard was a giggle.

"That's below the belt and ungentlemanly. Either answer will incriminate me."

"Gentlemen seldom win this kind of battle, sweetheart. Go ahead and incriminate yourself; it may prove beneficial."

"To whom?"

"To both of us. Since you don't plan to give quarter, I'll take the heat. How about Skip and I drive out to get you? My older brother, Steve, has practically demanded that I bring you to meet him. We'll drive you back out there. What do you say?" He held his breath, certain that she would deny him this chance to see her.

"That would mean ten hours of driving for you in one day, because I can't leave Casper overnight. Today's Saturday. So why don't I take the train in to New York tomorrow morning; you and Skip meet me; we go see Steve; eat lunch or something; and you drive me back? I think that's a better plan."

His heat slowed to its normal pace and he let out a long breath. What had happened to make her agreeable to seeing him and, especially, to meeting his brother?

"What time will your train get in to Penn Station?"

"Ten-twenty."

"Good. We'll be there."

"Who'll be with Skip? The doctor or the man?"

Relief. He laughed for the joy of it. "Woman, you don't give up easily, do you? Well, neither do I. Which one do you want?"

Her laughter rang like bells, warming him long after he replaced the receiver.


Jeannetta stepped off the near-empty train with one thought; if he hadn't forgiven her, why was he taking her to meet his brother? She had agreed because she meant to earn that forgiveness if she could, and she wanted the chance to teach him what love meant. She saw Skip running to her, his face shining with pleasure, and quickened her steps.

"Jeanny! Here she is, Dad." She hugged him, surprised that a boy his age would welcome an outward display of affection. She looked up into Mason's glittering eyes. Eyes that invited her to drown in them.

"Hi."

"Hi." From the corner of her eye, she saw Skip elbow Mason in the ribs. He looked down at his son.

"Aren't you supposed to kiss her or something? Like, this ain't cool."

She watched for Mason's reaction and relaxed when he grinned and said, "Kissing should be done in private. And don't forget: you're still twelve; you don't run my private life; and don't use street language. Right?"

"Right. But you *are* going to kiss her, aren't you?"

Mason looked up and tortured her with the hot gleam in his eyes. "Trust me, son."

Her heart galloped throughout the ten-minute ride to Steve's apartment.

She liked Steve at first sight. A big, handsome man, he wore the same demeanor of competence and strength as his brother.

"I've wanted to meet you for a long time, Jeannetta, and I appreciate your coming all the way from Long Island to see me." They entered the living room, and her heart seemed to drop to her stomach. The elegant woman sitting on the sofa fitted Betty's description; surely Mason wouldn't…

Steve introduced her. "Jeannetta Rollins, this is Vivian Allen; Viv is what we call her."

Mason's secretary. She acknowledged the introduction, not surprised to learn that Viv knew about her. But why was she there, and why wasn't Mason surprised at her presence?

Skip quickly put an end to her puzzlement. With an arm slung around her shoulder, he whispered, "Don't sweat it, Jeanny; I think she's Uncle Steve's new uh…girl."

She couldn't help smiling, both at his familiarity and at his words.

"Yeah," came his smug confirmation, "that's exactly who she is." *I could love this kid,* she thought, as the realization struck her that he was exactly her height.

"Jeannetta, how about helping me in the kitchen while we get acquainted," Steve said. "Mason wanted to take us all out to lunch, but I can cook as well as the next guy. Come on." She followed him in the kitchen, took a towel from the rack and secured it around her waist.

"What can I do to help?"

He pointed to a high stool. "Sit over there. Don't get it in your head that I'm meddling; I'm not. I looked after Mason from the time he was seven and I was twelve until he graduated from medical school. What happens to him is my business. *Are you in love with him?*"

Her mouth opened and her breasts heaved sharply; he had to see that he'd stunned her.

"I believe in cutting to the chase, Jeannetta. There's a lot at stake here."

Might as well go for broke, she decided, when she could get her breath. "Yes. I'm in love with Mason, and I have been since shortly after we began that tour."

His stare, so much like his brother's, but harder, nearly unnerved her.

"But you don't want to marry him."

Don't let him see that you're perturbed, she cautioned herself. "I don't want to settle for what he's giving me, when I know that we both would be so much happier if he could share himself fully with me. I've tried to explain this to him, but he doesn't understand. Steve, I have no idea what pains him, and

I wouldn't have dreamed that he would adopt a young boy. I love him, but I don't truly know him."

"I expect you never know a person until after you're married."

Her withering look didn't seem to bother him.

"I at least ought to know what makes him angry."

Both of his eyebrows arched sharply. "In this case, you sure oughta. It doesn't happen often, but when it does, it's something to deal with."

She decided to voice her own problems. "Mason has reservations about me, as I'm sure you know. The way I see it, my error was in not telling him the truth about why I took the tour and that I'd had a P.I. investigate him. I did both before I ever saw him, and I didn't tell him because I feared he'd walk away from me and sentence me to blindness. I don't know how to earn his forgiveness."

Steve propped his foot on the rung of the nearest chair and studied her for a long time. She let him. At last he asked, "What about Skip?"

"I could love Skip as dearly as if I had given birth to him. He's already in my heart."

Steve nodded, topped the eggplant Parmesan with mozzarella cheese, shoved it in the oven and sat down.

"I can't advise you, because there's so much I can't know in this case. But I will tell you not to let it slip through your fingers. It's too precious."

"But it isn't up to me."

He smiled. "Love him. That's all you need to do." She must have seemed uncertain, because he stressed it. "You heard me. Just love him."

"But I do love him." She watched Steve's frown fade into a grimace. Didn't he believe her?

"A couple of months ago, I might not have understood any of this, but I can tell you now that, if you love a person, you don't keep tabs on what you give each other. My brother hasn't known a woman's love since our mother died when he was seven. How do you expect him to peel off a thirty-year habit of shielding himself without some help? He loves Skip without reservation, and he can love you the same way if you guide him. But if you wait out there on Long Island until he sees the light, and he hangs tough in the city questioning your every motive, the two of you will squander what you have sure as heat melts ice." He took a pan of biscuits from the freezer, wrapped them in foil and put them in the oven, looked at her, and shook his head.

'You won't catch me doing that."

A cold soul-sickness settled over her. Had she failed him? Failed herself? Her own slice of love hadn't been oversized, she reflected; was she bargaining for a sure thing? She looked up into Steve's knowing gaze.

"Doesn't look good when you strip it down, does it?" he asked with merciless accuracy.

"No. It isn't easy to see one's own shortcomings." She slid off of the high stool, removed the towel from her waist, and asked him, "Sure I can't help with this?"

"I've got it under control. Thanks. And, Jeannetta… They say Rome wasn't built in a day, but I hear it's one of the world's great beauties."

She put a smile on her face and walked back into the living room, and a strong sensation flowed through her when she looked into Mason's face. Expectant. Hopeful. But he quickly covered his feelings with a broad grin.

"Well," Mason said, "don't tell me you're a closet gourmet cook like Steve."

She didn't feel like meaningless banter, but now was not the time for seriousness.

"I'm not much of any kind of a cook, if you take my recipe books away from me."

That remark evidently didn't please Skip.

"You can't cook either? Yuck. You oughta taste Uncle Steve's lasagna, and Viv says she can cook, too. I'm gonna stay over here a lot and let Uncle Steve teach me; one of us is gonna have to know how to cook."

Mason glanced down at him. "Who told you that I can't cook?"

"Well, you said you're going to do your best by me, and about all we eat is pizza, so I figured…" Mason interrupted him, laughing.

"When I asked what you like to eat, you said pizza."

Skip fidgeted uncomfortably. "That's right, but my mouth has been watering for some pork chops and some of that roast beef ojo that Uncle Steve makes."

They all stared at him for a second, until Mason corrected him. "You mean roast beef *au jus.*"

Jeannetta chuckled at the boy's look of incredulity.

"Whatever," he said with disdain. He sat on the sofa beside Mason with his legs stretched out, his feet wide apart and his hands in his pants pockets, his pose and gestures identical to his father's. She wanted to hug him.

Steve served a memorable lunch and, as the conversation flowed, Jeannetta thought she might find a new friend in Viv. She marvelled at Skip's easy acceptance of his new relationship with Mason; a stranger wouldn't know that they hadn't been father and son since the boy's birth. Somewhere in their loving connection lay a message for her, and for Mason. Mason asked Steve whether he and Viv would ride out to Long Island.

"Thanks, but there're only so many hours in the day, Mason, and I aim to spend as many of them as I can making my case with Viv. Wouldn't hurt you to think along those lines."

Jeannetta's gaze caught Mason's unflinching stare, and the silent movement of his lips told her that she might well do the same.

Two weeks later, Jeannetta mailed her manuscript to her editor and decided to take a vacation from work, to loll on the beach and enjoy the environment. She hadn't figured out how to approach Mason to tell him that she needed him and the terms didn't matter, and she knew that was because, in her heart, they did matter. At the least, she had to hear it from his lips that he loved and needed her. She dressed in woolen slacks and a bulky wool sweater for a walk on the beach and started out, just as the phone rang. Her hello was greeted by a distraught Skip.

"What is it? What's the matter?"

"My adoption and christening ceremonies are next Sunday, and my dad said he hasn't asked you to come. Can't you come, Jeanny?"

Cold chills streaked through her; Mason was moving on without her. "Honey," she began, as she struggled to control her voice, "I can't be there if your father doesn't invite me."

"But the only people I want there are you and Uncle Steve. I'm inviting you, so you have to be there."

She hurt for him and for herself, but she couldn't crash Mason's party. "Skip, I'm sorry, but I…I'll have to wait until I hear from your dad."

"If you won't come, I'm not having any christening."

*"Skip!"* He hung up. She checked the telephone directory, got Steve's number, and begged him to speak with Skip, not to let the boy hurt Mason.

"Mason didn't say you weren't invited; he said he hadn't done it, because you two had a breakdown in communications and he didn't know how to approach you."

"You won't speak with Skip?"

"What for? Skip wants a family. He's decided he wants you for his mother, and he refuses to have such an important experience without both of his parents."

"But I'm not his parent, and I may never be." She heard the deep breath that signaled his shortage of patience.

"Skip started out with nothing, not even parents, and he got where he is by setting goals and going hard after them. I refuse to interfere with his strategy."

She changed from the heavy sweater to a cotton shirt and tried to think. Her manuscript. Maybe if she sent it to Mason, he'd understand her misgivings, her needs. She put a copy in an envelope and called Federal Express.

Mason closed the door behind the last of his patients for the day. Noona Shepherd always made sure she had the last appointment, and her complaints always centered near her chest or her pelvis. He'd told her that he wasn't an internist or gynecologist, but she still pestered him. All five of his office rooms reeked with her perfume. She'd had her very last appointment; let her chase some other doctor. He opened the window wide, sat down at his desk, and glimpsed the red, white, and blue envelope. He slit it open and stared at the first page: *The Naked Soul of a Man in Love,* by Jeannetta Rollins. He read three pages and leaned back in his chair, perplexed as to where the story would lead. Then he put the manuscript in his briefcase, took that and his medical bag, and went home. Tension marked his dinner with Skip, as it had for the last three days, so he went to his room early, switched on the light beside his lounge chair and began to read. Sometime after midnight, he finished the story and laid the manuscript aside.

Is that what she wanted from him? He couldn't get the scene out of his mind. The hero, strong, competent, and seemingly invincible, had wept in his woman's arms when the man he'd defended was found guilty and sentenced to life in prison.

He'd wet her body with his tears, but she had given herself to him with a passion that might have suggested their last opportunity to make love before an approaching Armageddon. He found the lines, reread them, and mused over their relevance. The woman had never loved the man so much as when he came to her stripped bare of his public persona. Vulnerable. Jeannetta had said she wanted *him*. Is this what she meant? And would she share his doubts, misgivings, and pain, his disappointments and uncertainties, and still love him, as her heroine had loved her man? He remembered her having told him that she had left him in Zimbabwe because of his nightmare, and because she hadn't wanted to be the source of his guilt. And he remembered the times right after that horrible accident when pain had nearly ripped him apart, and he hadn't been able to share it with anyone, not even his brother.

Sunrise found him reading the manuscript for a second time. At seven o'clock, he showered, dressed, and went to the kitchen, where he found Skip setting the breakfast table.

"Good morning."

"Hi, Dad. You gonna call her? Huh? If you ask her, she'll come. I know she will; she said so."

Mason rested the egg on the counter and turned to Skip. "You called her?"

"Yes, sir. I invited her, but she said you have to ask her. Something like she didn't want to go against your wishes. Will you ask her?"

"Yes. I'm going to call her." He'd known that Jeannetta's presence at the ceremonies was important to Skip, but he hadn't realized how much. The boy showed almost no emotion, but sat down, propped his elbows on his knees, and held his face in his hands.

"I just couldn't do it, Dad. I mean, it's a big thing, a preacher holding an adoption service for us and me getting christened and all that…I couldn't do that without Jeanny. Next to you,

I love Jeanny the best." Mason laid a gentle hand on Skip's shoulder.

"I didn't want to do it without her either, son. Now, hurry and get ready for school. Breakfast will be ready in five minutes."

The door closed behind Skip, and he dialed her number. If only he could be sure that she was asking him to let her stand with him through every adversity, to dance the slow pieces as well as the fast ones, to sail with him and crash with him. To go to the wall with him. Was there such a woman *anywhere?* He had to find out if that was what she wanted to offer. But not now.

"Mason. I...I'm glad to hear from you. Did you get a chance to read my manuscript?"

"Yes, I did; you're a fine writer, but that isn't why I called. If you don't mind, we'll talk about that later. I'm calling about the adoption service for Skip and me and his christening. It's this coming Sunday, and we want you to stand up with us." She had to grab a chair and sit down. It hadn't occurred to her that he would give her an important role in their service.

"Jeannetta?"

She pulled herself out of her mild shock. "I'm honored, and I'll be happy to attend. You caught me by surprise. I hoped you would ask me to be there, but to stand up with you...well, I didn't dream of it. Of course, I will."

"Thanks. I'll send a car for you."

"Mason, it isn't..."

"I want to do it. The driver should be there at eight next Sunday morning."

She stopped short of protesting. If she wanted the whole man, she'd have to accept all that he offered.

"Alright. I'll be ready."

"Jeannetta, your novel impressed me, but I don't want to

discuss it right now, because I have to go to work. We'll talk about it when we're together."

"Okay. I'll see you Sunday." She waited for an endless minute and, finally, he said, "I miss you. See you." She listened to the dial tone, bemused. He seemed to have been at a crossroads, and her hammering heart prayed that he was.


Jeannetta didn't own a hat, so she substituted an elegant bow of green satin that matched her wool crepe suit. Only Laura would complain that the skirt stopped too far above her knees, she surmised, and Laura wouldn't be there. But she was, and so was Clayton.

Jeannetta had to hold back the tears when, at the end of the adoption service, Skip squeezed her hand and looked at her with joy blazing on his face.

"I put your name down to be my godmother. Okay? Uncle Steve will be my godfather."

She nodded and glanced at Mason beside whom Steve stood with glowing pride, and she thought her heart would burst with joy when Mason smiled and winked. The minister beckoned to Viv, Clayton, and Laura to come forward for Skip's christening and, after the ceremony, Mason took them to lunch at the Plaza.

"Laura and I are getting married in a couple of weeks," Clayton announced. "She wants me to know that marrying me isn't contingent on whether I clear my name."

"Of course, it isn't," Laura put in, "though I'm just tickled to death about your getting a retrial and that those seven women have agreed to witness for you. Betty helped a lot, so I guess she isn't such a bad egg."

"Who said she was?"

"Now, Clayton."

Jeannetta marveled at her sister's fashionable haircut, short-skirted designer suit, and the bloom that loving Clayton had put on her face. The old Laura had ceased to exist.

It amused Mason that Skip always managed to sit beside him, but had stopped sitting or standing *between* Jeannetta and him. The twelve-year-old was a master matchmaker, and an interesting study, too. He didn't believe he had ever seen such joy on a human face as on Skip's when Steve stood and welcomed him into the Fenwick family. His hand went of its own will to find and enfold Jeannetta's, and his heart bounded into a gallop when she squeezed his fingers, looked up at him, and smiled with love in her eyes.

"I've got something to tell, too," Steve announced. "I've asked Viv to be my wife, and this beautiful woman has done me the honor of accepting me." He touched her hand, and she stood up and brushed his mouth with her lips. Mason blinked rapidly in astonishment. He'd known that they had become close, but their engagement came as a surprise. He walked over to Steve and hugged him, then leaned down and brushed a kiss on Viv's cheek.

"I never dreamed that I'd be your sister-in-law," she said. "I hope you're happy for us."

"I am. If I had tried to stage this, you can bet it would have flopped. I've always wanted a sister, Viv, and I couldn't be more satisfied."

Steve beamed at her. "I've also decided to accept Mason's offer of a partnership in Fenwick Travel Agency, so now, Viv and I will be partners in every respect."

Ever business-minded, Skip sat forward. "What about your office-machine repair business, Uncle Steve? You're not gonna trash that, are you?"

"Thank goodness I don't have to. I've got a new man who can manage it. Mason, you remember Ralph Harper. That guy's the best thing to come along since air conditioning. He's one fast study, but of course, he should be; he's an engineer."

"That's the homeless man, Dad."

"Not anymore," Steve informed them. "In six weeks, he's acquired an apartment and a whole new life. He's going to train a couple of his old buddies, and I think they'll work out okay. He knew an opportunity when he saw it, grabbed it, and took off."

Skip smiled up at him and then frowned. Mason steeled himself against what he knew would follow, and Skip mumbled, "Everybody's got it together but us, Dad."

He patted Skip's knee. "I'll drop by home so you can get your books and pack an overnight bag. You're staying with Steve tonight."

"Okay, but where're you...?"

Mason didn't think he'd ever seen such a rapid change in anybody's facial expression. He would have laughed, but he couldn't afford to encourage him.

"Good. You're learning that some things aren't your business."

"Yeah." The boy's grin was downright beatific. "If she doesn't say yes, call me and I'll talk to her for you." He regained his composure and glanced down at the woman beside him, relaxed and serene, and wondered how much of that was real. They hadn't resolved their differences, and everybody around them appeared to have done that, so she shouldn't exude so damn much bliss. He told himself he'd soon know once and for all where they stood.

Mason parked in front of the house and hoped Casper remembered him, as he got out of the car and walked around it to open the door for Jeannetta, who fumbled with her seat belt. He unhooked it for her and suggested, "Why don't you put on some comfortable shoes and let's walk along the shore."

"I'll just take these off," she replied. "You aren't the only one who likes the feel of sand. Turn around so I can take off my stockings."

He repeated the order in his mind and wished he understood the female psyche; he'd seen every inch of the woman, but she wouldn't let him watch her remove her stockings. With his shoes and socks in his hand and his pants legs rolled up, they strolled hand-in-hand along the water's edge with the cool waves lapping at their bare feet. She stooped down and got a handful of sand, opened her fingers and let the wind take it away. He watched, mesmerized, at the smile that claimed her face. Previously, when he'd seen her do that, her expression had been that of a deeply troubled person.

"What pleases you so much?"

"The sand. This time, when I watched it falling, sifting through my fingers, I didn't think that every minute that passed brought me closer to blindness. That's over, thanks to you."

So that was it. "Come over here," he said, leading her to a nest of large rocks. He dusted the boulders with his handkerchief, and they sat quietly for a long time, looking out at the ocean.

"Are you going to forgive me, Mason? Try to remember that I did those things before I ever saw you, and that my crime was in not telling you. I have relived my opportunities to tell you one thousand times; you can't know how sorry I am." She folded her hands in her lap to steady them.

"You're asking my forgiveness. Does this mean that you can accept me as I am?" She rose and held out her hand to him, and they walked back to the house. He had to be aware, as she was, that this might be their last chance. As she stood with her hand on the doorknob, his piercing gaze unnerved her.

"You haven't answered my question."

"I accept what I know of you; I admire what I know of you."

When he reached past her to push the door open, his forearm brushed the tips of her breasts, stunning them both and bringing a blaze to his eyes. He stared down at her.

"I don't want you to compromise; I need you to love me for who I am, as I am."

Her head jerked back, and she looked at him, breathless with anticipation. He'd never said that before. She grasped his hand, hopeful now for their future, and led him to the living room.

"I won't settle for less than I need; don't let that worry you. I'm after what's inside you that you never let me see. That's all. I want you to open up to me and let me love you without reservations. I want to know you as no other human being does and, until you let me, you won't want to know who *I* am."

"Oh, yes; I read your novel, and it riveted me. I thought about my own life, the hard knocks, raw bruises, disappointments and uncertainties. I never had many friends, because I was too busy making my way; Steve was the closest person to me. But I couldn't tell Steve when I had a setback or missed out on something I wanted badly, because he sacrificed his youth, his education, everything, for me, and I wanted him to know that his trust was well placed. So I locked everything in, kept my problems to myself."

She gave silent thanks; the tide had begun, and she hoped it would bring a flood.

"I'll never forget the day I walked away from medicine," he went on, as though oblivious to her presence. "I tried to tell Betty, whom I was seeing at the time, what I was going through, and I had never before attempted to reach a woman at that level. She threw a tantrum about my foolishness and reinforced what I'd suspected: she didn't care about me or my feelings; she wanted the doctor, the socialite, not Mason

Fenwick. I remember the hollow, sickening feeling I had as I turned away from her. I still dislike the smell of lilac perfume, because she was wearing it, and the scent hung in my nostrils.

"Three weeks. Three agonizing weeks of waiting and watching beside Bianca Norris's bed after I'd done all I could for her, praying that she could come out of that coma. You can't imagine the loneliness."

Her heart swelled, and moisture clouded her vision. Hurting for him, she moved closer and laced her fingers through his, but didn't speak. She wanted him to let it all out.

"Would anyone have understood that, if it had been possible, I would have exchanged places with that woman? I couldn't dump that on my brother and, when I walked away, I couldn't make him understand, and he never accepted it."

She decided to risk a question. "Why did you leave it all?"

He leaned back on the sofa and propped his right ankle on his left knee, and she let herself relax when she saw that he would continue. "I had become a society doctor, treating the wealthy, squiring around rich women—black ones, white ones, Latin ones, foreign ones—all decked out in designer clothes, wearing designer perfume and starving themselves to death in New York's most expensive restaurants. I was in great demand, socially and professionally; doctors sent me their toughest cases, and I began to believe that I could do no wrong. In that operating room that morning, I got straightened out. I was not infallible. Later, I looked at myself and didn't like what I had become. I no longer had time for Steve; I'd stopped going to church, quit volunteer work, and had even begun to neglect myself. No surgeon can make it indefinitely on five or six hours' sleep, sometimes less, each night. I was busy at everything but what I should have been doing. I wouldn't have noticed Skip, and I shudder to think what I would have missed."

Her heart bloomed, a rose unfolding its petals, hammer-

ing an erratic rhythm, and she squeezed his hand in an effort
to communicate to him the love that swelled inside of her.

He didn't recall ever before having spilled his guts to anyone, and still more churned inside of him, struggling for release.

"I'm boring you with all this."

She had wanted to know him, and he had opened himself to
her. He started to draw himself inward, to put some distance
between them, but her arm slid around him and tightened.

"Oh, no, my darling. You're not boring me, you're loving me."

"What?"

Her other hand slid across his chest, and her head rested on
his shoulder. "I said…I heard somewhere that to love is to give
yourself, imperfections and all. And that's what I wanted, all
I wanted. Assurance that you'd let me be there for you when
you needed love and understanding, because if you'd do that,
you'd accept who I am as well."

She was too good to be true, and he couldn't help stiffen-
ing. From where he sat, all the saints were above.

"Nothing I told you makes you anxious? You don't think
less of me?"

Her soft hand caressed his face, and he leaned into it. "How
could it? What I feel is sadness that, when you most needed
someone who loved you, you had no one. Oh, you survived
it; you'll always do that, but life is easier and sweeter when
it's shared. Are you sorry you told me?" She watched his
fingers dance on his knee as he strummed the way in which
pianists exercise their fingers. Part of his thinking process,
she realized.

"No. Oddly, I'm not sorry; I feel as though I've dropped a
weight." She snuggled closer, and he voiced a belated thought.

"Do you realize you called me darling? That's a first. Why?"

"I feel closer to you."

His pulse raced, and he had to gasp for the breath that lodged in his throat. "You're saying nothing's changed your feelings for me, that you love me?"

"More than ever. I realize that I hurt you when I said I didn't know you and that you didn't meet my needs, but I didn't know any other way to express it." Tears pooled in her eyes and wet his hand.

"Honey, don't cry. It's alright. I understand a lot of things now. Don't... Ah, baby...it...there's nothing to forgive. Sweetheart, I just wanted you to love me."

"I do. Oh, I do. I..."

He covered her mouth and kissed her with all the passion that fermented inside of him, with love that screamed for his admittance.

"I need you," she whispered. "Mason, *I need you*. It's been so long. So long." Shudders racked him when she parted her lips for his possessive kiss and pressed his fingers to her breast.

"Is that door locked?" She nodded impatiently, and he rose and raced with her up the stairs to her room. In the heat of passion, they couldn't strip each other fast enough. Her fingers stumbled over the buttons on the front of his shirt, and he finally pulled it over his head. Her skirt zipper caught the woolen fabric, and she wanted him to tear it off of her. At last, he lay her on the bed.

"Let me," she whispered, when he reached for his bikini underwear. Hot arrows of desire sliced through him, and he jumped to full readiness when she hooked her arms around him, drew him to her and kissed him. And he could hardly withstand the torture of wanting her when she lay back and opened her arms to him. He eased into the heaven of her embrace, his body screaming for gratification inside of her, but he gazed into her trusting, loving face and brought himself under control.

Jeannetta lifted her body to accept him, but he denied her, worried her mouth with his lips and traced a hot frenzied path to her neck, while his fingers toyed with her breasts. Her body began to beg for what she wanted, undulating from side to side, but he stilled her and covered a nipple with his lips, blowing on it until she begged him to suckle her. She couldn't help crying aloud when at last his mouth began to pull on it, and his knowing fingers found the core of her passion and teased it until it released its love liquid.

"Mason, please… Honey, please. *Please*."

He didn't answer. His busy mouth found her other nipple and brought a keening cry from her. Frustrated, she hooked her leg over his thigh, reached for him, and tried to get what she wanted. He leaned over her and asked permission to enter.

"Yes, yes. For God's sake, *yes!*" She tensed with anticipation as he gathered her in his arms, positioned himself at her love gate and thrust into her. She bucked beneath him, begging for immediate satisfaction, but he withdrew, held her still, and entered with a powerful surge. Slowly, he began the dance, and she caught his rhythm and let herself go.

"Are you with me, honey? Am I where you want me to be?"

She let her legs tighten around him. "Yes. Oh, yes. Mason, darling, I want to burst."

"And you will." Shower after shower of hot darts penetrated her feminine core as he began a lover's kiss that simulated the movement of his body and duplicated the wizardry of his fingers between them. She couldn't help crying out as the spasm began, and he accelerated his powerful strokes until her screams filled the room and she surrendered herself to him.

"Mason. Oh, Mason, love, I love you so."

Her body clutched at him, demanding his total capitulation, and he splintered in her arms with words that he had never uttered before. *"I love you, Jeannetta. I love you. Love you. You're my life. Everything."*

Sated. Enervated. Drained. Long minutes passed before they spoke.

"I thought we were perfect together, that we'd reached the pinnacle of ecstasy," he whispered, still secure within her, "but it was never like this. Never." He propped himself on his elbows, and hugged her to him.

"I know. I used to feel empty inside for a long time after you sent me flying practically out of this world, and that bothered me. But now I know what it means to be fulfilled." He pulled her closer.

"I...I love you, and I don't mind saying it. I've loved you since Istanbul, do you know that?"

She could feel the smile that spread over her face, a smile of contentment. "I thought you loved me, because you acted as if you did, but I didn't know whether you knew it."

"I knew it alright. You're a wise woman."

"How so?"

"That novel of yours, it set me to wondering."

"I'd hoped it would."

"And what a title! *The Naked Soul of a Man in Love.* It's heavy stuff. Look. If I don't have anything good to tell Skip tomorrow, my credit with him's going to suffer. Do you know he actually offered to talk to you on my behalf if you turned me down? I ought to be as good at this as my twelve-year-old kid thinks he is."

"What would you like to tell him?"

"That you're going to be my wife and his mother."

She gazed into eyes that blazed with love, knew that he offered more than she'd ever dreamed of wanting, and snuggled closer to him. But he moved away as though to emphasize business before pleasure.

"Well?"

"Fine with me. You're just what I want and need. Both of you."

He reached down beside the bed, took the old keys out of his pants pocket and pressed them into her hand.

"What's this?"

"The keys to our home, the one we'll build on a hill where we'll see the sun rise in the morning and set in the evening." She closed her fingers around them, snuggled closer and smiled. He gazed at her for long minutes, then turned to the business at hand, and she opened to the sweet honey of his love.

* * * * *